Ruin Mist:

Keeper Martin's Tale

Robert Stanek

Ruin Mist Chronicles

This is a work of fiction. All the characters, names, places and events portrayed in this book are either products of the author's imagination or are used fictitiously. Any resemblance to any actual locale, person or event is entirely coincidental.

Ruin Mist: Keeper Martin's Tale

Reagent Press
Published by Virtual Press, Inc.
6134 86th Ave. SE
Olympia, WA 98513

Cover design & illustration by Robert Stanek
ISBN 1-57545-042-9

Reagent Press Books by Robert Stanek

Ruin Mist: Elf Queen's Quest
Ruin Mist: Fields of Honor

Ruin Mist: Keeper Martin's Tale

Magic Lands: Journey Beyond the Beyond
Absolutes: Race to Infinity

Praise for Ruin Mist

"A gem waiting to be unearthed by millions of fans of fantasy!"

"Brilliant... an absolutely superior tale of fantasy for all tastes!"

"It's a creative, provoking, and above all, thoughtful story!"

"It's a wonderful metaphor for the dark (and light) odyssey of the mind."

"The fantasy world you have created is truly wonderful and rich. Your characters seem real and full of life."

The Kingdoms

Great Kingdom

Table Of Contents

Preface

In 15 BD, the Watcher, Xith, is recorded as saying that "History belongs to the teller and is only as reliable as the teller's recollection of it." This is the truth of the matter, and why Keeper Martin, head of the lore keepers, chose to pen his own version of the histories of Ruin Mist before and after the return of Dalphan the Wanderer. Through Keeper Martin's gathering of history from various individuals, the story of Ruin Mist is retold in these pages. Keeper Martin would like you to think that his version of the history is the only truthful and correct account but then again, history belongs to the teller and is only as reliable as the teller's recollection of it.

Chapter One: Those Destined

Sunrise loomed across the horizon, pale as a jasmine and mostly obscured by dark, feral clouds. The early morning air held an unusual chill and Adrina gathered her light shawl more closely as she stepped out onto the catwalk atop the wall. A stout breeze blew long strands of hair across her face. The hair, black as the receding night, flowed to her waist and while it was normally braided and folded over her left shoulder, it wasn't now.

Summer must surely be at an end, Adrina surmised, for the breeze came from the North and not from the direction of the West Deep.

Adrina walked to a place where the wall jutted out and cut its way into High King's Square. Behind her the palace parade grounds were empty and silent, as was the square before her. The silence seemed a shroud over the whole of Imtal clear to the Braddabaggon. Many stories below, the city's residents would soon awake. The square would fill with sounds as merchants began to unpack their wares. Palace guardsmen would muster for breakfast. City and palace would stir to life.

Yet Adrina preferred the empty moments just before all this happened, for the silence echoed the aching of her heart. She pressed her chin into the palm of her hand, her elbow glued to the stone framework of the wall. She sighed mournfully. The palace was truly dead, all *real* life having long since been gnawed away.

She could have passed the day dreaming about things beyond the gray stone edifice, the cold palace wall, with its portcullis tucked cleanly out of view. She had sauntered through many a day thus, envisioning magnificent journeys to the four corners of the land.

Great Kingdom had many holdings. High Province in the north—the far, far North—where amidst mountains of ice and stone the rivers boiled and filled the air with blankets of fog. South, beyond a forest of great white trees called giant birch, lay South Province with its capital city enveloped by the majestic Quashan' valley. East through the Kingdom along the East-West road were the Territories, divided east and west. The untamed Eastern Territories were awaiting discovery. The Western Territories held but two Kingdom outposts: Zashchita and Krepost'. Traders claimed the walled city of Zashchita was carved from the very trees of the forest and its building lifted so far into the heavens that they were lost in the clouds. Beyond Zashchita lay Krepost' and her ferryman who took travelers across River Krepost' so they could begin the climb into the mountain city and where afterward the gatekeeper may or may not chase them over the cliffs into Statter's Bay and to their deaths.

But today Adrina was frustrated to the point of tears. She wouldn't pass the day dreaming of things she may never see. She didn't understand what difference the passing of a year made. Why did it matter so that she was a year older? This year seemed the same as the last.

She would have done anything, given anything, to be a little girl again, free to wander the city in her brother's shadow. Together they would wander Imtal's cobbled streets. She would pretend not to notice the press of guardsmen around them and see only those who had come out to greet them.

A fleeting smile lit her face. She knew this could be no more. Valam was gone now, gone to South Province, gone for good, and she, Adrina, was leaving adolescence.

The echo of footsteps against hard stones startled her. Her eyes went wide and she wondered if Lady Isador would venture to the walls. Her governess had threatened to before.

Adrina didn't want to be reminded of all the things she should or should not do, so she slipped away to the northern watchtower. At dawn the tower would be vacant and she could be alone without fear of interruption.

Adrina wound her way up a long spiral staircase. She stopped only at the very top to catch her breath and here at the landing was a large, open chamber whose broad windows were normally used to keep watch on the city's north wall and the fields beyond. Adrina crossed the empty chamber to a window. The cool breeze on her face tingled her nose and brushed the sweat away.

"No lessons today," she whispered to the wind. Lessons Chancellor Yi and Lady Isador would surely chastise her for missing—if they found her.

Not today, Adrina vowed, not today.

Always more reminders of the things she should or should not do—her proper place, always her proper place. She knew all about the proper things, the proper mannerisms, the proper greetings, her proper duties, her proper place. She had even been taught, though only recently, the proper things to do to invite a man's attention. She was to begin courting. But why?

What did she need a man for? Moreover, what would she do with one once she caught him? Was there anything she couldn't do on her own?

Leave Imtal, the wind seemed to say. That was right; on her own, she would never leave Imtal. The palace would be all she would see for the rest of her days, but did it have to be this way?

The wind howling as if in answer spurred Adrina on. "Courtship, marriage," she shouted back, "maybe it wouldn't be so bad, for surely all suitors don't live in Imtal."

As quickly as she said it, Adrina cast the notion away. Marriage had taken Calyin away. Adrina told the wind, "No, that's not for me."

She reveled in memories now, slipping back into the past and a time when everything seemed simpler. The minutes slipped away, and then Adrina pictured a beautiful sad face. Tears came to her eyes. Simpler times were not easier times.

"Why mother, why did you have to go? I have never forgiven you, never, and I never will. I am all alone now. Calyin is wed. Valam is in the South. Midori went away, never to return. And you, you are... gone. What am I to do? Can you know how much I loved you? And you always in that stupid garden."

Adrina waited. The wind howled, but no answer came.

"Queen Alexandria was beautiful. Land and people loved her very dear," said a figure from the shadows.

Adrina screamed; her heart stopped. Then in a sudden flood of thoughts, her young mind began to race—surely this must be a rogue come to steal her away.

Adrina said coyly, and hoped the other knew she wasn't telling the truth, "What manner of rogue are you? My father would hardly pay ransom for his third daughter. I am of little worth."

The robed figure still enveloped in shadows spoke again. "By the Mother, I never heard such a thing."

The figure moved toward Adrina who edged closer and closer to the open window behind her.

"Child, I will not harm you."

"Who are you and what are you doing here?" Adrina asked, brushing back hair from her eyes. "Your face it is covered in soot. Stop where you are or I will scream again."

"Go ahead, none will hear. I come to speak to you, Highness. I have seen you standing in this tower often."

"Who are you?"

"I live here. I clean. You *will* journey beyond Imtal. I have seen you in a far off place."

"Seen me?"

"In a dream… Smell the wind."

"Smell, the wind?"

"Child, smell it. It comes, can you not tell?"

"It?"

The strange woman took Adrina's hand and turned her to the window. The chill breeze was still howling out of the North. "Change, child. Sadness cannot hold forever the land."

Adrina turned to look at the woman's face. The woman directed Adrina's gaze away and pointed to the distant horizon. Adrina squinted her eyes and stared long. She imagined she could see Solstice Mountain and the whole of the Rift Range. In her dreams, she had journeyed there. The border country all around Great Kingdom was wild, to the north especially so. The sole purpose of the elite High Road Garrison Guardsmen was to provide travelers with safe passage along the Kingdom's High Road and to shield the Kingdom from bandit incursions out of the north. Beyond High Road was a vast desert called Barrens, a no man's land. Beyond the Barrens was the untiring Rift Range—ice-capped mountains of jagged black rock that climbed perilously into the heavens. Or so she had been told.

"Is that where I'll journey to?" Adrina asked, turning around. The woman was gone. "Hello?… Are you still here?"

The chill north wind howled. Adrina turned eyes filled with expectations back to the fields beyond Imtal. Calyin had told her once that in the North there were mountains that breathed rivers of fire.

Hearing what sounded like a foot slipping across the stones of the floor, Adrina spun around. "Hello? Hello?" she called out.

From the shadows the woman whispered, "Be careful what you wish for."

Adrina stepped toward the woman. "What do you mean?"

The woman, her face suddenly appearing aged beyond her years, took Adrina's hand. She kneeled then and as she kissed Adrina's hand, Adrina felt the moisture of tears on her arm. The woman whispered, "I cry for the children who at the end of the journey will never be the same. Child, I cry for you. I cry because I see you standing in the midst of a killing field. I cry for the thousands dead at your feet..."

***

Crying out into the darkness, alone, afraid and drenched in sweat, Vilmos awoke. His thoughts raced. The whole of his small body shivered uncontrollably. Opening eyes and uncurling his huddled form from a corner, moist with his own perspiration yet still cold from the night's chill, was a slow, time-consuming process.

"It was only a nightmare," Vilmos whispered to reassure himself—a nightmare like no other. In the dream he had used the forbidden magic once too often and the Priests of the Dark Flame—opposers of all that is magic and magical—came from their temples to slay him.

Vilmos stood uneasily and dipped trembling hands into the washbasin beside the bed. The cool water sucked the hurt from his eyes and mind and gently began to soothe and awaken his senses as nothing else could.

Carefully he dabbed a wet cloth to the corners of his eyes and only then did he became something other than the frightened boy who in his dreams huddled into the forlorn corner because of the sense of security it gave him to know his back was against the wall and that nothing could sneak up on him from behind.

Only then that he became the boy of twelve whose name was Vilmos. Vilmos because it was a trustworthy name. Vilmos because it was his father's name, who was named

Vilmos because it had been his father's name. Vilmos, the Counselor's son.

Readying for the day's chores, Vilmos pushed the last of the dream from his thoughts. He dressed quickly and slipped on his ill-fitting boots as he stumbled toward the kitchen.

The aroma of fresh-baked black bread and honey cakes pungent in the air about the kitchen, mixing with the growling of his stomach, made him aware of an enormous hunger. The night had been unbearably long and he had not eaten since supper of the previous day.

"Late again. You'll sleep your life away. Already an hour past first light," said his mother. She stood in front of the hearth. The words were not meant to be harsh, nor were they taken thus. They were a standard greeting.

"I know mother, I am sorry," replied Vilmos, tossing gnarled hair to one side surreptitiously, hair that should have been combed. He started to hurry away.

"Vilmos, where are you going?" Lillath asked. "Must I always remind you of your lessons? Someday you will fill your father's position. Someday you *will* be Counselor of Tabborrath Village. Now, recite the lore of the peoples."

"Mother, do I have to?"

Lillath didn't say anything, she just stared.

"Can I use the book?"

"From memory."

"The tale of the four people is the lore of four kingdoms," Vilmos began, beaming with Lillath's smile upon him. "Small in number, strong of will, united they stood against powerful kingdoms of the North. Four vast kingdoms would conquer the four peoples, but the will of the four people was too strong. Lycya, mightiest of the kingdoms, was swallowed by barren desert. North Reach and the clans over-mountain were consumed by the twenty-year snow. Queen of Elves and all her people were washed into West Deep by the three-year rain.

Only the Alder's kingdom, once the smallest kingdom of the North, survives.

"To survive, the Alder's kingdom formed an alliance with the four people. Their Graces, King Alexas of Yug, King Jarom of Vostok, King Peter of Zapad and his Royal Majesty, King Charles of Sever, are the wardens of the four people. The four wardens maintain the alliance and protect the four people."

Lillath maintained her smile. "Well, yes," she said, "that is the lore of the four kingdoms and thus the tale of four peoples. But it is not *the* lore of the Four Peoples. You need to take great care in your listening. Listening is the counselor's greatest skill. Each tale, each bit of lore, tells a lesson. Relate the lesson through the lore; it is the way of the counselor. Choose the wrong tale, give the wrong advice. Do you understand?"

"Yes, mother."

"Now tell me the correct tale and guess the lesson."

Nervously Vilmos played his tongue against his cheek. "From memory?"

"You may use the book if need be, at times even your father reads from the book."

"Mother," began Vilmos, looking into her eyes with much sincerity, "is it not time to—"

"Run along," she said. "Wood for the day's fire." There was a hint of mirth in her voice as she watched him wet his hands and apply this to unruly hair to settle the cowlick.

Vilmos briefly, but closely studied his mother's features as he did each morning. Offset with a slight touch of gray, dark black hair the color of a starless night sky fell to her waist. Her face, ripened with age in a pleasant way, was deep-set with eyes of hazel that seemed always to be calling out. This morning they said, *Hurry along or you'll be late.*

He looked like her not like father, thought Vilmos each morning as he did this—a father who barely tolerated him. Harsh words chased through the boy's mind. "Vilmos, why did you do that? I told you not to!" or "Vilmos, go to your room."

With an occasional, "I should send him away," thrown in when his father thought Vilmos couldn't hear.

"He is only a boy," Vilmos often heard in rebuke. "He will change in time. Give him more time." There was a deep love between the two, mother and son.

Wood for the hearth could be gathered easily from the brambles on the edge of the thick woods near the outskirts of the village and it was to this place that Vilmos started to go but the outside air this morning was chillier than usual and it sent a shiver racing down Vilmos' back. It carried with it sadness and a sudden flood of remembrance. In the back of his mind, Vilmos knew the real reason he watched his mother so closely. One day he would indeed be sent away, far away, because one day the dark priests would come for him.

Vilmos returned to the house to collect his short cloak. As he ran through the kitchen, he stopped beside his mother. Rising up on the tips of his toes, he gave her a single peck on her cheek. For an instant, a smile broke the middle-aged woman's tired face and fondly she touched hand to cheek.

"That's better," Vilmos shouted to no one in particular as he ran outside, slipping the sleeves of his shielding cloak into place. He could endure the cold now, and in a way, the remembrance as well.

"Hurry, breakfast!" shouted Lillath after him, while unconsciously raising a hand to her cheek once more where soft, young lips had touched. Vilmos looked back only for a moment to see this and to catch her eye. She added as he dashed away, "Remember to be careful… Remember what happened to the girl from Olex Village."

***

Guardedly Seth walked beside Queen Mother. His mind carefully searched while his eyes scanned every shadow the two passed. As First of the Red, her safety was his responsibility. He was against remaining in Sanctuary, but Queen Mother wouldn't speak of leaving.

For reasons that escaped Seth, she wanted to use Sanctuary's High Hall. Its crystalline walls were specially attuned to reflect the feelings of a particular host despite even the best efforts of a mental block or mind shield and although it was a feat Queen Mother could have easily performed herself, she had said that she wished to conserve her will power. For what, she hadn't said.

Queen Mother, is it true, has he truly returned? Has Sathar survived the Dark Journey? Seth sent into her mind as he walked.

Even now he joins forces with King Mark of West Reach and still others flock to his banner. It is as we most feared. The time has come... May Father and Mother watch over us...

Will there be war?

Queen Mother regarded Seth. *I will miss you in my thoughts.*

The words caught Seth by surprise. He didn't understand. The link between protector and queen was unbreakable. He was the watch warden of her body and of her mind. He felt her pain. He knew her anguish, her every anxiety. This *was* the link. *My Queen, I don't understand. If you break the link, how will I know if you come to harm? I must be able to find you at all times, no matter the circumstance.*

In time, you will Brother Seth. Even traditions that stem the ages cannot remain forever. Soon it will be time to guard my own thoughts and my own being, just as the first queen had to do. Centuries ago we abandoned our ancestral homes. We fled to this barren land out of fear. We have lived in fear of repeating the past and only succeeded in repeating it.

Seth was confused and the emotions he cast along with his words showed it. *But my queen, you mustn't. You must direct your will to keep land and people.*

Shh, say no more. We are at High Hall.

The two passed through the outer antechamber and entered High Hall. Seth remained at Queen Mother's side. He was pleased to see Brother Ry'al seated behind Brother Samyuehl, First of the Blue Order.

Greetings, sent Seth to Ry'al, guiding the thought solely to Ry'al's mind. Seth had not seen Ry'al since the two had been together under Samyuehl's tutelage, a time during which Seth had learned a great deal—being of the Red Order meant that he had endured the seven teachings as one of each order and the training with the blue had been especially interesting.

Just as Queen Mother took her place and sent her own greetings to the foremost six, each dressed in the appropriately colored robes of their order—Yellow, Brown, Blue, Black, White and Gray—Seth contemplated his long period of tutelage. He then turned to the long rows of cushioned pews to the left and right of the colorful six where the members of High Council sat. As all seemed to be in order, he took his place two paces behind Queen Mother.

He noted that she attuned High Hall's crystalline walls to her own mood, which at first was both pensive and somber. Reflecting this, the walls shone mostly in various shades of black and gray.

Queen Mother's expression became grim and determined as she levitated into the air above the gray satin-pillowed couch that dominated the center of the immense hall. The gray of the couch again reflected the somberness of her mood.

For a few moments before he settled behind the shields in his mind, Seth knew and felt Queen Mother's every thought and emotion. She was reminding herself that she had been annoyed this morning and had been annoyed many times over many previous days, but not now. Now she needed to keep her mind clear and her thoughts focused. She needed to keep her emotions centered and directed.

She chose her words carefully now and directed her thoughts outward. *Greetings to wise council. Thank you for a speedy assembly...*

Those words were the last Seth heard before he entered the quiet solitude of his mind. His duty was to be present and not to listen in unless directed to. He had many other things to concern himself with besides squabbles amongst High Council or the First Brothers. Again, he feared for Queen Mother's safety and wondered what would come of his fears.

Within the folds of his mind, Seth was barely aware of the outside world. Time passed slowly. Then for a single instant, it was as if a breeze had entered his mind—a presence in his thoughts.

Seth opened his eyes and turned to Queen Mother. She regarded him for a moment then dismissed him by saying, *Go now, return to your studies.*

Seth stood his ground, the indignity he felt at the dismissal showing briefly on his face. Then he exited High Hall, speaking not a word.

A time will come when you will know there are things greater than the self, Queen Mother whispered after him, *things greater than our people, and then you will come to terms with the sacrifice I make, but for now return to your studies. You study the ways of Man for a reason. A time of great change comes, a time of change for all. The battle for East Reach is far off, but the battle to save all is already beginning…* She paused momentarily then added, *Call Brother Galan to my chambers.*

Chapter Two: The Winds of Change

Evening found Adrina in the East wing of the palace. She had been wandering its quiet halls for the last few hours. Hunger had roused her to conscious concerns. She still hadn't changed into a dinner gown and the evening meal was less than an hour away. She would have to hurry to meet it and this she did with urgency. She didn't want to be late, especially after avoiding her duties all day.

Her chambers were on the upper level of the West wing and while Adrina could have gone down two flights of stairs to the ground level and crossed the gardens to the West wing, she decided to use the private royal access ways. Although this route was longer because Adrina had to go through the North wing, she wouldn't have to go up or down any stairs. Also she didn't want to stumble into Lady Isador before she changed into her gown—she didn't want to stumble into Lady Isador at all, especially after avoiding her duties all day.

Adrina ran full stride down darkened corridors that she could have closed her eyes and ran along. There was no fear of bumping into anyone, no one but her used them now, and she knew well ahead of time their every turn by the count of her strides. She turned a sharp corner and knew she was entering the North wing. A mostly straight stretch of hallway was ahead and then another sharp turn—the West wing.

She slowed her gait to catch her breath; the line of light ahead was from the door to her chambers. She stopped outside the door and peeked in. Inside, attendants were waiting to help her with her gown but she didn't see or hear Lady Isador. She paused a moment more to ensure the governess wasn't waiting somewhere out of eyesight, then entered.

The attendants fussed over her hair for a time and helped her put on the gown, but Adrina knew she couldn't wait for them to finish properly. She rushed out of her room even just as they fully secured the ties of the gown around her waist and neck.

She raced so fast down the broad central staircase that she nearly ran down the captain of the guard. She stumbled through a curtsy, and then rushed away.

In the great hall, Andrew, her father, was seated at his kingly chair with its high raised back and stout, straight arms in the true fashion of his office. Catching the gleam in his eye as he looked upon her, Adrina sighed then sat. An attendant pushed her seat forward, and she nodded in response. She was not late, though only barely so.

"Good evening, father," Adrina said, while trying to hide the sudden smile that came to her lips. "I trust I am not late?"

King Andrew swept his gaze around the enormous oblong table to the faces of the honored guests. "Only so, dear Adrina. Only so."

Adrina looked to the stone figurehead that was Chancellor Yi. He stood rigidly behind her father. The old chancellor did not move as he stood there, nor did he ever unless summoned. This was a strange thing since otherwise he was plagued with a habitual cold. A cold complete with runny nose, continuous sniffles and sneezing. A cold that he could turn off and on at will. To Adrina it was a warning sign of the deadening effect of the dreary, gray castle upon the senses, numbing everything away, leaving only the dead and the dying.

She would watch him while she ate, as she often did, searching for that small, scarcely perceivable shift of muscle or limb that told her he was still alive and not quite dead like some of the courtiers who dined with them and might just as well have been made of the cold stones of the gray wall behind her—they cared just about as much.

Her stomach rumbled. Adrina looked to the attendants waiting to ferry food to the tables, knowing that the prayer would come first and waiting for Father Tenuus to rise to his feet and clear his throat.

Father Tenuus was the palace's only in-residence member of the priesthood. Others of the priesthood, like Father Jacob, first priest of Great-Father, had chambers tucked away in the East wing of the palace this was true, but mild times mandated a breaking with old traditions. Now only Father Tenuus remained. The others had long ago abandoned Imtal Palace.

When the aged priest, given to habitual forgetfulness nearly to the point of annoyance, finally began the invocation, Adrina said her own silent prayer. She hoped he'd finish in record time. Her stomach rumbled again. She was hungry, very hungry.

Adrina's eyes wandered to the aged priest as he spoke. Long ago, she had stopped listening to the words he spoke, and so she figured it wasn't necessary to bow her head or close her eyes either. She told herself she would relish the day when he passed on, and then she cursed herself for thinking it. It had been Father Tenuus who had placed the crown on her father's head on coronation day. Father Tenuus who had joined her mother and father, Alexandria and Andrew, queen and king, in matrimony. And Father Tenuus who had brought her into the world.

Adrina sighed. The prayer seemed finally over. She watched attendants descend upon the tables carrying plates overloaded with fresh baked breads, platters with golden brown game hens, decanters of wine and an array of steaming dishes carrying wonderful aromas. Her mouth watered. Yet, just when everyone thought Father Tenuus would say "amen," he began to speak again.

Adrina tucked a wayward strand of dark hair behind her ear and scowled. She looked around the table. Her father, apparently midway through a smile, frowned, yet made no comment. He never did.

When Father Tenuus finally did finish, it was a mad dash to get food to the tables while it was still somewhat warm. Adrina watched in earnest as she was served. The rather pale looking man to her right, clothed in a purple velvet overcoat and blue silken shirt, turned a whiter shade of white as he raised a handkerchief to his puffy red nose. He was pretending to be aloof but Adrina knew inside he was probably seething because she was ignoring him.

King Andrew smiled as Adrina began eating without waiting for his approval. Adrina knew he liked her independent nature, for he had fostered this especially in her. Yet she also knew a great deal could be hidden in a simple smile. Its uneasy weight made her cringe and turn away from her father's gaze. Her independence was exactly what she and Lady Isador, her maternal nanny—governess—had discussed in length just the previous Seventhday.

"His Majesty is getting along in years, as am I, young Adrina," Lady Isador had told her in her frank, motherly way. "Some day you will be alone. His Majesty favors finding you a suitable mate in the near future. Already several prospective lords have been made aware that you will soon be of courting age. His Majesty has charged me with preparing you to begin courtship. Yet, it is well known—" And this is the part that made Adrina cringe then and now, for Lady Isador had come to tears. "—that you are not a courtly lady. I am afraid I have failed miserably in my duties as your governess. I asked to be dismissed, but His Majesty wouldn't hear of it. 'She is strong willed, strong minded, not easily pleased, and quick to anger, which is perhaps my own fault,' His Majesty told me. Young

Adrina, I gasped at the hearing, His Majesty is never wrong nor at fault. 'Lady Isador,' His Majesty went on to tell me, 'you have a lot of work to do if you are to retire at summer's end.' I agreed with him on that point.

"South Province is calling me home young Adrina. Only Great-Father and Mother-Earth could keep me from it. I long to see my father's house, walk amongst the great white birch trees that line the yard, and smell strong southerly breezes. Breezes that make you want to curl your toes up and walk through tall midsummer grass..."

A smile did come to Adrina's lips then, and she turned to look back at her father-king. There was a far away look in the monarch's eyes and Adrina could only wonder as to his thoughts. Surely, he was considering the progress of the search. She had heard that not a single one of the upper lords had responded. She wagered that presently he was considering which nobles of the middle and lower houses had suitable sons.

Momentary delight came to her eyes as Chancellor Yi seemed to twitch—King Andrew had nodded ever so slightly to get the other's attention. No doubt having mentally completed the list, he was whispering a notation in the chancellor's time-bent ear.

Adrina played with the bit of honey-glazed hen that remained on her plate. No longer hungry, she probably could have pushed the mostly empty plate away, but soon afterwards one of the dreadful courtiers would have undoubtedly moved in and she would have been locked into a meaningless conversation. No, she thought, let them think she was only interested in eating.

When Captain Brodst, the man Adrina had nearly collided with earlier, entered and approached the king's table, Adrina's heart raced—even the captain of the guard did not interrupt the evening meal without justification. Adrina tried to listen in but could only hear some of what was being said.

"—it is urgent Your Majesty," Captain Brodst said, "a messenger has arrived this hour from the South."

King Andrew furrowed his brow. "I gather the news is more than urgent?"

Captain Brodst nodded.

"I see, have council chambers prepared. I will be along presently."

"Yes, of course, Your Majesty," said Captain Brodst, kneeling appropriately, preparing to make his exit.

"And captain?"

Captain Brodst nodded again.

"Rouse two guards to council doors."

A pained expression crossed the captain's face. Captain Brodst took great pride in his position as captain of the king's guard and apparently being told to do the obvious was an insult. Adrina sympathized with the burly captain. She liked him, though he seemed to have little love for her.

"At once sire," said Captain Brodst. Then he quickly departed.

Adrina was left to amble through the scattered remains on her plate. Her hope was to escape the dining hall and find a strategic position near the council chambers.

She waited, and waited, patiently thinking to herself that the matter wasn't too urgent or else her father would have departed immediately. Then again, her father had never been one quick to stir to action. Sometimes it seemed that he mulled over the simplest of decisions for hours—like the color of a new flower to put into the gardens—and then those decisions that she assumed he would deliberate over for days were made in the blink of an eye. Still, she had seen him take seven days to contemplate a heated land dispute when a decision had been desperately needed that same day to keep two of the lower lords from mauling each other.

As King Andrew laid his dinner knife aside and rinsed his fingers in the dipping bowl for what appeared to be the last time, all eyes around the great oblong table rose to greet his. The time for Adrina to make her move was now or never. She shot a withering grimace to the pale little man to her right—stay where you are, she warned with her eyes—and attempted to follow in Andrew's wake.

She glanced back as she gracefully but hurriedly exited the hall to see if anyone followed. Most of the courtiers were caught in the tangle of attendants swarming over the tables to remove the remnants of the meal. Some of the courtiers had guardedly returned to their fare as they always did. Some were already deep into meaningless conversations with whomever was to their right or left. These were the ones who had either decided they'd never gain the king's favor and it was nearly time to depart Imtal Palace, or those who were just present because it was *the* thing to do. There *were* those who had chosen the evening meal as their final battling ground—their last chance to confer with His Majesty—and these were the ones that sought to follow but were caught in the tangle of attendants.

There were also those whose task it was to watch. They were the eyes and ears of many a lord and even the paid spies of other kings. Adrina was suddenly sure the rather pale looking man in the purple velvet overcoat and blue silken shirt was not only pretending to be aloof but was also listening to the King's every word. He did not get caught up in the tangle of attendants. In fact, he moved rather adroitly through the crowded room and into the adjacent hall.

As she reached the wide open-aired corridor connecting the central wing of the castle with the West wing, Adrina's heart and mind began to race with the possibility of excitement ahead.

"A messenger with grave news," she whispered to herself.

Change.

***

Crystalline walls mirrored Queen Mother's innermost feelings. The day held promise. Her mood was bright. The room, bright.

Walls, ceiling and floor of the modest meditation cubicle were clean-swept, and this broken only by the frame of the door before her. The chamber, designed for ascetic purposes, was meant to hold no distractions.

Queen Mother herself was outfitted in a flowing white robe. It too was without adornment, designed to hold no distractions. It dangled several feet beneath her crossed legs and levitated form. Her arms were also crossed. Her eyes, appropriately closed. Her head, level and directed toward the closed door. Her thoughts dwelled solely on cleansing meditation.

She did not respond to the soft summons the first time it entered her mind. Instead, she held persistently to her meditation. She was trying to forget.

My queen... came whispered words into her mind a second time.

A second time Queen Mother cast them away. She didn't want anything to spoil her pleasant mood, especially as troubled as her mind had been upon waking and considering how long it had taken her to soothe those troubles away. The day held promise, she reminded herself.

My queen... the voice came more urgently.

Annoyed now, Queen Mother opened her eyes. A light wave of her hand stirred the cubicle's door and swept it quickly open. *Do come in Brother Liyan... What brings First Counsel to my door?*

Following the unspoken whisper, the timeworn elder outfitted all in gray entered the room—the gray of the robe was a symbol of office, unlike the white of Queen Mother's robe, which was a symbol of her whims. Brother Liyan nodded to the Red Brother who stood watch just inside the chamber. Dark brown eyes regarded him for a moment and a chill ran the length of his spine.

The crystalline walls slowly adjusted to reflect agitation. At first they dulled and darkened to a metallic bronze and then settled on a murky brown. Taking note of the falling and deepening of the cubicle's glow, Brother Liyan turned pale.

My queen, Brother Liyan said as he stepped across the threshold. He kneeled appropriately, and awaited her response to make further comment. Under other circumstances, he would not have been so formal and formality would have been the last thing expected of him, but here in the halls of Queen Mother's sanctuary when Queen Mother herself had called a retreat it was expected of him and so he did his part.

Queen Mother responded again, only with feelings as she often did when annoyed.

Brother Liyan looked up into Queen Mother's eyes and uneasily rose from his knees. *My queen, a thousand pardons for the interruption, but this matter is urgent. You did not address it directly during the assembly, but I gather that Brother Seth prepares for the journey?*

Yes, that is so.

I do not understand. Why Brother Seth, First of the Red? His strength is needed here in Kapital, especially now.

Queen Mother held her position, her long white dress cascading to the clean, cold floor. *It must be.*

You yourself said the chosen wouldn't survive the ordeal. The chosen will never return to East Reach… Brother Seth must not go. Who would protect in his stead? Surely then… Brother Liyan paused and looked to the brooding figure standing beside the door. *As the second, Brother Galan must stay…*

That is a truth you would do well never to impart again… Only those of the assembly know the fate of the chosen… Brother Seth is free to choose as many Brothers of the Red as he feels necessary to accompany him. If it is in his will to choose Brother Galan, then she too must go.

Brother Liyan paled visibly again, yet would make the protest he had repeated over and over in his thoughts in preparation for this very moment. *My queen, have you considered what it is you do? The Red are your chosen protectors. It will soon be too late to—*

Shielding their thoughts and slamming the cubicle's door abruptly, Queen Mother didn't allow Brother Liyan to finish. Black walls mirrored her increasingly somber mood, for these were the very thoughts she had sought to cleanse away through her meditation. *Precisely,* was her response and the Brother Liyan's eyes went wide.

My queen... Brother Liyan didn't understand.

Good Brother, savor this feeling on a future day, but for now know that I am fully cognizant of my actions. I am the living prophet of my people, am I not? I know very well what it is I do... If I as Queen Mother, the heart and soul of my people, cannot pay the dearest of prices for the ridding of the greatest of ailments, then I, and all, fail the greatest of tests... Brother Seth is our only hope. He will fight to survive where others would surely succumb. Never have I seen such faith. Never have I seen such determination. He must believe he can succeed. And he must truly strive for this.

My queen, Brother Liyan gasped. *I truly did not know or understand, forgive me.*

There is no need for forgiveness. There is nothing to forgive. We each have our parts in this and we must play them out. We have waited too long to act. Sathar has the ear of King Mark. Our people return to the lands of Man... There was evident sadness in her voice.

Brother Galan, called out Queen Mother.

Galan opened her brown eyes and cleared her thoughts. *Queen Mother?*

Leave us now. Tell Brother Seth, I await his presence...

Galan fixed her eyes upon Brother Liyan. Remember your place, her deep-probing stare said. Then she quickly departed the chamber.

***

Out of breath from the long run, Vilmos doubled over. The sharp pain in his sides told him the run had been especially good. The way he figured it, if the walk from his father's house to the edge of the woods took thirty minutes one way and he ran it in five, he had nearly an hour to do whatever he pleased.

After the pain and the spots before his eyes passed, Vilmos quickly stretched. He knew from experience if his leg muscles were too tense or if he strained a muscle, he'd have to walk—or limp—home. Upon finishing, he put on his boots. He preferred to run barefoot; otherwise, the boots gave him blisters.

The air grew suddenly cold as an icy wind howled up the little country path that parted the dark wood. It was then that Vilmos noticed how quiet the woods were that morning.

He stared long into the dark wood—keeper of his secrets—as he often did. Here his childhood dreams had been realized. In the shadow of the great trees, he could run screaming as loud as he pleased, slay fire-breathing dragons by the score, discover incredible lost treasures, play with imaginary friends, and still return home on time—well, usually.

Vilmos easily collected a large bundle of light wood from the nearby thicket, and then laid it aside. The wind howled. He stared up the overgrown path. He never ventured very far into the woods, only far enough to be within their shadows yet close enough to still see the sunlight of the clearing beyond.

He heard what sounded like footsteps. He turned and stared, but saw only shadows. An alarm went off in his mind. He picked up a large branch and wielded it before him.

"Hello?" he called out, "Is someone there?"

Movement in the shadows caught his eye. For an instant, he could have sworn he saw an old man carrying a gnarled cane.

"Hel-lo?"

Holding the stick before him, in what to him seemed a menacing pose, Vilmos crept into the shadows of the dark woods. Leaves crunched beneath his boots. He grimaced. Movement caught his careful eye again. He turned, raising the stick, ready to strike, then stopped cold. He saw a mound of black fur and dark eyes, a great black bear, kin of the much smaller browns the village huntsmen often sought.

The giant bear was no more than five feet away.

Two days ago in Olex Village, one of the three villages in their cluster, a young girl had been mauled to death by a bear. Vilmos didn't want to share a similar fate. He stood perfectly still, his heart racing so fast it seemed to want to jump out of his chest. Then the great beast reared up onto its hind legs. Terror gripped Vilmos' mind. Warm urine raced down his legs. His every thought told him to run, but he couldn't. It was as if he was frozen to the spot where he stood.

His eyes bulging, he stared at the bear, sure any moment it would swing one of its mighty paws and that would be the end of it. He didn't want to die; he had so many dreams left unfulfilled.

Again, a voice in his mind screamed, Run! But he could not.

Images from his nightmare became real. In the nightmare, the dark priests had come for him and, like now, he had been unable to run. In the dream, blue flames conjured from his fright and desperation had lashed out at the priests. The priests had merely laughed and still they had taken him.

As if conjured again from his fear and desperation, the forbidden magic came. Vilmos felt a prickling sensation—raw energy—in his fingertips. In his mind, he screamed No! at himself and the bear. What if this was the one time too many? What if this was the time that made the dark priests come for him? Then he asked himself the final what if. What if the bear charged now?

One swipe of its powerful paw was all it would take to end his young life. The girl from Olex Village had been taken nearly so.

What *had* the village huntsmen said about bears? Had the girl not run when she should have? Or ran when she shouldn't have? Vilmos couldn't remember. He stared directly at the bear. It was sniffing the air as if insulted that it was crosswinds from him. Then suddenly it dropped to all fours—Vilmos was sure this was it, this was the end. The bear would charge, swipe and he would die.

The bear roared.

Vilmos squeezed his eyes tight. A scream built in his throat, but died as it escaped his lips.

Silence followed.

Vilmos waited—surely the great bear must be charging—and waited. The forest was deadly still. Vilmos inched one eye open, then the other. The bear was gone. Astonished, both his eyes grew wide. He stared into the shadows. Listened.

Nothing.

He sniffed the air; there was a strange scent in it. Scorched wood. Burnt flesh. Singed hair. All three?

Slowly, Vilmos edged forward until he was directly in front of one of the forest's giant oaks. He ran his hands along two still warm scorch marks in the tree's trunk. He swallowed a lump in his throat. He had done what he shouldn't have. Somehow he had conjured the blue flames.

Suddenly remembering breakfast and the woodpile, he turned his gaze to the forest's edge. He saw the sun in the clearing and ran for its safety.

***

Seth glanced at the piles of scrolls and tomes spread across his desk. No matter what Queen Mother had told him, there was no way he could remain unaffected by such writings. The fact that she wouldn't listen to his protests only served to agitate him.

Focus, Seth told himself. He set one of the leather-bound tomes before him, tried to convince himself he wanted to read it, then after a long pause opened it. The book was titled, "Courtship rituals of the noble class." He read the first page without any difficulty; it was an introduction. In fact, he waded his way through three entire chapters without any difficulty.

Yet, he wasn't expecting to find a drawing as he turned the page to chapter four. Disgusted, he pushed the book away. There was no way he would continue to study such perversity. His thoughts were cluttered, so much had happened yesterday.

He focused his thoughts on the breeze blowing outside the protected fields of Sanctuary. He raced with the swells, danced in the swirls and accompanied the currents into the heavens. There was moisture in the clouds. This was good. The rain was needed to quench the dryness of the earth.

Peace of mind swept over Seth. The will of the land found him. He pushed away the troubled thoughts of today and yesterday, and returned to the book. Hastily, he turned to the next page and began to read.

Without announcement, a figure clad in red burst into the room. Seth looked up from his studies only long enough to see it was Brother Galan. He glanced up once more to see her prepare for a bath, then his thoughts returned to the book.

You study too much. You need to relax... whispered a soft voice in his mind, *You should join me.*

Seth looked up again to see Galan standing before him. *I wish I could.*

Is it true then what I've heard? Galan sent strong emotions with the words, longing and curiosity.

For the first time as he looked at her, Seth saw Galan as different, beautiful. Suddenly uneasy and not understanding why, Seth stared down at his books. *Their strange ideas pollute my mind even now.*

Then it is true.

Seth wavered his head left and then right in acknowledgment.

Galan asked, *What do you find most odd about them?*

Seth smiled. Galan had the insatiable curiosity of a preborn child. She held the same view of looking at the world. She saw things as flashes of colors and feelings. Only Galan would ask what he found most odd about them. *I find them most odd.*

Everything about them. This notion of marriage. Their idea of distinct gender. Their class structure. They would find me naming you, Brother, very odd.

Why is that? Galan scratched at her side. *Why has Queen Mother told you to study their ways?*

Will you stand my watch again this day?

Galan answered not with words, but with feelings, playfulness.

There *were* times Seth could easily forget Galan had only recently ascended. At times like now, however, he was painfully aware of it. Galan had many seasons of maturing ahead. Yet, Seth also knew that beneath the facade of youth lurked a mind that was quick and strong, already nearly a match for his own—which when he had ascended had also been advanced. In twelve short seasons, Galan had become the second highest of the Red Order.

Galan sent him impatience.

Seth shook his head again. *All right, all right, I'll join you... One hour away from my studies will do more good than harm.*

Chapter Three: It Begins

Days passed. News of the messenger from the Far South spread throughout Imtal Palace. Word in the halls was that it had been a personal message from King Charles of Sever. Something was terribly wrong in the small Kingdom of Sever, though none knew what it was. To Adrina it seemed servants knew more about the visit than she did. She had always been adept at gathering bits of information and tying them together, finding connections between the smallest of occurrences when there seemed none, which gave her enormous pleasure—a small triumph in an otherwise gray, boring world. She *had* truly done her best to listen outside the chamber doors, but had not succeeded.

Now it seemed she had a second chance. She was sure another messenger had just arrived. The palace heralds had just sounded in greeting, and minutes earlier she had heard the outer city heralds' trumpeting calls. Adrina glanced at the flowing blue gown Lady Isador was still in the process of hemming—Lady Isador wouldn't hear of allowing a servant to do the work. "Proper hands do proper work," she had said and chased the servants away. That had been hours ago. It was now well past midday.

The clatter of hooves against the stones of the outer courtyard caused Adrina to jump and turn.

"Stand still, Young Highness," said Lady Isador. "Look, look what I've done. I've to begin again."

Still on her tiptoes, Adrina stared long. The sight of a sweated mount passing to the stables brought despair to her face. If she didn't hurry, she might never find out if she was right about the messenger. Think quickly, she told herself, think quickly.

"Down, down, down my dear," said Lady Isador, "no wonder that hem looked all wrong. Mustn't stand on tiptoes."

Isador stopped her work and looked up at Adrina. "Oh, child, you look definitely peaked. Are you hungry? The day is long. Shall I order the mid-day meal?"

"Could we finish this tomorrow, Lady Isador?"

"Sixthday is only a few days away. We wouldn't want to disappoint his lordship, the son of Klaive, would we?"

Adrina rose to her tiptoes again and turned a longing stare toward the stables.

"There goes that hem again," muttered Lady Isador. "My eyes aren't what they used to be, perhaps they do need a rest."

Adrina asked, "Is that a yes?"

"Yes, Young Highness, it is."

***

Seth returned from the bath to find Brother Everrelle waiting for him. *Queen Mother wishes you to High Hall and would have you wait in the antechamber until her summons to enter,* Everrelle said, and Seth rushed off.

Seth found the antechamber empty. He waited, his thoughts filling with dread. Hours passed.

The walls of the antechamber oscillated through the cast of gray, hovering just slight of brilliant silver and then fading to a quasi-black. Oblivious to this light show playing out before his tired eyes, Seth sulked. He had seen it a thousand times before and would probably see it many thousands more. The subtle but swift changes were supposed to be soothing, though he didn't think so.

Seth felt utterly helpless as he waited. He considered eavesdropping on those behind the closed doors. It would have been an easy enough feat to do, a simple projecting of thoughts, nothing more. Those within would not have gone to the trouble of masking open thoughts, for the chambers did that for them. That was what the adjoining chambers had been designed for. The thoughts were enclosed within the sanctioned walls and went no further. The antechamber was considered part of the hall. There was another such chamber at the northern end. Guests could be seated in either of these chambers, and often were, and thoughts needed to pass back and forth freely. So no, the thoughts would not have been blocked to Seth. He would have only to reach out to them. Yet he did not do this for it would have breached the bounds of ethics ingrained into him since birth. He would wait and bide his time.

Seth turned his thoughts to Galan now. As they had walked to the bathing pool, distress had replaced her playfulness. Later, she had told him of Brother Liyan's visit yesterday. Afterward she told him she had not masked her thoughts during their conversation. She had heard, seen and felt everything.

I am afraid for you my brother, but I must not say why... Galan had said. *Will you promise to return to the chamber afterward?*

Seth had said he would.

Seth's thoughts became unfocused for a time. Then just when Seth thought he could wait no more, the doors swung open and the summons came.

He was shocked to see that all the members of the three councils attended and that many others streamed in through the far door. Many eyes were directed at him now and he did not know why.

There was an unusual amount of energy in the air accompanied by a strange silence, which to his prescient mind was like an unwholesome numbing. People flitted around in their cushioned seats or floated just above them nervously but voiced no thoughts.

Seth was beckoned to the fore, though not by the flow of words or feelings to his wildly spinning mind but by the briefest stroking of his intuitive senses, a presage bundled in the form of a picture and thrust upon his mind, which was done for effect. It was such an overpowering tool that only Queen Mother would have ever resorted to its use, for any other would have provoked open wrath in the recipient and retribution would have been called for. Sure, Queen Mother could have sent simple thoughts of hot-cold and thus directed him, but any child could have done that. She had wanted to stun him, and she had.

Head slightly lowered, eyes wide and upturned, Seth lurched to a perplexed halt. Words whisked through his mind as through a dream and he heard only a part of the message.

… I send my chosen protectors to return to the lands of Man as a symbol of my resolve…

Then suddenly an avalanche of voices cascaded into his head as Queen Mother's words spawned a heated debate. Seth could only stare blankly ahead, still half in a stupor as he sought to digest the multiple conversations.

Queen Mother lowered her gaze and when their eyes met a smile passed her lips—only in that instant, did Seth realize that none of the others knew what she had done to him. She had in a way stolen the words from his thoughts before he could offer protest. When he finally did come to protest it was already too late, only Seth had the misfortune of not realizing it then. He began his protest.

How can this be so? he demanded, *Surely this is some sort of…*

"Brother Seth, the decision of the High Council is final as is the word of Queen Mother," the voice that permeated the air of the great hall was Brother Liyan's. It was not often that one of the Brotherhood spoke aloud, but this too was done for effect. Immediate silence followed.

"But I must stay here. Here is where I belong. I have sworn to the Father to protect. Send another. The Red's first duty is to protect Queen Mother."

"No, Brother Seth," the voice again spoken aloud this time was Queen Mother's and now audible gasps crisscrossed the chamber. Queen Mother never spoke aloud. "It was I who offered your services. The Brotherhood shall serve in this undertaking. It was I, who said the Red would be the chosen ones."

What of the Brown? Is this not a duty of the warrior order? Seth was just as purposeful when he responded in thought, as when Queen Mother had spoken aloud. It was a small defiance, yes, but it was a defiance far greater than offering his opinion when she had obviously warned him that she wanted to hear little more than silence from him.

The presage had been her warning to him and now Seth had defied her, yet those of the council were not privy to her earlier act. So while gasps audible and inaudible—those of the mind—passed around the chamber again, Queen Mother fixed her open gaze upon him again. Under the weight of her stare, he must hold his tongue, or suffer the accompanying wrath.

"Brother Seth, their part will come. It is not now." Queen Mother again spoke aloud. "Why do you think you have been studying their ways these many past weeks?"

It is our duty, my duty, to stay. I will not go... Seth closed his mind to further thought. He did not wish to listen to any more nonsense. He had sworn with his life's last thread that he would protect Queen Mother for all times. He would not leave her now or ever.

There was a trace of anger in Queen Mother's countenance and the naked rendering of such a strong emotion in the company of the Council and so many others was in itself significant enough to send Seth's knees to trembling. It wasn't that he feared her wrath. Queen Mother held no malice within her—her eyes held only caring and her heart only love. There was greater pain than physical pain and the greatest mental anguish to his kind was shame and dishonor.

Seth? Brother Ry'al of the Blue thrust the word into his mind.

Seth refused to open his thoughts.

Still the stubborn one aren't you. Seth the protector. Can you not see? Surely, you must see it. The time is upon us. All is up to you, chastised Ry'al.

All this from Seth's final refusal to Ry'al's final entreat occurred in the interim between one heartbeat and the next—the speed of pure thought.

If I must use my rank of office on you, I will. It is as it must be; no others could make the journey. What lies ahead is preordained for you to do, said Brother Liyan, *whether you want to believe it or not, you know in your heart it is the truth.*

The force of Liyan's thoughts thrust into his mind confounded Seth and nearly sent a wave of anger rushing over him yet he was able to turn that very anger to his advantage. "I see the truth of your words, Brother Liyan of the Grey, Queen's Counsel, greatest of the wise." Seth spoke aloud, the precise phrasing of his words brought a partial smile to Liyan's face.

"I make formal apology to High Council and to Queen Mother, who is the heart and soul of her people and who has wisdom second to no living mortal."

Now Brother Liyan's smile blossomed and broadened into a full-blown smile—this naked emotion was allowed. *Wise words,* he sent to Seth alone.

Seth turned to face the Council, waiting for acceptance of the apology.

Council accepts your apology, Brother Seth of the Red…

Relief passed over Seth, though the most important expression of forgiveness had not been passed yet—Queen

Mother had not spoken. This never came, though Seth waited for what seemed nearly an eternity to his turbulent thoughts.

Who will accompany me? Seth asked, breaking the silence.

I shall leave the choices up to you, Brother Seth. The voice in his mind was that of Queen Mother. *I know it will be a difficult one but I have confidence in you, Brother Seth of the Red, First of that order, Queen's Protector. You are the chosen one.*

***

After piling the light wood cleanly on the floor next to the wood stack, Vilmos crossed to his room and changed clothes, heedless of the fixed scowl aimed directly at him. He was tardy, but only barely so. Somehow during the tangle with the bear he had lost the rope to tie around the bundle of wood. Instead of running home with a neatly tied bundle over his shoulder, he had had to walk. The walk hadn't bothered him though; his legs had been shaky and unsteady after the encounter.

His eyes wide, Vilmos told his mother of the encounter with the bear and later about his inadvertent use of the forbidden magic. Lillath's face turned white with horror. She swept Vilmos up in her arms.

"You poor, poor dear, frightened to death like that."

Vilmos' father put aside the Great Book and directed angry eyes at him. "Bear or no bear, there is no excuse for magic."

"Yes, father, I know, but the power just comes to me. I can do nothing to stop it."

Despite a mother's pleading eyes, the angry words continued. "No excuses. If you had returned after gathering the wood, you never would've encountered the bear. You must resist the temptation to use the forbidden. It is the work of evil. You will spread it to the land and you will be damned!"

"Now don't be harsh on the child, Vil." Lillath called her husband Vil to keep words directed at father and son separate. "Go ahead, Vilmos, eat, you look beyond starved." The objection finally said, the woman returned to her meal.

Vilmos started to smile, a flicker of hope that was cut short.

"I'm not being harsh. Do you want them to come? Do you want them to take him away?"

Vilmos gritted his teeth; here came the lesson.

"Salamander dweller amidst flames; Sylph light and dainty as air; Elf of forest and water; Gnome under mountain and stone; inhabitants of the four elements no more. All because Queen of Elves took pity on Gnome and so wed King of Gnomes under Solstice Mountain. Unknowingly she brought with her the gift of Elf magic. Elf magic in the hands of Gnome—pure evil.

"Sylph, Salamander, Elf and Gnome, no more. Only the four offspring of King Gnome and Queen Elf survived. Naiad dweller of river and springs. Nereid dweller of sea. Oread dweller under mountain. Elf dweller of forest. In the end, even though they fought the evil of this new magic and directed it toward good ends, all perished save willful Elf who was in the end washed into the sea with her people. This is the lore of the Four Peoples. Go now. Contemplate this lesson and the error of your ways."

Cheerless eyes of a worried mother silently followed Vilmos. He could feel her eyes upon his back. He retreated to the sanctuary of his room, plopping onto his bed where he began a vigilant watch of the ceiling.

A long time passed before his mother entered the room, carrying with her a large tome, the Great Book, and a plate crammed full with breakfast goodies: still-warm black bread, honey cakes, country jams, dark yellow cheeses and three varieties of smoked sausages. She sat the plate down and began to read from the Great Book.

Vilmos only half listened.

"After He was cast from our world, those among us, the wise, foretold that someday He would return. If we allow him to escape the darkness through our use of magic, He will survive the endless journey of darkness… Magic draws upon the threads of the whole of the world. Eventually the threads will unravel. A rift will be created. When He has finally regained his powers, He will use this rift…"

Such teachings had been lectured many times before and though they were not lost on him, Vilmos didn't give them much thought. The Dark Lord had perished a millennia ago. How could he return by the simple use of magic? Besides, there seemed a never-ending list of lessons pertaining to the use of magic. It was true that tales of the Dark Lord and Queen Elf were the two that he heard constantly, but he was tired of them all.

"I try hard not to use it, mother, but I slip on occasion."

"The use of the magic is expressly forbidden. Never use it. Do you understand me? Never."

Vilmos appealed to her with his large, innocent eyes.

"I know but the power just comes to me. It is growing stronger, mother."

A look of shock spread across Lillath's features. She gasped. "You must not use it. Vilmos, promise me!"

"I can do nothing to stop it!"

Lillath, now appearing older than her years, swept Vilmos up in her arms. She held him for a time in a motherly embrace, and then let him go. She knelt beside him and placed both hands on his cheeks.

"After He was cast from our world those among us, the wise, foretold that someday He would return, but only if we continued to use magic. Magic is evil, Vilmos. This is why you must never use it. Promise me." Her voice had never sounded grimmer.

"I will try, mother."

Overtures of desperation, also a hint of vast knowledge, touched her words now. "*Even* I could not stop what must be done if you don't do as I ask. Soon, mind you. Do you understand?"

"You wouldn't let them take me away, would you, mother?"

"No, I would never allow the priests to take you away, Vilmos. I promise." Lillath was crying now and on those words she returned to her kitchen.

In his heart, Vilmos believed her. She wouldn't let them take him away, yet if they came he knew she would have no choice in the matter. They would take him away. He would never see the Kingdom of Sever again.

Vivid images from the nightmare returned to his mind and with them came clouded, troubled thoughts. He did not want to be taken away from his home. He did not want to go away. He did not want to leave his mother. He loved Lillath desperately. She was all he had.

Vilmos closed his eyes then escaped to the place he went when troubled. A deep, majestic valley spread before him. Its view was breathtaking as he stared down into its depths, imagining himself a great, giant eagle lazily circling high above the valley floor. This was his special place, *only* his, he thought. He was the great winged beast, master of all it surveyed, who could swoop, soar and dive to the valley floor or glide up on a light puff of air.

Alone and free, the great golden eagle flew.

Vilmos had always been different from other children. His powers separated him and he knew and understood this as bitter reality. Other children wouldn't play with him. He was an outcast and he had been ever since the fateful day he had mistakenly loosed his magic during Three Village Day two summer's ago.

A tear rolled down his cheek. The blue flames were the cause of all his anguish. Two summer's ago he had nearly killed Willig of Olex Village. Over a game of catch-and-seek, the big boy had pinned him down and had beaten him mercilessly—Willig was a poor loser. Vilmos had used his only means of protection and now he was cast out, alone, forsaken by all—except by Lillath who loved him with a mother's devotion.

He didn't care, thought Vilmos, as he soared above the valley. He knew who he was. He was himself and that was all that mattered. Besides, now he didn't have to go to those silly celebrations and he no longer had to take lessons with Willig or Erik, the other counselors' sons, either. His father had hired private tutors to continue his education—a difficult undertaking since there were few in the land that could read or write with much skill.

A mocking grin broke the internal corners of his mind. Temporarily the image of the great eagle and the valley faded. Many tutors had come and gone since that terrible day. Yet his current teacher, Midori, was warm and generous. She did not overtax him with studies like the others. And although Vilmos did like her, he still had tried to frighten her away with his use of magic, as he had those before her. He had even resorted to his most resourceful trick—levitation: the floating of objects. The prank had only brought laughter and was ignored, to his utter dismay and befuddlement.

Devious thoughts clustered through his mind, scaring off another teacher would surely even out the score with his father. The frustration on Vil's face would suffice as repayment for many chastisements—besides, it had taken a very long time to find this newest teacher. He would use the blue flames, the blue flames that he had unleashed upon the unsuspecting boy, the blue flames that scorched and decimated, the blue flames that stemmed from his anger. He allowed the thought to settle upon his mind in a fanciful way.

However, the tutor had been so kind to him. It suddenly seemed an injustice to think such thoughts about her. Could he have really hurt her? he wondered.

She was unlike any other teacher he had ever had. In fact, he usually enjoyed her visits very much. With effort, the thoughts slipped away before the anger that would sweep him away found him.

The transition back to the valley was made with a single folding of thoughts one on top of the other. The eagle with its stout, generous wings soared above the pristine valley. Floating on a pleasant pocket of air, sinking to the valley floor, scouring for prey, it filled Vilmos with life.

Vilmos did not know that in this form he also breathed life into a creature nearly as old as the valley itself.

***

Brother Liyan closed his eyes and listened to Seth's tale. After the council meeting Brother Seth had wandered the halls aimlessly and caught himself from time to time staring down from above his own thoughts as if he were aloof from them and during one such time he remembered Brother Galan. She had been waiting for him since early afternoon.

Seth returned to the room they shared then and did a thing he claimed not to understand. Galan was sitting on the edge of her bed, running a comb through her long hair. He sat beside her and the next thing he knew his lips were pressed against hers.

Immediately afterward, Seth fled the room and in his confused state of mind, Seth said he knew of only one person he could turn to. Brother Liyan had been meditating in his private chambers and without announcement Seth burst into the room and in one great rush of thoughts explained all that had happened since he left the hall.

Liyan opened his eyes. *Brother Seth, you have hardly committed an unforgivable transgression.*

Seth sent Liyan tortured thoughts. *These ideals of Man corrupt my thinking.*

Brother Liyan had been Seth's mentor for only one season now, his appointment at Queen Mother's request. Just now he understood what it must have been like enduring the teachings of the seven orders and after every phase of the training beginning anew like a child and always in training with children. He was suddenly less afraid of the mysterious and powerful Red. *It is Mother-Earth herself that corrupts your thinking… Have you never been beyond Kapital or Sanctuary?*

I have traveled the canals of the city from end to end with Sailmaster Cagan, and I have traveled the road to Sanctuary. Is there anything beyond that I would care to see?

It seemed that Brother Liyan also understood why Seth had fought so hard in High Hall. Seth was genuinely afraid of venturing into the world and Liyan had perhaps discovered the one thing that could bring true fear to one of the Red. *The whole of the world, Brother Seth, the whole of the world. Sights so marvelous you could hardly begin to imagine them all.*

Liyan sent Seth a mental image, the green of a forest against the backdrop of a white-capped mountain, the sky so blue it was almost purple. *That is our ancient home. Is it not truly beautiful?*

What of my act? Is my mind perverted?

I should think so, said Liyan, quickly adding before Seth could fly into a panic, *but I do think it is treatable.*

I am being serious and you mock me?

Brother Seth, I will tell you a secret I have never told another. Liyan paused and collected his thoughts. Tears came to his eyes, for now he also understood why Queen Mother had appointed him as Seth's mentor. *Just as you fear what you do not know, the unknown in the world, I have always feared the Brothers of the Red. In fact, terror is a better word to describe the emotion—*

That is an emotion we are trained to evoke.

That explains much, but it is not the point I am trying to make. We all have our fears, and what we fear most is a thing unknown to us. From birth, your kind is secreted away from all of society. By the time you complete your training you are passed youthful adolescence and then we dub you protectors of Queen Mother, never thinking that up until now all your dealings have been with teachers and children.

You were wrong about the Brown Order. They were the chosen warriors only out of necessity. Before the Brown there was always the Red and, since the establishment of the Brown during those dark centuries when brother turned against brother, the Red are still, first and foremost, the warrior-protectors of Queen and people.

Perhaps it is a good thing that Queen Mother wishes you out into the world, and a good thing you studied the ways of Man. Their culture is not so different from our own that you could not learn from it. Liyan paused, though just for a moment. *With Elfkind mating instinct often skips generations for reasons only Great-Father and Mother-Earth truly understand. Your feelings are not wrong Seth; they are as natural as wind.*

With Brother Galan, I would suggest you follow your instincts, perhaps it will bring good. There is however, one thing you should know, these feelings may never find her… It is one of the tragedies of our kind. For now, you should turn your thoughts on the journey ahead— Brother Liyan put a hand on Seth's shoulder. —*Are you prepared to greet the world? Is the world ready for you?*

***

Adrina still harbored hopes that a messenger had arrived from the Far South. Her father hadn't been in the study, nor had she seen Chancellor Yi—both sure signs something was afoot. Fussing with the buttons of her riding outfit, she raced down the hall, down a stairway, along a set of corridors, and then stopped. As she ducked into the shadows of the hall, she covered her mouth to muffle a squeal of glee. Guards were outside her father's private council chambers—that cinched the premise!

The door opened. A lithe figure entered the hall and darted away—a messenger. He bore Kingdom insignia; no doubt, he carried a response to the message King Andrew must have just received. Minutes later, a second figure entered the hall—small-statured and obviously fatigued. Adrina watched him pass. He bore no insignia save one on the upturned collar of the cloak draped over his arm. It had white and gold bands—a king's messenger.

Adrina came out of seclusion in the shadows, wandered past the closed chamber doors and tossed a wink to one of the guards standing without. She knew they listened—even when they knew they shouldn't. She also knew how to make most of them talk, especially the younger man on the right. A number of ways to touch his heart and stir his tongue crossed her mind. Perhaps she would use some of the ploys and deceptive promises she had so recently been taught.

"No man can resist your eyes," she whispered to herself as the words echoed in her mind.

Another wink delivered, Adrina meandered up the nearby spiral stair. She knew where she would find that particular young guardsman later. It was to this place that she went, intent on waiting.

She stared down into the deadly stillness of the garden from the balcony where she waited. She had once imagined it contained all the colors of the world, though not now—now it seemed just as dead as everything else around her. Queen Alexandria, her mother, had put the array of gardens together, flower by flower, into one great garden. Now she too was dead: a victim of the cold, uncaring death that shrouded Imtal Proper.

Adrina paced as she waited and chuckled to herself about the pompous little courtier in his purple velvet overcoat and blue silken shirt. He was still attending dinners in the great hall, and still lent an ear to the king's every word. She laughed at him because she hurt and because there were small tears welling up in her eyes. She laughed until the pain went away and then she laughed a little bit more because the laughter sounded good in her ears.

The sun had already set by the time the young guardsman approached and the tears were long gone. Adrina waited until he passed her and then tossed a well-timed girlish giggle into the air, only then stepping from the shadows.

"Your turn at watch at an end so soon?" she asked.

"Your Highness, you know it is," said a mild voice, "sunrise and sunset are the times of the changing of the guard."

"Guardsman Emel," Adrina said several times. She said this to slight him, and Emel knew this very well, just as he knew they had been friends practically since birth. This was her way of reminding him of his place and also reminding him that he had something she wanted.

"Acting Sergeant," he said, "now if you'll excuse me—"

Obviously, he was still angry with her for what she had done to him and in a way, Adrina didn't blame him.

"—*Acting* Sergeant Emel, who'd've guessed?"

Emel's pace quickened. "Just until Sergeant Stytt's group returns from the Free City."

"From Solntse?" inquired Adrina, "Really from Solntse?"

She collected herself, recovering skillfully her slip of composure. "I could see to it that he is re-positioned there permanently."

She threw the offering at him, hoping he would pounce on it.

Emel deliberately chased away a spark of awe from his face. He could still and quite vividly recall what had happened the last time he had told her things he shouldn't have. Yet, he couldn't help wondering if she really could do what she proposed.

"What do you want in return?" he asked.

"Information, that's all."

Emel had his own skill of tongue and he knew the exact words to pull Adrina in and seal the offering. She would not get the best of him this time. "Something about *trouble*, though I'm not exactly sure what. You know how hard it is to hear anything through those damnable stones…"

Adrina thoughts swirled. She quickly equated trouble with excitement. She linked her arm in Emel's and pulled him to the edge of the balcony, saying nothing until she hid her glee.

"Geoffrey of Solntse owes me a debt, did I ever tell you that?"

"What kind of debt?" Emel called her bluff. He wouldn't fall for her lies anymore, as he had so many times in the past. He was now an acting sergeant. He must behave accordingly.

"Well, ah... ah," began Adrina, stumbling, stuttering, at a temporary loss for words, "a passed down one, actually. One really owed to the crown prince, one he must repay out of duty... and gratitude."

At his hesitation, she directed probing eyes—it could have been the truth.

Emel didn't believe her, but he did find it hard to be cross with her, especially when she was so close to him. He could feel her warmth. He missed the friendship they had, but he'd never admit it.

"There is a squabble in the *Minors* again." Emel used a double-edged slang for the four lesser kingdoms.

Adrina's eyes went wide. She tightened the link of their arms, pulling him a little closer.

"Between Sever and Vostok," added Emel, setting his own hook.

"*Again?*" asked Adrina, "Really?"

"King Peter stepped in... but... that's all I know. I could hear no more." Emel broke off intentionally.

"Emel, I'm sorry, really and truly sorry. I shouldn't have let you take all the blame before. I shouldn't have let your father send you away to High Road. I missed you the whole of last winter and into spring. I've wanted to talk to you since your return, but, but—Oh, if you know anything more, anything at all, you have to tell me. I'm going to die, just shrivel up and die, if I have to remain here in this boredom."

Adrina paused as her face flooded with emotion.

"Please."

Emel pulled away from her.

"Fair-weather friend," he shouted back as he stormed away.

"Emel, please don't leave. By the Mother, I missed you."

Hearing this, Emel hesitantly turned to look back at her, a thing he shouldn't have done. He couldn't wander long in her eyes without giving in to her desires.

Adrina repeated her plea and Emel swallowed a bit of his pride. "If I tell you the rest of what I know, do you promise to tell no one and can I rely on your word and swear you to secrecy?"

Adrina nodded.

"No, I want to hear you say it."

"I promise Emel, I will tell no one."

"Not *even* the Lady Isador?"

"Not *even* Lady Isador."

"Remember your promise, and that you are only as good as your word." Emel was hesitant to say more, but he began again just the same. "The rumors of unrest are true. I mean *really* true."

He was excited now and did nothing to hide it.

"King Jarom is supposedly behind it all, that is according to that page of King Charles, if you can believe him. He seemed the trustworthy type though. Yet, his kingdom is at stake. Quashan' garrison is to be roused to full alert status. Can you believe it? I'd give anything be in South Province now. Wow!

"That's it though, I don't know any more. I could get into *real* trouble for telling you this."

"I will tell no one," Adrina said, hiding hints of elation with a steady tone.

Emel eyed her.

"*Really*, I will tell no one, you have my word."

Adrina touched a spontaneous kiss to Emel's cheek and walked away, extremely pleased with herself. She tidied this away with rumors of the Bandit Kingdom's insurgencies around the northern borderlands—proof again that life beyond Imtal was *exciting* and *vibrant*. She knew enough about the Alliance of Kingdoms to know the chances of war were slim, but some good strife always mixed things up a bit. Attendance of court would be more exciting if she knew angry words were going to flare. The bitter place in King Jarom's mouth for the Great Kingdom was well known and goading this along would bring her distinct pleasure, if given the chance. She wouldn't let it get too far though, just enough to stir things up. It was about time that Andrew showed the Minors to their proper place.

Adrina descended a long flowing stairway that lead down into the central gardens and moved along its paths without seeing much of what she passed. When she reached the far end, Adrina stopped for a moment and looked back toward the upper balcony. Barely visible amidst the deepening shadows was a single figure bent over the railing with arms crossed. Adrina knew it was Emel and she paused for a moment more. The conversation they had just had hadn't been a conversation between good friends. She had always intended to make up for what she had done to him, but the time had never seemed right.

Feeling tired, the day at an end, Adrina returned to her chambers where she was sure Lady Isador waited. Having avoided the old woman all day, she could endure just about anything right now.

Chapter Four: Discovery

Imtal palace held an unusual silence even for the late hour of the night. Adrina tossed and turned, enduring a fitful dream from which she had awoken more than once. Dreams had descended upon her normally soft world of slumber of late—one in particular had plagued her sleep for many weeks, though she told no one. On this particular night voices in the hall passing her door wrested her from sleep. The old chancellor with his coughs and sneezes—which at one time she had thought of as endearing, though not now—was the next to pass, followed by the low, baritone moaning of Father Tenuus.

"Sire, please wake," called out Chancellor Yi with much reverence, "Keeper Martin wishes to speak with you."

"A keeper!" said King Andrew, rising up in his bed with a slow persistence determined by old age. "At this hour? What is a keeper doing here at this hour?"

"Please sire, Keeper Martin says it is a matter of utmost import."

The monarch stretched arms to full length and began his long, slow turn to put feet to floor, causing the chancellor to scramble for the royal slippers.

"Keeper Martin did you say?"

"Yes sire, Keeper Martin, head of all the Keepers of the Lore," said Yi, sighing with relief, as he just barely placed the slippers beneath his sire's feet as the king touched them to the hard floor.

"What is Keeper Martin doing here at this hour?" King Andrew cleared sleep from his eyes. "A king needs his sleep you know, especially at my age."

"I assure you sire, I wouldn't wake you unless it was a matter of import—which I am assured it is—though the keeper would not address the matter directly, sire. There is a look about him, as if he has just returned from a very long journey—a look of fatigue in the eyes, an unkempt beard. It is unlike Keeper Martin to have an unkempt beard.

"He wishes to speak to you alone. Rather mysterious, I must say. I will go talk to him if it is your wish, sire, and tell him to come back at a more appropriate time."

The king raised a hand to the chancellor's shoulder, using it to lift heavy bones from his plush bed. "There will be no need, Chancellor Yi. I am already roused. Tell him I will be along presently."

Father Tenuus shot a worried scowl to the chancellor as the two returned to the hall.

"I told you we should have waited a few more hours," he said in his lowest baritone voice. "Who is it that is here again, Keeper Q'yer or Keeper Martin, I always get the two mixed—"

"Come along, and lower your voice!"

"Oh, that's right, the Keeper Q'yer is that nice, younger man. Keeper Martin is distinguished and graying… His hair, that is… It must be Keeper Martin that has arrived."

"You're the one that's graying, and it's not your hair," said Chancellor Yi in a barely audible voice as he strode away down the hall. Father Tenuus had managed to annoy him as usual and he drowned the other's further comments by blowing his reddened nose a few dozen times into a long white handkerchief.

Further disturbed by the boisterous voices in the hall, the young princess had listened with great enthusiasm. Images of the troubled dream quickly fell away as she waited until the two old men passed by her door. A keeper here in the palace—and especially at this hour—was a sure sign of trouble. For a brief instant, she was almost sorry her wish had come true, but she quickly waved that off. Anything that brought a breath of life into Imtal Palace was more than welcome.

The balcony overlooking the entrance hall was not far from her chambers. After she pulled a robe loosely over her shoulders, she ran to it. A flood of thoughts exploded through her young mind and several expressions of glee escaped her anxious lips during the brief walk.

While she looked on a still drowsy king greeted the great Lore Keeper. She chuckled a bit at her father's dowdy appearance in his night robe and slippers, and at the gauche waddle due to the slickness of the smooth floor. The special significance of the meeting struck—especially when private chambers were entered without Chancellor Yi who was the king's principal adviser. This was further compounded by the arrival of a second visitor in the night shortly after the two had entered the chamber and closed the door.

To get a better view of the newcomer Adrina had to slip from the shadows of the balcony, for his back already had been turned to her when she spotted him. The distinct robes of his office were an easy clue as to who the man was as he removed his riding cloak and wrapped it over his arm. Father Jacob was first minister to King Andrew, head of the priesthood, and there was no mistaking the great swirling circles of white that decorated the sleeves of his otherwise black robe.

A visit by both men, especially at this late hour, was unprecedented and in her mind Adrina found only one answer.

"War," she whispered in reverent tones. The Minors were at war.

***

"Your Highness, Princess Adrina?" called out a distant voice in her ear.

Grudgingly Adrina stirred.

Her room was still dark, the world still blurry. It couldn't have been day. She closed her eyes and attempted to return to sleep.

"Are you all right, princess?"

Adrina recognized the voice of the burly captain of the guard now. She felt his hands on her legs and screamed. The scream, a long and high-pitched wail, brought guards from down the hall, Lady Isador and roused King Andrew from his bed.

"Get your hands off me! Go away!"

"I think you should come with me, princess," said Captain Brodst.

Again he attempted to help her up. Again she screamed.

Motherly Lady Isador came barreling toward the captain screaming, "Hurry, hurry!" to the guards that were right behind her.

"Get your hands off her. Guards, guards!" she continued.

Eyes wide, Adrina watched Lady Isador tangle with Captain Brodst.

From down the hall, she heard her father's moaning and the clamor of heavy feet running toward her. Suddenly she realized she was lying in the hallway beside the balcony. She slapped a hand to her mouth as the events of last night came flooding back to her—the voices in the hall, Keeper Martin and Father Jacob's unprecedented visit.

"By the Mother," Adrina whispered as she broke out in laughter. The scene *was* comical. Her lying in the hall. Small-statured Lady Isador barreling down on the burly captain. Her father waddling down the hall in his night slippers. Guards running to her rescue.

Lady Isador stopped wrestling with the captain and stared at Adrina.

"She's lost her mind." The governess gasped. "The strain must've been too much for her."

Lady Isador swept Adrina up in a motherly, smothering embrace.

"You oaf," she screamed at Captain Brodst, "what did you think you were doing?"

King Andrew stopped directly in front of Adrina and Isador, and then turned to stare at the captain. Uneasily four guardsmen were pointing their long spears at Captain Brodst. One of the guardsmen's hands was shaking so violently that the spear was swaying back and forth mightily.

Embarrassment replaced Adrina's cheer. She had no idea how she would diffuse the situation. She looked from the captain to the guards to King Andrew to Lady Isador. Apparently, no one else knew what to do either. The guards maintained their stance, spears pointing at their beloved captain. King Andrew scratched his head and attempted to wipe sleep from his tired eyes. Lady Isador was trying to hug the life out of her. Captain Brodst was staring down the four guardsmen, almost tempting them to charge.

Adrina let Lady Isador help her to her feet, and then she walked toward Captain Brodst and took his hand.

"Thank you," she said, "will you escort me to my chambers now?"

The captain walked her to her chambers, where Adrina thanked him again, then closed the door. For five days afterward no mention of the incident was made to her, though she did notice that any time Captain Brodst came near Lady Isador became very defensive. When this happened, Adrina would hide a smile with her hand and usually Captain Brodst would turn away, an irritated look in his eye.

Adrina spent those days trying to piece together what had transpired behind closed chamber doors the night of the unexpected visit. That is, when Lady Isador or Chancellor Yi weren't giving her lessons on courtship and etiquette, and discounting the horrible day she spent with Rudden Klaiveson. The more she probed for answers, the more intrigued she became. No one in the whole of Imtal Palace would talk about the visit—Emel included.

She was working on a plan to change that. Emel would talk. She had only to find the right time and the right words.

***

Across a vast open courtyard, on the far side of the summer parade grounds, lay the palace stables. Performing his perfunctory duties as acting sergeant had delayed Emel and by the time he had arrived at the palace stables the others of his company had been and gone.

His steed, fittingly dubbed *Ebony Lightning* because it was jet black and could outpace even stallions bred for the king's swiftest messengers, still waited in its stall. He had known the appointed time of first formation and so he had not hurried—then he had still had a full half hour.

There was a reason *Ebony Lightning* was the swiftest steed in Imtal Proper and maybe even in all the land, and that was because of the special bond between horse and rider. Before and after every ride, Emel rubbed the horse down from the poll of its head to the dock of its tail, up and down each powerful leg. In his proud eyes, Ebony stood more than twenty hands tall and when Emel rode him, it was from this height that he looked down upon the world.

Emel would have given anything to be like the Kingdom huntsmen, free like the four winds. His skills as a tracker stemmed from these desires. He had even pulled several short assignments at High Road Garrison—the last being during the past winter and spring—which allowed him to exercise these desires. He had not been able to take Ebony Lightning with him then, but now things were different—since the animal was from the king's stocks and while he had cared for the great steed for many years and been its only rider, it was only recently that he had been given the horse, a reward for services rendered.

He had been putting the finishing touches on the rub down when the unexpected visitor had found him. Now he could only watch from afar as the other riders began to file through the outer palace gates and listen to the ridemaster's call, knowing the evident anger in the tone. A determined Princess Adrina had found him. From the expression in her eyes and the saddlebags beside her, Emel knew without doubt what she wanted, yet he maintained his plea one last time.

"Adrina, I will say this one more time, please give me back the harness and let me go. They're passing through the palace gates. Damn you and your foolishness."

Adrina batted thick eyelashes. "Emel, please, I want to go riding with you. I'll have my father talk to the ridemaster if need be."

"Adrina, it's not the ridemaster I'm worried about. Now let me go."

Adrina dangled the harness in front of him, the only harness that remained in the stables—as far as Emel knew. Adrina had carefully hidden the others.

"No, not until you say yes."

"I'm late and I am going to be in real trouble." Emel was clearly flustered.

"Just ask, my horse is already saddled, I won't complain or anything, I promise. I'll even be quiet. I won't say a word the entire way. You know how much I want to leave the palace... It's so dead, Emel, it's all dead... I see nothing but these damned gray walls and all I want to do is scream, shout at the top of my lungs and curse the whole of the world."

There was evident sadness in her words and Emel understood it. He understood what it was to be swallowed by the sense of loss, to mourn for so long that all you remembered was the sadness—forever retreating to that hollow place in the pit of your gut where sadness swells from—yet his oath was to the Kingdom and not to her.

Also, he had sudden visions of spending another winter and spring at High Road Garrison.

"I never hit a girl before, but if I have to, I will," said Emel.

"I am not a girl, I am a woman, and I if you hit me—" The princess paused. Still determined, she continued with a cool tone that was almost callous, "If you hit me, I'll hit you back."

Emel believed her. She had been trained in hand-to-hand combat the same as he had—an actuality that Adrina was proud of—and the fact that she had bested him once or twice on the competition field led him to believe that she could be capable of it again.

"Okay, you win, I'll ask. Now let's hurry," said Emel, hoping to snatch the harness from relaxed hands, and that is just what he did. He put the harness in place and was in the saddle nearly as fast as the wind—by his standards—but, by the time that he had finished, the persistent princess was mounted and cleverly awaiting him just beyond the stable in the parade grounds.

"Adrina, please, just forget it!"

"I've never been on an adventure. I'm all set for excitement," answered Adrina, pleading her case with the tone of her voice, still holding to the melodramatic.

"We aren't actually leaving until tomorrow. Today was to be practice. There are a dozen other guardsmen who will willingly take my position. Please just leave me alone. I have to show the ridemaster I know what I am doing. Besides the ride to Alderan City on the edge of West Deep is hardly an adventure. I'll be back in a few weeks. I'll take you riding then."

"I don't care, I just want to be away, as far away from Imtal as possible. Besides, I know something of the reason we are going to Alderan by the sea."

Adrina directed her eyes at him—it was mostly true.

"*We* aren't going. I am going. If I don't hurry, I'll miss my chance too. Ridemaster Gabrylle is sure to be angry."

Adrina knew the departure was shrouded in secrecy. Ridemaster Gabrylle had been told to make the journey look like training for the young palace ridesmen. Adrina had heard this from a kitchen cook that bedded the ridemaster. She owed the rather large woman a string of favors for the telling.

"Seven days ago, my father had two important visitors in the night. One was Keeper Martin, head of all Lore Keepers. The other, Father Jacob, first minister, head of the priesthood. Keeper Martin brought grave news from the Far South."

"Really?" asked Emel, "You're not jesting are you?"

"Do I look like I am? By the Mother, I tell you it is the truth. You didn't know this, did you?"

The thought of lying outright crossed Emel's mind, but the truth was that he didn't know. As far as he knew no one had been told of this, though he was admittedly extremely curious.

"No," he said truthfully, definitively.

"I heard the whole plan," said Adrina. She was lying and vowed to repent later, if it worked.

"How do you know? I wasn't even told, and I am a Sergeant at Arms." He made the title sound lofty.

"And I am the king's daughter, aren't I? I am privileged to certain information that you aren't."

Emel was taken aback by her words, but believed her. Possibly she really did know, he thought.

"All right, but you have to tell me everything you know. Deal?"

"Of course, first you must tell me the reason we travel to Alderan. Then if you tell me the truth, I will tell you what I know."

"We travel to Alderan to meet a ship that sailed from Wellison in the South three days ago."

"Thank you."

Adrina spurred her mount on.

The two moved across the pristine green of the open parade grounds at a slow trot. Emel purposefully reined his mount in despite its urge to race away and chase the wind. He wanted to find out what Adrina knew, for then he could ride off, leaving her behind without a care—or so he hoped.

"Well. Aren't you going to tell me something?" asked Emel.

Adrina wasn't about to fall for this ploy. "Yes, I'm going to tell you, just not right now. Only if you talk to the ridemaster. Is it a deal?"

Flustered and confident he'd never find out what Adrina knew, also sure she would chase him down even if he charged his mount out the gates, Emel waived his better judgment. He agreed to her wishes. Anyway, he knew the final words of approval were not his. Maybe if King Andrew said a final no, Adrina would tell him what she knew anyway—if he stayed on her good side.

"Deal," Emel said, "I'll talk to the ridemaster."

Chapter Five: Realization

The hours passed slowly in the peaceful hollow Vilmos had retreated to, its gentle serenity carefully lulling him into mindless complacency. Thoughts of returning home seemed so distant, so very distant. After all, he could dwell in the valley forever, couldn't he?

There was a finality in the thoughts that frightened him, and it was only this that ended his feelings of complacency and propelled the urge to return home to the foremost thought in his mind. With one last look down over *his* valley, Vilmos turned and walked away, leaving the peaceful vale far behind in a few powerful strides.

Strange though it seemed, the return trek was never as easy as the initial folding of thoughts one on top of the other that it took to get to the peaceful vale. No, the trek home was a long and arduous journey through a darkened land. Vilmos had to pass along the little country path that parted the dark wood and run for some distance veiled from the sun, with a perpetually icy wind at his back. He had to cross the distance from the woods to the village.

The next step of the journey was to enter the quaint country home that was his father's. His face set in a heavy mask of personal anguish, he did so on his tiptoes, moving slowly and quietly. He crossed to his room and closed the door without a sound. Approaching the bed, *his* bed, he sat down unaware of the gaunt, still figure already present. A moment for adjustment taken, Vilmos opened his eyes and retreated from his special place—the place he could have retreated back to with a simple folding of thoughts but which never relinquished him without first warning him that the world was a cruel and callous place.

That he would remain in his room throughout the rest of the morning was already a given. He found contentment by idly sitting on the edge of his bed where he could gaze out the clear open window and think of nothing in particular. And when he finally did venture out of his room, it was not until the midday had come and passed.

Upon cursory inspection, Vilmos discovered his father had already departed. On Seventhday, which was today, his father met with the Three Village Assembly. He was sure they would discuss the recent bear attack. Goose bumps ran up and down his back. He could have ended up just like the girl from Olex Village—and only Lillath would've cared.

A cherished notion to run away vaulted from his mind. There was work that needed to be done. Helping his mother, Lillath, brought Vilmos happiness, even though he considered "housework" a woman's chore.

Whistling a little tune, quaint and cheerful, he diligently started. Sweeping the floors was an easy task, so he tackled it first. He swept out the kitchen and the long, oblong floor of the visiting room in a matter of minutes. Bedrooms and halls were next and after them, as always, the porch. He was sweating now and the cool perspiration felt good. It was "honest work" he did, or so his mother said.

He paused for a time, though not long. Wood blocks still needed to be split and piled by the wood shed. His room needed to be cleaned. The bed made. His few belongings gathered and placed back into the wooden chest that lay at the foot of his bed.

After several hours of continuous labor and an examination by his mother, Vilmos was finished. Joyfully, he scrambled into the kitchen to sneak something to eat, yet as always it was his ill-fated luck to be caught.

"Vil-MOS! What are you doing?" Lillath asked. She tried to hide laughter with her hand. "Never cease eating do you?"

"But I am hungry."

"Go ahead. Don't eat too much. We'll have an early dinner. Don't forget today is Seventhday and we'll all go to the service, won't we?"

Vilmos frowned, then replied, "Yes, mother," but in his mind, he wished they would not go. He hated the long sermons, during which he often fell asleep, which got him into even more trouble.

In a moment Vilmos knew that without fail he would be told to review the history and as he didn't want to do that, he gathered up his bread and cheese, and tried to leave.

"Not so fast. Hold on a minute Vilmos," Lillath said, "forgetting something?"

"No mother. I put the bread back into the box, honest."

In a blur he was out the door and headed toward his room, sanctuary one solitary step away when the voice reached him.

"Mustn't forget to study your history. Someday you'll fill your father's position. Even with your faults." She added the last part in jest, but Vilmos didn't catch the false sarcasm in her voice immediately.

"And what faults are those?"

Lillath tried to hide her smile with a shielding hand. "I'm only joking. Go study the Book."

Vilmos lifted the heavy book from its resting place. Usually the Great Book would lie before him the remainder of the day, but mostly his mind would wander. Vilmos turned back to his mother and asked, "Mother, are there other books? I mean, surely all knowledge cannot be contained in one book."

"Don't ever let your father hear you talk like that." Lillath paused and stared at the boy. Her tone became milder. "Books are a rare, rare thing in the land. It takes years, lifetimes, to pen a single tome. And only a true book smith can press scrolls into such a leather binding as befits the Great Book."

Vilmos smiled. He opened the book about midway, and then set it down. Normally he would have turned away immediately and stared out the window. But today the book seemed to want to open to a particular pair of pages, a group of pages shuffled and he was staring at a new section of the book. Thinking fondly of what his mother had said, he mumbled his way through the inscribed words.

With the simple lives of children, the story began...

Thousands of years ago wars ravaged the lands, spread by the slow incursion of the race called Man to the brother races until it seemed that humankind would not endure.

Great-Father had not intervened until this time, he had spread his gifts thinly out to each of the brother races, imparting each with but one simple gift, but even the wise and the great could not have foretold the coming of the scourge of evil spread by a maligning of those same simple gifts...

Time eternal evolves in great circles and the All-Father knew and understood this only too well. So as the evil scourge was finally defeated and the First Age came to an end, he planned carefully for the future by selecting and gathering a few of those last children and imparting upon them greater knowledge and wisdom than most. Some he taught how to outwit time itself. Some he conditioned as watch-wardens to look for the signs of the next Coming, the next Age of mankind. Others he cast into the never-ending circle of time itself so that their spiritual forms could wind their way through its realm. These were the lost children and he appointed a single guardian over them all...

To balance it all, there was one who was both good and evil, fated by destiny to become part of time itself...

Vilmos frowned and stopped reading. He'd thought he'd read, or had read to him, every page of the Great Book at one time or another, but he had never read this page. It puzzled him, and he reread it. What did it all mean? What was the lesson?

Confused, he closed the book and stared at its cover. Later he opened it to a different section.

***

Vilmos' father did not come home until late that evening. Vil had been delayed in a special advisory session. Apparently a series of bear attacks had taken place in Two Falls Village a day's ride to the north and, huntsmen and trackers from the surrounding villages were preparing to track down the great black bear. There would be no one allowed to travel outside the village until the bear was caught.

Vilmos, who had been listening intently at the door to his room, suddenly found he had an entire evening to do as he pleased—that is as long as he didn't venture into his father's eyesight. He thought Great-Father was truly smiling down upon him.

"What luck!" exclaimed Vilmos as he jumped onto his bed. "What to do? What to do?"

With final commitment, he closed his eyes and retreated to his special place. The vale was a beautiful place toward evening with a red-pink haze held in the darkening sky spreading outward into the heavens in striking hues of orange and red. The hunter eagle was gone from the sky now so Vilmos contented himself by sitting on the very brink of the high cliff he had chosen. Occasionally he would throw a rock up in the air, catch it midair and then let it lazily float down to the ground like a feather.

Suddenly tired, he yawned. His vision began to fade out as slumber entered his thoughts and within minutes he fell asleep. Lulled by his fatigue, he was caught in the *quasi*-world he had created. Sleep for him was always accompanied by dreams, although unlike others who often forgot their dreams upon waking, Vilmos remembered his.

The dream began. It was a strange and frightening dream, the only dream that had played out before him the whole of his life as far back as he could remember.

The words of the Great Book that had lain before him most of the day came to mind, corrupted by the evil of the dream...

The creature of darkness descended to the earth from the heavens, wreaking havoc across the land's face, once more reclaiming that which was his, that which was denied to him.

Look weak creatures! Look what you have let loose! Look what you have freed to provide for your demise! I am what you most fear! I am He. A name cursed for all eternity. I possess the forbidden name, never spoken lest it invoke the greatest of all evil. I am that evil. I can speak its name. Do you know what that evil is? What does mankind fear so very much?

You fear yourself. You fear that which mankind was, and still is. You fear the darkness of your soul...

The boy, who was Vilmos as he looked in upon his dream as if from a distance, saw the evil one and looked into his eyes. The darkness within was well known to him. Its origin of rebirth was known. Held entranced by its call, he moved his hand forward to help it but was stopped by a sharp, stifling pain that shot through him. The shock and ache made his small body writhe as it carried him away.

Unconsciousness befell him, yet the images and the agony were still clear in his thoughts when he awoke some hours later crying out into the darkness, huddled in a cold, sweated corner, his body clenched and trembling.

"No!! No!! It will not be!" screamed Vilmos, perspiration dripped off his forehead.

"No, no, no," he continued through the sobs, unable to block out the lingering picture of the shadows in his mind, especially the evil, mocking grimace that laughed a deep, hideous laugh and the cold jet black eyes that seemed to haunt every corner of his mind.

This was the worst dream he could recall. For a time the dreams had stopped completely, then they returned with renewed fervor. Each night the vision came. Repeatedly it played, relentless. Each time growing worse, because each time it became more realistic. Now it was as if the Dark One was in the very room Vilmos occupied.

Normally he would have simply escaped to his private point to stare out across the vast expanse below, feeling more at home and at peace there than he had ever felt in his own home. However, this night Vilmos did not want to return there. Something was wrong, though what he didn't know. Content to remain in his room in the dark, staring into nothingness, desperately trying to remember something that he knew was important, his mind raced in a million different directions.

Throughout the night, he lay gazing into the darkness, searching for something that appeared to be just beyond his grasp. His concentration was so great that he had not moved in the entire time and when the sun rose bright and beautiful into a clear sky, he did not enjoy its beauty. His mood only turned from pensive to dreary. The new day brought him only misery, as he knew it would. His body, stiff and sluggish, moving with the aches and pains of one well beyond his years, did not respond well to his desires and again it was a long, slow process to coax stiff muscles into movement.

After eating breakfast and methodically performing his perfunctory chores, his thoughts filled with dread. The tutor would come this day. Weary and fatigued, Vilmos trudged back to his room, slumped onto the bed, all his energy spent. Utter exhaustion played out on his face, though he didn't understand why.

The instant eyes closed, consciously or unconsciously, he drifted away to his special place. It had been calling to him in the back of his mind all that morning.

***

A chilling breeze blew through the vale. A wind that had never before been cold. Today something felt different, as if he were not alone. Worriedly, he scanned the little vale, its steep slopes and its large open floor. He was indeed alone or so he hoped.

He became a great silver eagle, fearless and swift. The dive from his favored cliff was accomplished in one powerful leap. Wings sliced the air and made it sing. Down into the vale's depths the eagle swept, with great speed and agility. The silver eagle's keen eyes had instantly spotted its prey and now it raced toward the unsuspecting valley hare.

This was the intruder in his domain, thought Vilmos. He would crush the life from his prey and then would indeed be alone.

He swept up the valley hare in razor sharp talons. The warm and fleshy hare writhed pitifully and cried out for escape. The eagle did not heed its cry, but a part of Vilmos did and he forced the great eagle to release the hare.

"Do you know what it is that you are doing?" beckoned a voice into his mind.

Vilmos was startled.

"N-no," he replied warily. The voice was somehow familiar.

Momentarily the vision of the eagle faltered. For an instant Vilmos stood on the high, raised cliff staring into the cold northerly wind. Then he was propelled back into the razor-taloned, silver eagle.

"It is called non-corporeal stasis, an out of body experience," said the other with evident wisdom.

"What are you saying? What does that mean? Are you here to take me away?"

Vilmos ceased being the eagle altogether, yet the cliff was not the place he returned to. Instead, he stood in the middle of the valley and searched in all directions for the source of the mysterious voice.

"<*Look!*> Look about you. What do you see?" commanded the voice.

Vilmos did as bid.

"I see the valley and nothing else."

"Yes that is correct, now look beyond the valley. Extend your thoughts and open your mind. Now what do you see?" The voice flowed with warmth and again Vilmos sensed a familiarity in it.

"I see only the valley," Vilmos replied.

"No!" said the other with vehemence, "<*Look, look again!*> Search beyond the valley. What do you see?"

Vilmos didn't like this game and clenched his fists in anger. "I see nothing!"

"<*Open*> the window to your soul. You *will* see. <*Look!*>" said the presence.

Compelled to do as told Vilmos looked inside himself. He saw the door to his soul and he opened it. Beyond, in the shadows, he saw himself, lying in his bed, in his father's house.

"What do you see?" the other asked.

"N-nothing!"

"<*What do you see?*>" commanded the voice.

"I see myself, I see myself!" Vilmos paused. His voice filled with surprise as he continued, "but how, I don't understand?"

"That is what the experience is. Your body remains on the physical plane and your spirit searches beyond. You were truly flying. You really were the lone eagle flying over a valley of your own creation." The ominous voice seemed to close in on Vilmos. "You are a master of non-corporeal stasis, yet do not forget that all things have mirrors on the physical plane."

"How is this possible?" the skeptic in Vilmos inquired.

"Think, before you speak. <*Look within, you know it is possible.*>" The tone of the voice became sinister. "As is everything."

"I am afraid. I want to go home—I want to go home now."

"But Vilmos you are home. <*This is your home.*> This is the sanctuary you alone created," the voice rang with heavy truths.

"No, I want to go home," insisted Vilmos, "I am afraid."

"Well you should be Vilmos, you should be very afraid." Vilmos pictured black eyes drawing up before him. "This experience leaves your physical self completely without defense. It is open to attack from any force or forces that wish to enter it. Any spirit can enter your body while your own spirit travels. And there it can grow and thrive!"

Vilmos jumped back, his face drawn and pale with shock. Bewildered eyes looked out. His body shivered beyond control. Everything within him told him to run away, to hide, though he could not. It was then that he recognized the voice, though vaguely. It was then his panic grew to despair and he feared for his very soul.

"It is you! This is what I was trying to remember!"

"Yes it is," said the voice with mocking overtones.

***

Gripped with fear, Vilmos stood unable to move. He looked out over the valley that had once seemed peaceful, only now regaining the point as he fought to focus his mind. He felt alone, very alone, though he knew he wasn't. He cocked his head, left and right, forward and back, searching. But his search was in vain because he truly was alone. There was no one else with him.

Waiting to hear the voice again and ensure he wasn't just daydreaming, Vilmos remained absolutely still. Only his own gasping breaths broke the silence, nothing more.

"Where are you? Show yourself," Vilmos called out. The only answer Vilmos received was the sound of wind rushing over the point and the returning echoes of his voice as it faded away and blended into the wind.

The vale was empty; the ridge, empty.

"Looking for me?" came a voice from behind him.

Startled, Vilmos jumped. His heart pumped faster and faster. Breathing became taxing. It seemed he could not grasp any air. He spun around, faltering and falling to the hard, rocky surface of the vantage point. He pulled himself to his feet, and shook defiant fists in the air.

"I will not hurt you," said the now charismatic voice from behind him.

Vilmos spun around again. "Where are you? Show yourself."

"I am here."

"But how? A moment ago, I was alone," said Vilmos as he turned to look in the direction of the voice.

"A moment ago, I was not here," said the venerable man who now stood in plain view in front of Vilmos. He was by far the oldest man Vilmos had ever seen. His appearance was one of such frailty and weakness that Vilmos imagined a heavy wind lifting him from his feet and casting him about in the air like a feather.

The aged man leaned his weight against his long, misshaped, walking stick, edging poised lips closer to Vilmos' ear. "Do not let the body fool you boy," he whispered, "I will not *<blow>* away in the wind."

Just then a cold, harsh wind started to rip across the point. With each passing second, it increased in force until it was a gale of great strength. Very soon, Vilmos found he could no longer stand in its face. He crouched to his knees and then to his belly. The old man did not so much as twitch.

"Please stop it!" screamed Vilmos.

"I cannot. Only you may stop it."

Not wanting to fall from the ledge to his death, Vilmos huddled close to the ground trying to maintain his grip with desperate fingers. "I don't know how to stop it. Let me go. I want to go."

"Then surely you shall perish." The man spoke sternly, his voice lacking any hint of remorse.

Vilmos trembled. "Do you mean die?"

"As surely as you were born."

Truth in the other's words stung Vilmos, similar to the dirt in his eyes. He knew without a doubt that he would indeed perish if he failed.

Wind whipped at him. Dust stung his face and blew into his eyes. And while Vilmos could barely see through this dust and dirt, he felt he had to see the old one again. Gazing through stinging dirt proved a difficult task accomplished only with shielding hands. To Vilmos' dismay, the man stood straight and tall, tall as the twisted staff he carried. He faced the wind and his stance still did not vary.

Suddenly the man did not appear so aged to Vilmos. In fact, somehow he seemed different, as if Vilmos saw another standing there in the old man's place. "I do not deny that you have powers beyond my grasp," began Vilmos, "but I don't understand the point of the test. I don't know what to do."

"Vilmos, <*use*> that which you already know. <*Use*> the skills you possess! <*Use them now!*>" The man spoke powerfully.

Compelled by the enchantment of the voice, Vilmos made a vigorous attempt. He concentrated, trying to make the wind stop. He clasped his eyes tightly together, held his breath, clenched his fists so firmly that his fingernails dug into his palms. The wind did not desist; it continued to lash at him with increased vigor.

Fearing for his very life, Vilmos tried again. He thought about the wind and wanting to stop it. In rebuke, the blast of the wind started to push him toward the edge of the cliff. Vilmos dug his fingers into the dirt trying desperately to hold on, grasping and clawing until his hands were bloody, but to no avail.

His fingers pulsated with pain. Vilmos screamed and pleaded desperately for assistance. He turned his head wildly back and forth, wary of the approaching drop. "I don't want to die... please help me... how can you just stand there, help me! Please, I beg you."

"<*Reach inside yourself for the power!*> It is there. The power lives within you. You have used it many times before, though you didn't know why or exactly how. <*You are the power Vilmos.*> It yearns to be released from within you. <*Release it.*>"

"Please help me!" Vilmos sounded pathetic. "P-please."

"Release the power Vilmos," repeated the other, "let it go. I am giving you a reason to use your power. I give you your life! <*Do it now, quickly, or you will DIE!*>"

The voice was commanding again, Vilmos felt compelled to do as invoked. He had to prove he could stop the wind. Somewhere within was the key, a key that must be found. It had been so much easier before. He had never really tried to use the power. Previously it had just come to him when he needed it. He needed it now, and it wouldn't come.

"Hurry, Vilmos. You must hurry!" spoke the man with a hint of anxiety in his voice.

In time, Vilmos found the object of his inward search. The strength was there.

Still unsure exactly how he was supposed to make the wind stop, Vilmos decided to let his mind drift. His thoughts wandered until he found a helpful clue. As he anticipated, the solution to his dilemma seemed to seep into his mind.

It had always been there.

"Quickly, Vilmos!" The man spoke frantically. "<*You must release the power now!*>"

A test of the power within forced the wind to flicker. Strength flowed to Vilmos unbidden. He bathed in its caress; it felt so wonderful.

Magic isn't evil; it is beautiful.

Vilmos knew what he had to do to make the wind cease. Now he would do it.

The man screamed, "Vil-mos, release the power, release it now before it is too late!" His anxiety increased with each passing second. "Hurry Vilmos! You must release the power now! <*Let it go, feel it flow!*>"

Vilmos perceived a peculiar scratching at the back of his mind, something loomed closer. Magic isn't evil, he reminded himself, the words flowing to him again.

"Go on try it," whispered the voice, "set it free."

Vilmos shook his head to rid himself of the irritating scratching.

"I will, I will," Vilmos said.

For an instant, Vilmos toyed with the wind. The gale stopped full, then started again with sudden vigor. Vilmos shook his head again to rid himself of the irritating scratching at the back of his mind.

Was it a whisper?

Seemingly as if simply acknowledging the whisper existed was enough, the voice came again. "No Vilmos," it whispered.

Vilmos shook his head again, his concentration faltering. Irritated the old man grabbed Vilmos about the shoulders and lifted him from the ground, shaking him violently.

"Do as you were told boy!" he screamed, his razor sharp finger nails pushing into Vilmos' arms.

With untold power captivated in a crisp, clear voice, the newcomer spoke again. "It is a trick Vilmos. Look closely, see his true form. Evil comes in many shadings, but you can always see through it if your vision is clear and your mind is centered. Search its form. <*LOOK!*>"

The wind stopped dead; the old man released his grip. Vilmos fell to his knees.

"No Vilmos, it is not true. Release the power. Do not listen to foul lies! <*Release it now!*>"

Heeding the will of the voice, the power of magic within Vilmos soared. Torn between the two choices, unsure which to follow, who spoke the truth, or what to do, Vilmos clasped his hands to his head. His mind reeled with pain. He wanted to curl up into a ball and disappear.

Unchecked the power within grew to a crescendo, reaching beyond Vilmos' control. His wild eyes stared in disbelief as crazed thoughts continued to spin through his mind. He was the power, the master of all he surveyed; he would release the force within.

"Vilmos, in the name of Great-Father, I command you *<AWAKEN!>*" spoke a third voice with overwhelming sincerity and vast fear. In the haze of Vilmos' consciousness, the voice was a distant untouchable shadow. The power within was so inviting and warm, he did not want to let it go.

The old one grew greedy and smiled an evil grimace. "YES, Vilmos, can you feel it? Yes. That's a good boy. Now, *<USE>* it."

Vilmos discerned and separated the perceived voices. The newest, the faint, distant one overridden with fear and heart wrenching pain, was feminine. The crisp, clear voice of the newcomer was calm and compelling. The voice of the old one demanded action.

"Are you the evil one?" Vilmos asked.

The instant disbelief entered his mind, the enchantment was lost. The energy within him dissipated. Vilmos looked dead into the old man's eyes and understood the guise.

"You truly are the evil one," said an amazed Vilmos. As he spoke, both strangers disappeared. The words reverberated in his thoughts.

With the releasing of the deadlocked gaze on the wall opposite his bed, the vision ended. Complete and utter confusion played across Vilmos' face. The sepulchral dream had ended, though its images were still held in his mind's eye. It had seemed so real, but how could it have been? He had never left his room; he would not have perished. It was only another daydream, a dreadful one.

He reflected upon what he had seen there and was deathly afraid, for normally when the dream ended the evil of the Dark One disappeared. This time the dream was different, Vilmos could recall shapes and images, even the form the evil one had taken.

It no longer seemed that the evil one was just part of a dream. He remembered the raging winds and the fear. It was then that an alarm of distress sounded within. Again there was a small part that he just couldn't remember he had seen something, but what was it?

The images became steadily less clear as he strained to focus on them. Pain in his hands caused all thoughts to drift away and when he looked down at them, opening and closing them with evident agony, he knew the pain had been real.

Physically and mentally drained of all its energy, his body was an empty shell with all its stamina gone. Vilmos wanted to sleep, yet he dared not close his eyes. The dream had been real, not imagined, he reminded himself.

Aghast, he curled up in the corner, fitting his small form into a tightly curled ball. The pain had been real, the dream been real, his mind repeated relentlessly.

Chapter Six: Permission

A strong wind out of the northwest blew long strands of dark hair into Adrina's eyes. Every now and again as she looked down into High King's Square, she tucked the errant strands behind her ear. Sunset was near, and the square was bustling with activity. Merchants packing their wares onto pack animals, townsfolk haggling for last minute deals and the inevitable array of jugglers, musicians, fire-eaters and the like trying to earn a pittance for their supper.

Adrina disliked the busyness in the square; nevertheless, she stared down into it. She was waiting for Emel to return with news from Ridemaster Gabrylle and the square afforded the best vantage point to witness the return of the horsemen. She was worried. Emel should have returned to the palace an hour ago—at least that is when he had told her he would return when she had parted with him at the palace gates.

Briefly, Adrina cast uneasy eyes westward. The sun was already beginning to dip below the horizon, soon it would be dark. Just then she noticed the northerly wind and a smile crossed her lips.

"Change comes," Adrina whispered.

As she turned back to stare down into the square, a distant sound came to her ears. It could be the clatter of hooves on cobbled stones.

She heard the sound again, though this time it seemed even more distant. Then trumpeters in the palace gate towers and at the city walls sounded off in response to the distant call and Adrina knew the far off call had to be that of a trumpet. Her eyes set with worry, she stared westward. Someone in the foothills beyond the green fields that stretched out of view was in trouble.

Trumpeters at the city walls sounded again—a cavalry call. Adrina knew the calls well—Emel had taught them to her—there was no mistaking the distinct call to arms. Imtal garrison riders would soon respond to the trumpeters' summons. Adrina's face flushed white. Emel was out there somewhere with Ridemaster Gabrylle and a group of unproven young guardsmen.

Her heart pounded in her ears, another call came from the city walls. A mounted guard was passing through the gates. Somewhere in the foothills a battle was surely taking place. Adrina had sudden grand visions of a full-scale invasion by the Bandit King of the North. Emel gallantly defending land and king. And the king's cavalry charging into the fray.

She held her breath until the call ended, realizing only as the call to arms faded into the wind the true consequences of such a thing. "Please Great-Father not Emel. He may be brash at times, but he is brave and true as any. The truth is, I would miss him dearly."

The silence that followed became unbearable and Adrina retreated to her room. For a long time, she stared out her window. The dusk sky slowly darkened and night arrived. The trumpeters made no further calls and Adrina eventually let sleep take her.

***

Unsure what had awoken her, Adrina stirred. She dipped her hands into the basin beside her bed and eased sleep from her eyes with the cool water. High overhead the light of a full moon was filtering in through her window, casting long shadows about the room.

An attendant was replacing the coals in her fireplace. "Sorry Your Highness," she whispered. "I shouldn't have let the fire go out, but I wished not to disturb you. It looks to be a cold night and I was concerned."

"Yes," said Adrina, "summer is surely at an end."

The attendant finished her work and as she departed she said, "Good night, Your Highness."

Adrina nodded. She was watching the flames in the hearth slowly build.

Soon a low but cheerful fire began to fill her chamber with warmth. As Adrina bent down to put on her slippers, she noticed she was still dressed in her riding clothes. She changed into her nightclothes. Thankful Lady Isador hadn't found her sleeping thus. She would never have heard the end of it. She could hear the old governess now, "Proper ladies do not sleep in their day clothes."

A soft knock on the door followed by whispers caused her momentary alarm. "Lady Isador?"

"Do I sound like Lady Isador?" replied a voice in a hushed tone.

"Emel?" asked Adrina.

"Of course Emel. Are you going to let me in?"

"Just a minute." Adrina slipped a robe around her then opened the door. "Hurry up, hurry up. No one saw you come up here did they?"

"Do I look stupid? Close the door, close the door."

Adrina closed the door. She almost ran into his arms, but caught herself on the first step. "Must remember your station, dear," she whispered to herself—Lady Isador's words.

"You're muttering, I can't understand you. I nearly ran into that attendant of yours. I told her I was making my rounds. She seemed to believe me. I think she rather likes me. She is pretty don't you think?"

Noticing how handsome Emel looked in the pale light, Adrina stared—here before her was twice the man the son of Klaive was.

Their eyes met, she averted her eyes from his. "I was worried. I heard the trumpet calls and when you didn't return I thought something dreadful had happened to you."

Emel chuckled. "Something did happen and you're not going to believe me."

Adrina directed her eyes at Emel. Okay tell me, they said.

Emel started laughing again. "You wouldn't believe what happened to Ridemaster Gabrylle."

Go on, Adrina's eyes said.

"We were skirting the Braddabaggon foothills on the return. Twelve new recruits, never been on a mount before in their lives. Twelve more that'd done border patrol once or twice, but still rather new to riding. Three others, acting sergeants like me. Ridemaster Gabrylle been cussing all day long. And out pops this lowland cat. The thing was seven feet long head to tail, all claws and teeth.

"It let out a cry and up went Ridemaster Gabrylle's bay. Ridemaster Gabrylle fell clear from his saddle and there he sat. One more hiss out of that cat sent the new recruits running scared. And they didn't just go in one direction. They all went in different directions. Half were clinging to their frightened mounts' necks and the other half were just trying to stay in the saddle.

"Ridemaster Gabrylle started screaming and cursing—it was then we noticed he'd broken his leg in the fall. He was spitting fire and those new recruits heard it and they panicked even more. They thought the cat was devouring poor Ridemaster Gabrylle. I didn't know whether to laugh, cry or help the ridemaster. It was comical as you please."

Adrina was laughing heartily now. She motioned to Emel to sit and hesitantly he joined her on the bed. He sat on one side, she on the other.

"Tell me the truth of it," Adrina said, "you ran too didn't you?"

"I did think about it. I didn't want to be there when Ridemaster Gabrylle got back into the saddle."

"What of the trumpets?" asked Adrina, tucking her long black hair back to one side.

"Oh that is even better." Emel paused and took a deep breath, his eyes following Adrina's hands. "Ridemaster Gabrylle's leg is broken and he demands that one of us snap the leg back into place. I'd never done it before and neither had anyone else. Gabrylle pointed at me and screamed, 'Brace the damn leg boy, I'll do it myself!' I gritted my teeth, closed my eyes and did it. Then I hear this snap, snap, SNAP!

"Gabrylle lets out this scream that chilled my bones and then we hear this trumpet call from Braddabaggon way. Gabrylle points at me and three others, 'Get that idiot boy back here,' he screams. We mounted. Then the call comes again. By that time, the city trumpeters are already responding and it's too late to do anything about stopping the garrison riders—you can't countermand a call to arms.

"We ride into the Braddabaggon a ways and at the bottom of this long round, we find this boy sword in one hand, trumpeter's horn in the other. His mount gone and half crazed hearing Gabrylle's screams, he wouldn't let anyone near him. Finally the four of us get the sword away from him—by force—and we were returning when we see two entire columns of riders approaching lances, battle armor, shields. They were ready for a fight. Gabrylle buried his face in his hands and wept.

"Well actually, I thought he was weeping. Turns out he was trying so hard to hold in the laughter he was crying, broke leg and all."

"What happened next?" asked Adrina. She moved a little closer to Emel. "What happened to Ridemaster Gabrylle?"

"Oh he's all right, no riding for a couple months."

"No riding for a couple months," Adrina sounded disappointed as she suddenly realized that no ridemaster probably meant the end of their hopes for the trek to Alderan. "What of the journey to Alderan? Did they select the twelve guardsmen?"

"It would seem that the matter is more pressing than the ridemaster's injury." Emel paused, Adrina moved again closer to him. "I think we'll still mount and ride tomorrow."

"Think or know?" demanded Adrina, moving back.

"Well, I was told to rise before dawn and have my bags shouldered when I go to morning meal."

"So you made it, you're one of the twelve. Congratulations!"

"Wasn't much of a choice after the cat. But I won't be riding as a guardsman, Ridemaster Gabrylle says I'm to continue my apprenticeship into the rank of sergeant."

Adrina was glad of her friend's good fortune, still disappointment played on her face. "I guess you never got the chance to ask the ridemaster about me, did you?"

"In all the excitement? No, I never got the chance. Still it seems the company will be very much larger than expected. During the day something happened that I'm not privy to. I don't know what it was but it's sure to be the reason why two full columns answered that alarm call.

"Seems Ridemaster Gabrylle wouldn't have lead the party anyway. Captain Brodst, my father, will. He's been elevated to King's Captain for the task. They'll be at least three garrison captains to boot. Seems half the city garrison is being roused and sent to the South. I don't know what's happened, but remember those two distinguished visitors in the night?"

Adrina nodded her head.

"The word is they'll be accompanying us."

***

Adrina greeted the new day with bleary eyes. After Emel had left, she hadn't slept at all. She had been busy plotting; somehow, she would find a way to join the company. With half the city garrison on the march, surely there was no need to fear for her safety.

"If only to see the sea," Adrina called out to the wind, "to smell salt air and wiggle my toes in the sand."

"Wiggle toes in the sand?" asked a voice from behind her.

Adrina quickly brushed her hair back and sat up. "Sorry Lady Isador, I thought I was alone."

"Talking to yourself are you now. You need more fresh air dear. You look peaked. Did you sleep well last night?"

Adrina considered lying. "Not really. It seems the world is passing me by and all I can do is watch. Do you know what I mean?"

Isador sat down on the bed beside Adrina. "You're talking about the departure today aren't you. When I was a girl of sixteen, I wanted to see the whole of the land. Odd though it is, all I want to do now is go home. You see, home is the place you try so very hard to get away from only to miss dearly when you are gone."

"Oh Isador, are you making fun of me?"

"No dear," said Isador taking Adrina's hand, "I'm not. Have you considered simply asking His Majesty?" No, Adrina hadn't. "King Andrew can be very open-minded at times. Look to the Princess Calyin. Your sister traveled more times to the East than I care to count."

"That was because of her betrothal to Lord Serant of the Territories."

"Yes, yes it was, but the Barony of Klaive is not far removed from Alderan City."

Adrina winced. "I do not want my life decided for me like father tried to decide Midori's."

"Your sister's affiance to King Jarom was purely a matter of state and for the good of Great Kingdom," Isador said with a stern tone. "You may never know His Majesty's anguish over that decision, but I knew, and your mother, bless her soul, knew as well. His Majesty was simply attempting to make amends for a transgression of youth."

"Did my father really win mother's hand over Jarom?"

Isador smiled and brushed back a wayward strand of Adrina's hair. "His Majesty won more than her hand, he won her heart, and, when Alexandria came to Imtal, she took with her Jarom's own heart."

Adrina's eyes wandered to the sunshine playing in the window. "Do you really think he would listen, Lady Isador?"

"You know I do, Young Highness."

***

Adrina awaited her father's response. Despite frowns and stares, she maintained a smile.

Father Tenuus, silent and brooding, stood off to King Andrew's right, a sour frown set to his lips. The king frowned likewise, probably agreeing with the captain's statement—the open road and a long, hard journey were no place for a young princess. Still, Father Jacob had added a rare touch. His blessing for her to accompany the group came as a surprise to say the least and thus was surely the reason for the sour grimace Father Tenuus bore before him.

Andrew rose from his high-backed chair and spread his broad shoulders wide. He looked first to Captain Brodst and then to the two distinguished visitors, Father Jacob and Keeper Martin. "Three years have come and gone since your mother's passing. Each day I grieve. Each day the pain does not diminish, it grows. I am beyond healing Adrina. Queen Alexandria *was* my life. You look so very much like her my dear, sweet Adrina.

"Each day I also see this pain mirrored in your eyes. I ask myself what I can do to end it. Yet, if I cannot solve this for myself, how can I solve it for another? I think the time away could be the time to finally heal. You may go with my blessing, my dear."

King Andrew looked to Lady Isador, "And, I understand you will visit the Barony of Klaive on the return. You don't know how much that pleases me, my dear. 'Tis a beautiful place come spring. Often I've envied Klaive his place by the great sea. Rudden Klaiveson is an apt and likeable fellow. When you announce your betrothal to him you will have made a wise choice, my daughter."

Adrina began to hurry away. She turned to look back at Lady Isador. "What of you, Lady Isador? I mean, you will come with. You do want to go home, don't you?"

"South Province will wait." Lady Isador sighed. "If you're bound for Klaive, I'd never resist the temptation to go with you. Hurry along now, before I come to tears. I'll be along in a moment to help you pack."

***

Glowing with delight at her father's approval, Adrina guided her mount through the palace gates, her head held high. She cast thoughts of Rudden Klaiveson away—nothing was going to spoil her day. The Barony of Klaive was at the very least a six-day ride away, and first they would journey to Alderan by the sea.

Adrina rode along the cobbled streets of Imtal toward its southernmost portcullis. She knew she would miss the city. So often had she looked out her window, stared at its tall gray walls, and dreamed of things beyond that the lands beyond seemed just that, a dream. She would miss Lady Isador, her maternal nanny, and her father, Andrew, this was true. But oddly, most of all she would miss those tall gray walls. They had housed and symbolized her fears, her loss, her anger, even her hopes and dreams for so long they truly seemed a part of her. The future without them to look out at, even if only for a few weeks, seemed frightening.

Her dreams had held her and carried her through those three long years. But now she finally had what she wanted and suddenly she felt an overwhelming urge to turn around and race back to Imtal Palace—for there, she could dwell in her dreams and hide from the truth, the cold bitter truth.

"Pleasant thoughts," she whispered, "only pleasant thoughts today."

She let her mind wander along the cobbled city streets and small shadowed alleyways they passed, pieces of her thoughts falling into every nook and cranny.

As the iron grate clambered closed behind her the excitement of the open road before them, the open green of a large inland plain and the gentle rolling of soft hills in the distance swept her away. She held no remorse for leaving now, only hopes for the thrills that lay ahead.

With but a gentle touch of moisture in it, the air that morning was fresh and cool. Overhead the sky was cloudy and dark and even though it held the promise of rain, it held an appearance of serenity. Adrina inhaled a deep breath and drank in the early morning aromas—the smell of grass and of early morning dew—then tightened the reins in her hands and bid her horse to speed swiftly onward.

Three squadrons of garrison troops filing through the city gates in ponderously long lines four abreast had been an awesome spectacle, yet the sound of hundreds of hooves and thousands of feet plodding along muddy ground, filling the air, was equally as spectacular.

"Half the city garrison," Adrina whispered to herself and to the wind, "all headed south, south to Alderan by the sea."

Chapter Seven: Meeting

After the ordeal, sight had been the first sense to return to Vilmos' tortured world. The other senses followed at a pace of their own accord—except pain. Pain it seemed had always been there, overshadowing the sense of touch. Taste came in the form of a pasty film that covered his tongue, which as he rubbed it away made his stomach sour. A vague odor came to his nostrils, the smell of his own sweat. The last sense to return was hearing. Rapid breathing burst upon him and Vilmos started.

"You are truly the evil one," Vilmos repeated in hushed tones.

The sound of stifled, irregular breaths fell upon his ears again. Realizing the sound was not his own, Vilmos shrank back into the corner. He would not have been amazed to see the dark-faced one sitting beside him—this he expected—yet as he turned, meeting a warm smile, he nearly wet his pants.

"Mi-do-ri, is that you?"

The tutor seated at a chair next to the bed, stared intently at him. The expression on her face was one that Vilmos did not recognize, one completely out of place, a look not of dismay or terror but of understanding and approval.

Vilmos pinched himself to insure he wasn't somehow still dreaming, and then asked excitedly, "What are you doing here?"

The teacher answered with words he had not expected. "Watching you Vilmos," she whispered softly.

In reaction to his anxiety, she shuffled the chair away from him.

"Why didn't you wake me? I was having a terrible, terrible dream. I was probably even talking in my sleep." Vilmos halted only for an instant to intake a breath. "I do that sometimes, just go on and on and on about nothing. The dream was scary, I think."

"Don't be silly," said Midori, "we both know you were not sleeping. I am a friend, Vilmos; there is no need to fear me. I am here to help you."

"Then was it real? Did it really happen?" asked Vilmos with renewed vigor in his words.

Midori glanced at Vilmos' hands and the blood dripping from his shoulders. "If you believe it occurred, then it did. If you believe…"

"I'm afraid," admitted Vilmos, "are you here to take me away?"

"No, Vilmos, I will not take you away, nor will I let the black priests take you away." She moved the chair closer to the bed once more. "I am here to help you."

"I don't need any help. Please just go away," said Vilmos feeling suddenly brave.

"I can't go away Vilmos. You need my help more than you know." Midori glanced nervously out the window. "Vilmos, you are very special. All you have to do is to trust me and let me help you. Can you do that?"

Vilmos nodded. Midori touched a dark yellow stone to the palms of his hands. "It is a healing stone," she said, "it will ease the pain."

"Is it magic?" asked Vilmos warily.

"In a way, perhaps," said Midori, upturning warm green eyes to ease Vilmos' fright, "but this stone comes from the temple of Mother-Earth." The stone began to glow, bright yellow, then slowly dulled to a charcoal gray. The pain gone from his hands, Vilmos suddenly noticed the sharp throbbing of his shoulders. "I am sorry. The stone's power is gone, but I could not have undone that anyway. I must go now. Will you come with me?"

"Wh-wh-where," stammered Vilmos, "are you going?"

"I am going to meet someone. A very good friend, who is special like you. He has waited a long time for you to be ready."

An internal voice told Vilmos if he were to leave now he would never be coming home again. "Midori, I am afraid."

The gentle woman offered Vilmos her hand and hesitantly he accepted. Her touch, sympathetic and soothing, put Vilmos more at ease. He looked up into her soft green eyes and suddenly worries and reservations about her intentions faded away. He would go wherever she would take him.

"We have to move swiftly," Midori said as she led him from the house. "The woods are a strange enough place with the light of day, let alone without it."

They had just reached the edge of the village, when the sound of drums burst into the air. Midori began to run all out, dragging Vilmos behind her. "Hurry, hurry," she said. "They come."

They made the trek from the village to the dark wood at a record pace, Midori dragging Vilmos behind her. Coming to a path, they took it. It was a seldom-used path, so it was largely overgrown with weeds and underbrush, but still visible to an observant eye.

High overhead the sky was turning dark and yet they followed the little trail. Many questions flooded into Vilmos' young mind. Where were they going? What of his mother and father? What of the bear? What of the drums?

Several times he tried to speak, though no words ever escaped his lips. He simply followed as Midori led him along the tangled trail, holding tightly to her hand. A sickness was welling up from his stomach. He felt the whole of the world was suddenly somehow different and the feeling didn't end as the trail did, coming to an abrupt end near the forest's edge.

The two emerged from the forest's shadowed darkness. The sun had already sunk low on the horizon in front of them. Soon it would be night. A large meadow spread beyond the forest's veil and soon they found themselves trudging across it. Vilmos could not see beyond the meadow's brink due to the rolling hills beyond it. He wondered what they would find on the other side, or perhaps if their destination lay beyond the hills, somewhere off in the unseen distance.

Determined now to quietly follow his silent companion, trudging on tired and sore feet, Vilmos began to wonder if they would ever stop to rest or sleep. His answer came as they marched up into the soft, rolling foothills beyond the meadow. They quickly found themselves on a rocky precipice over looking the most beautiful sight Vilmos had ever seen—the deep valley of his imagining.

"Hello Vilmos," simply stated a strangely familiar voice.

Vilmos was startled by the sudden appearance of the other. He stared at the peculiar tiny man for a time. His skin was the color of rough leather; the face deep set with wrinkles that covered its entirety was the best indicator of his great age; hair long and black with whispers of gray neither accented nor subtracted from his appearance of age and wisdom. Vilmos stared into eyes as silver as the moonlight, and found the man had a special energy about him. It seemed like an inner flow of light and, it intrigued Vilmos, and perhaps beguiled him.

Vilmos finally responded with a timid, "Hul-lo."

"I am Xith," spoke the man in a clear unwavering tone, "shaman of the great North Reach, perhaps the last of my kind, the last of the Watchers."

"How do you... Watchers? There is no such thing as a Watcher. That is only legend."

"Ahh, yet here I stand before you and you better than anyone else should know it to be true."

Vilmos searched his mind. The words appeared to be true, but how could it be so. The tiny man who stood before him could not possibly be a Watcher—Vilmos quickly discarded the thought. He would not judge others so hastily anymore. He had already learned his lesson once before about incorrectly judging people.

In the history written down in the Great Book, he recalled mention of the Watchers. He closed his eyes and concentrated, trying to find the words that momentarily eluded him. "...and the Watchers shall return from their long vigil. They shall bring word of the Coming..."

Vilmos opened his eyes. "You do not look like one of the great Watchers. You look more like a gnome than anything else."

Xith paused and took a deep breath. "Gnomes have not been seen in the land since Father Gnome sealed Solstice Mountain five hundred years ago."

"Father Gnome and Queen Elf are dead," said Vilmos, "and Oread was cast to the four winds with her siblings."

Xith sat and motioned for Vilmos to do likewise. He said nothing for a time afterward and simply stared at the boy, then spoke. "History belongs to the teller and is only as reliable as the teller's recollection of it."

Far off Vilmos heard the sounding of drums again. He saw Midori nervously glance to the woods. "Why are you here?" Vilmos asked.

"You already know the answer."

"Huh? I do?" said Vilmos without thinking. He slapped a hand to his mouth and raised his eyebrows. A realization entered his mind. He remembered something that had been gnawing at him ever since he had heard the shaman's voice. He had almost recalled it before, but he had lost the thought. Now, he did remember. He knew what had been lost in his subconscious. "You were there last night, in my dream and again before. I saw you."

"Yes," Xith said.

"Then was it all real?"

"It was very real, more real than you will ever know." Xith leaned forward and touched a hand to Vilmos' shoulder; the raked flesh was already beginning to fester. The shaman shook his head in disgust.

"But, but how... How did you... and now you are here... Thank you!" exclaimed Vilmos, clutching Xith's hand. "I remember now. I remember it all. I have seen you often in my dreams."

"I did only that which I must," Xith's voice was calm, unchanged.

"What do you want of me? Why have you returned?" Vilmos searched for a clue that would somehow indicate the shaman's intent. He continued to gaze into the shaman's eyes, and a feeling of exhilaration swept over him.

"We will camp here tonight. Get some rest Vilmos," said Xith, "tomorrow I will answer your questions. <*Do not worry, for there is nothing to worry about. All fears are behind you for a time.*> You will <*sleep*> peacefully this night. <*Sleep,*> young Vilmos."

Overcome with sudden fatigue, Vilmos found a dire need for sleep. Xith motioned with his hands and a fire appeared. Its warmth carried with it a healing touch and as soon as Vilmos lay down on the hard ground next to the fire, he fell asleep.

***

"Midori, come here. Let me look at you," said Xith, after a brief lull, "it has been a long time since I last saw you."

Xith stretched out his hands to greet Midori's. The two took a seat beside the fire opposite Vilmos. Xith's silver eyes glowed with joy in the firelight. He was obviously pleased at how Midori had grown. The years had surely developed her.

"Yes it has. I have not seen you since that day long ago when you left my dreams. I was only a child then," somberly stated Midori.

"Yes, you were. You have grown into a fine woman and have learned very well. I am proud of you," said Xith matter-of-factly. His words of praise the absolute truth. He was indeed proud of her achievements, although he was not completely surprised by them. He had seen great promise in her when he had chosen her.

Midori's lips rose into a knowing smile. Xith had been her greatest mentor. She respected him deeply for it and held his approval in the highest regard. "Thank you, Master Xith. I am honored by your kind words. Do we go together to Tsitadel'?"

"No, I am afraid the circumstances have changed. I must take Vilmos with me. There is another that I must take to Tsitadel', one with greater need. But that is not for sometime now. There is much to be done before then, so much to be done before then..." his voice trailed off. He heard drums sounding in the distance again.

Midori honed in solely on the one part of the statement that struck her as inconceivable. "With you? Not with the others?" she asked, a spark of fear entering her mind.

"Yes, I am afraid so. You should return now, there is much to do. We will meet again soon. Do not fret. There is nothing to worry about. Just explain to the council that I was wrong."

"But, you've never been wrong." Midori didn't know how she could tell the council Xith had been in error. No one would believe her. She knew something was drastically wrong, and an alarm sounded in the corners of her mind, though she tried to remain calm.

"I am an old man and old men should be allowed an occasional misjudgment. Besides times are changing. Tell them, I know they will believe you. <*Mention nothing of what you have seen. Clear the thoughts from your mind. Believe in me, Midori. What I do is for the best,*>" said Xith, his words flowing freely.

"I do believe in you, my friend. I will do what you say." Midori took his hand and added with an emotion filled voice, "I will not fail you."

"Please go. And take my blessing with you."

"I will worry about you my friend," Midori said. "Will you be safe?"

"My child," began Xith, using a soft-handed tone, "of course I will come to no harm. <*There is no need to worry.*> Time is short dear Midori. I have a great deal to say. Listen well."

A short pause followed while the words echoed in Midori's mind, <*there is no need to worry.*>

"Promise me you will forget what you know and what you have seen. Think of the boy no more. He is under my care. This alone should ease your woes. A great change is sweeping across the land. Great events are beginning to unfold. Things even I can only wonder at. The Kingdom of Sever is no longer safe. Do not return here.

"Take my mount. In the saddlebags, you will find several weeks of dried rations and three scrolls. The first must go to Master T'aver, you should know where to find him and yes, dear, I recall your dread of the swamp. I have inscribed the scroll with a special seal. The seal can only be broken by his hand.

"Still, choose your messenger with utmost of care. <*This message must reach his hands.*> He *must* know what to do when the time comes. The second scroll, you are to read only after you have departed the council. <*Do not read it before then!*> Among its instructions it lists the time when you should open and read the final scroll. <*Under no circumstances are you to read it before the appropriate time!*>

"Go now and take my blessing with you, it is you that I fear the most for." Xith's face grew dark and shadowed. "Watch your way with care, and I will see you many more times."

"Many more times," Xith repeated, waving to Midori as she departed. Then he looked to the heavens and sighed.

Nestled among a few shining stars under an otherwise obscured sky, a pale and somber gibbous moon smiled down. He bedded down beneath this thick blanket, his worries turning from the girl who ran away into the stark, hostile unknown to the boy, Vilmos, who was cradled in the known.

Taking the boy to Tsitadel' would have proven the easiest route, though he had already followed this path to its end in his mind. No, this path was reserved for another.

Xith had other plans for the boy, and in this he must not fail. He did not know if he could cheat fate or even if it was wise to try, though try he must.

Chapter Eight: Guidance

Storm clouds of early morning were blown south by strong winds out of the north and a clear bright sky quickly replaced dark clouds. Adrina rode quietly, content for a time simply to watch the scenery they passed, scattered trees, farmers and work animals in fields, and the occasional traveler. The swelling rounds of the Braddabaggon quickly replaced the green of flat-open plains. Though the gentle foothills weren't wild country, Adrina kept her eyes wide open. She didn't want to end up like Ridemaster Gabrylle. No lowland cat was going to ruin her day.

She thought about the long southwesterly trek to Alderan. The coastal port city, a mere day's ride south of the Free Cities of Mir and Veter, was rumored to be beautiful beyond compare. In days of old Alderan City had been the capital of the Kingdom. Named after the first king of the land, the Alder, it was once considered the meeting place of the North, South and East.

Adrina maneuvered her mount between Keeper Martin and Emel's, and attempted to spark a conversation with Emel, though without success. She didn't know why he was angry with her but she aimed to apologize quickly. She needed someone to talk to.

"Emel, I am sorry. I won't do it ever again, whatever it was. I promise," said Adrina softly.

"Are you at least going to tell me what you know?" Emel asked. "Or do I get nothing in repayment?"

Before she might have decided to come clean and admit she didn't know anything, but as she considered his question, she decided instead to feed him along. "Well, you actually didn't help me. It was Father Jacob who did, and he already knows the plan."

In response, Emel spurred his mount and rode to the front of the party. Her intent hadn't been to anger Emel, only to carry on a conversation with him. Now she felt doubly poor for what she had done. An earlier promise would be kept, she would say an extra prayer this evening to repent for the subterfuge.

"Dear, he will forgive you in time. For now, just let him be. Enjoy the morning and the fresh air. Drink in its beauty," said Keeper Martin.

Adrina was aghast; the Lore Keeper had spoken to her. She didn't have the heart to tell him that she had already enjoyed the morning and was now becoming extremely bored. Her reply instead was an easy response of agreement, a few more hours of silence would be tolerable, but just barely so. She hoped Emel would speak to her soon.

At midday Captain Brodst called the column to a halt. The abeyance would only be long enough to give horses and tired foot soldiers a much needed rest and to grab a light repast. Adrina was very pleased to rid her bottom of the saddle for a short time. After dismounting and leading her horse to where Keeper Martin, Father Jacob, and a few others were gathered next to a small stream beside the road, she readily dove into her saddle bags. To her delight, she found dried beef, still warm rolls and a skin of kinder-ale. In all the excitement, she had not even remembered to eat this morning.

While she ate, Adrina looked to the Lore Keeper and the king's first minister. She wondered at Father Jacob's approval of her presence. His words had surprised her then and puzzled her now as she contemplated them. Why did a man who spoke directly to Great Father care about a mere girl? Why did a man like that do anything?

And then there was Keeper Martin. Rumor had it the great keepers communicated in dreams and that is how they recorded the histories of all that went on in the land. Rumor also had it that Martin was unlike his predecessors. Martin was forever traversing the land. Heading over-mountain, braving the wilds of the Territories or journeying to unknown places in the Far South. Before Martin the head keeper never left the Halls of Knowledge.

"It is impolite to stare, dear," whispered a voice in her ear.

Hastily, Adrina swallowed a lump of half-chewed meat. "I didn't mean to stare. Do you know everything, Keeper?"

Grey-haired Martin chuckled. "No, Your Highness, I don't, though there are those who say I would like to."

Adrina took a sip of kindra-ale, a bitter tasting drink with an unpleasant aftertaste that was strangely satisfying. "Will you be going all the way to Alderan with us, Keeper Martin?"

"I was planning to turn south at the crossroads and press on to South Province with the detachment heading to Quashan' garrison, but I think I will continue to Alderan. My business in the South can wait a few days."

Not knowing what else to say, Adrina smiled and returned to her meal. After eating she wandered to the edge of the stream. There was a small pool here, formed where white waters rushing from upstream found themselves blocked by two large boulders. Bending down, she dipped her hands into the water of the pool. Finding it clear, she rinsed the dirt of the road from her face and neck. Then she slipped off her riding boots and dangled her toes into the cool water.

She looked back to the soldiers milling about on the road and finding not a few stares directed her way she blushed. "Not a proper thing to do," she imagined Lady Isador telling her. She quickly slipped her boots back on and pulled the collar of her riding blouse into place.

"Adrina?" called out Emel timidly, approaching slowly. "I'm really sorry about earlier. I was just frustrated that's all. I heard the news about your upcoming betrothal to Rudden Klaiveson. I guess I was just being petty. After all, you are a grown woman, but I thought you would've told me first. We are friends, aren't we?"

"Heard it from your father no doubt." Adrina frowned. "Rudden Klaiveson is days away and at the end of our journey. We'll have no talk of him or anyone else that'll ruin our fun, deal?"

Emel nodded in fast agreement.

Hearing the bantering of a large group of men, Adrina turned. "What are they discussing so heatedly over there?"

"Scouts. They left the group a few hours ago. Must've just returned," replied Emel. He cocked his head in their direction. "Sounds like they're worried about something ahead. The rains returning perhaps. You see the three approaching just now with the gold lapels?"

"Captains?"

"The one on the right with the grizzled beard is Captain Trendmore. The tall southerner is Captain Adylton. The other is Captain Ghenson. He's quick-witted. I like him."

Adrina grabbed Emel's arm. "Were they just talking about the ship from Wellison?"

"I don't think so. It wouldn't be a prudent thing to do—" A horn sounding the end of the rest cut Emel short. "—Time to mount. Do you wish to ride with me? I can show you a few things, about riding and scouting."

Adrina puckered her lower lip and bit the corner of it. "Really?" she said wide-eyed.

***

With the afternoon came the autumnal rains that the dark clouds of early morning had hinted of. At first it was only a gentle mist coming down upon them, later heavy sheets of icy moisture. The travelers quickly became bogged down in gooey, sticky muck. With no place to hide and wait out the storm in the open fields, stopping served no purpose. For safety sake the great column slowed to a crawl, yet Captain Brodst kept the group traveling onward. With any luck, the storm would be behind them in several hours.

Despite hood and cloak pulled tightly around her, Adrina was drenched through. Rain streamed down her face and though she felt helpless, she was happy—the dreariness was comforting and reassuring.

"Isn't this great?" shouted Emel, raising his voice above the ruckus of hundreds of hooves plodding through thick trail mud and the heavy downpour. "Castle watch is monotonous when compared to this, nothing compares to this!"

"Are you kidding?" screamed Adrina, pointed frustration flushing her face. She edged her mount closer to his, then reached over and slugged him on the arm. Emel didn't respond. He just smirked rather broadly.

Wet clothes and wet saddle were now chaffing and irritating. Adrina was cold and drenched and wanted desperately to stop for another rest. She turned to look back at the others through the shroud of rain. Father Jacob wore a solemn, thoughtful expression on an otherwise expressionless face. Knowing that the good priest was always like this—true feeling hidden on the interior of a hardened exterior—she wondered what feelings were hidden behind the clear impressionless mask. For therein lays the heart of the man—her mother had told her that once long ago.

The rain notwithstanding, Keeper Martin had his eyes wide open. He scanned the horizon ahead. His face, with upturned eyebrows and slightly furled lips, showed little complacency. Clearly he didn't like the rain or the trail conditions, yet as always he sought to maintain a clear awareness of their surroundings and find the good in ill. Something troubled him, noted Adrina. She guessed that it probably had something to do with their journey—the keeper had too much wisdom sometimes.

Besides the ever-present scowl, Captain Brodst had an otherwise expressionless countenance. For Adrina, the scowl signified order. The captain kept his companions and his subordinates in check with it—the guards, the soldiers, not even the distinguished guests, Adrina included, dared to speak their thoughts. They would endure the rain for as long as the captain ordered.

The others in the long line of garrison soldiers fore and aft, still four abreast on the muddied kingdom road, and the palace guardsmen that encircled her, Adrina noted, were disheartened. The rain was bogging down their thoughts. Some of those whose faces she could see despite the murky rain were thinking of other places—perhaps home and loved ones, perhaps just the local ale house—but still it was clear they were thinking of someplace else.

Her special talent, a learned talent for knowing what others were thinking from their expressions, a gift perfected during numerous court sessions, ended as she turned to regard Emel. She had a hard time discerning his feelings from his expressions. This especially troubled her and attracted her to him. As she considered this, her eyes wandered toward him once more—quickly turning away down the muddied path as her gaze met his. The message in his eyes, mixed feelings—feelings she didn't like—was confusing.

As the rain persisted and the day grew long, Captain Brodst signaled another slackening of the pace. Afterwards, he signaled the young sergeant to fall in place beside him. Adrina followed, then after slowing her mount, she did her best to listen in.

"... Remember it will be a light camp, no tents, " reminded the captain, "so find us a good thick spot in a forested canopy."

To Adrina's surprise, he addressed her next.

"Sorry Your Highness," Captain Brodst said, "we will be unable to reach an inn. I had hoped we would be able to make up some time, but the rain is slowing us to a crawl. Our file is too long to risk much faster travel."

"You considered stopping at an inn," said Adrina, more to herself than to the captain. "Even after what you said before we departed Imtal?"

"Come on, Adrina!" yelled Emel, as he urged Ebony to race the wind. "Catch up!"

Captain Brodst was part way into a response that was quickly drowned out as Adrina raced to intercept the retreating figure. She did toss him a final probing stare though as she swatted her horse to speed the weary animal's lackluster pace. She was also quick to turn back to the trail ahead as the captain sought to raise an objection. She was certain she was right about his constant scowl. It was his shield.

"You see, my father..." shouted Emel, looking back over his shoulder as his horse plodded through the thick mud and rain, "... the captain has a heart after all."

For a long time the two sped along the trail despite the greatly reduced visibility compounded by rain, diminishing daylight and their speed. Adrina had a difficult time maintaining her focus on the figure ahead. Soon she became completely absent of her surroundings, and watched only for the spray of mud from hastened hooves ahead.

"Emel, wait up! We aren't in that much of a hurry are we? The others are well behind us by now. Besides, how can we find a suitable place to stop if we can't even see what we are passing by?"

Emel reined Ebony in. "I don't need to see where I am going. Even in the rain I know this section of the road like the back of my hand." He stroked Ebony Lightning. "My first apprenticeship was as a king's messenger. I know exactly where we'll find a sheltered site away from the rain."

"Then why are we racing?"

"Imtal Palace Guardsmen and guests shall have the base fire. The garrison troops will have to fend for themselves. They have their own detachment and squadron commanders. It is my father's way of telling the palace guard he cares. Garrison soldiers will also see him as one who cares well for his own and perhaps there will be more than a few who at the end of this trip will wish to enlist his confidence. At the end of a long journey soldiers remember the little things. Food, water and shelter are held in the highest regard.

"And we race for sport!" said Emel urging Ebony faster and faster.

Mud and dirty water propelled high into the air and fell just short of Adrina as she fought to catch up under a flagging mount.

After they had rounded several bends in the road and breached several low hills, Adrina momentarily lost sight of Emel. Her heart still pounding from the race, she held her breath as she tried to discern shapes in the dim light. Then she spotted horse and rider racing off the trail and hastened after them.

Just before he reached the edge of the woods, Emel turned Ebony about and raced back toward her. In one swift move he wheeled his mount along side Adrina's and reaching down, seized the horse's reins just above the bit, bringing the mare to a rigid stop. Not expecting this, Adrina tumbled from the horse into the mud.

Emel dismounted. "Can I help you up, Your Highness?" he asked smugly.

Adrina could see he was trying to contain the humor within from bursting into raucous laughter. Her face was red and tears came to her eyes. Mud clung to her hair, her clothes, her cloak, and frustrated hands did little to remove it. "No, I think you've done enough already. I am quite fine!"

Emel tossed her an impish look and if she hadn't have burst into laughter, Adrina would have cried deeply. The laughter, a much need burst of cheer, was oddly cleansing, but short-lived.

"Damn you Emel!" she screamed, "You did this on purpose, didn't you?"

She was crying now and suddenly screaming at him again. "Damn you, damn you—" She realized she was whining and then how pathetic she sounded, she laughed—and the laughter felt good.

When Emel offered her his hand in assistance, she pulled him forward, and didn't let go until he landed face first into the mud. Then she tried to run out of his reach, but was too slow.

"Why you," yelled Emel, as he grabbed the retreating foot.

A backwards slip landed her, with a muddled thud, on her backside. She squirmed to get away from him as he dragged her toward him.

"Let me go! Let me go!"

Emel continued to drag her by one leg backwards through the mud as she fought to break free while the rain beat down upon them in a sudden strong drove. With both hands, she scooped up a large clump of mud and threw it at Emel. It landed with a splat, squarely on target and she finally broke free of his grip.

"So that's how you want to play it," Emel said, grabbing a large handful of wet muck.

Adrina returned the volley. "Serves you right!"

The mud flinging continued back and forth until they were both drenched and covered in mud from head to toe. Adrina was laughing so hard she fell backwards into the mud, adeptly tripping Emel as she went down. As she pushed a sodden handful into his face, both burst into hearty laughter. Then content to sit idle, allowing the rain to splash down upon them, the two passed a quiet moment.

"Stand up," Adrina said to Emel, offering her hand to him as he stood. "We have to get all this mud off of us before the others catch up. I don't want to get you into any more trouble."

Emel looked at her, eyes agape, as if he had just remembered something that his life depended on. Warily, he accepted her offer, quickly returning to reality from the momentary reprieve. They waited in the rain just long enough for it to wash the majority of the mud from their clothing and then prepared to move under the forest canopy.

"Grab your horse, follow me," said Emel.

Hurriedly, he led her into the large stand of nearby fir.

Quickly the rain became scarcely noticeable as they entered the thick folds of the shielded canopy and as they moved deeper and deeper into the heart of the great fir stand the rain was soon only a pleasant sound in the distance. The world became suddenly quiet and calm.

"Gather some sticks and small branches for kindling. I'll get the larger branches," said Emel. He loosely tied off Ebony's reins to a low branch and retrieved an axe from his saddlebags.

Adrina collected dry twigs and small branches into a pile as Emel had asked. When she had finished, Emel had already returned with a plentiful harvest of large branches. A tree had fallen nearby and its great boughs would be put to good use.

After a circle was cleared around where he would start the campfire, Emel quickly assembled the wood into a neat pile with the kindling at the base and the larger branches at the top forming a huddled triangle. Flint and steel were retrieved from saddlebags and then an instant later its spark lit the kindling. A few tender puffs spread the tiny flames and soon a gentle fire was crackling, replacing the soft sound of distant rain.

Adrina was almost impressed by his expertise. "Pretty nimble," she said, "how much longer before the others catch up?"

"Soon," Emel said, "so hurry up and take off your clothes. We don't have much time."

Both flattered and outraged, Adrina's face flushed and then became bright red. "What do you mean?" she shouted. She slapped his face. "Why I never! What do you mean get undressed?"

Emel swallowed harshly, then his face turned bright with embarrassment, a close match to the princess'. "What I meant to say was, hurry up and get out of those wet things so we can dry them over the fire."

"Why?" demanded Adrina, still upset.

"I didn't mean it the way it... I mean, what I'm trying to say is..." said a flustered Emel, "You need to dry your things before the others arrive. Otherwise, you know, it might be difficult for you to get them dry. I'll tie a line up between those two trees for you, and then you can hang your clothes to dry. I'll go watch for the others by the trail, just yell when you are finished."

After a moment of silence, Adrina laughed. Now, she understood what he was trying to say. "I'm sorry Emel," Adrina said, quickly adding, "I mean for hitting you, I'm sorry."

The fire was blazing brightly by the time Emel had tied up a secure line. He would have preferred to gather more wood as he should have done, but he didn't. The great fallen tree was close by though and it could serve as a source for many, many fires to take away the chill of the rainy night.

"Good-bye," he said, "just call out when you're done. If the others get here first I'll call out in greeting to them and you'll know they are close. I'll need to build a watch fire near the forest's edge but that will only take a moment."

***

The watch fire built, Emel was hesitant to leave its warmth. Returning with Ebony Lightning to unsheltered skies seemed an unpleasant proposition and he did so with quick regret. Almost immediately, cold rain drenched any part of him that had been partially dry.

An easterly wind blown from the direction of the distant sea made the rain feel that much colder. He knew, even on an evening such as this, the red glow of the watch fire from the darkened wood cutting into the darkened land could be seen a long distance. He needn't wait here on the trail for the others, for they could have easily followed the building light to its source. Here, he felt safer, safer because he was away from the young princess and the desires of his own young heart.

Safer? he asked himself, immediate alarms sounding in his mind. He had just left the Princess Adrina alone in the woods. He had not checked for signs of other passersby. Nor had he checked for signs of other creatures seeking shelter from the rains.

He mounted Ebony then charged into the thick woods, passed the watch fire, ducking low hanging branches as he went. Dark silhouettes of trees passed by in blurs as he raced for the red of the base fire. Reaching the base fire, he found the hollow under the canopy empty.

"A-dri-na, Adrina?" he screamed, his mind filling with dread.

Hastily, Emel dismounted. Panic mandating his every move, he began a frantic search.

"Adrina, where are you?"

For an instant, he felt a breath of air on his neck—perhaps the wind from beyond the forest. Then a hand clasped firmly to his mouth.

"Do not scream. I not harm you," whispered a dark figure, whirling him around so he was left staring into heavy gray eyes. "We bring word from land and people."

The figure then led Emel deeper into the forest. Emel counted the figures in the shadows as he was led passed them, twelve in all. He soon found himself in a large circle of dark-robed figures. All save one had the hoods secured, masking their faces. Princess Adrina sat in the middle of the circle beside a tall light-haired woman. Dark skin said the woman was surely a southerner, but the light blonde hair seemed out of place.

"Who is your friend?" asked the woman of Adrina, not turning to look at Emel.

"He is the son of the captain of the Imtal guard."

"Sit, Emel Brodstson," said the woman, beckoning with her hand. Then to Adrina she said, "We do not have long, I can hear the column approaching. I must speak fast."

Emel heard nothing save soft rain and perhaps wind.

"Travel not to Alderan by the sea. The ship you seek from Wellison will not arrive. You are in grave danger princess. A great evil has put its mark upon you. It is good you have a friend who cares for your welfare. You would be wise to care as much for yourself."

Adrina glanced at Emel, then asked, "Why me?"

"The struggle is long and many are its participants. The journey you have embarked upon is but the first step along the path. The evil has chosen you because of your position of influence and because of the emptiness within you."

"Can I not rid myself of this mark?"

The woman began speaking more swiftly now. "Look to two strangers for aid, for fate brings them to you. Beware those that are not what they seem and the traitor. A traitor among you will insist you continue to Alderan when it looks you should not. Remember, only death awaits in Alderan."

Adrina regarded the woman and started to say something but Emel cut her off. "What is so important about this ship from Wellison? Why should we even listen to you? You should flee before the garrison soldiers find you and run you through."

"Speak not words in haste, oft you may regret the reply. Yet if this is what you truly wish to know, I will tell you. Know there is a heavy price. Once a thing is known, you may not so easily turn away." The woman paused and stared into Emel's eyes, seemingly pleased with what she saw, she continued. "The ship from Wellison has a most precious cargo, the heir to the throne of Sever. At this very moment, King Charles lies dying in his bed. An assassin's poison is slowly eating away at him. Alas there is no cure, a terrible poison it was.

"The evil uses King Jarom's lust for power just as it uses you and many others. He sees himself seated in the throne room of Imtal Palace. He means to plunge the kingdoms into war. To be sure, he will use the death of Charles and the fears of the heir to his own ends."

"Can I not rid myself of this evil?" repeated Adrina.

"Please leave us now," said the woman to Emel, "go to your watch fire. The soldiers are near. I would speak to Adrina alone."

Emel hesitantly turned away, his pace just slow enough to hear their continued whispers.

"The evil brings the change you so wished for. It has found a home in the emptiness of your heart. You care too little for those around you. You see not the servants who toil for you, workers in the fields on their hands and knees with the whip at their backs, drudges scouring the kitchen floors—"

"I am not heartless," protested Adrina.

"Did I say heartless?" asked the woman. "Tell me, what is the name of the servant girl who cares so much for you that she remains awake through the night to re-stoke your hearth only to feel the lashings of a whip at her back the next day for laziness?"

Adrina fumbled for a name. "She is a servant girl, nothing more."

"Myrial," whispered Emel.

"Queen Alexandria, your mother, would have shed tears at the hearing. Your position has made you forget there are others in the land that suffer. Your father is not the strong and caring king he once was. Fault him not; there are those who use his grief to their own ends. You must open your eyes!"

Adrina tried to raise an objection. The lady continued. "Go now. Look for the two strangers, find the son of Charles, beware the traitor and those that are not what they seem. Say nothing of our conversation to anyone."

"But what can I do? I cannot rouse the southern garrisons to arms."

"I did not say to rouse the garrisons. Would you so foolishly provoke war?" The woman paused and stared into the shadows. "And Emel Brodstson, if you've heard enough, continue on your way. Remember, there is always a heavy price."

Chapter Nine: Ambush

What do we do now Brother?

We die, Brother Galan, Seth said coldly, simply, *but not until we fight honorably and die honorably.*

All eyes keyed to the hulking masses of multi-sailed vessels that hungrily approached.

Cagan? Seth directed the thought to the mind of the ship's captain. *We must get through. We cannot fight them all at once. Can we make it to open water?*

"Perhaps, if we use the escort ships as decoys while we break through—a hard strike to the right side of the blockade should do it. We can try to circle them and make for open seas. Once there, with the wind in our sails, this ship can outrun anything they can throw at us." Cagan spoke aloud as was his chosen fashion.

Running is pointless, Bryan said. *It would only show that we are cowards. We should strike the enemy head on, with our eyes wide open.*

I agree, Galan said.

After a tug at his grizzled beard and a scratch at his large rounded head, Sailmaster Cagan said, "We are not running, but surviving."

You are wrong, Bryan said.

Cagan's open thoughts streamed to Seth who stood beside him. Seth had passed more than a few nights sailing the canals of Capital with the kind sailmaster. They knew each other well, he knew no one whose love and respect for the sea was greater. It was Cagan's life. He also knew the venerable captain would not let them down, would not let him down, would not let Queen Mother down. *No,* Seth said, *Sailmaster Cagan is not wrong. Go ahead with your plan. I trust your judgment.*

Sailmaster Cagan passed instructions to the ship's broadcaster who in turn relayed them to the escort ships. A maneuver was dealt out to their small, honest fleet—one that would cost them greatly. The escort ships turned sail from their current position, and headed directly into the enemy blockade. They struck hard and to the right side as instructed and in a few terrible, fate-filled minutes, they were over swept. A heavy toll would be brought for their fall, Seth was confident of this.

Sailors from both sides swept over the decks. Tiny specks leaping from tiny ships, images that floated farther and farther away. Seth looked down to the deck of the Lady L. Those of the Red were lost in silent meditation, a thing Seth did not presently allow for himself. He knew well why they closed their minds to the screams they perceived—screams of pain, anguish and demise. He knew they were preparing for battle, a battle they must win.

Dark pillars of smoke and flames rose into the air far behind them. Seth saw tiny white sails engulfed in those deadly, dark flames and dark shapes, the broken hulls of fallen ships, sinking into the waiting, black waters. *They found open seas, but at what cost?*

***

Of the many enemy ships that had formed the blockade, only two were able to raise full sails and remain in proximity to them. The chase was on.

A master at the helm, Cagan turned sails to catch maximum benefit from the winds. He guided the ship into the head of the gull, a maneuver that would eventually steal the draft from the sails of the pursuers as they closed in, and force them to scramble to catch a fresh breeze.

Clever, Sailmaster Cagan, very clever, said Seth.

Cagan's retort was swift and his eyes never broke away from the sails or the wheel. "I had some help did I not?"

The forces of the Mother are at the call of all who know how— A peculiar sight caught Seth's eye and for an instant his thoughts broke off. *—who know how to use them.*

The wind ebbed on the fore-and-aft rigged vessel, which forced them to lose some much-needed speed. Meanwhile, the enemy cutters had finally found their sails and were gaining.

"They will not catch us, they cannot catch us," said Cagan as much to himself as to Seth, "not a chance, not a chance."

"Bo's'n!" he yelled, "Tighten that riggin', attend to that rope, check the trim."

The boatswain's response was loud and shrill. In brief, precise thoughts, he spit out the orders and, in short order, the swift craft lurched forward under proper sails.

Cagan, to the east, look!

A single ship grew from a speck along the horizon in front of them to a dot on the water. They could not afford an engagement now. The pursuers were too close behind.

"It is over, my friend," Cagan said, "one way or another, we must move to engage, either to the rear or front..." The wily sea captain paused. "Yet, perhaps—Yes, if we tack directly toward them we will surely catch them off guard."

Yes, maybe we can gain the upper hand before the others join the match, said Seth with twisted hope.

Cagan ordered the vessel turned against the wind, their nimble sloop could cut well in the tack. The cutters behind them, on the other hand, were much slower in the turns.

Cross-winded the Lady L rapidly approached the ship that a short time ago had been but a mere, distant speck. All onboard readied for the inevitable. Silent prayers were sent to Father and Mother to protect and watch over them and to keep them.

Seth looked down at his small group of dedicated followers. He knew that each prepared their mind and spirit for the end. Death was not a fear, though failure was. To pass in such a way would mean dishonor and disgrace. Therefore, they must succeed.

Readily their nimble sloop approached the oncoming vessel with expectant hopes that its captain would not expect a direct assault.

"Captain, she has square foremasts and two lateen rears," yelled the lookout from his perch.

An expression of dismay and fear passed over Cagan's face. He had not expected so great an adversary. The speed with which the vessel had moved through the water had led him to believe it was another cutter. He had not expected a full-sized galleon. His fears permeated the air, and flowed to Seth.

Seth was also worried. King Mark was better prepared than they had thought. He only wished he could contact Brother Liyan and warn him—galleons were not quickly or easily built. Many skilled craftsmen had labored long on such a vessel as they now faced which, as they drew closer, loomed larger and larger against the pale blue backdrop of the waning day. There could be no turning back now. Fate was locked in.

The two ships, galleon and sloop, were nearly within striking distance of each other. They were dead on course for the galleon, with the other enemy ships reduced to unseen dots along the horizon to the distant rear. For now, it would be just a one on one engagement.

Seth was proud of Cagan's sailors. They held no fear in their thoughts, only determination which was strong and growing with each passing moment. They followed Cagan's orders and kept the sails perfectly trim and rallied for the coming fight.

A questioning voice came into Seth's mind, *Brother Seth?*

Yes, Everrelle, responded Seth curtly. He was angry at the untimely interruption.

Do you mark any of our kind on board their ship?

... I do... not. Seth paused then gasped.

Nor do I, said Galan.

Yes, that is it, my Brothers! There may yet be hope. The enemy may be well prepared but they may also have underestimated the lengths Queen Mother would go through to ensure success. Mere numbers are no match for the power of the Brotherhood.

What if they are merely shielding their thoughts? Bryan said. *We should probe to make sure.*

Seth agreed. Bryan cast his will into the wind. Cagan continued on a direct course for the galleon.

There is no trickery, Bryan said.

Seth smiled, thinking that perhaps the day was not lost.

The galleon captain began to scramble to turn the large ship. He barked out orders, which carried across the darkening waters even above the sound of rising frenzy from both sides. He tried gallantly to fill sails for maneuvering speed though it was a useless effort.

Cleverly, Cagan turned toward the galleon's broadside, the bow of his ship locked straight on the exposed side. With a resonant rending, sloop and galleon collided. The air filled with the cacophony of crunching timbers and shrill screams as the battle was joined.

The galleon had received a potentially lethal blow and was gaining water fast. Still, her sailors would not go down alone. Grapples were swiftly set and tied off tight. The two ships would go down together if the sea had its way.

Cut lines were cast back relentlessly, yet this alone was not enough. Over the bow the enemy forces swept with blades readied in angry hands.

"They do not stand a chance against us!" cried Cagan to his sailors as he swung across to the galleon's low side on a rope tied to the upper rigging.

With a cheer, his men returned his chant and charged, their blades clashed with the enemy, and drew crimson blood.

Still one small group had not moved nor did it seem they had registered the attack. They were the members of the Red and they waited until the mournful screams in their minds reached a crescendo. Then Seth took charge of his fellows and as one they screamed in fury their chant of war, the chant of their ancient brethren.

Blood bathed in rage, they raced forward to the bow, pouring forth like a deadly red rain. A blur of brutal force, they dropped the enemy, each where they stood, with but a single precise touch. Such was their evident anger and the might of their invoked will.

Yet with a cry of ironic agony, their charge ended. Feet no longer tread solely upon enemy dead. Seth felt vivid torment in his soul. The first of the Brotherhood fell, a blow from behind piercing the brother's heart.

Seth vowed to spare no suffering on the one who had delivered the deadly blow. With a jump and a kick, the guilty was knocked stunned to the deck, his demise not instantaneous like the others before him. He would be forced to lie and watch with eyes that were purposefully allowed to move as life slowly dripped away. Seth's blow struck the spinal cord just below the neck on the right side.

Nine and one trudged onward toward the high deck where Cagan now battled the enemy captain. Three sailors were all that remained of his once proud group and they protected his rear as he struggled against the galleon's surly captain. Although thick lines of evident fatigue held to his countenance, Cagan persisted. For now his determination could not be extinguished. Yet the numbers were not on his side and soon the enemy would overwhelm Cagan and the last of his sailors.

Desperately, Seth continued the assault. The enemy was strong and skillfully wielded their weapons. Two more brothers fell.

Seth pushed onward with regained ferocity, as did his companions. He and seven others reached the stairs to the high deck and surpassed them. Only Cagan remained standing, all around him were the dead and the dying and, his sword lay deep in the enemy captain's chest. With the heel of his boot, Cagan smashed downward, and retrieved his cold steel blade. In disgust, he spit into the dead man's face.

Drained, Cagan stumbled. Seth rushed to his aid, and cradled him in still strong arms. "It is only us at the last." Cagan choked on his own blood and weakly added, "... my friend." His clothes blood splattered and shredded revealed multiple lacerations beneath.

There was no time to attend to Cagan's wounds, Seth knew this. The two remaining ships were near, and within minutes their ranks would sweep over the decks toward the place where the last few survivors stood. The middle decks of the sinking galleon were already being claimed by the yearning sea and their own small ship was beginning to founder under the yearning weight. The end was surely near.

Seth spoke to the seven yet fated to remain, words that exited his mind with powerful intent, words that he truly meant. *They are what stand in the way of our victory. We cannot fail! We* will *not fail! Do not still your fervor, nor your fury. We shall make them pay well beyond their expectations. Eight against the many shall be triumphant!*

"There are... nine!" said Cagan.

Chapter Ten: First Lessons

Vilmos bolted upright, unsure what had awoken him. Thoughts from the previous day came flooding into his mind. The Shaman. Midori. The drums, he heard the drums again. And voices.

Then for an instant, all thought stopped. No dreams, he realized, no dreams. He had slept peacefully during the night and nothing had awoken him, until just now. The drums, he heard them again.

He was about to speak when Xith clamped a hand to his mouth. The shaman stared meaningfully into his eyes. "Not a sound. Take my hand."

Vilmos nodded. His knees were trembling. He sat as Xith indicated he should. Quietly the two waited. The sound of voices and drums grew steadily clearer and closer. Soon it became readily apparent that whoever was out there was in the hills just beyond their clearing.

Vilmos was ready to run but Xith sat very still, his eyes closed, his face pale and drawn, and his hand clasped tightly to Vilmos'. From high overhead came the distant call of a hunter. Staring long, Vilmos caught sight of the grandest eagle he had ever seen. It was circling lazily over the hills and as Vilmos peered up at it, it turned a glistening black eye in his direction.

Suspicious, Vilmos stared at Xith.

The eagle called out again, a long piercing call, and then it folded its powerful wings and dove from the heavens. Vilmos held his breath as he watched it fall. It soared over the cliff's edge and down into the depths of the deep valley.

Color slowly returned to Xith's face and he released Vilmos' hand. "Huntsmen and trackers," he whispered, patting Vilmos on the back reassuringly. "They are from your village and the neighboring two."

Vilmos turned a watchful eye to the hills. "Are they looking for me?"

The shaman shook his head. "As far as I can tell, they hunt an animal of some sort."

"The bear, the black bear," said Vilmos, wide-eyed. "Is it near?"

Xith asked Vilmos to explain. Vilmos told the shaman of the bear attacks, the death of the girl from Olex Village, and his own encounter with one.

"Bears you say," Xith said, "that is interesting. Bears are not easily stirred, nor easily angered. Animals of the forest have a keen sense about them. We will have to keep our eyes open as we move north. To be sure, it would not be wise to travel north through Vangar Forest and a descent into the valley from here shouldn't be too bad."

Vilmos saw a puzzled expression cross the shaman's face and his eyes darted toward the hills. "You weren't expecting hunters and trackers were you," said Vilmos, sounding suddenly older than his years. "Who were you expecting, shaman?"

"There is no need to trouble over the could have beens," replied Xith. "Are you hungry?"

Vilmos agreed he was. The shaman removed a thick slab of finely smoked beef and a loaf of hard black bread from his saddlebags.

"Better eat all you care to," Xith said, "it will be a long day."

"I am going home then?" asked Vilmos. "My parents will miss me if I am not home soon."

Xith had been busily cutting thin strips of beef. He paused, and then laid the knife aside. As he began to speak, his bright and shiny eyes lost their gleam and there was evident sadness in his voice. "Many, many years ago, I made a promise to a young couple who were very much in love. Five years they had been wed and still they had no children. They so wanted a child. I told them of a girl heavy with child in need of caring hands.

"The girl, your mother, needed a secluded place to stay, a place where none knew her or that her child was without father. Death by stoning is the punishment for such a child and mother.

"I told the couple they must harbor the child's mother and see that the child entered the world without harm. Afterward the child would be theirs to keep and raise as their own. I also told them there was a price. One day I would return for the child. Until that day the child was in their care—"

"—I want to at least talk to my mother," cut in Vilmos. "I'll tell her I am fine and that I am with you. She will understand, though I am sure she will tell you to make sure I am back before the next Seventhday."

"<*You will not be home before the next Seventhday,*> Vilmos, <*or any other day.*>" Xith paused to ensure Vilmos understood. "Your father was among those from the three villages. I could sense his anguish. He knew the day I spoke of those many odd years ago had come. Your feelings for him are wrong you know. He loves you more than the air he breathes.

"I stayed with them for three days when I escaped from the North with your mother. I told them the signs to watch for, the signs that would tell them I would return." Xith stood and walked to the rim of the valley and gazed across the great span. He said nothing for a time, and then turned to look back at Vilmos. "Your magic is what brought me to you, Vilmos, and the reason your father was so exacting. He knew your use of magic would only hasten me to your door."

Tears in his eyes, Vilmos looked away from the shaman.

"<*Do not be sad,*> young Vilmos. To be sure, Great-Father and Mother-Earth will not let their sacrifice go unrewarded. <*Look now to the future*> and the days ahead. "—There was a distinctive quality to the spoken speech that was consciously inaudible to all save cautioned ears, this was the power of Voice, and Xith played upon its dominion with the touch of a maestro's hand.—"<*In your heart, you have always known*> one day <*you would leave your home.*> You *know* this is true."

Vilmos nodded in agreement. Closing his eyes, he pictured long black hair touched with gray and tired eyes of hazel.

Xith turned to fully face Vilmos and stared directly into his eyes. "It is time we started our journey. There is much to do, so very much to do. I would ask you now to come into my service—sort of an apprenticeship. There is much I can teach you of the powers within you. I would have you enter my service of your own free will but there are things I must first tell you.

"Know that you *can* stay if it is your intent. Know also, the dark priests will surely find you. They will not be as kind as I. They will bring a sentence of death upon those you love, as this is the law."

Vilmos shuddered at the mention of the dark priests. Their task was to purge the land of magic, a task they and those that served them had carried out across the centuries.

"Or you can come with me now. I will do my best to teach you control over your powers. And though I am not human, I *can* teach you the way of Magus." Xith's expression became stern. "A very difficult trial awaits in the coming days. In this, I need your help Vilmos. Will you help me?"

"Lillath will be lonely," Vilmos said, wiping tears away from wet cheeks. "Will they ever have another child?"

"In time, Lillath *will* bare your father a child."

"What of the dreams, are they gone?"

Xith stared directly into Vilmos' eyes. "Have you made your choice, Vilmos?"

"I wish to go with you."

Xith's face betrayed no emotion, pleased or otherwise. He waved his hand, beckoning Vilmos to follow him.

***

The descent into the deep valley had taken hours. Picking their way along the broken trail to the valley's floor had been akin to torture. Four times the trail cut out of the face of perilously high walls had ended, and four times they had used ropes to continue the descent. Each time Vilmos had muttered under his breath that there had to be other trails and each time Xith had responded with, "Perhaps, perhaps not. At any rate this is the path we have chanced upon." Xith had spoken the words with such vigor that Vilmos was sure there was a lesson in the words but what it was he didn't know.

Vilmos craned his neck to see the lip of the wall they had just descended. He was panting, and sweat dripped from his chin. Vilmos sighed and fought to take in one lengthy breath to get his breathing under control. The hard work had been oddly cleansing.

A soft breeze cutting through the valley brought cool air swirling beside the wall. Vilmos smiled, cool perspiration against his skin felt good. "Where do we go from here shaman?"

"The northwesterly curve of the valley will carry us to the upper bounds of the Vangar," Xith said, indicating it was time to begin again. The brief rest was over.

The shaman spoke as he walked, "From there, it is at most a day's trek to the plains beyond. We do not want to delay long in the forest. Hearing the news of bear attacks puts me at great unease. For something that surely isn't human or oreadan has taken up residence there."

"Oreadan," mused Vilmos, turning to regard the shaman more closely. With the high sun at his back, the shaman seemed even more intriguing and mystical. Perhaps it was the wrinkled, timeworn face or the troubled, weary eyes that although the sun dulled them were still of a silvery gray.

Perhaps his height which measured Vilmos' equal—but Vilmos was a boy with much growth ahead. As Vilmos considered this, Xith's words struck a chord—nothing was north. "Do you mean to leave Sever? There is nothing but desolation beyond."

"That is what you have been told, this is true. But the whole of the greatest kingdom in all the lands is north," answered Xith, as he slung his leather satchel over the opposite shoulder and changed his walking stick into his left hand.

"The Alder's Kingdom."

"Yes, the Alder's Kingdom, known as Great Kingdom to those who dwell there."

Methodically, Xith picked up his staff and placed it in front of him with each plodding step. Although well in his years, he didn't show the signs of it. He didn't need the walking stick though it looked very appropriate in his hand.

When it seemed Xith would say no more, he said, "And, the Borderlands are north of course."

"Is that where we will go?" asked Vilmos, "I do not want to go there. I have heard strange tales about the Borderlands—evil dwells there," a direct quotation from his mother. Vilmos was well practiced at recalling such things. His eyes grew wide. "What of the Hunter Clan? What of the Bandit King?"

"We must first enter Great Kingdom at a place called South Province."

***

The first night in the valley they camped beneath the stars. Vilmos learned the deep valley was a harsh place without a warming sun. Soon after dusk, the land lost all its warmth and the cold only worsened during the night.

Two hours before sunrise, they started their solitary march. By the time the evening sun arrived, they hoped to reach the river at the valley's center. If they could cross the river an hour or so before nightfall they could, with luck, dry their clothes by the last of the sun's rays. If they didn't reach the river in time they would camp on the close shore and cross the river the next morning, but this would mean many wasted hours.

Xith set a furiously fast pace. Any rest periods this day would be few and short. Vilmos couldn't be sure but it seemed the farther north they went, the more eager the shaman was to quicken the pace. The sores about his shoulders had grown scabs but still they ached with a dull pain. To him, the pain was a constant reminder of what waited ahead.

***

"We walk to teach a lesson—your first lesson," replied Xith. Vilmos had been asking him questions ever since they crossed the river this morning and though he was growing irritated, he was pleased. Vilmos was genuinely interested in just about everything. "<*The most important lesson of all.*> There is <*no simple path to follow.*> Once you begin a course of action, you must follow it through. Yes, it would be easy to teleport to our destination, but then you would learn nothing."

"Teleport?"

"Yes teleport." Xith held back a chuckle, knowing a secret yearn the boy was not aware of. "True teleportation, or moving from one place to another through magic, is very powerful magic. You must understand that. <*It is a feat few magicians may attempt.*> <*To fail is to bring your own demise.*> It is a special kind of incantation that draws heavily upon the threads of the universe. One must also know exactly where they are going in order to teleport."

"You don't know where we are going?"

"Yes I do, but you do not. For the spell to be successful, to teleport the two of us to where we travel, you must also know precisely the point to which we go."

"Then tell me—"

"—I am afraid it is not that simple. For now, <*we will walk,*>" Xith said, using the Voice to end the conversation.

Xith stopped for a moment to open the leather bag that had been slung over his left shoulder. "Here, eat this."

"What is it?"

"Dried fish."

Vilmos invoked a sour face in disgust, but he was hungry. He disliked fish and decided after he swallowed the last bite that he especially disliked dried fish. Xith raised a warding hand as Vilmos started to speak again, waving his hands wildly and pointing to the ground, meaning for Vilmos to stoop low.

"What's wrong?" whispered Vilmos, not moving.

"Shh!" responded Xith, "<*Get down.*>"

The response automatic, Vilmos sank low and moved to the tall grasses that grew along the river's course. For a time silence followed, then abruptly his ears filled with the cacophony of thundering hooves. Vilmos hugged the grasses closely and clung to the ground for safety. The sound of hundreds of charging horses, the clash of whips and voices soon became overbearing. Vilmos had to block them out. He clasped his hands tightly to his ears and pushed vigorously until the sounds were muffled.

The ground trembled in the wake of the riders' procession and in his fright, Vilmos pushed with such force his head began to throb with pain.

"Make it stop," Vilmos whispered. The unmistakable rasping and creaking of a wagon's passing in proximity to his position swelled to his ears despite the intended barrier. Wanting to run became the most prevalent thought in his mind, but would he be caught? What would they do to him if they caught him? And where was Xith?

Hesitantly, Vilmos opened his eyes and craned his head up slightly. Wagons were still passing and behind them came many more riders. Carefully Vilmos checked the area to his left and right, his hands never shifting from on top of his ears. Xith was nowhere in his eyesight and now Vilmos was really feeling frightened and alone.

The voices he heard seemed harsh and cruel and, the cracks of their whips sent shivers down his back. *Please, oh please, don't let them hurt me.*

Seconds ticked by to the pace of his heartbeats. Vilmos prayed to Great-Father to keep him safe. Eventually though the sounds grew distant and as quickly as they had appeared, the men and horses disappeared.

Before daring to crawl from the high grass cover, Vilmos waited until he could no longer hear the sounds of movement. Hesitantly he rose from his crawl to a half stoop, and stared along the trail in the direction that the sounds had retreated.

"Xith? Xith? Where are you?"

Xith's answer was calm. "Yes, Vilmos I am with you."

"Who were those men?"

"They are the reason we must travel swiftly."

With his eyes filled with fright, Vilmos asked, "Would they have killed me?"

"There are worse fates than death, Vilmos."

Vilmos brushed the grass and dirt from his clothing. "Where are they going? And why are they in the valley?"

"Most likely they use the valley for the same reason we do. It is safer than the forest."

"Why would such a large group fear the forest?"

Xith turned to stare at the trail of dust rising from the valley floor. "Why indeed."

***

Two long and uneventful days followed the encounter near the river, and on the eve of the fourth day in the valley, Vilmos and Xith completed the crossing to the northern rim. Low bluffs on one side and gentle hills on the other replaced the high cliff walls of the southern rim. The two weary travelers found a small cave nestled in a low wall and they stopped to pass the night. The cave was just as dreary as Vilmos had always imagined a cave would be—damp and dark, offering nothing that appealed to his senses. He almost would have rather slept outside on the hard ground.

"Well, what are you waiting for? I am sure you will find some brush just outside that will make us a good warm fire," said Xith.

Vilmos considered another time when Xith spoke those words. It seemed now a distant memory—not altogether forgotten, but rather something that had occurred long ago. Yet now, he recalled the thought fondly and smiled as he retreated from the cavern.

After a small bundle of assorted twigs and small sticks was neatly stockpiled Vilmos went in search of larger firewood and found some not far off. When Vilmos returned a second time, Xith indicated that he need gather no more wood. They would have plenty to carry them through the hours of darkness and to cook their breakfast over if they so chose.

"Good," Xith said. "Set the wood in the center of the chamber and start the fire while we still have a little light from the outside."

Vilmos did as Xith stated and built the fire base. When finished, he looked to Xith, waiting for the shaman to give him something to start the fire with.

Xith rummaged through his bags for a few moments, then set them aside. "Sorry, I must have lost the flint and steel."

"Lost? How can I start a fire without it?"

"Are you always so stubborn? Use that which you have. You must always <*use the tools*> that you have been <*provided.*> Do not be afraid to use <*your natural gifts.*>"

Vilmos searched in the dim light until he found something he could use: two stones, which he picked up and began to strike together trying to make a spark. Xith watched enthusiastically. Vilmos had such determination that Xith almost believed Vilmos would light the fire by striking the stones together.

Several frustrating minutes later, after Vilmos had smashed his fingers a few times, he gave up. He looked to Xith for a hint of approval or some sign to stop but Xith offered no response.

Vilmos didn't want to disappoint the shaman. He snarled back a frown and returned to pounding the rocks together. Yet after smashing two more fingers, Vilmos cast the stones against the cavern wall. "I give up, I simply can't do it."

"You just aren't trying hard enough."

"What do you mean, I'm not trying hard enough?"

Xith stood and moved toward Vilmos. "I mean you're not trying hard enough."

"That's it," Vilmos said, "I've had it."

"<*Calm down,*>" said Xith, "listen to me closely. All right?"

Vilmos nodded.

"You are going about this in the wrong manner. I said, '<*use your natural talents*>'. <*Magic*> is one of your greatest talents, Vilmos."

"But, I don't know how to use it that way."

"<*Try,*>" invoked Xith. "All you have to do is try. You have the ability, <*it is easy.*>"

Vilmos mulled over Xith's words for a moment. Still, he was afraid of his magic. Nothing good had ever come from using it. "No, I will not do it."

"There is nothing to fear, just <*listen*> to me. Draw the energy into you, but slowly. Only <*build the power*> that you need," instructed Xith, watching the boy's face carefully. "<*Can you feel it?*>"

Vilmos did as told. He drew the power in slowly. "Wow!" he exclaimed, "I can feel it!"

"Good, now <*focus*> on the <*fire*> and turn the energy inside you onto it."

"H-how do I do that?" Vilmos was confused.

"Do not think about the how," said Xith, "just do. <*Focus*> the energy on the fire, think about lighting it."

Vilmos thought, enough already, I'll do it. A minute spark lit the room for an instant. Vilmos started, and then became frustrated. "I can't!"

"You mean you won't do it. You block the energy flow. You must <*think positive.*> You must <*know you can do*> something simply because you can. Do not worry that you won't be able to do it. Follow my instructions closely. <*Are you ready,*> Vilmos?"

Vilmos shrugged.

"Take a deep breath. <*Breathe*> it in slowly."

Vilmos inhaled a deep breath as Xith had instructed, his lungs filled with air.

"Feel the air inside your lungs," Xith said. "Feel it fill them <*full.*>"

Vilmos did.

"Now exhale, continue to breathe deeply, feel the air flow in and out. <*Feel*> the <*life*> within you."

Vilmos did as he was instructed.

"Continue to breathe, clear your mind." Xith's eyes glowed. More stirred within the boy than magic alone.

"I'm trying—"

"—Shh… <*Listen*>," commanded Xith. He smiled. "Clear your mind. <*Concentrate*> only on breathing."

Vilmos cleared his mind until his only thoughts were of his breathing.

"<*Focus*> the energy. <*Concentrate.*> <*Gather*> it in slowly."

Xith waited. Vilmos brought the power in slowly as instructed.

"Find your center! <*Draw upon the power*> around you, drink it in—but only a small amount. Focus the energy! <*Use it now!*>"

Vilmos did as Xith stated. The energy was there and thankfully, he was able to focus it. Suddenly a brilliant, blue-white flame burst amidst the wood.

"Wow, I did it!" Vilmos exclaimed, eyes wide with amazement.

"Yes, but next time try not to waste so much energy."

Missing the false sarcasm in Xith's voice, Vilmos elected to ignore Xith's comment and enjoy the fire. It was after all warm and did offer some cheer to the otherwise dank cavern. He removed his boots and placed them next to the fire, stretching out his short, stubby toes to the warm blaze to soothe his blistered feet.

Xith opened his pack and pulled out some foodstuffs, splitting the last of the supply of bread and cheese between the two of them, offering the largest share to Vilmos.

"Eat hearty, Vilmos, and then get some sleep. You will need a good rest, for tomorrow will be a long day."

The day's trek had left Vilmos ravenous and he attacked the food vigorously. He was always hungry. Eating was almost his favorite pastime. Within minutes, he had gobbled down his share and was staring intently toward Xith's, which the shaman had barely nibbled at.

"Go ahead, Vilmos, take it. You are a growing boy. Eat."

Vilmos raised his eyebrows. Are you sure? His expression read. Xith nodded.

***

Vilmos' mind was teaming with questions, so many that he didn't know which to ask first. He considered them one at a time, and then selected the one he deemed to be the most important. "Xith, will you tell me NOW where we travel to?"

"Get some <*rest,*>" replied Xith, "tomorrow is another day."

Vilmos leaned back and patted an excessively full belly. "Then tell me about your people. What are they like?"

"<*Sleep,*> Vilmos."

"But Xith, I'm not really tired."

Xith eyed Vilmos. "Yes, you are, now <*sleep.*>"

Xith waited, interested in the response and the apparent rejection of the guile's of Voice.

"But—"

"—No more questions, go to <*sleep*!>" yelled Xith.

Vilmos stretched out next to the fire and with eyes almost closed, he feigned sleep. Bodily tired but with a mind too full of unanswered questions to sleep, he eventually turned frank eyes cautiously to the place where Xith sat, eyes wide, feet stretched out, hands happily stroking a long wooden stick, whittling it away with a short tooling knife.

"Xith?" Vilmos called out with a hint of boldness.

"Save your strength, you will need it," said Xith, not looking up. "Tomorrow will be a long day in Vangar Forest."

Vilmos sat up, his eyes filled with sincerity. "But why was it safe to use the magic now and not before? Are the dreams gone? And why did Midori have to go? And why—"

"—Shh," Xith said. Xith set aside his knife and stick, and then waved a hand over the fire. The flames sprang back, seemingly into the wood, until only a few tiny flames remained.

"A great many things will be explained at a time when I know you are ready to hear them. Too much awaits in the days ahead for me to properly begin your education. You have chosen to accept the way of the Magus as your way of life, and as such, you must know that nothing is ever simply revealed all at once, rather in bits and pieces.

"Your use of magic alone didn't bring me to you, it was also your dreams. Once I sensed them, I sent Midori to watch over you until it was time. When the time was near, I came."

Xith waved his hand over the fire again. The flames turned white. Vilmos saw images playing amidst them. He leaned forward, his eyebrows knotted together as at first he became confused then alarmed.

"Pieces of your dreams," Xith said. "All those who have special gifts are troubled by such dreams. They are the playing out of good and evil. They are the reason magic is forbidden, for during the dismal centuries before and after the Race Wars, the unwary so easily succumbed to the destructive nature of dark magic that in the end it became more prudent to destroy would-be mages than to try to save them from themselves.

"The Watchers were born of this period, and we took it upon ourselves to save those we could, for we knew what peril lay in a world without magic." Xith's tone became melancholy. "That I am the last of the Watchers, there is little doubt, and when I breathe my last breath, there will be no more watch wardens and magic will surely fade from the land."

Xith picked up the staff he had been working on, and then he reached back into his pack and pulled out another. Even in the pale light Vilmos could see that the second staff was the one Xith normally used.

"But in the interim, I do what I can, and what I must." Xith moved the staff he had been whittling toward Vilmos but didn't let him touch it. "When I finish this, I will give it to you. And, on that day, you will know that your education is truly beginning."

Vilmos grinned, then frowned. "But what of the dreams, are they gone?"

Xith put the staffs away. He regarded Vilmos for a time, then said, "To any other, I would say yes. To you, I say we will have to wait and see."

Chapter Eleven: Decision

The plains beyond Imtal Palace, the rolling foothills of Braddabaggon way and the green of the forest were all far behind Adrina now. The day before they had passed through the quiet village Captain Brodst had been trying to reach the night of the heavy rains—the night Adrina had met the mysterious lady in the forest. Early this morning the column had crossed into Mellack Proper.

The new day surprisingly brought a beautiful, clear sky. Adrina's mood became quite cheerful despite her saddle sore backside and her heavy thoughts. The southern road, though still muddied, was readily traversable and the column was able to travel at a remarkably good pace considering their rate the previous days. Adrina had seen very few passers by this day—only a few merchants which Captain Brodst had sent immediately away to peddle their wares elsewhere, and the infrequent travelers who hurried along on independent goals.

Over the past day and a half, Adrina had thought of little else other than the words of the mysterious lady and the heir to the throne of Sever—Prince William. She had only met the young prince once, but that had been three long years ago at her mother's funeral. She remembered little of her distant cousin, only that he had the bluest eyes she'd ever seen.

Adrina watched everything and everyone she passed—thinking every pair of peddlers would be the two strangers or that every guardsman that came near her was the traitor. "You must open your eyes," the lady had told her, and Adrina had.

Emel had stayed as close to Adrina as his duties allowed. The two had discussed several plans of action but nothing they came up with seemed appropriate. The lady had told them to tell no one of their conversation, but how could they do otherwise? They had to tell someone—for how could they stop the column from proceeding onward to Alderan. But who?

A sounding of the horns signaled a slackening of the pace and as Adrina looked up, she saw Emel racing back to the middle of the column. Two hours ago he had been sent out to lead a scouting party.

Adrina nodded her head as he passed her. She noticed he looked nervous and knew he would return as soon as he reported the group's findings. Captain Brodst had been sending out scouting parties at regular intervals ever since they had crossed into Mellack Proper. Adrina guessed that this was because Mellack Proper was a king's holding without a garrison. The citizens of Mellack looked to the Duchy of Ispeth that bordered it to the west and to Imtal to the north for its defense.

She didn't have to wait long though. Emel was reining Ebony Lightning in beside her a few minutes later.

"Did you see something?" she excitedly asked him.

"I wish," Emel replied. "Nothing but fields as far as the eye can see."

"Why are you sweating so? You look peaked. What is wrong?"

Emel smiled devilishly. "Ebony wanted to race, so I pressed the group hard. I saw no harm in it. We are nearly upon the borders of Ispeth now."

"Isn't much to Mellack Proper, is there?"

The expression on Emel's face grew grim. He lowered his voice to a whisper as he began to speak. "Did you know that tomorrow a detachment will break from the main company?"

Adrina turned frank eyes upon Emel. "Have you thought of what I said earlier?"

"I've thought of little else." There was evident tension in Emel's voice. "Do you really think it is wise?"

"Do we have any other choice? The way I see it we have to talk to someone about this and who better than Father Jacob, Keeper Martin or Captain Brodst."

"Why do I have to be the one who makes the choice of which to talk to?"

Adrina said nothing in reply.

"I never should have turned back," muttered Emel, thinking Adrina couldn't hear him, but she did. She winked at him.

"I'm glad you did," admitted Adrina. "I couldn't have shouldered this alone. You are a true friend."

"This is not a choice I want to make hastily." Ebony nickered. Emel stroked the stallion's mane. "I need more time. Besides, my father wants me at the fore of the column. We can talk again later. Agreed?"

Concern in her eyes, Adrina watched Emel ride off. Afterward her thoughts turned back to the road. An afternoon sun was just starting its descent and passing clouds brought dark shadows to the land. She hoped it wouldn't rain again and as time passed and rain did not come, she counted herself fortunate.

She listened to the clatter-clatter of hooves and heels along the hardening ground. The company had returned to a four-abreast formation with one squadron of garrison soldiers to the fore of her position and two to the rear. The palace guardsmen and the distinguished guests made up the middle of the formation with protective files set up along both sides of them.

Great Kingdom had few bandits in its heartland but Adrina knew Captain Brodst thought one could never be overcautious. As she looked on, the captain surveyed his group from end to end. He was conferring with the three commanders. From his especially grave scowl Adrina guessed it wasn't pleasant words he spoke to them. Among the three, Captain Adylton, Captain Ghenson and Captain Trendmore, it was only the Captain Trendmore that she thought warranted closer attention. Trendmore was an ambitious and manipulative man, or so Adrina had once heard during a session of her father's court.

Adrina chased after Emel in her thoughts now and, preoccupied with this she had not taken notice of the keeper's presence beside her nor had she heard his words of inquiry until he spoke louder. She started at the voice, jumping in the saddle and then had to rein in her mount to slacken its excitement which matched her own.

"What troubles the mind of one so young and beautiful?" asked Keeper Martin.

Recovering her senses, Adrina said, "Beautiful day, keeper."

Martin mumbled something inaudible.

"Have you decided if you will continue to Alderan with us or not keeper?"

"The East-West crossroads are but a day away. I may yet change my mind and go south with the party to Quashan', dear." Gray-haired Martin paused. "In truth, I am awaiting response to the message I sent to Keeper Q'yer. If all goes well I should receive it this night."

"Tonight?"

"Keeper Q'yer has had his week to recuperate from the last sending."

Adrina turned frank eyes on the keeper. "A dream message?"

The keeper smiled knowingly, but didn't say anything immediately. Adrina knew little about the mysterious Lore Keepers who in recent years had detached themselves from palace proceedings yet still seemed to know everything that went on in Imtal. She knew the keeper to be a man who preferred his records and his tomes to human companionship—at least that is what she had heard.

"You have careful ears dear. Where did you hear such a thing?" asked Keeper Martin—a check for honesty, among his other duties as Head Keeper was to track the history of the royal family. At the age of consent, it would be time to draft a new tome, one with the young princess' name inscribed upon its leather binding.

"Why from your own lips keeper."

"A dream message is a form of communication," said Martin, his words sounding like an oration, "a keeper can deliver a message to another keeper in the form of a message that enters their awareness and takes the form of a dream."

"But how is such a thing possible?"

"Actually, very simply. The real difficulty lies in the proper use of your will. To begin you must clear all thoughts from your mind and reach into the center of your being. A spark of power lies there that is your soul. You reach out with that power until you touch the consciousness of the one you wish to communicate with. You speak through images and feelings that you create in your consciousness and pass... Boring you dear? I am sorry, I tend to babble."

Adrina tried to remain focused on her goal, which was to find out what the keeper knew of their destination, but she was caught in the interest of the ideas he presented to her and this perplexed her. "No, Keeper Martin, you're not boring me. Can anyone do this? How come you can't use words?"

"Slow down dear," said the keeper with equal enthusiasm. "Only a few know how to properly utilize their conscious to create the message. It is part of the knowledge passed down from Great-Father to us alone, the Keepers of the Lore. Throughout time there have been others who learned to use this power. Unfortunately, though, only the keepers retain this skill now."

"But I don't understand. How can you comprehend the dream if you do not use words?"

"I did not say that words could not be used." Martin paused, adding extra meaning to the statement. "It takes an extremely powerful center to create a vision in the form of thoughts that enter another's awareness as audible words. The simpler form is to use images and feelings."

"Keeper can you teach me, I mean… can you teach me how to use the dream message?" Adrina was excited now and did little to hide it.

"I can teach you the theory." The keeper sighed with lament. "But I am afraid it is a mute undertaking."

Adrina thought about his words for a moment. She still wanted to know what he knew about their destination but she *was* genuinely intrigued. She also hoped this would give her a chance to talk to the keeper alone. She had made her choice, she would tell the keeper of her troubles. She had only to tell Emel this now. "I do not mind. There is nothing better to do with my time at present—if you do not mind imparting your wisdom on me, of course?"

The keeper's eyes gleamed as he said, "Of course I don't mind. In fact, I'll take great pleasure in it. We'll start this evening."

***

Captain Brodst called the column to a halt near the borders of Ispeth. "Eat well and rest your feet and your mounts," he advised. "If the good weather holds we will try to make up the distance we lost to rains the days before. The earlier we reach the crossroads tomorrow, the better."

Adrina eagerly dismounted and followed Father Jacob and Keeper Martin to the top of a small rise where the commanders and the guests would have their midday meal. Mostly she wanted to listen in on their conversations but she was also very hungry.

From atop the hill she could look down on the whole of the extensive company. Ridesmen were tending their mounts. Foot soldiers were resting tired feet. Obviously unhappy guards were posted fore and aft.

Not far off Adrina saw Emel and the small band of young ridesmen—twelve in all—that had survived the encounter with the lowland cat of Braddabaggon way. Little of their conversations rose to her ears, but she could tell the foul weather hadn't dampened their high spirits. To them, the journey to Alderan was still high adventure. Adrina wasn't so sure anymore, though she still longed to feel hot sands between her toes and taste the salty spray of wind-blown seas.

True to his word, Emel found Adrina shortly after Captain Brodst called the column to movement. But before she could say anything of her conversation with Keeper Martin, Emel spoke his mind. "I have given it much thought," he said furrowing his eyebrows and borrowing his father's scowl, "I truly do not know Father Jacob or Keeper Martin. I am sure they are both men of honor but I cannot vouch for their word. My father, the captain, on the other hand is a man who lives by his sense of honor and I can vouch for his word. He has never knowingly broken a trust."

Adrina didn't know what to say. She had tried to interrupt Emel but he hadn't let her. Just as she was about to say something, her mare whinnied. For some reason the horse liked her to run her hands along its withers and the base of the mane and scratch. She also thought the mare was fond of Emel's Ebony.

"There, there girl," she whispered to calm the animal. Then turning to Emel she said, "What of Keeper Martin? He is by far the wisest man in the kingdom."

"See, there you go. I make a choice and you don't like it."

Adrina was quick to explain about her earlier conversation with the keeper. "So you see," she concluded, "isn't Keeper Martin the best choice?"

"But when will we ever get him alone? He's never alone."

"This evening. He promised to talk to me. We'll find a quiet place to converse and you'll join us."

Emel signaled agreement and for a time afterward no words passed between them.

It was not long before the company crossed into the Duchy of Ispeth. The quiet fields of Mellack Proper were left behind and now groves of fruit trees lined the road. The apples of Duke Ispeth were the best in the land and often graced the king's table.

It was nearly autumn. Many of the trees were laden with fruit. The sweet scent of apples, heavy in the air, was mouth watering. Adrina saw more than a few soldiers climbing trees and filling bags—no doubt, they were claiming the apples in the name of King Andrew.

Barely an hour after crossing into the Duchy of Ispeth, a vanguard of the Duke's small army was already on its way toward them. Adrina watched Emel and the riders around her grow agitated at the show of force. She didn't know why though because the soldiers of the column outnumbered the small group of Ispeth knights a hundred to one.

Captain Brodst commanded the column to a halt and saying, "Stand at ease. Two runners. Banners high. Forward," dispatched messengers carrying the king's banner to greet the approaching riders.

"There's Duke Ispeth himself," said Emel unhappily.

Adrina maneuvered her mare closer to Emel. "You've met him?"

"I *was* a king's messenger. Crossing into Ispeth uninvited isn't wise."

Emel made no further comment on the matter even when Adrina pressed him. She imagined that he'd met the duke before. She'd heard about the eccentric duke and seen him on several occasions, though he rarely attended the king's court.

"What are they doing now?" Adrina asked. "Are they setting up a tent?"

Emel didn't need to respond. The duke had apparently ordered that two tents be built and workers were busily staking out the lines for the canvas. After the tents were erected, Duke Ispeth and Captain Brodst met in conference. Keeper Martin, Father Jacob and the three commanders were summarily summoned.

"What's going on?" asked Adrina.

"Duke Ispeth is not the most trusting of men. I've had the pleasure of his company on several occasions, I know. If he sees plots and spies in the passage of a mere messenger across Ispeth who knows what he thinks seeing this mob… We'll not be traveling anymore this day."

"At least we may get the chance to talk to Keeper Martin earlier than we planned…"

***

Long after Adrina had bedded down the previous night Captain Brodst and the others had been in Duke Ispeth's tent. What they had talked about during those many hours Adrina didn't know, she only knew her hopes of talking to Keeper Martin had faded hour by hour.

"Emel," called out Adrina, flagging him down with her hands as he rode past. She attempted to make conversation with him as she had tried earlier. Again he cut her off and rode on ahead. It didn't seem intentional though because he seemed worried about something. She thought it possibly related to the conversation the captain had with the *acting* sergeant before they broke camp. She hadn't been able to discern their whispers but the conversation had seemed rather one sided with Emel doing most of the listening.

Aggravated she wrapped the reins tight in her hands and spurred her mare on. "Oh no you don't, Emel Brodstson!" she screamed after him.

Emel reined Ebony in and wheeled about to face Adrina. He didn't say a word. He didn't need to. His stare was angry and cold.

"Did I do something?" asked Adrina near tears.

Emel cast a glum stare toward the rear of the column. Adrina could only guess that it was directed at the captain. "I am sorry, Adrina," he said, turning away and chiding Ebony into movement, "I tried, I really did."

Adrina brought her mare along side Emel's Ebony. "Slow down, talk to me."

"My group has forward position throughout the morning."

"Is that all that's wrong? You don't have to protect me at all times. I saw you relieve the central guard again last night. You can't keep standing watch all night and riding all day. You'll drop out of the saddle."

"The Duchy of Ispeth is not all sweet-smelling orchards you know. At one time, this was swamp as far as the eye could see. That is, before Ispeth River and its tributaries dried up, or so it is said. The farther south you go, the wetter the climate becomes. In a few days, you'll reach the swamps and if you're lucky the company will skirt them, if you're not you'll take the Kingdom road through them.

"Since you have to keep pace with the column, it'll take you a week to skirt the swamp. Or at the very least three by the King's road. Ebony and I cut through the Bottoms *once*. There's things in there without names, but they'll try to take you just the same. They don't call it the bottom of the world for nothing.

"Fog rolls in so thick by mid-afternoon that you can't see your hand in front of your face. I dropped my torch, *my torch*, and nearly lost it. It was the longest twelve hours alone of my life. I nearly lost my wits. It's a good thing Ebony can chase the wind. Just before sunrise we went in, and an hour past sunset we came out."

"There's nothing that will *get* me," said Adrina. A proud smile came to her lips. "I have Emel Brodstson to guard me."

Emel's next words were drowned out by the sounds of the column.

Adrina shrugged. "I can't hear you?"

"I am to go south with the detachment to Quashan'," said Emel, in a soft, sorrowful voice. Afterward he spurred Ebony on and didn't look back.

Adrina returned to her place in the column. A dull pain in the pit of her stomach told her of emotions she sought to hold in. No tears ran down her cheeks though several times she fought them back as they welled up in her eyes. Emel was the only one who shared her secret.

Anger and disillusionment found her. Hadn't the lady in the forest said Emel was now a part of that secret? Didn't that mean he should remain with her at least until they decided what to do? They hadn't decided anything, except to talk to Keeper Martin, which they hadn't been able to do.

She listened to the clatter-clatter of hooves and heels for a long time afterward. Only the far off angry calls of birds from amidst the apple orchards aroused her to the world around her—apple pickers were chasing the birds from the trees.

As she turned to watch a flock of black birds rise from the trees, Adrina caught sight of Keeper Martin and Father Jacob returning from the rear of the column. Suddenly resolved to talk to the keeper, she slowed her mare and allowed them to overtake her. Determination in her eye, she said," Beautiful day, Keeper Martin, Father Jacob. Keeper, what news of the dream message? We will reach the crossroads in a few hours."

Gray-haired Martin grinned sheepishly. "I did not hold to my word did I, Young Highness. I am truly sorry. Duke Ispeth is both persistent and long-winded. He would have rambled on and on through the night if Captain Brodst hadn't put an end to it when he did. And yes, Keeper Q'yer's message arrived."

Adrina flashed her eyes at the keeper. Well? They asked.

"Indeed," said Martin, tugging on his unkempt beard and turning to Father Jacob.

Jacob who had been nibbling on an apple cast the core away. Adrina caught sight of the great swirling white circles that decorated the sleeves of his otherwise black robe. The circles that had once been bright white were now dull and dirty, coated with the dust of the road.

"I have given it much thought," said the priest, pausing to sigh. "You are right. I can sense it too. It is all around us."

"Then you have considered what we discussed?" asked Keeper Martin.

"I have, but I do not think this is the right time to discuss this."

"Indeed," said Martin, scratching at his beard again.

Adrina didn't say a word. She hoped the two to would forget she was even there.

"Please forgive us, dear," said Martin turning to her. "Our thoughts are on other things at the moment. Perhaps it would be best if we talked later."

"Then you will be continuing with us?"

The Lore Keeper turned to Father Jacob then said, "Yes, I believe I will."

***

The column reached the East-West Road late in the day and here they stopped. The great road stood barren before them, its wide span thick with mud and seemingly sullen. There had been a settlement here once but all that remained were dilapidated and decaying buildings.

West along the sea lay the Barony of Klaive, across the swamps to the great sea lay the Twin Sonnets, the Free Cities of Mir and Veter. East, a long, long way along the great road lay the end of Great Kingdom and the outset of the Western Territories. Here the land was shrouded in ancient woodlands, a forest as deep and rich as the whole of the Territories, Eastern and Western. Directly to the south lay South Province and its capital Quashan'. To the north, Imtal awaited their return.

From here, a small complement of ridesmen, two detachments and the acting sergeant at arms, Emel Brodstson, would continue south. The remainder of the great company would follow the gradual westward slope of the road for a few more hours.

Adrina watched as the detachment rode away to the south and she rode westward. Decidedly, she would miss Emel. She wanted to chase him down and wish him a safe journey or maybe mumble through an apology, but held back.

She would have continued riding west and never spoke the good-bye she was harboring if a few moments of hesitation hadn't changed her mind—she did want to chase after him. She wrapped the leather straps tightly in her hands and pulled them sharply to one side to turn the mare quickly. A swift kick to the hindquarters sent the mount charging.

Not quite sure what she wanted to tell him, she was slow to call out to him.

"Emel, Emel!" she yelled.

She wanted to tell him that it wasn't his fault. She wanted to tell him what she felt for him in her heart. She wanted to tell him that she would miss him. Yet as he turned to look at her, she found her tongue growing limp.

"Please give my regards to Prince Valam. Tell my brother I can't wait until his visit next summer," she said, saying what was safe and not what was in her heart.

Emel returned a pithy, acknowledging smile.

Chapter Twelve: Vangar Forest

Three hours after dawn, they entered the forest. Almost immediately, Vilmos felt the crawl of unseen eyes upon him, but he did not really start to worry until the sun disappeared, blocked out by the forest canopy.

Despite ever thickening undergrowth, Xith maintained a steady pace, trying to stay directed north. At times, it seemed as if the forest had a will of its own. Sprawling rows of brambles seemed to close any gaps as they approached and the two would have to travel either west or east until they finally chanced upon a break. Sometimes this distance was only a hundred yards. But more than once, it seemed as if the brambles had stretched on for miles.

"Stay close," Xith advised for the second time.

"I still don't understand why we didn't use the road the soldiers cut through the forest," complained Vilmos. "Surely it went directly north."

"<*Silence,*>" commanded Xith.

Vilmos turned as the shaman had and saw movement out of the corner of his eye. His heart started pounding in his ears and a lump swelled up in his throat.

"<*Run,*>" shouted Xith, pushing Vilmos. "No matter what happens do not look back. Do you understand?"

Vilmos said nothing. Xith twisted him around and stared into his eyes. "Do you understand?"

Vilmos nodded.

The two ran at a flat out race. Trees became black blurs. They no longer turned at brambles; instead they plowed through them with Xith pushing Vilmos ever forward.

Cuts and scrapes on his hands, face and arms, bruises on his knees, Vilmos trudged on. He ran as fast as he could. Every now and again he saw black shapes out of the corner of his eye that he was certain were not trees. But it was only when he heard the first tormented howl that he became certain he was running for his very life.

Soon the tormented cries of the unknown beasts came from many directions then gradually the howls grew closer and closer. Xith pushed Vilmos faster and faster, surprising the boy with his seemingly endless endurance.

Nervously, Vilmos glanced to his left and to the rear. His feet lead him to the right—there were no cries coming from the right. Then suddenly the shaman stopped. Vilmos nearly collided with him. His eyes grew wide with terror and his heart pounded so loudly in his ears that he couldn't hear what the shaman was saying. Vilmos only knew the shaman was staring into the shadows of the forest.

"They are leading us," Xith said, "do not let your feet stray."

The two started running again. Terror helped Vilmos find his second wind and soon he was outpacing Xith.

Coming down a ravine, Vilmos stumbled and fell. Xith picked him up by the scruff of his collar and lead him on. They breached a hill, crossed a stream, trudged on in soggy shoes, on and on they raced.

Vilmos was running to the pace of his heart, which was still pounding in his ears. He stretched his small body to its limits, again surprised at the shaman's seemingly boundless stamina. More than once he doubled over in pain and fought to catch his breath, and more than once the shaman forced him into movement. Sometimes dragging him by the arm or the collar.

Sometimes pushing him. Sometimes just his wild stare was enough to force Vilmos to find his next wind.

Then suddenly they burst into a clearing. A midday sun shining overhead told Vilmos they were safe, they were out of the dark forest. A sigh of relief escaped his lips.

Then just as Vilmos paused to catch his breath, Xith directed his gaze to the other side of the clearing. The forest stretched on endlessly, the trunks of trees fading into the gloomy shadows.

Vilmos tried desperately to catch his breath. "Can we rest, please?"

"Not long," cautioned Xith, "those beasts aren't far behind us."

"What are they?"

"Some things are best left unnamed. To be sure, their masters are the reason the animals of the forest are angry." Xith's eyes darted to the shadows. "Run now, run as if your life depends on it, because it does."

"I need... more rest," said Vilmos, panting, "can you not use your magic on them?"

"For every one I sent back to the pits where they spawned, two more would come. No, we <*run,*>" said Xith, launching Vilmos into a run by pushing him forcefully with both hands.

***

Vilmos stumbled, fell, came up on his feet again. For a moment in his confusion, he thought Xith wasn't with him anymore, but then he caught a glimpse of the shaman's brown robe. Exhausted, Vilmos no longer ran. He simply plodded along, forcing himself to put one foot in front of the other, required great effort.

Time progressed slowly. Most of the tormented howls faded to distant echoes and now it seemed only one of the strange beasts followed them. Vilmos heard its high-pitched howl sound off to his left.

By now they had gone so far and so deep into the forest and strayed off course so many times that Vilmos thought surely even the shaman had lost his way long ago. The beasts *were* leading them, forcing them to take an increasingly easterly course.

Vilmos could no longer determine shapes in the shadows. Everything was shadows and dull grays slowly turned black. Night was surely near.

The touch of a hand to his shoulder caused Vilmos to start. He jumped and nearly screamed. Xith whispered in a low voice, "Tie this rope around your waist. It will keep us from being separated."

Vilmos took the offered rope and began tying it about his waist.

"Follow where I lead you," said Xith. "Keep your hands out in front of your face protectively."

Vilmos finished securing the rope. He caught sight of a soft glow from the shaman's eyes. They were glistening silver once more. "Do your eyes allow you to see in the dark?"

Xith grinned. "It is the gift of Oread to her people."

Vilmos stretched his sore muscles, and eased the fire away from aching legs, then finally asked the question that had been bothering him for what seemed hours. "Are we lost?"

"The sense of direction of the peoples of Under-Earth is keen. Do not worry my young friend. Soon we will leave the Forest of Vangar and all of this will be behind us for a time."

Xith said nothing more, but suggested they should begin moving again.

***

Vilmos followed where the pull of the rope lead him, the world around him was now so black that he couldn't discern anything from the darkness that surrounded him. Not knowing when they would come to a rut, a hill, a ravine, he placed each foot down softly and uncertainly. He tried to keep his thoughts from wandering and think only of placing one foot in front of the other. This was a difficult chore as he fought exhaustion.

The single hunter continued to follow them, howling out at seemingly regular intervals—perhaps telling companions that followed silently the hunt was still on.

Staring into the darkness and not being able to see anything was at times overwhelming and during those times, Vilmos felt utterly helpless. He could only follow the tugs at the rope and hope that the person tied to the other end was still Xith—for exhaustion made him doubt *even* that.

His thoughts did wander though, even as he fought to keep them focused on putting one foot in front of the other. He thought of home, the villagers, and Lillath and Vil. Surely if the powerful shaman feared the creatures that chased them, the three villages were in danger. Yes, days of forests separated them, but how far did these creatures roam?

Vilmos answered the question for himself. Far enough to chase a great black bear south. Far enough to make it attack and kill the girl from Olex Village.

He groped his way around a tree that seemed to suddenly sprout in front of him. The ground beneath his feet was now damp. Vilmos knew this because of the thick mud clinging to his boots, making heavy feet that much heavier. Far off he heard the sound of running water as if a stream lay somewhere ahead. For a time his thoughts filled with a longing to drink of its cool waters.

They were coming down a long, long hill when suddenly the rope went slack. Vilmos' mind filled with alarm. Xith normally signaled with a double pull on the rope when he was going to stop.

Vilmos groped with his hands about his waist until he found where the knot in the rope began. Then he began to take up the slack in the line. When he had pulled in about five feet without the line going taunt, he stopped. He was almost afraid to keep pulling. His hands way ahead of his thoughts kept working though and Vilmos soon found the end of the line in his hands.

Vilmos tried to rationalize. He told himself Xith must have untied the rope from around his waist. Perhaps the stream was just ahead and Xith wanted to tell him this. The running water did sound awfully close.

Bravely, Vilmos took a step forward into the darkness, then another, and a few more. The stream was there all right. He found it by stepping into it with a slosh—the water *was* cold.

"X-Xith," Vilmos whispered, "where are you?"

No answer.

Vilmos whispered in a slightly louder voice, "X-Xith?"

Vilmos heard movement behind him and spun about, nearly losing his balance. He saw the dull glow of a pair of eyes about halfway up the steep, forest-covered hill—but the glow wasn't soft silver.

He stood deadly still. He heard growling now and then a howl, joined by many more. Confusion, exhaustion and panic mandated his actions. Instinct and human nature took over his thoughts. The will to survive became his only objective. Blue sparks danced across his fingers tips without him even realizing it.

The light only served to fill in the images missing from his mind's eye. Halfway up the hill he saw them, a pack of the creatures that though they looked like wolves he knew they weren't. No wolf he'd even seen had two heads. No wolf he'd ever seen was as large as a bear.

Vilmos slowly backed into the stream. The creatures inched forward. He inched backward. When the waters swirling around him were knee deep, Vilmos stopped. The lead creature, the largest one of the whole pack, stood no further than ten feet away from him now. Vilmos was suddenly sure this was the beast that had hunted and howled after them while the others in the pack had hunted silently at its side. It seemed to signal to the others to wait as it approached.

Instinct and the will to survive still at the forefront of his thoughts, blue sparks continued to dance across Vilmos' fingers. He waited, staring down the strange two-headed creature, wondering why it did not attack him, wondering if it could lunge ten feet in a single, swift move using the powerful legs he saw.

Vilmos began to back up again, and the creature continued to approach. Each took one small step at a time, and stared the other down. Vilmos' two eyes matched against the creature's four, each daring the other to make a move.

The water about his legs was now only ankle deep but Vilmos gave it little thought. He dared not waver his eyes from the position they held locked to the creature's. Soon Vilmos found that he was no longer sloshing backward through water. He had come to the far bank. The strange beast waited on the opposite bank, only a few precious feet away.

In the soft blue light, the creature's double set of fangs glistened white-blue. Two heads meant two mouths filled with up-turned and down-turned canine fangs. Vilmos and the creature stared each other down, seemingly to find out whose will power was stronger.

Something brushed against his shoulder. Vilmos let out a scream that echoed long into the night. He whirled about, fists poised ready to fend off the unseen attacker, only to find soft gray eyes fixed on his.

"Xith!" Vilmos shrieked, "Thank the Father!"

"Do not thank him yet," Xith said, "back up slowly now. The Wolmerrelle will not normally leave such a sanctuary, but let's not give them any reason to think they should."

"W-Wolmerrelle?"

"Suffice to say that species from different realms were not meant to mate, for when they do, the result is not for the greater good."

"Where did you go?" Vilmos asked as he inched backward.

Xith held out something in his hand that the boy didn't dare to look at. "They were leading us all right. Another pack was shadowing us, waiting until they had us cornered."

Xith put a heavy hand on Vilmos' shoulder, indicating they should stop. Vilmos noticed there were no trees around them. He stood in tall grass that stretched to his chest. The lead Wolmerrelle was still staring them down, but now it was a good twenty to thirty feet away. Vilmos groaned and put his hands to his face to rub bleary eyes. As Vilmos did this, Xith lost the support he had been using to keep upright. He staggered and fell.

Vilmos grabbed Xith's waist to help the shaman to his feet. He felt moisture against his hand. Xith's robe was saturated from his neck down.

"Don't worry." Xith's voice was weak. He coughed. "Most isn't mine."

Vilmos knew then that it was blood he touched. For a moment, a small sliver of the moon shined down upon them as it broke through heavy clouds. Vilmos saw the shaman's prize. It was the head of one of the beasts; up close it was far larger and even more frightening than he had imagined.

Vilmos tended to Xith's wounds. He did as the shaman instructed and cleaned the wounds against infection then touched the stones of the river to them. "The stream is a tributary to the distant river Trollbridge that divides the Free Cities of Mir and Veter. It runs a long way from Rain Mountain in the center of the forest to where it joins the Trollbridge and helps feed the swamps. Its stones are healing in their own way," Xith had said, and Vilmos did not question that they were.

For the next several hours, Vilmos lay at Xith's side, afraid to let sleep take him. Several times as he stared through gaps in the tall grasses to the far side of the stream, Vilmos saw the strange creatures Xith had called Wolmerrelle. Xith had been right about one thing; they were best left unnamed. Putting a name to the horror he saw only aided their terrifying grip on his mind. Somehow he was sure that one day he would return to Vangar Forest and when he did, the Wolmerrelle would be waiting for him.

Next time Vilmos knew he would not be so lucky. He would not escape as easily.

Chapter Thirteen: The Bottoms

Captain Brodst called the company to a halt. The low road that lead down into the murky lowlands, aptly dubbed the Bottoms by both those few who dwelled there and by those who frequented these southerly lands, lay before them.

He cast a glance heavenward, the sun was well past its zenith and the storm clouds of morning were gone. His customary frown lengthened. He reconsidered his alternatives, to take the king's road or to skirt the mire. He had discussed these choices with Keeper Martin, Father Jacob and the other captains the day prior. The obvious choice was to take the short cut through the swamp. They were already behind schedule, yet something Duke Ispeth had told him the night before last was bothering him now.

"Not a single messenger—and few travelers—have come north for more than a week," the duke had said, "tis a strange occurrence indeed."

At the time Captain Brodst hadn't given it much thought, he had been tired and angry. Duke Ispeth could be a stubborn man when he wanted to be. Captain Brodst remembered that just after the duke had said that he'd scratched his head and said, "It's probably nothing. In another week or so, I'll probably find that the roads were washed out again… Damned rainy season approaching, you know."

But there was something in the way the old duke had said it that told Captain Brodst he didn't really believe what he'd just said. It was true Duke Ispeth was eccentric and suspicious of everyone; even so, Captain Brodst had never seen anyone as agitated as he'd seen the duke that night. He had ranted and raved for hours. He had told them about reports of strange travelers passing through his lands at night, peasants complaining that whole crops were disappearing and many other things.

Captain Brodst took in a deep breath. If the weather had been better, surely they would have been ahead of schedule and he could have opted to skirt the swamps. He had discussed this route with King Andrew because they both feared the closeness of the rainy season. Captain Brodst found it ironic that since the rainy season had arrived early, that he now seemed forced to make a completely wrong choice in an attempt to save time.

None of this worrying will save time, he told himself. They were at least one day behind schedule and needed to make up for lost time. The only way to do it would be to turn south. He gave the signal, pointed to the southernmost road, then spurred his mount on. In a few hours Captain Brodst planned to call a halt for the evening and, by mid-morning of the second day along this route, they should enter the outer mires.

***

The passage along the rolling hills that gradually sloped down into the dreaded Bottoms was moderately paced. Unfortunately, the seasonal rains returned with vigorous fury, forcing a deficient, sluggish rate upon the travelers. But fortunately, after several hours of intense storms, high winds carried the storm front away to leave the skies clear and the grounds muddied though passable.

The group retreated from the confines of heavy cloaks, dropping hoods and loosening the ties about the neck as the air grew warm. Adrina had been in a pensive mood all through the morning. Her thoughts were with Emel. She felt so alone without him and what made this even worse was that everyone around her seemed to notice this, especially, Keeper Martin and Father Jacob.

Adrina's unease began to grow as they moved ever closer to the Bottoms and not only because the thought of traveling through such a place filled her mind with dread. She had been counting on the extra days the longer route around the mires would have provided. The road through the Bottoms would only hasten them to Alderan and this more than anything else filled her mind with alarm.

Keeper Martin, who had been keeping a watchful eye on her and not letting her out of his sight, spoke, "There is nothing to fear, dear, the passage through the mires will be swift and we'll be smelling sea breezes before you know it."

Adrina expressed a sour grimace in response. Keeper Martin may have had an intuitive wisdom, but she knew better than to think there was nothing out there. The putrid smell of rotting vegetation that the wind carried had to be hiding something.

Father Jacob added to the keeper's words, his voice trembling with emotion, "He is right Princess Adrina. Tonight we will stay at a palace of such great beauty that it rivals that of Imtal's. And, Baron Fraddylwicke is a most excellent host."

"Imtal is hardly beautiful," said Adrina.

Father Jacob burst into laughter and said cheerfully, "The palace once belonged to King Jarom the First of Vostok before he lost the lands to the Kingdom long, long ago. At one time, it was the gateway into the whole of the South. The Lord and Lady Fraddylwicke await us..."

His voice trailed off, but Adrina thought she had heard him finish with, "or so I do fear."

"And it has only fallen into the mire three times since then," said Captain Brodst, adding melancholy to the cheer.

Surprised at the Captain's joining in, Adrina said nothing.

"A trivial fact, I assure you," said Keeper Martin, "it was rebuilt each time with increasing care and magnificence."

Adrina smiled and responded, "I can't wait to see it. It sounds wonderful." She added for the keeper's benefit, "Full of history."

Her thoughts took a turn toward expectations and away from disappointment and unease. She was again surprised that Captain Brodst had spoken to her.

"His scowl is his shield," Adrina whispered to herself.

Adrina relaxed in her saddle and soaked up some of the warm air. She undid the ties on her cloak and removed it. However, the warmth that had fed their momentary good spirits came to a quick and not-at-all-subtle end. The ground seemed to readily suck up the warmth and a chill rapidly returned.

***

The long file entered the outer mire. The coolness of the air entwined with the warmth of the ground caused wisps of mist to swirl underfoot even in the early hours of afternoon, giving the area an eerie haze. Adrina felt her body begin to shiver uncontrollably at the cool touch, a touch similar to the play of cold fingers along the exposed areas of her skin.

She pulled her cloak tightly about her and brought its hood up stout, retreating far into the recesses of the cowl as she had this morning. Although the cloak was still moist from the rain, it did manage to provide a little bit of extra warmth. She was thankful for its touch of comfort and hopeful that they would reach the castle soon for she was growing very weary. She sank languidly into the leathers of a saturated, irritating saddle, almost wishing that she had heeded Emel's words along with her common sense and remained in Imtal.

Torches were mustered from the supplies and spread through the long line as insurance that, should the mists turn to fog, the group would not get lost in its midst. Captain Brodst, using his flint and steel and a few pieces of his precious stock of dry kindling—some of the torches had gotten damp—lit the initial torch, which he passed to the sentinel to bear at the front of the column. For the present, this was the only one to be lit. The others were not yet needed.

The sun's rays were soon lost in a shroud of haze and the hours appeared to drag by. Dampness was held so thickly in the air that it caused the moisture to sink into the very souls of those present. Adrina was caught up in deep feelings of portentous dread and she petted her mare's mane to soothe it—or so she told herself. But it was really herself that she sought to calm, to rid her mind of the eerie thoughts it held.

She tried to think pleasant thoughts. She didn't like the swamp they traversed and she liked the dense fog even less. The combination of the two elements overwhelmed her mind and only the thought of the castle that lay somewhere ahead in the distance turned her woes toward eventual ease.

She could imagine the Lord and Lady of the castle, him dressed in a purple overcoat and a blue silk shirt, his court best, and her in the long flowing gown of the day properly coordinated to the purple and blues of the Lord Fraddylwicke, her attendants forever at her side. She imagined their greeting a grand affair at the great palace gates. The castle walls were not a dead and dreary gray but cheerful silver.

They delved further and further into the mire. It seemed as if they had suddenly passed under a great thick blanket of endless gray. Captain Brodst was forced to call another halt. The double file that they had begun the gradual descent into the mire with was dispensed and a long drawn-out single file unfolded into the shadows.

Torches were ignited from the sentinel's and though this should have been reassuring under most circumstances, it only assisted the uncanny veil's pervasion of their thoughts.

Progress through the ever-thickening sheets of fog materialized as a feeble inching forward. The cries of the cricket and the frog, the buzzing of insects and the stirrings of other smaller beasts ground to a halt. Only the sloshing of the horses' hooves and boots in the soggy trail remained and it was as if nature itself had paused, waiting for the next puff of freshness and life.

Adrina witnessed the line of lights assemble in front and behind her. Then as she watched, the former disappeared one by one into the veil ahead. Those behind she didn't turn to look back at.

Carefully following the movements of those ahead when it was her turn, she coaxed her mount by gently slapping it with the reins to start it moving at a relaxed gait. Still she stroked the animal's mane with her free hand. Briefly she looked back now to ensure the rider behind her noted her passage and followed her lead.

She gazed intently ahead and tried to maintain a bearing on the dim glow of the torch Keeper Martin carried in front of her. The fog seemed to swallow any hint of the flame, leaving only a slight trace of its glow to guide her movements. The pace appeared to quicken instantly to a slow gallop and then suddenly decrease to a saunter, making it extremely difficult for her to preserve the integrity of the file. She wondered how the rider behind her faired in her wake. She hoped that the other could sustain a bearing on her torch but for now she dared not look back for fear of losing sight of the elusive glow in front of her.

The cold mire air grew steadily damp and stagnant as the last remaining hints of the earlier wind disappeared for good. Adrina began to shiver uncontrollably once more. It was as if unseen hands groped their way across her skin and the touch was cold and sinewy.

She tried to find warmth and security in her heavy hooded cloak but she found none. Then just when she thought she could tolerate no more, it was as if those same unseen hands had reached out and grasped her throat, squeezing down with slow, firm pressure.

Suddenly she was afraid to move. What if she raised her hands to her neck and really did find an unseen hand gripped about her throat? But what if it was only her imagination? What then? She wanted to scream out for help, to lash out at the unseen specter, to cry out to the dead land that she did not want it to claim her.

She began to whimper and plea with the unseen hands to release her but this only caused a flood of suppressed emotions—three years of pain and anguish, sorrow and denial—to descend upon her. The dead, gray walls of Imtal were around her, looming up dark and deadly before her—like in her dreams—and all the land was dead and she, Adrina, was dead.

The specter was there with her—like in her dreams—to take her away. But now she didn't want the specter to take her away. The prune-faced man with his twisted wooden staff had saved her before, but he wasn't here now and this wasn't a dream. She began to scream. Frantically she kicked her mount and pulled on the reins sharply. Her shrill scream cut short by a rationalization that came too late.

The horse beneath her confused by the mixture of opposing signs given it, reared upward. To regain a tight grip on the reins, Adrina twisted the leathers in her hands. This again sent misleading signals to the confounded and uneasy animal beneath her. It reared upward again.

A second pull on the reins caused the mare to shift sideways as it landed. The steed stumbled, and then faltered as it lost its balance on the uneven roadside. Adrina's tumultuous, wanton eyes spun around as horse and rider tumbled.

No longer a participant, Adrina became an observer. The torchlight seemed to dance around in circles before her as she felt herself falling to the ground. Her head was still spinning and her thoughts yet dazed as she landed with a splash into the murky waters and mud of the mire.

In a blur of frenzied thought, she felt herself sinking downward. A split second passed and she relived the fall into the water, eyes wide, cheeks puffed gasping at air, hands flailing, the light of the torch spinning wildly before her and then dying the instant it hit the dark waters with a sizzle.

A scramble to free feet from stirrups ended as she felt the movement of her body come to a sudden stop. Had she hit bottom? Was this it?

She held all the time in the world in the palm of her hands and she released a sigh of thankfulness, cut short by the horse landing on top of her with a horrific crunch. Adrina's pain was sudden, excruciating and vividly real as her world careened to darkness.

Chapter Fourteen: Rest's End

A full day had passed before Xith felt strong enough to continue the journey northward, but in the three days since, he and Vilmos had made excellent progress. They were now in the land known as South Province, a holding of Great Kingdom. The wounds Xith had suffered at the hands of the Wolmerrelle were healing nicely and now he looked to the days ahead.

The evil presence that had been with them those many days seemed to be gone—gone with Vangar Forest. Xith knew that all too soon the gentle wind-blown plains of this section of South Province would be gone as well. Their journey was taking them, north to Great Kingdom and west to the great sea.

Soon it would be time to again work on awakening the power within the boy. Xith knew he must do this slowly and cautiously. To prepare Vilmos for the task ahead, one that only he could do, Xith must make the boy face his fears. In the end, there would be nowhere left to run *from,* only places to run *to.*

***

Vilmos had never been beyond the limits of the secret place he traveled to in his dreams, the confines of which he had been content to live in and *would* have been content to live in for the rest of his life. Suddenly a new world was opening to him. In it, he discovered new definitions of the boundaries around him and a thirst for knowledge of the outside world. The great windswept plains of South Province were truly beautiful—and a far stretch from the lands of desolation described in the Great Book.

With the same hunger, Vilmos listened to the shaman's words. Concentrating on this gave him something to focus on, which made it easier to forget all that was behind him.

"The element of fire is the most basic of the arcane elements to grasp initially. It is also the trickiest to control because of the tremendous raw power it taps," Xith had warned him and Vilmos had taken this to heart. After only his third attempt at producing a spark to ignite wood he had performed, "well" as the shaman had put it, "magnificently" as he put it.

He had mastered his first incantation—the first incantation of the element fire. He could now touch delicate power to wood with apparent ease and produce a soft red-orange blaze. Vilmos looked forward to the next lesson, which Xith promised he would teach him soon.

Now it was time for a reprieve from the heavy cares of the world. Before they moved on to the next lesson, Xith had told Vilmos he intended to take them to a place where they could rest for a time.

Ahead in the distance lay a rustic trade center. It was built along the eastern bank of a river, near a ford. Its three small buildings in various stages of decay stood at the fore of the road huddled around a two-story clapboarded building on which hung a tiny sign that read simply 'Inn, All Welcome.' Other than this sign the settlement was void of the appearances of habitation.

Closer inspection of the small inn showed that although it was in an equal state of disrepair as the buildings surrounding it, it was a relatively new structure. Xith paused momentarily in the middle of the path and turned to look at Vilmos, then raised the hood of his cloak up over his head and pulled it forward to hide his face in the shadows it created. He motioned for Vilmos to do likewise. The sense of caution in Xith's features told Vilmos to act without hesitation.

The interior of the inn was as untidy and unsightly as the exterior. The ground floor of which was largely dominated by an open, dimly lit chamber that contained several tables and many chairs, which were twisted and broken. Near an elongated staircase that led to the second floor sat a portly man upon a lonely unbroken chair. In front of him was the sole upright table.

The obese man, who Vilmos surmised to be the inn keep, had a rather unpleasant odor about him. He didn't budge until he heard the sound of coinage dropping onto his tabletop and even then, his only action was to point to the stairs, then raise three of his chubby fingers to indicate the respective room number.

Without a word, the weary travelers climbed the stairs and went to room number three. They closed and bolted the door behind them. Though it was only midday they found sleep came very easily and, it was not until many hours later that either stirred.

Vilmos awoke to find Xith staring at him.

"No dreams," Vilmos whispered reverently, as he had each day upon awaking since joining Xith. Then he turned frank eyes to Xith. "Where are we?"

"We have reached the edge of the disputed lands."

"The Borderlands," exclaimed Vilmos. "Bandit Kings and Hunter Clan!"

"No, not the Borderlands of the North, but—"

Vilmos cut Xith short, "—Then the stories are true?"

"Vastly overstated."

"Well, are the stories I heard true or not?... Tales of great heroes of the Borderlands wielding giant battle swords and fighting evil two-headed..." Vilmos didn't finish the sentence.

"Those times are no more," said Xith, a twinge of sadness or perhaps longing in his voice—Vilmos could not tell which.

"We are nearing the disputed lands of the South. Here only brigands and a few traders remain. But we are only going to skirt the edge of this area. It is the fastest way to the sea."

Vilmos had never seen the sea, and in his wildest aspirations he had never thought he would. "The sea, really the sea?"

"We are at a last stopping place before we enter what was once the Alder's Kingdom, but is now mostly ruins, except for Alderan."

"Tell me more, please." Vilmos was babbling excitedly.

"There isn't all that much to tell. Besides, your version of the truth would very greatly from mine. You will see soon enough. We must turn our attention to other things first though," Xith said, a far off look in his eyes. "<*Are you there?*>" he called out in a scarcely audible voice.

"What do you mean?" asked Vilmos, responding not to the question but to the previous statement.

"Nothing. Rest," said Xith, relief in his voice, "we have a long trip ahead of us in the morning."

Vilmos sensed something was wrong, but whatever it was it seemed out of his grasp. He leaned back, touched head to pillow and closed his tired eyes once again. Images of the day's adventure danced before his sealed lids—the most profound of which was the image of the burly looking innkeeper whose figure played ominously in his thoughts, with his fat hands raised, pointing at him, provoking him, warning him.

After what seemed hours of restless tossing and turning, Vilmos opened his eyes in frustration and sat up in bed. The last light of day still had not given way to the darkness of night and as Vilmos peered about the room, he was shocked to find himself alone. Xith was gone.

Vilmos was puzzled. Would Xith leave him? Maybe he went to relieve himself or something, Vilmos thought. He ran into the hall, but found only greetings of darkness.

"Xith," called out Vilmos in a weak, half-whispered hiss, "Xi-ii-tttthhh."

Frustrated he sat back onto the bed, curled his feet up tight and wrapped his hands around his legs. He sat this way for hours, watching the sun slowly disappear behind the neighboring building. Periodically he looked toward the closed door.

The shadows in the room began to take on an eerie perspective, casting odd thoughts into his impressionable young mind. A half-burnt stub of a candle lay atop the stand beside the bed. Vilmos reached out and grabbed it. He thrust it back into the pricket it had been removed from, with the apparent intent of replacing it though the new one had never been brought and the old one had never been discarded. With a flick of absent thought, Vilmos sparked it to life.

The brilliant orange of the flame danced in front of his eyes as if it played out a song to him. Vilmos was captivated and motivated by it. Yet a heavy breath unknowingly extinguished its fragile flame, forcing him to re-ignite it. It had been quite accidental, but Vilmos was amused by it. He took to blowing the candle out and then lighting it again and again with his mind. He laughed a soft, silent chuckle to himself as he did this.

He played with the candle for a time, flicking it off and on, the light of the fire reflecting off his face in the otherwise dark chamber.

Mesmerized by the candle light, following its on and off blink, eventually, quite accidentally and without even realizing it, Vilmos learned to gingerly manipulate the flame with his mind. He could put it out and then touch it again with his power to relight it, which was quite an accomplishment if only he would have realized it.

With a sudden twist the doorknob turned and the door opened. Vilmos heard voices from the hall.

"I'm sorry I couldn't be of much help old friend. I'm sure you are right. Alderan is the key. They'll surely travel along the coastal highway."

"Goodnight Misha. I am glad your other guests decided to depart ahead of schedule," Xith said. He laughed as he slipped into the room, and then took a sip of the drink in his cupped hand. "We will have to do this again sometime.

"And goodnight to you to Midori. Thank you. You have again done well. I truly did not expect to see you so soon. Guard well the final two scrolls. I will not see you again until after the Autumnal Equinox—after all this is behind us." Xith whispered the last in a voice barely audible, and then took another swig from the half-empty mug he cradled almost tenderly. He waved and then closed the door, trying only now to be quiet.

The scene was quite comical when Xith turned around and prepared to creep to his bed. Vilmos was waiting, and Xith could only smile as a child caught in the act of doing something he knows he's not supposed to be doing. Without a word Xith crossed to the bed opposite Vilmos, sat upon it, blew out the candle Vilmos held and then lay back and closed his eyes.

***

Xith opened the door and pointed down the hall. A heavy sweet aroma filled the air in the hallway and Vilmos' stomach began to growl as he inhaled the first mouth-watering breath. However, before Vilmos could think of food, he had to attend to more immediate matters.

He returned a short while later with a smile on his face and a hand on his belly, a sign that he was hungry. Xith lead him down the stairs to the kitchen from which the aroma rose. The behemoth of a man Vilmos had seen earlier upon their arrival and knew only as the innkeeper was busily working over a brightly burning hearth. Only today, he did not seem so unfriendly and detached as he had the previous evening.

Vilmos scrutinized the small kitchen. He could have sworn he had heard more than two voices last night.

"Beautiful morning Mish'!" Xith exclaimed. He walked over to the large man and patted him on the back.

The innkeeper, Misha, smiled and tossed Vilmos a wink, then he showed the two to a table that was tucked cleanly away in a tiny nook in one of the kitchen's many corners. While they ate, Misha stuffed several satchels with fresh baked breads, smoked meats and an assortment of various other foodstuffs whose aromas wafted through the air to the place where Vilmos and Xith sat and mingled with the pleasant smells already present, creating a feast for the senses of a king. And they both ate like one.

Not long after breakfast, Xith and Vilmos departed the inn. Misha had graciously offered them his wagon, and although old, worn and led by a pair of jades, the wagon was comfortable, and riding proved a very great respite from walking.

Vilmos thought Xith had been rather rude for not introducing him to his apparently good friend. He tossed Xith a snarled grimace but then turned to other subjects, visions of what lay ahead. Although he had never been to the Alder's Kingdom, he knew much about its lore from the Great Book. The Alder had been a very wise king. In signing the treaty with the southern kingdoms, he had ended the longest and bloodiest war in the history of all the lands.

The Race Wars, as they were later called by those few who had survived, had lasted generations. During that time, whole peoples and nations had perished.

A nearly forgotten lesson echoed in Vilmos' mind. He thought of the once great kingdoms of the North. Lycya mightiest of the kingdoms swallowed by barren desert. Queen of Elves and all her people washed into West Deep. North Reach and the clans over-mountain consumed by the twenty-year snow. And, he thought about the Alder.

Xith beat at the controls, driving the pair of jades faster than they seemed to want to go. Vilmos knew without doubt the rest was over. Something dread lay ahead, but what it was he did not know.

Chapter Fifteen: Disaster

Water, dark and icy cold, surrounded Seth. He groped for the surface, his lungs hot and ready to explode. His head stung, his vision clouded. Pain and darkness sought to overcome him. Then just when he thought his lungs would explode, he broke the surface and gasped for air.

Despair filled his mind as turbulent waters pulled him under again. Wildly, he grabbed at the surface, both arms flailing frantically. His hand found something wet and rough. He latched onto it. Coughing and choking, he held on.

The night above the water, nearly as dark as the world beneath the water, offered him little relief. Seth cursed his foolhardiness: He hadn't expected an ambush so soon after departing Capital and somehow Seth knew he should have. He remembered little of how he had come to be in the water. One minute he had been standing on the deck of the Lady L, Sailmaster Cagan at his side, preparing to make one last desperate stand. The next, a sharp sudden pain in his legs and then the long plunge into cold deep water.

Seth suddenly realized had no idea if anyone else had survived. He lashed out with his mind, *Sailmaster Cagan? Galan?*

Seth felt something pass underneath him, and then touch his legs. Fatigue, disorientation and panic overwhelmed him. Sailmaster Cagan had told him about dark beasts beneath the waters. Creatures called sharks that fed on all manner of beast alike. His left arm had caught a blade and his leg—*his right leg*—was gouged from thigh to calf.

Unwisely, Seth kicked out with his feet and slapped the water with his free hand. He lost his grip and again slipped beneath the dark waters. He reached for the surface and the handhold. The piece of wreckage had to be there; it just had to be.

Seth broke the surface, only for an instant, only long enough to fill his lungs with air and calm the red-hot fire in his chest. Then storm-tossed seas pulled him under again.

Great-Father, I cannot fail. My need is great! he called out in despair.

Seth? called out a voice weak in his mind. *Seth?*

His thoughts spun. He reached out, a hand found his.

Bryan?

Yes. Kick harder, I'll need your help. I can't do this alone. Grab on, hold on, don't let go... Just a little more... Just a little more... Seth, you must help me.

With Bryan's help, Seth crawled onto the small section of wreckage. He lay on his back, panting, for many long minutes. Exhaustion nearly carried him away to sleep, but he fought to maintain consciousness. *Did anyone else survive?*

I'm not sure, I saw you get knocked into the sea as the mast crumbled, and I panicked. Everything after that is a blur. The ships are all gone. Fire and water took them.

What about Sailmaster Cagan?

Seth, I don't know... It seems he went down with the Lady L, said Bryan. He paused, his mind filled with obvious anguish. *How did they know we had begun the journey? There were so many, so many...*

Seth found sudden resolve. *We survived Bryan. We have not failed yet... Wait. Did you feel that? The anguish, the sadness.*

That's me, Seth. I'm sorry, I'll shield my thoughts if...

No, someone is out there... Seth turned his thoughts inward and sought to concentrate his will. Then he groped outward with his mind, straining to maintain his strength while he searched. *Galan? Yes—yes, it is... By the Father, she lives!*

Seth pressed his weight against tired arms and sat. He stared into the inky darkness of a largely overcast night sky. He saw little, his mind filled in the pieces. *Wait, someone else is with her... She's holding Everrelle afloat... Galan won't last much longer. She's exhausted.*

Frantically, Bryan and Seth paddled with their hands through choppy waters. It seemed with waves slapping against the makeshift raft, they barely moved at all. Then suddenly, two dark shapes appeared out of the gloom. Everrelle, barely conscious, was near death and brave Galan was utterly exhausted from the struggle to keep two afloat in turbulent waters.

***

The night passed with eerie swiftness. Seth awoke to find a midday sun. Images from the previous day seemed a crazed blur, but the ache of his body told him it had all been real. For an instant, Seth felt sure he was alone, and then he saw the others. They were the last survivors. Frazzled and haggard from battle and exposure to the sea only four lingered in life, yet it was these four that had escaped. Now only faith in their service would take them to safety or deliver them from life.

Still exhausted, Bryan and Galan slept. Everrelle, weak from blood loss, slipped in and out of delirium. Seth turned bleary eyes to the sun, its warmth on his face felt good. He remembered now that during the night he had prayed for the day to end the bitter cold. He removed his cloak, which was still mostly wet, and allowed the sun to chase away any remnants of the night's chill. Then he worked to bind wounds that were already festering.

Each of his companions had many injuries—bruises, scrapes, lacerations—which proved to him how desperate the battle had really been and how miraculous it was that anyone still lived. Everrelle was by far in the worst condition of them all. Her right hand was missing four fingers. Seth was sure she must have reached out to block a blow and instead met the steel of a blade. Using strips of cloth from his robe, he did the best he could to wrap her hand. He hoped it would help stay off infection. He turned to Galan next, Bryan afterward. His own wounds he bound last.

Scattered debris from the great ships that the dark deep waters had claimed during the night was all around them. Seth worked against fate to gather what he could. As he worked, he thought of Cagan standing defiantly at the helm of the Lady L. He told himself that was how he wanted to remember the kind sailmaster and all the others that had perished with him. In the end, his search turned up an invaluable prize, a water bag. Half full, but still a water bag. He put it beside the one Bryan had managed to escape the Lady L with, and thanked Great-Father for his good fortune.

The day grew long. The utter exhaustion that held the others found Seth. Unwillingly, he slipped into delirium.

Days passed. Everrelle's condition worsened. Seth, Galan and Bryan took turns at the healing art, but weak from battle and hunger, they could offer little. Unbelievably, the raft held together with little more than prayers had kept them afloat through those endless days.

Seth had held the hope that land was just over the next crest of the rolling waves or just beyond the next horizon. Bryan and Galan had also been hopeful. But days of nothing save dark waters had tainted that hope and the possibility that land loomed over the next crest or beyond the next horizon waned. Now Seth could only lie idle with all his energy drained. Only his training kept his mind semi-clear and his thoughts open. *I am Brother Seth of the Red, First of that order, Queen's Protector,* he repeated many times in his mind.

He sought to cleanse his mind of questions he didn't want to answer. Nonetheless, the questions came. The ambush set by King Mark at the hand of Sathar the Dark had been too well planned. How could the enemy have known their plans so precisely? Was there a traitor amongst them? Had there been a traitor on the Lady L leading the enemy to them?

No, it can't be, it just can't be. The thought of a traitor having been amongst them was too painful for Seth to consider. Brother did not betray brother. *No, I must focus.* Seth returned to the cleansing meditation.

Seth, came the whisper into his mind.

I am Brother Seth of the Red, First of that order, Queen's Protector. I must maintain clear thoughts…

SETH?

Yes, my brother I am still here.

Seth, what will it be like in this land of Men? asked Galan.

Still lost in his meditation, it took Seth a moment to slip back into reality, a task accomplished only after Galan repeated her question. Seth said, *It will be different, far different from anything we have ever seen that is for sure. Long ago our people often journeyed to their villages and cities. Our lands and cultures were close together then. It had been a peaceful time, but then came the Great Wars. The last and most devastating treacheries were the Race Wars during which Man drove all their distant cousins away. Into the far corners of the world we fled and never in over five hundred years have we ventured back into their lands.*

Seth felt Galan fight to remain coherent. Galan asked, *What did you learn during those many weeks you studied them? Do you really think they will help us? Or will it all be for nothing…*

Her faith was waning and Seth knew this. *Once we explain what is taking place, it will be their cause as it is ours. They must aid us. But it could take a long time to explain. These Men,—* Seth said the word with distaste—*prefer to stay out of the affairs of others until they are sure they have a marked interest in what is taking place. They often wait until it is too late.*

Seth, began Galan, there was a serious note in the unspoken voice, "*there is something I should tell you that I haven't, something I overheard—*

—I do not wish to know thoughts that I was not meant to. Some things are best left unknown.

Like why you prepared for a journey to the lands of Man even before Queen Mother consulted High Council. And why, your lessons began even before we learned of Sathar's return.

Seth was unsure whether he should voice the truth or not—*but what did it really matter anyway?*

There is much more in peril than our homes and lands. Queen Mother knew this.

Seth, I grow tired. I must rest. Will you play the image Brother Liyan gave to you, the image of the green forest? I wish to dream...

***

Seth looked to Galan who was still sleeping and wondered if dreams of the forest still swept through her mind. He knew little of the sea and winds, but unlike, Bryan and Galan, he had been on the canals of Capital with Sailmaster Cagan. He used a makeshift hook and tied bits of colored cloth to it, then cast out his line, a length of string from his robe. Over these past days, he had enjoyed no luck and while it truly seemed there was no life in the deep sea, he was not about to give up.

A hazy dawn eventually gave way to day as the sun made its inevitable climb. With irony, Seth remembered now that he had once prayed for the day's arrival to end the bitter cold of night. But the night didn't steal precious moisture from his weary body, the sun did.

The day gradually grew hot and dry. Seth found that his thoughts were beginning to wander. He maintained consciousness, but only barely so while he cast the line out and pulled it in slowly, as he had once been shown.

At one point, out of the corner of his eye, Seth saw Bryan moving about the raft, but inevitably as the sun beat down upon him, thirst and hunger took over. His thoughts began to wander and shift despite his best efforts. Seth attempted to clear his thoughts, but this required a complete conscious effort, which under the torment of the blistering sun, with strength draining from his body little by little, Seth could not give it. He could only mourn the loss he could do nothing to regain. He perceived himself as a hapless child. He, First of the Red, with all his knowledge and skills could not resolve their dilemma.

Seth soon found himself drifting back to sleep.

We're in danger, warned Bryan. *Sharks!*

Seth came alert in an instant. It seemed he had just closed his eyes, but then he took note of the light of a virgining day on the horizon. Then suddenly Bryan's warning registered in his mind. *By the Father! Galan, Everrelle!... Everrelle?*

Galan awoke. Everrelle didn't. For some reason one of the great gray beasts began attacking the bottom of the raft. Bryan pulled in the fishing line. Seth noticed there was something on it. Seth asked, *You caught something?*

Bryan started to reply, *In a way—*

Bryan's voice was drowned out by Galan's scream. *Dear Father! Everrelle, Everrelle?*

Galan directed thoughts to Seth. *The infection it's worse...* Then she turned back to Everrelle. *Stay with me, stay with us, don't go! 'We'll survive the journey together,' you said. Hold on, promise me you'll hold on...*

Another of the gray beasts that lurked just beneath the surface of the water nudged the raft.

Get Everrelle away from the edge! exclaimed Bryan.

Days without food, meant exhaustion. Galan too was exhausted, and the exhaustion only magnified her alarm and her panic. Seth could see it in her eyes. He directed Bryan to crawl to the other side of the raft and help Galan with

Everrelle. Then he concentrated on angry thoughts and sent them into the minds of the dark shapes beneath the water.

The raft shook as it was buffeted by tail and fin. Angrily and relentlessly, Seth, Galan and Bryan beat at the dark shapes until the raft shook no more. The three stood quietly, huddled together, and stared into the dark waters.

One by one, fatigue overwhelmed them. Bryan was the first to collapse, Seth the last. Silence followed.

Galan broke the long silence, with a very soft whisper, *Everrelle is gone… She promised she'd hold on, she promised.*

Seth didn't answer immediately. Sleep was trying to lull him. He felt Everrelle's passing, but could do nothing more than wish her a safe journey. After a few minutes, he directed a response to Galan, *Sleep, my brother, save your strength.*

Chapter Sixteen: Passage

"Father Jacob, will she be all right?" demanded Captain Brodst. His heart pounded rapidly in his ears, a lump swelled in his throat. He paced back and forth, and waved a torch haphazardly about in the air, paying little attention to the water and muck that dripped from his uniform. The young Princess Adrina's face gathered in a deathlike throng was his only concern.

He feared the worst for Adrina as her face grew ashen. He was positive King Andrew would have his head for this. His despair grew, so did his anger and frustration. Again, he yelled at Father Jacob who apparently was not listening to him. "Father, will she be all right?"

Father Jacob had worked frantically ever since Captain Brodst had rescued Adrina from the murky waters of the mire. Although a male, he knew the art of healing well and had attempted to work its miracles on her almost immediately. Yet, he was growing annoyed by the captain's repeated inquiries and this distracted him.

"Perhaps, perhaps," he hissed back at the captain, "if you give me some silence!"

Keeper Martin touched a hand to the captain's shoulder and said, "Do not worry so. Father Jacob knows what he is doing. Give him some room and the silence he asks for, then trust in him and Great-Father." Then he returned the captain's cloak and sword belt.

Captain Brodst took the belt and cloak and donned them. He chased off the reassuring hand. He didn't want to be soothed. He wanted Adrina to regain consciousness and to insure this, he whispered numerous pleas to Great-Father.

There was doubt in Father Jacob's mind as he continued to labor over Adrina, his healing abilities were not as great as those who were of the Mother. It is most likely that Jacob would have offered his soul to have a priestess of the Mother stumble across their path if he hadn't believed that somehow he could save Adrina—after all, she had been in the presage. All he had to do was to overcome his doubt.

Instinctively, Father Jacob had laid Adrina on her side and managed to clear some of the water from her lungs, still she had not regained consciousness, nor did she breathe. Father Jacob could not touch enough of the Mother's will to draw upon her powers to cure. Only after special prayers were sent to Great-Father to give him the extra strength necessary did Jacob begin to chant the incantation—the ancient litany of life and healing. He wouldn't think it odd that fate had brought him to this path until sometime later as he reflected upon this happening.

Erase doubt, he reminded himself, think only of healing and life. He continued the rhythmic chanting.

A noticeable shift swept across Adrina's features, her chest rose once and then fell as her body convulsed. Soon Father Jacob heard the strangled sounds of the girl choking on water still in her lungs. He slapped her back repeatedly and forced her to cough.

Adrina choked on the water she spit up, and gasped frantically for air. She inhaled deeply and rapidly. Violently she vomited the mixture of water and mud she had swallowed—Jacob never broke the rhythmic tone of the litany of life and healing. After a moment, Adrina stopped her convulsing and regained her senses. Tears rolled down her cheeks as she reached up to embrace Father Jacob.

"I'm sorry," she whimpered, "I'm sorry." She closed her eyes briefly against the tears and let the elder hold her.

"Blankets! Get me some blankets, now!" said Father Jacob. He was clearly drained of all his strength. His face was pale and wet with perspiration. He sighed, he had done it, he had succeeded. "We must keep her warm. She will need to get some deep rest soon and, in a warm, comfortable bed."

Silence prevailed for a time afterward as Jacob's words settled on those listening—they must get through this damnable mire and reach the elusive castle somewhere in the distance. Night had settled upon them somewhere during the journey through the mire or perhaps in the frantic moments following Adrina's near fatal accident. Only Father Jacob truly knew how close Adrina had come to death's door, for he was of Great-Father and Great-Father knew all, especially in matters of death.

With unsettling certainty, Father Jacob knew that an unseen evil had been at hand. Great-Father had sensed it and so had he.

***

"We cannot just bed down here surely," came a grumble from a mixture of voices.

Captain Brodst's cold, dark eyes glared back. No further grumblings were made, yet there was truth to be found in those words. All their gear was soaked. Three men had worked furiously for many long minutes to ignite damp kindling and get a small fire started. The meager fire that warmed young Princess Adrina would not last long and then what would they do afterward?

They could not bed down here. The road was narrow and the mire was on both sides of them. Besides, a night in the dampness of the mire and they would *all* catch their death of colds.

Captain Brodst had planned to continue the march for a few hours past sunset and reach Fraddylwicke Castle, but it was already night and the castle was still a half day's march away. Ahead there was a place where hillocks rose out of the mires. Surely there they should have better luck starting a base fire from which they could light the many fires needed for the camp. But that still wouldn't solve their problems, for Captain Brodst knew those shallow hills, there it would be nearly as cold and as damp as if they had bedded down right where they were. No, Adrina needed to sleep in a bed beside a roaring fire, his men needed a place to dry wet clothes and wet gear. Fraddylwicke Castle and its commons was the only place where they'd find both.

Captain Brodst looked to Adrina then turned to one of his sub-commanders.

"Captain Adylton, command of the foot is yours. I want you to keep the men in good spirits and reach the castle as soon as possible. They'll be hot food and fires waiting if I have to rouse every innkeeper's cook within a mile of the castle."

Captain Brodst turned to his second in command. "Captain Trendmore, muster the horse, we ride for Fraddylwicke Castle."

***

The long file was quickly regaining the broken formation. Torches fanned out and faded into the dismal fog. Adrina seemed to be still dazed. She kept repeating, "I'm sorry, I'm sorry," as Captain Brodst picked her up in his arms and carried her to his horse.

A guardsman momentarily held Adrina while the captain mounted, then Captain Brodst took her gently into his arms. While holding reins in one hand, he held her tightly with the opposite arm. Captain Brodst joined the middle of the horse column, Captain Trendmore fell in beside him.

Despite dense fog, Captain Brodst urged the group to maintain a fast pace. They were in a race against time and bone-chilling dampness. The horse soldiers feared the captain's wrath, and none offered further complaints. Their thoughts and concerns were also with the young Princess Adrina. She was royalty and thus revered. There were none among the simple men who would not have given his life for hers.

The night air grew steadily colder as the mire seemed to drink in the last remnants of reassuring heat. When mixed with the dampness of the mire, it made the chill reach through thick clothing. An uncanny sense of portentous dread hung in the air and Father Jacob wasn't the only one who could feel it now. Soon all longed to reach a place where a hearty fire could be raised and the unchanging darkness of the mire left far behind.

With the changing of the temperatures toward freezing came a slow, subtle end to the fog. Gradually it faded into small patches of outlying mists and as the night drew on the captain increased the pace accordingly. Oddly, though, a relieved sigh did not pass throughout until much later.

A short distance ahead lurked a series of interconnecting low hills and upon reaching them, the captain stopped the group to release the stress from the intense pace. This gave the horses a short break for feed and water, and riders time to stretch sore muscles. Also, Captain Brodst wanted Father Jacob to check Adrina's condition to ensure it had not worsened.

While the good father checked on Adrina, Captain Brodst momentarily stretched tired muscles. He gazed back across the mire they had traversed and into the darkness that surrounded them. He tried to convince himself that Adrina's accident had not changed his plans. His hope was to reach the castle commons in an hour, at the most two. Once inside the castle, Princess Adrina would be safe and there she would stay. In a few days when she was well enough to travel, she would continue on to Klaive. He however, could not afford to waste precious days waiting for a recovery only Father Jacob could ensure. Five days, he told himself. Five days to reach Alderan.

Captain Trendmore who had been checking on the men returned. "It would seem our plans have changed," he said.

Captain Brodst shook his head, at times it seemed as if Captain Trendmore could read minds. "No, nothing has changed." He wasn't in the mood for a conversation, so he spoke tersely.

"With Princess Adrina in such a state—"

"—You are forgetting one thing, we haven't even reached Fraddylwicke Castle yet. For now, I will change no plans."

"The Prince's party will not leave Quashan' until the Seventhday, that gives us a week to reach our destination. A day's rest will be good for everyone."

"Less than a week. At the rate we are traveling, we are already a day or more behind schedule. We will obtain as many fresh mounts as we can and continue south in the morning as planned, unless I decide otherwise."

"Surely you do not intend to leave the Princess and continue on."

Captain Brodst turned away, ending the conversation.

Father Jacob finished his examination of Adrina. He told Captain Brodst her condition had not worsened. After more blankets were wrapped around her, Captain Brodst gave the order to prepare for movement.

Before Father Jacob went to his mount, he told Captain Brodst, "Try not to jostle her so. I know you wish to move swiftly, but you must exercise caution. I do not know what bones she may have broken."

"Thank you, Father Jacob, I will try to remember that."

Captain Brodst waited until Jacob was in the saddle then called out, "The princess' condition has not worsened. There is still hope, but we must move swiftly. Pray to Great-Father, all!"

With renewed vigor after the short reprieve and the captain's enthusiastic words, the riders began anew. The ground did not level off immediately after the last of the hills were left behind. Instead it seemed to slope gradually downward, its base enveloped in a bank of swirling mists.

Captain Brodst passed a warning along to the riders at the fore. "Watch the trail before you carefully!"

With great reservation and careful hesitation, they entered the gray veil of dense fog a second time. The captain hoped it would last only until they crossed the shallow point at the bottom of the long downgrade. For an instant he turned his eyes to look down upon Adrina to make sure his heavy woolen cloak was still pulled tightly around her.

"Soon," he said, "soon, we will stop. Rest, princess, rest."

Suddenly the crying whinnies of a frightened mare broke the air followed by the frantic yelling of the lead rider as he jerked harshly on his mount's reins. "Captain Brodst, captain! Quickly!" the rider shouted.

The others behind him came to a similarly abrupt halt. Captain Brodst urged his mount faster and raced to the front of the group. He was amazed at what he saw as he approached the first rider. Ahead in the distance he could see nothing but water and loose patches of dense fog. The road was gone, apparently washed away. His fears rang true.

A voice reached out into the darkness seeming to stir even the hidden creatures of the mire. "Bring up torches!" Captain Brodst cried out. "Hurry, you louts!"

A large gaggle of men stormed toward the captain. They raised their fiery brands high into the air. The only response to this was a scattered reflection off the water, a dingy yellow mirror of dull orange torch flames.

"It is only an illusion of the fog. The road is washed out at the bottom of the trail nothing more. You there and you, move out!" ordered Captain Brodst.

Those he pointed to shrank back and his scowl deepened.

"Mount and ride out into the water," he ordered again, this time he pointed to two palace guardsmen and made sure he had eye contact with them. "The trail must be there. Find it and be quick about it!"

***

The chosen two entered the dreadful darkness of the lurking waters with reverent care. Movements of their horses were slow and sluggish as the animals fought for every step through the sticky goo of the mire.

They passed through layer upon layer of swirling gray. It seemed dark waters stretched on endlessly before them with no hope of an end. Their mounts began to sink deeper into the muck with each step. Soon the animals, having better sense than the riders, refused to move further without constant coaxing and even then, they became disquieted and whinnied their disapproval.

The chosen two respected the keen sense of their mounts. When the yearning for a retreat out of the gloom became stronger than the urge to continue, they came to a frustrated halt.

They puzzled for a moment over possible solutions, then attempted to maneuver in different directions but to no avail. Their mounts only got more bogged down. Soon they would not be able to escape the mire's yearning grasp. And if strong beasts could not break free neither could simple men. The road simply was not there.

"Cap-tain... Cap-tain Brodst," screamed one of the men. "Sir, there is only water ahead. We are sinking into the mire... We cannot continue."

"You must continue. We must reach the castle... There is a path, find it!"

"But Captain," said the other rider, "we cannot go any farther. We will be lost."

"You must try, there is hope. Do not give up so soon. Push forward!"

The two bravely forced their mounts into movement. With each step the animals sank deeper and deeper into the mud. Soon cold waters lapped at the riders' boots and then there was no retreat backwards or forwards. They were completely stuck.

Kicked, swatted and cussed at, the horses felt the frustration of their riders and it caused them to panic. The scene quickly turned to turmoil, with neither rider retaining a clear mind capable of rational thought. Desperation fed their frenzied movements and their crazed thoughts.

***

Panic-stricken screams reached those waiting behind and created an alarm. No one knew what caused such desperation. Had something as black and as grim as the mire found the unsuspecting two? Was it waiting for them all out there in the swirling gray mists?

Captain Brodst called out, "What has happened? Do you need our assistance?"

He paused for a moment waiting for a response. The shouts continued unabated. He quickly dispatched two additional riders to tread into the murky waters and assist the others. They did as ordered, but with great reservation.

"Try to remain calm," shouted Keeper Martin—he sensed the cause of the panic. "Aid is coming to you."

Captain Brodst nodded in agreement as he also realized what had occurred. He began passing out orders. He told the riders to wait, ordered several squads to come forward and passed the princess into safe hands.

"Ropes," Captain Brodst shouted, "Ropes!"

He untied a rope from around his saddlebag and after he secured it, threw the coil to the closest rider. "Tie it to your length."

Then he turned to one of his sub-commanders. "Captain Ghenson, throw your rope to the other rider!"

Captain Brodst continued to pass out orders, his mind quick and calculating under pressure.

"I need two more lengths of rope," he said.

Another man handed two ropes to Father Jacob, which he in turn gave to Captain Ghenson and Captain Brodst to add to their lines for additional distance.

When all was ready, he turned back to the two riders who were awaiting his orders. "Take up the slack, move with caution. When you reach them, toss each a line and tell them to tie it off securely. I pray we can provide them the extra strength necessary to return safely. When you are ready, yell loudly. We will begin to pull on a three count..."

***

One of the trapped guardsmen had lost his torch in the frenzy. The other's had expired and now only darkness remained to add to the worries of their already troubled minds. Slight shifts in the air around them caused their minds to flee in all directions. What could be out there lurking around them unseen and unknown?

Alone and isolated, they searched for any sign or source of light to pierce the blackness. A barely audible splashing, slurping noise crept into range of their listening ears. One of the guards drew his blade and, after a brief moment, the other did the same. In the stillness of their surroundings, the sound seemed to grow in intensity until it became an unnerving clamor.

Two tiny points of light pierced the darkness as a glowing pair of spheres—eyes to the beholders—that grew in intensity with each passing moment. A shrill voice cried out and without heed to the message the trapped two prepared for the end, for they knew it came.

The voice cried out again. "Where are you? Say something, are you there?"

A moment of realization passed between both men. "Over here, over here! Here we are!" they cried.

The rescuers homed in on the direction of the voices. They saw only darkness and proceeded cautiously. The endless spans of the darkened mire pulled and played upon them, and took them deep into its folds. Soon they too could barely coax their mounts through the muck.

"We cannot reach you!" shouted one of the approaching riders.

His frantic partner screamed, "Where are you? We are sinking!"

Panic spread also to their thoughts. They didn't want to be stuck like the others. They had to escape before the mire swallowed them like it surely would the other two. After they had ensured their own ropes were properly secured they began to shout wildly. Several sharp tugs at the lines caused those waiting to quickly pull them back in.

Not entirely pleased with the performance of the two before him whom he now considered cowards and nearing the end of his patience, Captain Brodst began a thorough chastising. His anger forced him to become irrational. Sword withdrawn, mount turned, eyes glaring, he stared down the first, while he waited for the second to emerge fully from the darkness.

With his free hand, he motioned for them to dismount and step forward. They did so reluctantly.

In a series of lightening swift slashes, Captain Brodst lashed out with his blade, and cropped the lapels from their shoulders. The guardsmen had not flinched at the sight of the captain's blade, yet they had felt its wrath as if it had pierced their hearts.

Pity entered the thoughts of the onlookers, for they all understood the sign and knew it could have just as easily been their own fate. Even Keeper Martin who was not an initiate understood the unspoken meaning of the captain's gesture. The two were no longer members of the elite palace guard.

Stripped of the privileges of their rank and all its entitlements, the two nearly wept as they withdrew. Failure was not an easy notion for Captain Brodst to swallow. He sheathed his sword without regrets for his action.

"Give me a torch!" He yelled, his voice boomed. "Tie these ropes off and prepare for my signal… Father Jacob, keep Princess Adrina warm. We are going to get her to the castle if it requires my last breath to do it... Keeper Martin, can I have your long walking stick?"

***

"Hold on, keep talking so I can maintain a bearing on you," Captain Brodst yelled out.

He drove his stallion onward in the direction of the screaming voices.

"Where are your torches?"

"One is lost and the other is burnt out."

"If you have some flint lay a spark to it. It may yet burn."

Even in the fog, Captain Brodst saw the light the tiny sparks afforded as they were struck and knew he was close. Progress was becoming extremely arduous now and he had a difficult time persuading his mount to move ahead, but he did not retreat like the others. Inch by inch, his mount crept closer to the trapped riders.

"Find a dried cloth in your bags. Anything dry. Tie it to the top of the torch. Then lay a spark to it!"

Captain Brodst waited for a response. A shout of hooray erupted from the two as they managed to light the torch at long last and confidence began to replace their unease.

Captain Brodst now had a meager beacon to follow toward the two. He changed his harshness to gentility, and soothed his horse while he urged it to trudge through murky waters. The stallion, responding to his master's faith, pushed onward using its powerful legs to advance slowly and methodically.

Captain Brodst readied the rope as he approached. An ecstatic cheer erupted from the hapless two as the first line was caught in yearning hands.

Captain Brodst untied the rope from his saddle horn and tugged the line sharply three times to signal those waiting to start pulling. The slack was quickly taken up as the rope went taunt, the initial strain audible in the air as a loud twang that continued as a stretching noise caused from the heavy tension in the line.

Horse and rider strained as one, yearning to be free from the unwanted grasp. Instinctively, the horse fought to be free as much as the rider wanted to be free, its heavy set breathing and the painstaking plodding of each step it took clearly audible.

Sufficiently free, the first man untied the line and pulled it in several yards to throw it back to Captain Brodst who was now fixed approximately midway between the two escapees. It took several attempts before the rope reached the captain and when it finally did, he relayed it to the last man.

Knowingly, Captain Brodst kept his mount moving so that it would not sink too far into the muck of the mire. Once the second rider was at a safe point, Captain Brodst instructed him to make a loop and throw the line back. He secured it tightly to his saddle horn and then to the astonishment of the receding two who were moving back to the safety of firm ground, Captain Brodst turned and plunged deeper into the quagmire.

Defeat was another word he frowned upon.

His scowl was now plastered to his face in thick folds. "Think lightly," he whispered to his mount, "we will find a way."

Initially, he tried to circle around the area where the others had been stuck. Unfortunately, he was caught up in the same sinkhole they had been stuck in. He probed with the keeper's long stick. The search for a spot that was not excessively soft told him he had to retreat in the direction he had come from.

Undaunted by the small set back, he made the detour and then pushed on. He attempted to go around in the opposite direction, and moved outward laterally to the right until he found a spot where he could press forward.

Much to his dismay he came upon a tiny spot of land, an island in the middle of the muck, a minute area a mere five feet across and three feet wide, but it was a hard surface from which he could maneuver. Hiding his elation as reservation returned, he stifled a shout for joy. His exerted steed was rewarded with generous strokes and a brief reprieve.

One last time, he plunged into the muck of the mire, and after only a short jaunt again to the right across a small patch of dank swamp, he found the road. In a soft, steady voice he whispered, "Hold on young princess. I promise you'll soon rest in a warm, warm bed."

Captain started to call out to those behind. "A warm bed awaits!" he intended to say, but a faint sloshing, slurping noise caught his trained ear, and no words escaped his lips.

He turned in time to see a dim figure emerge from the gray of the fog. Instinctively he dropped the walking stick, his hand going to the hilt of his long sword, and his heart skipping a beat before he recognized the once grim shadow. He raised a hand in confused salutation.

"Captain, why did you leave ranks?" he asked.

Chapter Seventeen: Past Thoughts

Hot, it's so damned hot...

Endless waiting played heavily on Seth's faith. Yet, he knew it was faith that he must maintain, for there was nothing else. Only Mother-Earth would carry them to safety or deliver them from life.

Ah, please... please... make the sun go away... make it end...

A full day sun blossomed overhead. The struggle to keep squinted eyes open was borne. Once closed under the beating sun, blisters would return and with them infection, and then eyes might open no more. The ruinous combination of sun and salt water had already desiccated and blistered his body, yet it was the eyes that seemed his most sacred pride.

Seth struggled to his knees. He tested the strength of the pieces of ropes and tattered clothing that held the raft together. Salt water despoiled them. Still, they held well. *Thank you...*

A sudden tremor in his mind sent Seth's thoughts careening outward. *Bryan!* Seth called out.

He perceived no return response, though he could feel the other's anguish.

Oh please... please, hold on...

Seth carefully removed the cap from the last water bag they possessed and put a single droplet to his own parched lips.

Give me strength... He wanted more, he wanted every drop the bottle contained. *Give me strength...*

The water's caress as it moistened his lips caused a shiver throughout his body. The yearning for more increased, yet he could not, *would not,* allow himself to partake of it.

His hands were shaking. *Give me strength...* He implored.

Seth lowered the water bag. He reached over to where Bryan lay, and cradled his companion's head upward. Slowly and painstakingly, he dropped the precious liquid to Bryan's lips, and savored every drop as if it touched his own lips. He continued to drop the water to Bryan's lips, drop by precious drop, until the brother could swallow. Afterward, he did the same for Galan.

Bryan's and Galan's faces were covered with sun blisters, as was his own, but his thoughts were only for his fellows. *Two must survive no matter the cost,* he whispered to himself, *two must survive*—Queen Mother's last words of warning to him. Delirium enveloped his thoughts and the words echoed through his mind. Somehow he must shield them, somehow they must all survive...

***

More long hours under the burning sun did little for Seth's clarity of mind. He was nearing total delirium. The only thought that kept him near sanity was the one single thought that had kept him through the last three hours. *Two must survive, two must survive no matter the cost,* went the echo in his mind. Surely sometime ago he had ceased thinking it, yet the echo still clung to his mind.

With great persistence, Seth moved from a sitting position to a kneeling position—waves shifting the raft, and his fatigue, made the small accomplishment a difficult chore. He held there motionless for a moment and tried to recall why he had risen to his knees. Then, after a lengthy pause, he sank back down to his haunches. There must have been something he had wanted to do, but what, he couldn't recall.

Two must survive, he whispered.

Weary, Seth slumped down onto his side. He closed and shielded tired eyes, using the tattered shards of a once magnificent cloak to mask his face. For what seemed hours, the ceaseless up and down swaying of the raft lulled him. By luck or fate, or perhaps a little help from Great-Father, Seth managed to focus his will, though only for an instant. He reached outward with his mind trying desperately to reach a knowing consciousness. He found none.

Yet, the momentary clarity of mind also allowed him to concentrate. Surely there was an answer to their dilemma. He pondered this. Something had gone wrong from the start, but *what* had it been. Had there been a traitor among them? Was there a traitor among them now? Was it Bryan or Galan?

No, paranoia. Seth dismissed the idea of a traitor. No one of the Brotherhood would ever betray Queen Mother—*Sathar,* whispered his conscience. *No, Sathar betrayed all. Survival is keyed to the past, the answer is there, if only I can find it.*

Exhausted, Seth started to drift off to sleep and was quickly lost to his dreams. Dreams in which he could replay events that had unfolded against them.

No longer was he in his beloved homeland, surrounded by the peace and serenity of Queen Mother. Now he was thrust out into the strange and cruel world, *into an unknown fate.* Only Great-Father knew how the long struggle would end.

His mind wandered further, and floated through delirium to mixed conscious thought. He began to think back, *back to the time before they had left their homeland.* At first, in this mixed up delusion that to him seemed real, Seth heard only the voices, his and hers. Yet, as his thoughts cleared and he entered a deeper dream-state, he pieced together disconnected thought without much detail.

It was to this at first colorless world of dream with only the voices that he fled.

***

Quickly, Brother Seth. You must wake now or it will be too late! said a voice entering Seth's dream.

All thoughts of sleep were instantly gone. The voice sent a shiver careening down Seth's back.

Quickly, quickly now, the voice hastened.

Suddenly he was unsure whether the voice was within or without. Was it his own mind that called out the warning or another?

A shifting of the raft caused Seth to open his eyes. *Was the voice of alarm within or without?*

Seth stepped back into the dream-thought, which was difficult but successfully managed. He ran from his room, down of series of twisting halls and into the great monolithic entry hall. He slowed his pace here to a stately walk. After he had crossed the hall, he descending into the great open courtyard that spread out in gothic proportions in front of the wide translucent steps of alabaster that he used.

This is why I have chosen you, Brothers of the Red, he called out, greeting those already assembled. He spoke powerfully now into the minds of the chosen few. *You were each hand picked for the task that lies ahead. Queen Mother has spoken and her protectors have listened. Go now to the harbor, Sailmaster Cagan awaits you.*

Seth inspected each as they departed the courtyard. He stopped the last brother, and chased a whisper of thought after her. *Brother Galan, I had wished you to remain here leading the Red in my stead but it could not be so.*

Galan turned and the two locked eyes in a deep drinking gaze that spoke volumes. Her open thoughts streamed to his mind. She was remembering the kiss of many days ago. The meaning of it still confused her.

Shifting on one of his heels, Seth turned about and marched back up the long alabaster stair into the monolithic entry hall and swiftly along it. Queen Mother had retired to a meditation room and this is where Seth hastened to. But Seth did not find

Queen Mother there, and it wasn't until many precious minutes later that he considered checking High Hall.

Queen Mother was seated at her place in the middle of the hall, eyes directed straight at him. Seth said, *We leave now, Queen Mother.*

Yes, I know, she imparted softly, yet forcefully. *May Mother-Earth protect all her children who must now leave their home to journey to the world of Man. May the Father guide you on your journey to safety.*

Beckoned by feelings mixed in with the words, Seth looked into Queen Mother's eyes. He had been trembling though he hadn't known it until her soft eyes forced calm into him. *Good-bye, my Queen. We will succeed in this endeavor. We will bring word to the Alder King and persuade him to join our cause. As I have sworn my duty, nothing shall stop me from completing this.*

It was difficult to stare into eyes with such emotion for any length of time, yet when Seth attempted to look away, he was drawn back again by her words and her thoughts. *I have great faith in you, Brother Seth, though I regret your having to make this journey. Alas, all is set in motion. There can be no turning back now. It is up to fate and faith to bring you back safely to our shores.*

I have no regrets, Queen Mother. We will succeed.

Then by my leave, go swiftly, said the Queen as she touched her hand to Seth's brow. She left her index finger lighted there while she said these words, *and this, I whisper only to your mind my son. I as Queen Mother can see shadings of what is yet to come. While I am powerless to stop what has been set in motion, I can say this. You must always be prepared for the unexpected. Never let down your guard. You must accept what you alone are fated to do. Always retain your faith, never let it dwindle…*

Never let it dwindle, repeated Seth.

...Always make it burn brightly as a red-hot ember of your being. Your faith will shelter you. Fair-thee-well my son, and

remember that above all else, two must survive the journey, for only one will be able to return to our shores...

Never let it dwindle, repeated Seth as he turned away.

***

Waves beneath the raft shifted it and just as his thoughts were coming to a clear, full focus, Seth was jolted from his slumber. He opened bleary eyes to a night sky. He did not marvel at the arrival of darkness. The night sky only meant cruel heat was gone and bitter cold had replaced it.

He was thankful thought that Bryan and Galan were soundly sleeping. They had survived yet another day beneath the untiring fury of the day sky.

He opened the water skin and put several droplets to his lips. He could have easily finished that last bit of water in the container. It would have only taken a second more. Momentarily, he reveled in the fantasy of it slipping coolly down his throat. The fact that his throat was swollen and every such swallow would have brought sure pain did not taint the longing.

Give me strength, he implored.

Only as he raised the container back to his lips did he find restraint. *Thank you...*

Two must survive, went the ceaseless echo in his mind. He turned his eyes back to the dark waters and a thought from the dream found him. *The mind shield.* The mind shield could resist his probing thoughts. Anyone could be lurking out there in the darkness, waiting just beyond the next crest or trough.

High Hall, why High Hall? Seth thought suddenly, though he didn't dwell on this long. He was elated. Keys beyond the confusion in his mind could be found. *Bryan, Galan!*

He had considered the others a moment ago, though the thought had slipped away before he had a chance to focus on it. *Galan, Bryan?* he called out again.

Neither stirred.

A panicked probing assured him they were alive, although he didn't like the weakness that had come from Bryan and it worried him. Convinced that in order to survive the journey he must lose no more of his companions, Seth was prepared to go to any length to ensure their survival. He would have slashed his own wrists and fed them from the blood that oozed from the open gash if he could have. In the *very* real delirium of his mind, this notion was suddenly appealing until he realized it would quicken his own passage from life. And life, especially one's own, was sacred.

Suddenly he wished he had learned more about the sea. He knew little of the creatures that lurked beneath the dark waters, only that at night he saw them, the ones called sharks with the high dorsal fins, circling round and round their tiny raft. When he had been stronger, he had chased them away by sending harsh emotions into their underdeveloped brains. Now he was too weak to attempt this—and nearly too weak to care at all.

Somewhere in the convoluted corners of his mind, he made a connection between the circling predator and Bryan. Suddenly he remembered the water bag still clutched in his upturned hand. He awoke Bryan and forced the brother to drink a few precious drops, but no more.

Do not waste brother, you need this more than I. You must live… came the shallow whisper into his mind, the voice was Bryan's.

Drink, I will not tolerate nonsense.

Afterward Seth gave Galan an equal portion of the water. *Drink, drink,* he said to Galan. *The supply of water is almost spent, soon we will all be without its life giving essence*…

Although his teachings and his faith told him otherwise, he felt completely responsible for the fate of his two companions. *If* he had but one wish, he would do something, anything that would ease their suffering.

It is time you saved your strength, imparted Galan.

Surprised by the voice, for he had been sure his thoughts were sealed, Seth apologized. *I am sorry Brother Galan. I did not mean to trouble you with open thought.*

Seth, you know better than that. Our fate is predestined, you cannot alter it. You cannot stop the inevitable, you cannot hold back the winds, or the looming hands of fate…

Seth listened to her words yet he did not accept them. The weight of guilt had already scarred him.

Sleep well my Galan, he said, although he doubted Galan had heard him for she was already gathered in a heavy sleep. The presence of the Father faintly came to Seth, as he too, slipped quickly back to sleep and delirium. His dreams of remembrance grew surprisingly richer.

Two must survive, echoed once more in his thoughts, just before the dreams gathered full force.

***

The first shafts of light from an early morning sun shot over the horizon in the East. The light touched the haze of Seth's mind and caused him to rub his burning eyes. A dry yawn issued from his mouth, and then with one partially unclenched eye, he squinted toward the brightness.

It will be a clear day.

Seth both welcomed the sun's warmth to end the night's cold and feared its erosion of their bodies. For Seth, the days were longer than the nights and, upon reflection, he did indeed prefer the night despite the often bitter cold.

Time passed. The sun seemed to wither and weaken Seth even more this day. The dryness and excruciating pain of his throat aroused him to its swelling—it was nearly swollen shut. He attempted to squeeze down a lump of dry, pasty spittle, and cried out in a muffled whimper as he did this.

So much water around me and none to drink.

Their small supply of fresh water was nearly exhausted and this was now the only concern in his frazzled mind. *Seawater.* It was all around him and he could drink none of it.

Why can it not rain Father?

Still unconcerned for himself, Seth first touched a few precious drops of moisture to Galan's lips then covered her face and arms again with the tatters of his robe. He drank then, a little more than he should have, barely getting the drops to slide down his aching throat. Then Seth gave Bryan the last few drops the water bag contained.

Is it all for nothing Father?

The day turned to night and back again to day. Seth felt the vitality within him ebb. His consciousness fell to total decay. He could no longer focus his will to maintain him which frustrated him utterly. The forces of nature were all around him, yet he, Seth, First of the Red, could not touch them. He was losing himself and his center. Soon he would slip away to a peaceful bliss that he would have welcomed only a few short days ago. But now he had struggled too long to give in, fought too hard to give up.

Great-Father, is that you? Have you come to gather me home? What did I do wrong?... I do not wish to go... I could not have stopped the ambush... I... I... did not know. No... I cannot fail. I... I must think. I must focus...

***

The sun was midway in the sky before Seth finally came back from the endless world of gray delirium and dream. Visions of ships sinking into the dark, waiting waters that surrounded him even now, slowly fell from his eyes—*so much needless loss.*

A light breeze played soothingly across Seth's tormented skin. Hidden behind a murky cloudbank, a pale sun looked so distant and harmless, yet its ill effects had whittled away his body and his strength slowly and effectively.

Rain may come, Seth mused. If rain came, it may just save them. Then again, the storm unleashed with the rains could drown them just as easily.

Hours diminished to the slow pace of the passing of minutes as time slowly plodded on in agonizing increments of seconds and heartbeats. Ignoring the hunger pains in his clenched and swollen stomach, the brittle dryness of his lips, and the tremendous aching of his brutalized body, Seth attempted to center his thoughts.

He knew somewhere in his teaching there must be an answer to their dilemma. He searched the indexes of his mind. A wish sprang to mind, a wish that he had learned more about seamanship from Cagan, the crafty sea captain who he had known since childhood and who since his childhood had commanded the Queen's own fleet. Such learning would have proven a worthwhile investment, yet then he had not had time for such foolish endeavors.

Seth felt a faint prick of pain in his mind. He strained to focus his thoughts. As he did this, sadness swept over him and in an unexplainable way Seth knew something was wrong. *Is someone in my thoughts?*

A gentle whisper entered Seth's mind.

Yes? he answered.

If *I told you I was afraid, what would you say?* asked Galan.

Seth reached out for Galan's hand and took it in his. *We all have our fears, Brother Galan. It is not wrong to fear what we do not know.*

I fear death, said Galan sending feelings of hopelessness along with the words. *I fear in death I will find only longing and emptiness.*

Great-Father will not forsake— Seth felt another prick of pain in his mind. —*Is that you, Brother Galan?*

You are wrong. For those who have failed, there can be no joy in the next life. The voice nearly inaudible in their minds and edged with bitterness was Bryan's.

Seth disagreed. *While blood courses through your veins, it tells you that you live.*

I died long ago, said Bryan.

Bryan's sadness flowed strongly to Seth. It encompassed him and the whole of their bantam raft. Then Seth felt pain again. *What are you doing in my thoughts?*

I'm dying Seth.

Dying? Seth wheeled about the raft wildly. Frantically he searched for the precious water bag. His aim was to pour its every drop down Bryan's throat in the desperate hope that it alone would keep him. It was then Seth remembered they had no more water. He had used the last of it.

No Brother, said Seth. *It is not time, it is not your time! You must hold strong, you cannot desert us. We need you, I need you. There is so much, so very much…*

Bryan didn't or couldn't answer.

Bryan, please answer me… There is a way, there must be a way… The dream, the dream, the answers are there, please hold on. I will find them… I will.

Seth's eyes flashed to his wrists. The blood coursing through his veins gave him life, it would give Bryan life.

Go ahead Seth, whispered the voice, Bryan's voice in his mind. *Two must live.*

No Seth, it is already too late for him. It is not yet our time. Mother-Earth still has plans for us.

Galan cried out in sudden pain.

Go ahead Seth, it is your fault I die. You owe me your life. You bring shame and dishonor to our kind.

Paralyzing anguish shot through Seth's mind. *No, Seth, it is his time. Our time is yet to be destined.*

Again, Galan cried out in pain. Hands suddenly gripped Seth's throat.

Bryan, what are you doing? Remember, you pulled me from the water, you saved my life—Ga-lan, he's choking… me—Bryan are you mad?

You still don't understand, do you Seth? Bryan squeezed harder.

The hands still at his throat, Seth struggled wildly to his knees. Galan made her move and hit Bryan from the side.

What followed was outright pandemonium. Seth found Bryan unexpectedly strong and only with Galan's help was he able to break the hands from his throat. Together, wobbly and barely able to keep their feet, Seth and Galan fended off Bryan's blows. Seth ducked to dodge a blow. Galan lunged at Bryan, and knocked him off his feet. Together they fell into the sea.

Seth let out a high-pitched cry of anguish. He scrambled to the edge of the raft.

Galan and Bryan broke the surface. They were still struggling. On his belly now, Seth reached out to Galan. He felt the tip of her fingers touch his. Then Bryan pulled Galan under with him for what seemed the final time.

Seth lay still. He stared into the dark waters through red and burning eyes. Despair ravaged his heart.

Chapter Eighteen: Awakening

"Isador?... Isador, I saw him. I saw him!" screamed Adrina, as she roused from a feverish state. "He is hurting. He needs our help!".

"Princess, it was only a dream," said an alarmed Father Jacob. The sound of Adrina's voice had startled him. He took the moist towel from her brow, dipped it into the cold water of a basin beside him, then reapplied it to her forehead. The fever must have finally broken, he thought.

"We must hurry," continued Adrina heatedly.

"It was only a dream," repeated Father Jacob. He patiently dabbed the girl's forehead with the cold towel.

"His eyes were the bluest blue. He spoke to me in the dream." Adrina lurched up in bed, then after putting feet to floor, she stood. She looked around the unfamiliar room and stopped. A puzzled frown crossed her face. "Fa-ther Ja-cob?... Where am I and how did I get here?"

The room started to swirl around her, twisting and turning round and round. Adrina began to lose her balance. She fought to steady herself. Father Jacob caught her and ferried her back into bed. She looked up at him, her eyes wide and imploring, and said, "We must leave now. I know where he is. Just as the lady said, the ship did not reach Alderan."

Father Jacob was sure Adrina was talking gibberish again. She had said many things in her fevered state. "Child you must rest. Tomorrow will bring a new day. The others will return soon enough."

"No, you don't understand. Get Keeper Martin. He understands, he will listen to me."

"I am afraid they have already departed. You have been asleep for quite some time. Now please get some rest, my child," said Jacob. He pulled heavy blankets up around Adrina to keep the girl warm.

Adrina wanted to say something else but Jacob silenced her and again bade her to sleep. As Jacob turned away, Adrina grabbed his arm and squeezed as hard as she could to gain his attention. She didn't want to sleep—at least, not yet. Once she had his attention, she stared straight into his eyes and stated in a calm, portentous manner, "When did they leave?… We must go now before it is *too* late."

Father Jacob was taken aback by her words, something told him to listen to her. "Slow down, Adrina. I am afraid I don't understand. Tell me of the dream?"

After a brief moment of silence, Adrina said, "It was in my dreams, father. I saw Prince William and he spoke to me. I know where he is and he urgently needs our help… There is something wrong."

"You are full of fever. Prince William is in Alderan. No harm could have befallen him there."

Adrina closed her eyes for a moment though she did not let go of Jacob's arm. "No, the ship from Wellison did not complete the journey. The voices, the message, Father Jacob, it was all *real*… You must believe me. If only Keeper Martin were here. He *would* understand."

"I believe you young princess," said Father Jacob, "but you are in no condition to travel."

Adrina regarded Father Jacob with serious eyes. "Are you patronizing me?"

"No, child. You close your eyes and rest now. I'll see if I can arrange travel accommodations." Jacob nodded his head wearily.

He wasn't convinced it was a good idea to leave Fraddylwicke Castle. He departed Adrina's chamber with troubled thoughts filling his mind. His hope was that the girl would be fast asleep when he returned.

***

Adrina gathered her strength and sat up. She stretched her arms and her sore back with a hefty, stretching-yawn. A few minutes passed without movement as she attempted to shake dizziness away. Eventually the room did stop moving. She slipped over to the side of the bed and placed her feet onto the floor.

Carefully she reached out, grasped her boots, then slipped her feet into them. A bit wobbly, she stood up and looked about the chamber. Bright daylight pouring in through a terraced doorway instantly caught her attention. She walked out onto the balcony and squinted her eyes to the bright orange of the sun, which to her astonishment was midway in the sky.

She rushed back into the chamber, which seemed suddenly dark. She stumbled. She had moved too fast. She pressed up against the frame of the door and held herself there for several long breaths while her eyes slowly readjusted to the dimness of the interior.

After a quick scan of the unfamiliar room for belongings, she prepared to leave. Instinctively she checked her hair in the large mirror that stood beside the door on her way out. Her hair was a mess. She ran her fingers through it to straighten it. Abruptly she stopped what she was doing and stared at her reflection. Something wasn't right. It took her a moment to realize she was wearing a nightgown. To have put her boots on while she still wore bed clothes. Whatever was she thinking?

She wasn't thinking.

Her head ached on one side—a dull throbbing that numbed her awareness—as if she had been kicked and a large swollen area on the right side of her skull attested to this fact. She touched it gingerly and winced.

Think clearly, think clearly. She tensed up and took a couple of deep breaths, trying to concentrate. All right, now what was I doing?

It took her a moment to remember and only after staring into the mirror again did she finally realize what she needed to do next.

"Riding clothes, riding clothes," she muttered to herself.

At the opposite end of the large chamber was a partial wall-divider, which she finally realized was where the dressing area must be. I knew that. Where was my brain?

Adrina touched the lump on the side of her head. She screamed out, "Ouch!" Her brain was there—in pain.

It was a slow methodical amble to the divider and even slower changing into her riding clothes that were clean and thankfully dry—she recalled now that they had been wet, that she had been wet.

A dull thump sounded at the door as she was dressing and Adrina shouted, "Just a moment—"

"Oo, ouch!" she moaned. Her head throbbed with pain. No more screaming.

It took a few more careful minutes before Adrina finished dressing and walked over to open the door. She opened it to find Father Jacob standing solemnly, a deep-set frown on his face.

"I was hoping you would be fast asleep when I returned," he said, as he stepped into the chamber.

"No such luck," said Adrina with heedful volume so as not to cause her head to pound any more than it already did.

"You are still flushed with fever. A day's delay will cause little harm. I am concerned about your health, child, more than anything else. That was a nasty fall. You need to rest."

"There will be plenty of time to rest later, Father Jacob."

Father Jacob started to reply. Adrina reached out and took his hand in hers. "I must do this, Father Jacob." She spoke with sincerity.

Adrina started to lead Jacob into the hall and as he stepped back into the corridor, he stopped. "Wait a minute, am I crazy? I didn't want to do this, but if I have to... Get back into that bed this instant, you will sleep!"

Adrina stepped deftly passed Father Jacob. "This will not wait, father. He is dying, I know it. Did you know—" Hesitant, Adrina stopped herself from saying anything more.

Jacob took a step toward her. "Go on," he said.

"It was only the voice at first, calling out, but then I started to see things. It was as if I were traveling a great distance. There was so much I know I saw that I cannot recollect, so much, Father Jacob... The vision first led me out to sea, then to the southern coast—"

"Did you?" asked Jacob, "No, of course you didn't, did you?"

"Did I what, Father Jacob?"

"At any rate, we cannot leave until Captain Brodst recovers. I would not hear the last of it if I left him in Fraddylwicke Castle with the Baron and Baroness."

Adrina nearly fell as the words hit her. Father Jacob fought to ferry her back to bed but she wouldn't let him. "Who leads the column to Alderan?"

"The second in command *was* Captain Trendmore. He assumed command after Captain Brodst's unfortunate accident. He waited until late this morning, but couldn't wait any longer. With Prince Valam's arrival in Alderan in three days, he had to leave. It will take a miracle—" Jacob glanced heavenward. "—for them to make that march in three days. I am sure Captain Brodst said it would take at least five."

Adrina's face turned deathly pale. Now she understood why the detachment had turned south for Quashan'. Now she understood why so much was at stake in Alderan. "Prince Valam is to meet the ship from Wellison, the ship carrying Prince William?"

The lady's words flooded into Adrina's mind and piece by piece she started to put the puzzle together. *The ship from*

Wellison has a most precious cargo, the heir to the throne of Sever. At this very moment King Charles lies dying in his bed… King Jarom sees himself seated in the throne room of Imtal Palace. He means to plunge the kingdoms into war. To be sure, he will use the death of Charles and the fears of the heir to his own ends…

Adrina decided right then to confide in Father Jacob. She recounted the meetings with the strange lady. She told him of the first meeting in the palace tower at Imtal and the second meeting in the forest on the night of the heavy rains.

As Adrina watched, it was clear a flood of awareness swept over Father Jacob. He was silent for a time then he mumbled words Adrina barely understood. "This is the very message Great-Father sent—the message I have puzzled over these long past days."

"Father Jacob, are you all right? Is there something I can do for you?"

"Just let me stand here a moment, child." Father Jacob paused, took a deep breath then added, "On second thought, let's sit. Perhaps over on the bed…"

Father Jacob regarded Adrina with marvel. "I told no one about the voices and the portentous messages that brought me to Imtal Palace on a dark night what seemed so long ago. I did not even tell the cunning Keeper Martin… Great-Father does sometimes work in mysterious ways. Messages in dreams are not uncommon and the Lore Keepers often use them for long communication."

Father Jacob again became quiet and the wrinkles around his eyes grew thick. "You are right, child," said Father Jacob at long last, "we cannot wait. May Great-Father speed us on to Alderan…"

***

Adrina approached the low portcullis that separated thick walls midway along the castle's southerly bastion. She continued past it to the stables where a stately wagon was being prepared. The Lord and Lady Fraddylwicke had chased after her every step of the way from the inner courtyard to the wall, but neither the baroness' "Your Highness, please, the tea is ready," or the baron's "The wagon would have been ready in another hour," would slow her down.

Yesterday it had been the baron who had convinced Father Jacob that they should not leave the castle until this morning. It was true that by the time preparations had been made and they were ready to leave it was late afternoon, but there still had been a few hours of daylight left. What harm would a night in the swamp have brought? This morning, the baroness was dead set on having tea after breakfast. Who drinks tea at daybreak?

Adrina cast a glum stare behind her. Father Jacob hurried along beside the baron, and Adrina heard him again speaking an apology. "It seems we must leave at once on an urgent matter," he was saying. "Please give the message I left for Captain Brodst to him as soon as he wakes. You have been most gracious hosts. His Majesty will surely hear of this."

"Raise the portcullis," Adrina screamed to the guards inside the gatehouse.

"The wagon is most splendid," Jacob said, seemingly to drown out Adrina's words.

No doubt, Lord Fraddylwicke had chosen the stately wagon with its four-horsed team with clear purpose. Adrina knew this was meant as a symbol both of his wealth and his generosity, which he hoped would be relayed to King Andrew. She didn't find it odd that she could so intensely dislike a man who she had only met yesterday evening.

Behind her, Adrina heard men shouting, she looked back to the outer courtyard to see a small contingent of foot soldiers mustering. Adrina stopped and whirled about to face the baron. "A gaggle of foot soldiers will only slow us down. We need the wagon and the provisions you promised, nothing more. Tell them to return to their duties."

"Your Highness, I must object," Baron Fraddylwicke said. "I must see to your protection. The swamp is no place for a lady such as yourself to be alone."

Adrina started respond, but Father Jacob spoke first. "He is right, Princess Adrina. It would be best to have an escort."

"Fine, if they are to come along, have them mount up. They can ride, yes?"

"I am afraid—" Adrina held her breath. The baron was fond of those three words. "—that the scant few animals that remain are ill-fit for riding. Your Captain Trendmore took every horse in Fraddylwicke. Strangest thing, I told him I needed mounts for the King's messengers—you see, usually we trade out on a one for one basis—but he said he wanted them all and would keep his. Even sent men about the countryside. He left nary behind. It is only by the grace of Great-Father that my personal team remains."

Adrina started to say, "Great-Father had nothing to do with it," but then realized that it was fortunate the baron had hidden the animals away. Her irritation with the pompous baron decreased. She bit her cheek and smiled.

"That was a wise decision," she said, "my father, the King, will surely hear how you have helped me, for I will tell him personally."

Baron Fraddylwicke's face suddenly seemed to glow and the baroness touched her kerchief to her eye.

Father Jacob nodded approval and helped Adrina climb into the wagon.

***

The four-horse team eagerly responded to Jacob's heavy hands. At first the gentle countryside that encompassed Fraddylwicke Castle greeted them, but this was a short-enjoyed oasis in the midst of surrounding mires and after only an hour of riding the roads ahead began to slope gradually downward to be reclaimed by the wetlands.

Instantly Adrina and Jacob felt moisture in the air and smelled pungent odors of stagnant waters. Fortunately, the roads leading away from the castle in this section of the lowlands were well reinforced. The main road was built up a full three feet above the waiting waters. Adrina marveled at the feat of ingenuity and determination it had taken to build such an access way.

A dreary haze hung over the mire, giving it unparalleled uncanniness. This when added to the sense of foreboding Adrina felt, put her at considerable unease. She puzzled over a great many things, especially how Prince Valam fit into all this. To be sure, they must reach Alderan before her brother's arrival. They also needed to catch up to the column and warn them, but what would they tell them to watch out for? And what of Prince William? If his ship had not arrived in Alderan, why had no messages been sent? Why in the dream was he in such pain? And why had he stared at her so?

As she tried to think about all this, Adrina's head began to throb, the pain becoming so intense that all her thoughts eventually fell away. Ahead in the distance lay disparate crossroads that led to tiny villages whose buildings dotted the landscape. Mounted on top of tiny cross-sections of land that were barely habitable, the villages seemed much like the swamp's scattered weeping willow trees, waiting to be reclaimed someday by the dank surrounding waters.

Hoping to rid herself of a throbbing headache and troubled thoughts, Adrina turned to Father Jacob. And though he seemed deep in his own concerns, she endeavored to spark a conversation with him.

"It all looks so lonely, does it not, Father Jacob?" said Adrina, her voice mixing in with the thump-roll, thump-roll of the wagon's wheels. "I'm curious about Lord Fraddylwicke, such a grand castle in the middle of all this waste. Everything so well maintained, these roads as well. The villages we pass are impoverished. With tithing to the temples there can be little wealth left to tax. Does the Baron tax in blood?"

Jacob was slow to reply, but it seemed clear as he began that he grasped Adrina's intent, which was to rid their minds of troubled thoughts for a time. "I find these lands curious as well. Only the southern portion of the mire remains populated, you know. During the Great Wars, the castle was a major strategic point for King Jarom the First, but now it serves no useful purpose. There are other safeguarded passages to the southlands.

"The wars lasted generations and it does seem odd that anyone would chose to stay in so desolate a place afterward. Perhaps they stay simply because it is their ancestral home."

"Perhaps," said Adrina.

"In a way I pity them and not only because the desolation and isolation they endure seem overbearing. Also because generations of war and life in such a place left behind a bitter and superstitious people. Their ancestors are King Jarom's Blood Soldiers. Too brutal and uncivilized for the civilized world that emerged after the Great Wars and too many to exterminate, they are all but forgotten about by both the kingdom that gave them birth and the kingdom that conquered them."

"Blood Soldiers, why have I never heard about them?"

"You won't find anything I've just told you in any book in Imtal, this I assure, though Keeper Martin would verify the history. Yet, it is perhaps best they remain forgotten."

Father Jacob whipped the reins held tightly in his hands. Adrina took this as a sign to change the topic of their conversation. "Father Jacob, how long will it take to reach the coast?"

Jacob thought about it for a short time and then responded, "Great-Father willing and if we pray very hard and drive the horses as much as we dare, we might be able to reach it by midmorning tomorrow."

"And Alderan?"

"Early the day after, if we pray."

"Then we will pray," said Adrina matter-of-factly.

Weariness swept over Adrina like a storm. Her face turned pale and though she fought to stay awake, sleep came.

The wagon continued to speed along the trail although occasionally Jacob was forced to quarrel with the controls to maintain it. His thoughts were on the wagon and the trail ahead. It took great care to hold the trail steadily at the increased speed. He was so engrossed in his concentration that he did not notice Adrina's state. He only heard the horses' hooves thundering along the trail as he nervously beat at the controls.

The sky above grew overcast, the winds began to pick up, and an ill feeling intensified in Father Jacob's gut. His intuition told him a heavy storm was approaching. He cast silent prayers to Great-Father to protect them from the rains and to allow them to complete their journey unscathed.

But it was a losing affray that was being conducted against the squall in the good priest's mind. The clouds overhead turned dark and callous quickly. Jacob felt their presence as an evil spirit invading his privacy.

The air turned cold. The first droplets of rain fell. Jacob beat at the reins with increasing ferocity matched by the increasing fury of the wind. Sprinkles of rain thrashed against them, then the downpour began.

Jacob secured the top button of his cloak and turned up the high collar. "There are extra blankets in the rear—" Jacob stopped cold, the words frozen on his lips. Suddenly he saw Adrina, her face colorless, deathly pale, and fear entered his thoughts and took control. He commanded the horses to a halt.

With trembling hands, he reached out and touched Adrina's face. It was cold, sticky wet with perspiration and rain. He removed the extra blankets from the rear of the wagon and bundled Adrina in them. Then he drove the horses onward, faster and faster. Somewhere ahead, he hoped to find a crossroads that would lead to a village.

Anxiety swept over him as they sped along the road. He chastised himself repeatedly in his mind. Rain began to fall in mighty torrents as the storm engulfed them. Wind, rain and diminished visibility made the road treacherous but Jacob did not slow the horses. He continued to push the wagon to its limits.

Lost to the frenzy of the moment, his mind stressed and incapable of clear thought, Jacob panicked. Frantically he scanned ahead, his thoughts running in a hundred different directions and many times he glanced worriedly at Adrina.

Jacob drove the team on. He whipped at the controls, urging the animals still faster. The dirt trail quickly turned to mud and it was only the high sides of the road thankfully packed in a precisely built wall of rock on either side that held the mud in place. The horses plodded through this muck, kicking up a splatter of mud and small stones. The droning thunder of hooves and the racing of wheels rose above the clamor of falling rain and mounting winds.

Soon Father Jacob gave up hope of finding a village ahead. Recalling the villages behind them, he now sought a place to turn the wagon around. Again and again, his eyes darted to Adrina's still form. A relieved sigh came as he finally reached a spot with an adjacent path where he could turn the four-horse team and wagon around in a tight circle.

Jacob reined the team in and with a pair of leathers in each hand, guided the horses quickly through the twist. A sudden creaking of the wagon's wheels whining above the sound of rain and wind caused him to start. He pulled the reins in the opposite direction. The team turned back, but his reaction came too late. The axle was surely cracked. The left front wheel was out of kilter and it would only be a short time before the wheel broke free.

Jacob shook with dread. Still, he forced himself to think through the situation. Alone he couldn't fix the wheel should it snap. He would have to seek shelter from the storm and attempt to repair the damages later. He didn't move for what seemed the longest time. He just sat there, eyes wide, searching. He wanted to see a village along the horizon. The last village they had passed was quite a distance behind them. Perhaps he could reach it if the axle held long enough.

The air around him, which was already cold, grew icy as the storm raged on. Father Jacob wanted to curse, wished his vocation would allow him to curse. To scream aloud just once would have satisfied all his pent up frustration. Instead he found the wisdom of his faith and prayed to Great-Father for guidance. Briefly afterward, the will of the Father flowed strongly through him, but then it was as if the storm sucked away the renewed vitality as readily as rain and wind beat down upon him.

A portent of evil filled his mind like a sickness, yet even in this Jacob attempted to find good. The will of the Father had found him even in this hellish squall. Faith maintained, he continued his scan of the vicinity, his eyes wandering along the adjacent trail while the heavy downpour obscured his vision.

Abruptly he stopped. He squinted his eyes, and strained to fix them ahead in the distance where he thought he saw the outline of some low structures. Were they dwellings? Could it truly be? Or was he imagining them?

At a careful gallop, ensuring his pace did not upset the wagon too much, Jacob ushered the four-horse team on. The tiny road was no more than a raised path but it did appear to lead toward a village of sorts. Jacob held his breath with each bump, and prayed the axle would hold, and each time it did, he released it in a heavy sigh.

The mighty structures he envisioned were no more than a collection of thatched huts clumped atop a mound of dirt. But in his mind, Jacob was sure he and Adrina would find warmth inside.

The ailing wheel finally gave way with a resonant crack and the wagon slid to an awkward halt. Jacob held Adrina tightly as the wagon toppled to one side. Clinging to his faith, he wiped hopelessness from his face, then picked up Adrina in his arms—Great-Father would not let him fail. He would carry her the remaining distance. Relief was only a few steps away.

The next hundred yards seemed liked miles to Jacob. Step by step, he sloshed through the mud. His back ached and his arms tired, but he did not stop. A wooden door loomed in the distance and eventually he came to stand before it. He cried out into the stormy sky, a solemn thanks to Great-Father, and with a heavy fist he rapped on the door of the hut.

The dull echo of his blows was the only response. In desperation Jacob tried to force the door open but apparently it was barred.

"Go away!" said a meek voice from behind him.

Jacob turned around wearily, his face expressionless as he looked upon the small boy in front of him. Jacob said, "We need your help."

A middle-aged man appeared from out of the gloom. He approached the boy and put his hand on the boy's shoulder. "You must leave, we cannot help you."

Jacob didn't move.

"Please go, you must go."

"I am Father Jacob, First Minister to the King. I need your help."

"So," said the boy.

The man hushed the boy, and said, "You must go and if you truly be the First Minister to the King, you will know what peril it is to accept strangers during such an evil storm."

And with that, the man took the boy's hand and hurried away.

Chapter Nineteen: Magic Shield

A trek that would have taken many days by foot would be substantially shortened by wagon. Xith was deeply concerned about getting as far north as quickly as they possibly could. Time was running out. He could sense that now.

Xith looked at the innocence spread out simply on Vilmos' long face and was saddened by it. He wished he could explain to Vilmos the gravity of the situation they were in, how precarious the path ahead was, and how much of it relied on him, a mere boy. Xith only hoped when the time came for Vilmos to act that he would be prepared, that they both would be.

"Beautiful morning!" exclaimed Xith, breaking the silence in the air and casting the shadows from his thoughts.

"What?" asked Vilmos, broken from his own reverie.

"Can't you feel the energy in the air? Don't you just want to draw it in?"

Vilmos sniffed the air. It didn't feel any different from normal. "Not really," was his quick response.

In and out of his mouth with hearty puffs, Xith began to breathe the moist morning air. Vilmos imagined that Xith was beginning to glow and became entranced by this fanciful notion. Then, subtle changes in skin tone became increasingly apparent until Xith actually did glow. His voice peaking in the middle, Vilmos asked, "Xith, what are you doing?"

Playfulness cascaded away from Xith's eyes. "Sorry," he said after a long pause, "I was going to show you something, but now is not the time. We must wait a while longer."

The road Xith and Vilmos traveled along was arid. The horses' hooves and the wagon's wheels kicked up a large dusty plume, which marked their passage. Ahead in the distance lay a series of rocky hills covered mostly with tall grasses and patched with granite. Beyond, the trail disappeared as it wound through small canyons the hills created and beyond the hills was another open flat prairie with dry tall grasses dancing in the gentle winds traveling lightly across its face. With the slow creaking of the wagon echoing in their ears, they made their way through the hills to the far side of the prairie and beyond.

Vilmos' eyes grew heavy and his yawns became more frequent. His thoughts drifted for a time, unfixed, and eventually settled on images of his mother whom he missed. A happiness that had been absent for days entered his heart as he pictured her face. His next conscious thought was not until sometime later. A sudden shift of the wagon as it hit a large hole in the path thrust him from his sleep and the dream was gone.

Caught in the dilemma of how much he could teach Vilmos, not knowing if the boy was fully ready to begin the lessons and if he were, how fast was too fast to progress, Xith tried to reach a decision. It seemed there was time for one last lesson. He must teach it, but was Vilmos ready?

Unable to solve this dilemma, Xith concentrated on the road, which was pockmarked and pitted. He slowed the team down to steady the wagon, and the sluggish pace made the day's progression seem nonexistent. Xith retreated to thoughts of times past and old acquaintances, while Vilmos moved on to let his mind wander, and again enjoyed the passing serenity of the land.

After they had eaten and rested the horses and were back on the trail moving through a series of wooded knolls and open grasslands, Xith came to a decision. There *was* time for one last lesson. He would teach it as he had planned to.

As the day ended and early night settled in, Vilmos and Xith set up camp in the safety of a clearing within a small woodland oasis. The rather large stand, an oddity this far south, was a hearty growth of fine northern fir, the clipped boughs of which served as an excellent mattress upon which to rest. Lying upon these soft, scented pine boughs, arms crossed and head propped atop, tired eyes were allowed a tranquil view, a sedate, star-filled night sky with a gently shining liquid moon.

It was an autumn moon, a moon that was not quite full and loomed low in the sky with the distant, unseen sun casting a cool orange luminescence upon its face. In other times Xith would have called it a blooded moon and the portent would have been one of ominous foreboding, but under the current circumstances it moved him into a somber introspective mood.

While he didn't offer the omen much thought, he did not cast it away either. Rather it hung there in the back of his mind while he floated off to sleep and later invaded his few moments of private dreams.

***

Vilmos was the first to wake. Wet droplets of morning dew were the first things to greet him. At first he didn't want to leave the warmth of his blankets or the soft gentle fir bed to enter the cold uncaring air. A foot, an arm, a leg, slowly probed and eventually, Vilmos slipped from comforts into the cold. As he stood there not moving, adjusting, the only thought in his mind was to find some dry wood. With it, he'd make a fire to take the chill away. After a long gradual coaxing, he set himself to the task.

Xith awoke a short while later to the pleasant crackling sounds of a blazing fire, the warmth of which felt good against his face and hands. He sat up and edged his body closer to the fire, surprised that he hadn't even felt the energy expenditure

Vilmos had used to start the healthy blaze with. Perhaps, Xith thought to himself, the boy was ready for the lesson after all.

"Well good morning," Xith said.

Vilmos returned the shaman's warm greeting with one of his own and went in search of the food supplies that had been left in the wagon. He grabbed a little of this and of that, items that appeared most desirable to his sense of smell.

The horses were still loosely tied to a low hanging branch next to the wagon. Thankfully they had not gotten free. Vilmos stroked one of the mares, which was agitated for some reason until she calmed, then walked back to the fire and sat across from Xith. He offered the shaman a small portion of the carefully selected prizes he had brought back with him. Then he gingerly picked at the food before him, those selections he had not given away to Xith, hard pressed to decide which to eat first because too many arousing scents arose from the stores Misha had prepared.

Vilmos ate a honey cake first, then nibbled on a bit of spiced beef, salted pork and finally a tiny mincemeat pie. He washed it all down with several long swigs from a water bag filled with a sweet drink that tasted of grapes.

When Xith finished, he stood. "Are you ready?" he asked, patting Vilmos on the shoulder, a subdued deviousness was mixed over with half-warm tones.

"Sure," said Vilmos. He stood and crossed to the wagon. He started to climb onto the wagon's running board and stopped abruptly as something hard hit him in the back with a resonant thud.

Vilmos whirled around. "Ouch!"

"You said you were ready." Xith laughed and threw another rock at Vilmos, forcing him to dodge it.

"But you didn't say you were going to throw a rock at me!"

"You should always be prepared for the unexpected. This is the next lesson, our second lesson. You have learned well the forces of fire. Now you shall learn those of air..." so saying, Xith hurled two rocks at Vilmos.

The first Vilmos had expected and dodged successfully, but the second hit him in the back of the hand. Angry, frustrated and not understanding the point Xith was trying to make, Vilmos climbed into the wagon.

"Vilmos, will you ever learn," Xith said. "Here, pick up this rock with your mind." Xith pointed to the small stone in his hand.

"I can't, I don't know how."

"Yes, you do. Midori told me all about your magical pranks. Why do you think I came when I did? I came because I thought you were ready. You have done this before. <*Think!*>

Xith threw the stone at Vilmos. After waiting a moment, he then picked up another and did the same. Vilmos stood, unmoving and unyielding, not knowing what to do.

"<*Stop the rocks from hitting you!*> <*Do it now!*>" said Xith in a voice that shook Vilmos' mind and stirred his thoughts, but his response was still, "I can't. I don't know how."

"<*Think!*> It is a very simple process if you have already mastered the forces of levitation. Remember, when you were at home and often you circled things around you? How did you do it? Do you remember?"

"Maybe." Vilmos knew the pranks he had used to drive tutors away, but he didn't understand how it related to a rock being thrown at him.

"Levitation is the process in which you use the element of air to force an object to float. Remember flying, floating above your valley?"

Vilmos' thoughts returned for the first time in a long time to his special place, which he had thought lost to him and understood. "That is easy, but I don't—"

"<*Hush.*> <*Listen!*>" Xith said, slipping again into the compelling voice to grab Vilmos' attention. "Instead of using a positive force to lift the object, exert the force out as a wall and repel the object away from you. This is the first lesson, it is the easiest way to repel an object from you. The second lesson is a little trickier and requires a great deal more energy. <*Watch!*>"

Purposefully sluggish as he overemphasized the strain and the concentration, Xith called the rocks from the ground. One at a time, he slowly lifted the stones and pebbles around them until the air was filled with rocks of all sizes floating through the air. With a summons and a wave of the hand, Xith stirred them to movement as one would a swarm of angry bees. He hurled them through the air, then directed them at himself, where they were reflected harmlessly off an invisible barrier. "Now, do you see?"

"If someone is throwing rocks at you, I guess so."

An immediate pained expression crossed Xith's face, it was clear he was upset. One by one the rocks took flight again, yet this time they were volleyed at Vilmos. Several hit him before he collected his thoughts, his hand hurt, his legs hurt, and he was really getting angry.

It took a stone hitting him square in the face, knocking him to the ground, before he decided this was no longer a game. Vilmos had sudden flashbacks to a barren ridge and raging winds. Vilmos stood and brushed the dust and dirt from his clothes. For a moment, he paid no attention to the debris flying around him.

He collected energy into himself, slowly as Xith had taught him, pulling the energies of creation inside. His only problem was that he didn't know how to properly release it. The energy welled within him until he let it ebb and subside. He cast infuriated eyes upon Xith.

"Continue," Vilmos said simply, haughtily.

Xith smiled an eager smile and slowed the rate of the barrage to a steady, constant attack with fair interval between each wave. "Push them away, Vilmos." Again Xith paused and waited for Vilmos to gather his thoughts. A single pebble at a time, started moving again in slow motion.

One stone was propelling its way toward him. Vilmos pushed out with his energy. It wavered and fell to the ground.

"Yes," Vilmos cried out. He had successfully repelled it, yet the wall wasn't in place around him, but it was building. In one side with the new and out with the old, thought Vilmos to himself. His concentration was building and so was his confidence.

"Very good," said Xith, "try two."

Two rocks launched at Vilmos at a steady pace. He managed to stop one, but the second one hit him and broke his concentration. He threw his hands up in the air as a sign he wanted to quit. His head ached; he had enough for one day. "Can't we wait till tomorrow?"

"*<Try again.>* *<You can do it.>*" The use of Voice was mandatory.

As always Xith's words of praise inspired Vilmos. He knew this time he would not fail. Two stones fell away harmlessly, successfully repelled; but he wasn't prepared for the third that hit him from behind, again on the buttocks.

"Build the wall," Xith said. "Try again."

Especially goaded on by Xith's perky smirk as the last rock had hit him, Vilmos grew angry. He was not going to let Xith or anyone else get the best of him. He stopped one, two, three, four, five and even a sixth stone.

Xith picked up the tempo and changed the directions from which the stones came. Two and three pebbles homed in like beacons on Vilmos in groups from different directions, but again he successfully warded them off.

Sweat dripped off Vilmos' brow. He was tired but Xith would not stop. The air was filled, a clutter of tiny objects, launched at Vilmos. Vilmos cast Xith a lopsided smile, equal to Xith's own menacing grimace. He had built his invisible wall and nothing would get through.

"Nothing will get through," Vilmos whispered to himself. He was nearly exhausted.

Xith did not let up and neither would Vilmos yield though he was passed exhaustion and moving toward delirium.

"You waste too much energy, learn to conserve it. <*Shape your power,*> use it to your advantage."

"I can't do all that at once!" shouted Vilmos, breaking his concentration for an instant.

Xith answered by an increased volley. "<*Concentrate!*> Do as you did before. Use part of your consciousness toward the task of building the wall and another to shape it. Try to release the spent energy. From this lesson stems the basis of your magical shield, the shield that will protect and keep you in dangerous times. <*Now, concentrate!*>"

A part of Vilmos digested the words Xith had just spoken while the rest of him set to the task of building the repelling wall. It was so much easier to do before when he had not fully realized what the shaman was trying to teach him through the seemingly simplistic lesson of repelling rocks—*A magical shield, wow!*

Again Vilmos let the wall slip, only for an instant, and was smartly answered with a rock hitting him. The shock cleared his thoughts and jolted his mind into action; again he strove to perform the feat and this time succeeded. He could feel the energy flow within him.

"<*Control,*> always stay in control. You must control the energy, don't let it control you."

Vilmos had forgotten to exercise control in his momentary lapse. The energy was flowing through him like a tidal wave, flooding his mind. Concentrate, Vilmos thought to himself, I must hold it steady. Gradually, he gripped the energy and regulated it. The power flowed, but did not flood over him.

"Better. Keep it up. Don't lose sight of your center," said Xith.

The assault continued minute after exhausting minute for almost an hour. Xith pushed and pushed until he felt Vilmos had reached his limit, then he purposefully pushed him beyond it.

Vilmos learned fast to control the energy flow and maintain the wall. Soon it became facile, requiring less energy, less thought to maintain. He found his center. He knew exactly how much energy he could build and how to shape it. He was in control. He even thought Xith looked pleased.

An idea came to Vilmos, a plan that seemed easy. Devious thoughts spilled over into this plan. He gathered a small reserve in his energy flow, a slight store inside him. The energy caressed him and Vilmos bathed in it. He split his thinking into three parts, one for the wall, one to keep the flow, and one to begin to conserve the energy for his little scheme.

Vilmos' shield totally fell as he first attempted this feat. Vilmos thought Xith was clearly displeased, but Xith took it as a sign to end the lesson, Vilmos was progressing well.

"No, I want more," Vilmos demanded.

"I think you've had enough for today. You should rest. You have already discovered that from the simple stems the difficult, this is true with all things."

"Just a little more."

Xith waved his hand and began the assault.

A reorganization of his thoughts enabled Vilmos to build a reserve slowly. The wall didn't flicker and he attempted his ploy. Instead of just letting the rocks bounce off his shield, he hurled them away. It took great concentration to keep up all three, the flow, the wall, the casting away, but he managed and now maintained the energy flow, the shield and was successfully repelling the stones.

Xith didn't appear to notice the subtle change and Vilmos was pleased. At first, he could repel only one rock at a time in a given direction, but later with practice he achieved two and then three. He settled there, while he adapted to the strain and soon this too became easy.

Vilmos stared at Xith with a wide grin that Xith didn't even pay attention to. He was certain Xith didn't know what he was up to. He continued until he could deflect an entire barrage at one time and then he went back to throwing them in a few select directions. Although difficult at first, Vilmos succeeded and abruptly he was passing the rocks Xith's way.

Xith was almost taken completely by surprise. He hadn't even expected such a twist. He was pleased as he allowed the first rock to hit him, very pleased.

"There is hope for you yet. That is a very difficult feat to attempt when just starting," Xith said. He latched out with his magic and lay rest to all movement around him. "Enough for today. You need to rest. The lesson is ended."

Vilmos was beaming he had done it. He had bested the shaman if only once. Xith fixed Vilmos with a long hard stare and without a word, began to harness the horses.

Vilmos climbed onto the wagon's running board, then moved to the seat. He watched as Xith finished harnessing the horses.

"Can I take the reins?" Vilmos asked as Xith climbed into the seat beside him. Xith handed him the controls. The animals lurched forward under unskilled hands.

"I'm sorry, shaman!" said Vilmos turning to Xith.

"No apology is necessary. You performed excellently."

"Not well, not good, but excellently?" Vilmos' voice crackled in the middle of the last word.

"Yes, you really have! You've learned a great deal more today than I had expected. I had hoped… but then you did. You have learned one of the hardest lessons there is to teach—"

"I did?"

Wordlessly Xith took the controls from Vilmos' hands. "Yes, you have. You have learned to control your energy while your mind is occupied with other tasks, but most importantly you have learned to assimilate your thinking. By grouping the way you think into sections, that is a very great deed in itself.

"It may sound easy, but under duress it is often the hardest thing ever imagined to try. The more you can do at one time the better you will be. If eventually you can do many things without even thinking about them, you will truly be one to be respected.

"You will find the talent very useful. Now maybe you are ready to learn how to control and channel your energy while you sleep. But we will save that lesson for another time."

Xith spurred the horses on. For a time, the grasslands seemed to spread endlessly before them, then rolling hills returned. As they reached the summit of the last in a long string of green-covered hills, Xith reined in the horses.

"There," Xith said. He reached out with his hand and pointed. "The great sea, West Deep..."

For a few long minutes, they sat quietly and stared down at deep blue waters, then Xith chided the horses into slow gait. He steered them to a course parallel to the great sea, before whipping at the reins with heavy hands. As he did this, he nervously glanced skyward. The sun was hours past midday.

Chapter Twenty: Refusal

Her arms were shaking, weak. Still, she reached out for him and touched him.

A second time you pulled me from the sea, Galan said. She strained to move again, to give Seth back his robe that now covered her. "*What have you done? You must also survive, Seth.*

Seth stretched the tattered robe back over Galan, and covered her face and hands. *I'm no longer sure I want to survive, Galan. Why was I so blind?*

You did not betray your brethren. You could not have known.

But I should have—

—Faith, said Galan. She gripped Seth's hand. *I want to dream, may I see the forest again?*

Never let it dwindle, a voice in Seth's mind repeated, *never let it dwindle, faith will shelter you.* Had Queen Mother known? Seth wondered. And if she had known, why hadn't she tried to stop it?

Seth, said Galan. *Do not dwell on things that cannot be changed. Maybe Queen Mother did know and her words were her only way of warning you. It is not wise to try to change fate but there are perhaps ways to alter it slightly.*

I did not mean to trouble you with open thought. Seth projected the image—the green of a forest against the backdrop of a white-capped mountain, the sky so blue it was almost purple—into her mind's eye. The idea of such a place's existence truly did seem a wondrous dream to him now.

Confused emotions swept over Seth. Even now he felt the urge to hold Galan as he'd done when he pulled her from the sea.

You may hold me, said Galan, *I feel suddenly cold and empty.*

Waves that had been rolling moderately grew gradually choppier and the open sea became a disquieting place to be. Wind whistled in Seth's ears and the tiny raft began to creak and moan. In the shallow of a trough while the water on all sides of him filled his field of vision, it seemed as if the sea was opening up to swallow him.

Galan, said Seth. *We must lash ourselves to the raft.*

High seas washed over the raft. Seth strained his mind, and tried to discern a response amongst the tumult. He probed Galan's mind. *Galan? Galan?*

He found only emptiness. Galan was dying.

Their raft was chasing the edge of black clouds now. The scent of rain permeated the air. Soon they would be within the folds of a raging downpour and violent seas. On his hands and knees Seth scrambled toward Galan. He slipped and fell with each movement, and though it was only a short distance, his weakened and weary body was put to the test. Only his near-broken constitution kept him when endurance and stamina had failed.

Finally at Galan's side, Seth cradled her in his arms. He held her tenderly and firmly, as one might hold a newborn babe if they were afraid it would slip between their fingers. Tears came to his eyes. The moisture burned like fire across his dry eyes. And then as if in response, bitterly cold rains hit him. Rain, the essence of life—life that abounded with irony while Galan lay dying in his arms.

No my Galan… Do not leave me. I need you— Seth could not finish the sentence. He could not accept the thought of more loss.

No more loss, he promised himself, *no more loss*.

Seth worked to secure Galan to the raft while the storm bludgeoned him with wave after wave that washed the raft's face. Seth vowed that if he and the raft survived the storm so would Galan and only through the sheer force of his will did he maintain his grip.

When he finally got a knot in place, he gasped, and collapsed onto his back. Hungrily, he drank the rain that splashed his face. It seemed a lifetime since he had tasted anything so sweet. Afterward, he worked to lash himself to the raft. This was much easier, though still the work was strenuous. He had to fight the storm and guard against waves that sought to pull him into the sea.

Again, he was left panting. Again he drank as much of the rain as he could force down his burning and swollen throat.

It was then he felt Galan's spirit yearning to be gathered by Great-Father, to be taken home, but he would not let it go, could not let it go. He projected his will into the place her spirit sought to flee, and barred her passage from life. The place between life and death was a cold and empty place just as Galan had warned him it would be.

Right then he vowed he would give his own life before he would allow the last unraveling thread of her life to slip away. In the chaos of his mind, Seth truly believed he could deny death. If it would have been any other, they would not have been able to do what Seth was doing now. Such was the strength of his will and his conviction in his desperation.

He became oblivious to the bludgeoning of the storm. He knew only that he had to hold onto the raft, his precious cargo and maintain the projection of his will. His thoughts became lost to the internal struggle of his consciousness, his sense of justice over his sense of better judgment. He would not lose the focusing of his will. Barring all else, blocking out sound and sight, Seth escaped reality and slipped further and further into his thoughts, further from what was real and just, while voices filled his mind and his dreams, taking on the role of the just and the unjust.

What is the first law of life, Brother Seth?

Of course the answer is to preserve what Mother-Earth has created so all may enjoy it.

Ahh, yes, but what is the second law of life?

Not to interfere with the natural order of nature and most of all to heed the will of the Father.

Great-Father's word in such matters is final, is it not?

Yes Brother Samyuehl, it is, but the law also says that one is permitted to guide that order or to correct injustices.

To guide or correct yes, but not to interfere with the natural order and that means not to hinder the will of the Father.

When Seth opened his eyes, the world he found was surprisingly different from the one he had left. The sea was miraculously calm. Night had miraculously arrived and a soft soothing breeze blew upon his skin.

There was picturesque beauty in the face that he looked down upon, even when the eyes were closed and it was gathered in a deathly pale. Vast sadness grew within him, encircling him, and Seth averted his eyes. He peered out into the night sky and time became nonexistent. His only thought amidst mounds of confusion was to maintain his will and keep his vigil. He would not let lose the thread, that last simple thread of life and will.

In and out of consciousness his mind ambled, always reaching, always searching, searching for a way to cheat the inevitable, to cheat life and death itself.

Remember, when all seems lost and you cannot find the center of your being, return to that which separates you, distinguishes you, from all else. Return to your thoughts, for they are truly your own. They are you…

Chapter Twenty One: Crossing

"A curse upon them Father," Jacob said. He began the long march back to the broken wagon, mud and rain only increased his disillusion, disgust and utter disappointment. His arms and legs were on fire with fatigue, Adrina was a lead weight in his arms that he would not drop.

Jacob staggered and stumbled. He sank to his knees several times, only to return to an uneasy stagger moments afterward. Mud covered his cloak, his arms and even his face.

He began to chuckle to himself as an increased downpour ironically washed the muck away. A few more steps, he promised himself, not realizing he didn't know what he would do when he did reach the wagon. *Faith,* whispered a tiny voice in his mind, *faith everlasting...*

"F-a-ther!" crackled a distant voice, softly intermixed with the sound of the storm.

At first Jacob thought it was the voice of his conscience speaking to him again, but then the call repeated. He stumbled and turned back toward the huts. As he did this he fell to his knees and, still clutching the princess tightly, he looked up to see an ancient man with a long, white beard standing in an open doorway.

"Quickly, now!" the man hissed.

Finding renewed vigor, Jacob did as the old man bade. Rain beating down upon him washed away the mud from his most recent fall by the time he reached the doorway.

"I won't forget this Father! I will never forget this," Jacob called out to the sullen sky. He revoked his ill-spoken curse.

Quickly Father Jacob slipped off the princess' soaked jacket and the wet clothes beneath which were drenched both from rain and perspiration from a renewed fever. After throwing the wet things unceremoniously into a pile on the floor, he laid Adrina onto the bed that the kindly man indicated. Immediately, he pulled its thick blankets tightly around her pale, limp body.

"Get me some moist towels," Jacob demanded of the old man.

Directly the man returned with clean cloths and a bowl of cool water. He joined Father Jacob at the bedside. "Here, let me do that for you. You are tired, you must rest. I am Master T'aver and I gather that you are Father Jacob. I am sorry about before, but you must know of the superstitions of my people. I take great risk allowing you into my home on a night such as this. Can you not feel the malice of the storm?"

Jacob heard little of what the other told him. It wasn't that he was ungrateful, but his attentions were on Adrina and he cared of nothing else. He wet a cloth in the bowl, rung it out and placed it onto Adrina's forehead. The increasing fever magnified his worries and he bent his head in solemn prayer. He needed guidance. He prayed for strength and continued faith.

To Jacob it seemed hours later that he raised his head and whispered, "I am ready," to the fading echoes of voices in his mind.

He cleared his mind and set to the task ahead. Somehow, wisdom came easily to his thoughts. Power flowed through his mind and center. His will became centralized, focused, and this time there was no block between the power of his mind and his heart. He began the litany of healing and life, yet this time the song-prayer was somehow different from the one that he had tapped into before. It was animate and latent with power.

His words departed from those of the Kingdom spilling slowly over into those of another time, becoming for a time a blend of present and past, and then finally focusing on the old tongue.

It was an odd sensation to feel within himself the will of Mother-Earth so potent—few males had ever been granted such a gift from the Mother. Perspiration flowed down his brow and dripped from the tip of his nose to touch the floor below with a splash in the small pool forming beneath the spot where he stood engrossed in a litany of words so ancient they glistened with subtle hints of power. But it was not so much the words Jacob spoke that created the power, rather the delicate focusing they created in his mind to gather his will and direct it precisely.

Over the course of the hours that ensued, Father Jacob maintained the chanting rhythm and the healing began. Minutes became hours and hours unfolded one by one. The power of life flowed from Jacob's words and took new form inside the young princess whose face was still wrapped in a pale, deathlike mask, and as that strength flowed between them, Jacob could feel hours of his life slip accordingly away.

Utter exhaustion played out on his features and when he was finally forced to quit due to his fatigue, Jacob slumped over at the side of the bed. He rested his head on soft covers, arms raised and crossed over his knees. He was trembling and there were tears in his eyes. He knew he had succeeded. Already he could sense the fever lifting from Adrina.

But what had it cost him, he asked himself. They were miles away from Castle Fraddylwicke, miles away from the sea, and so very far away from Alderan. Soon exhaustion forced sleep upon him and Father Jacob fell fast asleep.

***

"Good Father Jacob, can you hear me?" a soft voice called out. "The dawn has come and gone, and still you sleep…"

Jacob stirred. He heard the unpleasant sounds of hammering now, which suddenly sounded to him as if someone was driving a spike into his head. Still half in a daze, he opened his eyes. He looked about the room. He was lying supine on a cot opposite the hut's only bed. His eyes flashed with surprise as he realized the bed was empty. "Where is Princess Adrina? Have you done something to her?"

The old man batted his eyes at Father Jacob as if the priest had just stung him. "That one is full of wind and fire. She's been directing my sons' efforts all this morning, fixing the wheel on that wagon of yours."

Jacob moved sluggishly to a sitting position. "And you are?"

"I am Master T'aver," said the old man. He scratched his long white beard. "You came upon my home during the devil's own squall yester eve. You truly are First Minister to the King. You performed a miracle last night that never in all my years have I seen."

Jacob cocked his head and looked out the window. "The banging has stopped."

"Yes, it is near midmorning. Some hours now my sons have labored at that wheel. It must be fixed. You should eat now and with godspeed you'll be on your way."

Jacob started to stand, T'aver put a halting hand to his shoulder. "Wait. The food will come. We should first talk. There are things you must know if you are to continue your journey."

"What can *you* possible know of my journey?" Jacob asked. Again he moved to stand. The fog in his mind was clearing now. He was worried about the young princess. He hadn't expected a full recovery and Adrina was just strong-minded enough to be out and about while still very ill.

T'aver moved a chair to Jacob's bedside. "Five days after the last full moon, I received a portentous message from an old friend. The message was in the form of a scroll, sealed magically—"

Jacob's eyes went wide at the mention of the forbidden craft—it was one thing to use prayers and gifts from Father and Mother, quite another to tap into the fabric of the world.

Master T'aver continued, "And meant only for my eyes. It told me things I didn't want to believe—not that I doubted the word of the Watcher."

Again Jacob's eyes grew wide with astonishment.

"But I truly did not believe until your arrival yester eve... Trust the girl's instincts Father Jacob. She walks under a charm..." T'aver seemed about to say something more, but just then the door opened and an old woman carrying a tray of food entered the hut. Master T'aver bade Jacob to eat and said no more.

***

The four-horse team seemed strangely unresponsive as Father Jacob directed it back to the main thruway. Aloft the sky was clear and deep blue. While Adrina was hopeful it would remain that way, she couldn't deny the ill feeling building up from within. She cast Father Jacob a concerned glance and wondered at his silence. He had said little to her since awaking and nothing of his conversation with T'aver.

In a quiet, unbroken pace the journey continued, with the musty and pungent odor of the swamp replaced eventually by a fresh, cool breeze that promised of the coast and the sea ahead. Adrina watched Jacob pound at the controls repeatedly, chiding the horses to swifter and swifter speeds. To her it seemed they raced time itself. She was sure they would arrive in Alderan too late to stop whatever was taking place. Also sure Father Jacob felt the same thing.

That night they camped only when it became too hazardous to continue along the shrouded road. Adrina slept bundled in many blankets in the back of the wagon. Jacob slept on the ground beside a meager fire.

Adrina came awake before dawn and, as the false dawn gathered, Father Jacob and Adrina began their race again. Soon the sea came into view and a wonderful sensory explosion of salt air and sea life followed. In the distance seagulls speckled the air and dotted the landscape of a rocky coastline, their calls raced to the approaching two on gentle breezes.

Adrina's face flushed with sudden color, turning from the ashen pale it had held to a rosy alabaster as sea breezes blew against her cheeks. A smile touched her lips and she touched her hand to Jacob's and momentarily held it tight. The sun and the breeze felt good. For a brief moment, she thought of Lady Isador. Lady Isador who longed for southern breezes and tall grasses.

"I made it to the sea," said Adrina glumly, her voice so soft and shallow that it blended into and was lost in the sounds of wind rushing passed her ears and birds in the sky overhead. Her eyes fixed on a point out along the horizon and out across the waters of the sea ahead. Somewhere out there was Prince William. Adrina was sure of that now. She saw his blue, blue eyes staring up at her again.

Adrina prepared herself to ask Father Jacob a question that had been in the back of her mind for some time. She was already sure what Jacob's answer would be, but felt she had to ask anyway. Either Jacob would confirm her fears or—and this is the reason Adrina felt compelled to speak—he would tell her that things were not as bad as they seemed. She took in a deep breath, laced her fingers together and then spoke. "Father Jacob…"

Jacob cast her a sidelong glance.

"Do you believe King Jarom would try to kill my brother?" There, she said it, but she didn't feel any better for the saying. She took another deep breath and braced herself for Jacob's response.

Jacob seemed to sense her anguish. He put the controls for the team in one hand and with his free hand touched hers.

"That is a question I have asked myself again and again, but I told myself I did not want to answer. The fact is that King Jarom murdered King Charles and that obviously he wants to stop Prince William from reaching the North to bring word of this terrible deed to King Andrew."

"What could King Jarom possibly have gained from killing Charles?"

"It could be that he wishes to restore Vostok to its former glory."

Adrina's eyes widened. She recalled something Keeper Martin had told her before they had entered the swamps. "Would that include Fraddylwicke Castle?"

Jacob's mouth dropped open. Adrina had never seen him at a loss. It was clear he hadn't considered this.

"King Jarom may lust for power," Jacob said, "but that would mean plunging the kingdoms into an all out war. As it is now, what he has done may already mean war, but that would depend on the evidence Prince William brings to King Andrew and the decision of the Alliance."

"The lady in the forest told me that King Jarom sees himself seated on Imtal's throne. Was Vostok once that vast?"

"Never that vast, but at the end of the Race Wars when only the five sons of the Alder remained in power, King Jarom the First controlled nearly all the lands from Neadde to River Ispeth. It was his Blood Soldiers that pushed the enemy back to the sea near River Opyl and, he with his own bare hands that committed patricide and started the last Great War."

Adrina felt suddenly sick and sorry she had spoken at all. She said nothing more, and neither did Father Jacob.

Upon reaching the rocky coast, Father Jacob turned the wagon in a wide semi-circle and took the southerly route. Alderan was now only a half-day's ride away. With luck, they would reach the city before dusk. Another question neither Adrina nor Jacob wanted to answer was whether this would be too late to stop what was already set in motion.

***

The section of the coastline they traveled along became a series of rocky crags with sharp, jutting spurts that jumped out into the yearning sea. Rough-hewn, carved by the forces of nature that acted upon the waters that enveloped them at times, they seemed somehow alive.

The wind, a steady gale with mixed patches of warm and cool, often carried with it a soft salty spray as waves crashed into the shore, and as the as the afternoon sun gathered itself full in the sky the day still held the promise of clear, cloudless skies.

Adrina sat silently, her hands clasped tightly together. She reflected on earlier thoughts, letting her gaze wander as the wagon twisted and turned.

The breezes became cooler as the sun began to settle toward the glossy blue waters of the sea and although the cool air felt good against Adrina's skin. Still, Father Jacob stopped the wagon for a moment to retrieve two blankets from the rear. He searched through the satchels of foodstuffs and came up with a rounded loaf of black bread and a dark yellow cheese.

The meal was a hurried affair. Soon after finishing, Father Jacob spurred the horses onward. It was a quick start, followed by an unwholesome lull. Even the sea breezes seemed to be aware of it as they softened. Then, the pleasant sounds of the great West Deep soon disappeared altogether. The calls of the gulls died out. The splashing of the waves became subdued. Even the rolling of the wagon's wheels became secondary.

Father Jacob slowed the horses to a sedate pace. His eyes searched. Adrina remained silent, her thoughts mostly idle and insubstantial now, though she could not shake the voice of the lady from her mind. It unnerved her. It called out to her and the fact that it grew stronger the farther along the coast they rode did not make her feel any easier.

A sudden change in the air around them came as a single, dark cloud passed in front of the sun, momentarily creating an eerie shadow across the land. With the momentary darkness came a spontaneous downward shift in the temperature. Jacob and Adrina clutched the woolen blankets more tightly and subconsciously shivered to erase the sudden chill.

The horses cast frightened whinnies into the air, their sixth sense warning that danger lurked near. Adrina's heart seemed to stop beating, in a temporary lapse until the sun's brightness and warmth once more covered her. Yet even with the warmth's return, the chill was not so readily cast away. Rather it lingered much, much longer. It was as if an evil hand reached out and stroked her, telling her, bragging to her, that it was near.

Adrina cast a glance heavenward. The sky was as clear as it had been a short while ago. The dark cloud was gone, vanished, as if it had simply evaporated after it had passed. As her eyes returned to the horizon, she grasped Jacob's hand and pointed to an object far in the distance. Jacob followed the direction her outstretched hand led him out along the coast and into the dark waters. However, what Adrina directed him to was not out amidst the darkening waters, but across them, back along the serpentine coastline. A cloud of dust arose and, it seemed a large group of riders rapidly approached.

"Father Jacob," said Adrina, "I don't have a good feeling about this."

Father Jacob seemed to still be shaking off the previous chill. He made a quick scan of the area, apparently looking for a place to hide, before he replied, "Rocks and squat grasses don't offer much cover, child. This wagon is too slow and awkward to maneuver in this rough terrain…"

Jacob paused in thought, Adrina cut in, "Perhaps, we could unhook the team and proceed on horseback."

"By the time we did that it would already be too late…" As he spoke, it seemed an idea came to Jacob. He had Adrina pull her long black hair back and tie it up in her scarf. Afterward he pulled the blanket around her so that it partially concealed her face and then he did likewise. The air was chilly and it wouldn't have been all that unusual for them to be bundled against the cold and the spray from the sea.

Jacob didn't stop the horses as he had thought to do, but instead proceeded at a slow pace. The riders steadily approached. Adrina's gaze grew gradually downcast until she was practically staring only at the dirt in front of her. The riders slowed as they passed for a cursory inspection, but quickly increased their pace and sped away.

Not raising her downward gape, Adrina saw only the riders' mounts, a blur of hind legs and forelegs, as they passed. She closed her eyes and nearly fell asleep until Jacob nudged her to tell her everything was all right.

Adrina lowered the blanket, but still kept it about her shoulders. The danger was gone, or so it seemed. She cast a nervous glance over her shoulder at the group of riders and then watched as Father Jacob flicked the controls to hasten the team.

They continued to wind their way along the serpentine coast, and Adrina cast her fears away. The trail became steadily rock-strewn, making passage over it rough and often very difficult. Large boulders that had to be circumnavigated sprang up in the middle of the trail and the width of the coastal road became steadily narrower.

Adrina followed and wandered among the empty waters breaking the coastline with her eyes, searching for that which was not there. The voice in her mind had grown sullen and quiet and, now her thoughts wandered free with the waves, rolling and sinking with each as they turned under, rising as each new wave was born, racing as they crashed into the rocky shore.

The emptiness was still present however, and the sounds of life still void. This lifeless droll played heavily on Adrina's thoughts. With each new curve, she wondered what lay on the other side. The coastal highway they rode along wasn't usually a bustling thoroughfare so she didn't think it was odd not to see any more passers by. It wasn't that she really wanted to see any, actually, but she wouldn't have minded seeing a friendly face—she didn't consider Jacob's pensive stare friendly or comforting.

Her thoughts slowly turned to the encroaching night. The sky was still clear but Father Jacob had told her storms here usually came suddenly and frequently.

Adrina cocked her head and listened to a sound carried by the wind. "Father Jacob?" asked Adrina with a timid voice. "What is that?"

"What is what?"

"Can't you hear it?" Adrina asked.

Jacob pulled the controls taunt and the horses slowed to a steady halt. "Can I hear what?"

"The singing."

"Singing?" Jacob tossed her an odd glance then put his hand to her forehead. "Stick out your tongue child?"

"Father Jacob, listen..."

A puzzled frown crossed Jacob's lips. "Maybe I do hear something, then again it doesn't sound like sing—" A distant low rumbling came from behind them now. "It is only thunder, child."

It took both a moment to realize that the sound they heard was the plodding of hooves against the rocky ground. Frantically they spun around and stared back down the trail behind them. A clump of dots trailing dust slowly became visible—the band of riders were returning.

"Still, that's not what I hear, Father Jacob," Adrina said.

"Wait a min—" Jacob gasped. "By the Father, I do hear something."

Adrina grabbed the controls from Jacob's lap and whipped them. The horses took off at a gallop, causing the wagon to jolt wildly. Adrina glanced behind them. She could make out single objects now, horses and riders. The group was gaining on them. "They'll catch us before we can get away," she said.

Apparently feeling suddenly inspired, Jacob shouted, "Give me those controls, child! We'll give them a run for it!"

Adrina didn't give Jacob the reins, the strong presence of evil had returned. She didn't know whether it was from behind her or ahead, but she knew it was there. She squinted her tired eyes ahead. A small sandy inlet settled where the ridgeline sloped down to the sea, forming a cove of sorts. This was the first place she'd seen where the road ran directly along the waters. The section appeared to have been washed away by the recent heavy rains and the inlet thus formed.

"There!" she shouted. Adrina didn't have to point to the object in the sand now, she knew Jacob saw it too.

"Halt!" sounded a loud, masculine voice that appeared drastically close.

Both Adrina and Jacob skewed their eyes left to see a rider that seemed to suddenly appear beside them. As a reflex Adrina halted the wagon. Her mind was filled with sudden panic. Why now when they were so close? She wanted to cry. Her eyes swelled with tears that slowly began to roll down her cheeks.

"Father, why?" she sobbed raising her voice aloft, not really asking Jacob and not really asking Great-Father, rather addressing them both.

The face that loomed over her, angry and fierce, seemed to lunge at her as it stepped from the horse to the wagon's deck. Just as the man reached his hands out to grab Adrina, Jacob snatched the controls from Adrina's hands and whipped them as hard as he could.

"Go away, leave us alone!" shouted Adrina.

The four horses dashed responsively forward and the rider, who had been struggling to maintain his balance as the wagon sprang forward, tumbled to the ground. A crunching sound an instant later said he struck the hard ground fatally. Adrina regained the controls from Father Jacob and a chase commenced with Adrina's only goal being the sandy inlet not far ahead. She was certain something was there, but exactly what she didn't know.

"I don't believe it!" shouted Jacob, "Look, there is another group of them ahead of us... Give me those controls back... We can't outdistance them, we have to think through this logically."

"No," shrieked Adrina. She slapped Jacob's hands away.

The wagon shook and rattled as it raced along the rough trail. Heedless, Adrina urged the horses on until the back end of the wagon was bouncing into the air. Jacob tossed nervous glances behind. It was clear he was more concerned about those that loomed up from behind than those that were ahead of them. The riders behind them were chasing them while from what Adrina could see of the group ahead, they weren't moving at all.

"What are they waiting for?"

"I wish I knew," Jacob said. "Wait a minute, are those Kingdom standards?"

"So what if they are."

Jacob squinted his eyes. "Great-Father, they are! It must be the column. We're safe, Adrina, we're safe."

Those were Jacob's last words as a mailed hand cuffed him. His head struck the wagon's deck below Adrina's feet with a crunch that sent chills up Adrina's back. Her terror-filled shriek was cut short as she fought off hands that sought to grab the controls from her. Panic gripped her mind. Her screams became wild and shrill. Suddenly strong hands snatched the controls away from her and the wagon was brought to an abrupt halt.

The same strong hands twisted Adrina and wrenched her from the wagon's seat, throwing her roughly to the ground. Momentarily everything became black as the wind was knocked out of her. Adrina scrambled backwards on the ground as the angry man swept down upon her. He picked her up again a moment later and began to shake her violently. Adrina's head bobbed and her teeth rattled. Her thoughts stifled with fright. Even when the man stopped shaking her, still she trembled uncontrollably.

"Treacherous murderer!" shouted the angry voice of the man whose strong hands squeezed into Adrina's shoulders with increasing vigor.

Frustration and despair lead Adrina to tears, but anger and pain soon took over. She clawed and kicked her captor, raking him across the face.

With one hand the large man aptly pulled back her long hair as she struggled to break free, while his other hand groped for something, Adrina didn't know what. Then out of the corner of her eye, she caught a glint of something shiny. She swallowed a heart-sized lump in her throat as a short, fine blade was applied to her upturned neck.

"A-dri-na?" came a distant voice.

Upon hearing her name, the terror-filled fog in Adrina's mind cleared. "Let me go, let me go," she screamed.

"Adrina?"

Adrina stopped kicking and clawing her captor. She turned. The first face she saw was familiar to her. "Emel!" she cried. She wiped the tears from her face, and reached her hands out to embrace him. Still, she shook uncontrollably. "But you were… that was… you then… Where is my brother? Has he already reached Alderan? Is it too late to stop him?"

The large dark-skinned southerner holding Adrina did not let her go. Instead he returned the blade to her throat. "By the Father, her blood *will* stain this blade."

"Hush. Let her go, what are you doing you fool?"

"But they killed Wrennyl!" The Southerner spun Adrina around and stared at her.

Adrina saw fury in his eyes. "It was a mistake, a mistake. We didn't know who you were and it was an accident that… that… he… fell, an accident."

Emel snatched Adrina away from the angry man. His free hand went to his sword in its sheath. "I said, back off, back off..."

Menacingly the large Southerner took a step toward Adrina. His blade poised ready to strike, he spoke, "Lord Valam will surely hear off this... Wrennyl was a good man!"

"I trust he will," said Emel, "especially since this is *the* Princess Adrina."

The man turned pale. "*The* Princess Adrina?"

"Yes, the Princess Adrina."

The Southerner began babbling an apology. "I'm sorry, Your Highness. You must forgive me. I didn't know... I didn't know, I swear it."

The man was sniveling and in tears, but Adrina said nothing. Her shoulders ached where he had gripped them and she just now got her shivers under control. She wiped tears from her cheeks, and turned away as the man sank to his knees.

"By Great-Father," moaned Emel in a low tone, "say something to him please. If they think you took offense, he'll get lashes. He is a family man. Do you know what that'll mean to him."

Adrina just then noticed the press of riders around her. "Lashes?" she asked.

"Say it now, please!"

Adrina turned back to the man. "Rise please, stand true. I accept your apology. Though in the future, I would ask that you treat a lady as a lady should be treated."

The Southerner stood and straightened his hunched posture. Evident relief passed over his face moments later.

Sadness and relief triggered something in Adrina. She looked around wildly, then started running. "Emel, come quickly!" she called back over her shoulder, "Come quickly, it is Prince William!"

There was a low moaning from behind them now as the two raced away. Uneasily, Father Jacob settled back onto the seat of the wagon, a hand raised to his cheek. Several riders quickly came to his aid and helped him down from the wagon.

***

A single figure lay washed onto the beach, folded into the area where the recent storms had formed a sandy hollow. Wreckage lay scattered on the shore around him. Adrina ran to him. She knelt in the wet sand beside him, and touched a hand to his cheek. She expected him to greet her with his warm blue eyes, but to her horror and shock, his skin was cold, cold and stiff with death.

"He is dead," Adrina said, "we are too late... Alderan? How far are we from Alderan?" Adrina grabbed Emel about the shoulders. "Where is Prince Valam?"

"Our party from Quashan' circled north around Alderan only a few hours ago. We expected to meet the column on the north side of the city, but we found nothing. His Highness sent our detachment north and another east to find the encampment. His aim was to proceed to the city outpost. Why aren't you with the column? Did something happen?"

Adrina explained as best she could what happened after Emel had left the column.

Emel swept Adrina up in his arms. Caught up in the reassurance of his touch and the warmth of his embrace, Adrina pressed her lips against Emel's. For a moment, Emel returned the passion of her kiss, then he stood stiffly and turned away from her.

"No doubt Captain Trendmore is our traitor," Emel said, "and more likely than not, he ordered the column to turn north at the sea instead of south. I never should have left you... This is all my fault. I didn't listen to what the lady said and look what has happened."

"It wasn't your fault, Em—"

"What about my father's accident?"

"Emel, I don't think you could've stopped it even if you had been there. Now is not the time to dwell on the could have beens."

"Indeed," said a voice from behind Adrina. Startled, she turned to see a strange small man and a boy. They were seated in the shaded part of the rocks behind her, and she had not seen either before.

Emel immediately drew his blade and stepped between Adrina and the stranger. "Proceed with caution friend, I'd just as soon run you through as not. What are you doing here?"

"Same as you," said a strange short man as he stood. "We were drawn here."

"Stay where you are," warned Emel.

The stranger took a step toward Emel. His hands were raised and, it seemed to Adrina he was unarmed. "Here is where the paths cross. The many become one for a short time," so saying, the man reached out his hand to Emel.

Emel lunged forward, his blade arched high, then it plunged deep into the man's side. Adrina's scream came too late.

Chapter Twenty Two: Alderan

Vilmos stepped protectively across Xith's prone form and waited for the assailant to make his next move. He was angry and magic raged unchecked through him.

"We are friends, not enemies," Vilmos said. "I don't want to have to kill you."

The man raised his sword defensively. Vilmos felt himself losing control of the magic.

"Put away your weapon," Vilmos said. "Please."

"Emel!" yelled the man's companion.

"Stay out of this, Adrina. I will let no one harm you." Emel turned back to Vilmos. "Tell your other companion to get up none too quickly. Or I'll likewise run him through."

"<*Trust*> is a two-way path. <*Put away*> your <*weapon,*>" said Xith, using the Voice to calm. Then he grabbed Vilmos' hand and said, "<*Control!*> Remember that anger and that hatred for another time…"

Xith gasped for breath. "The stones… in my bag, you'll find… a sack with five stones, bring… it to me…"

Vilmos brought the small bag of stones, but never looked away from the one who had attacked Xith.

"You are… swift… with a blade," Xith said through gasps, "we may soon… have need… of your skills."

Voices called out from the road now, "Emel, are you all right? We heard shouting?… Emel, do you need help?"

"<*Answer*> them. Tell them you are fine. <*Tell them you will be along presently…* >

"We are fine," Emel shouted. "We will be along presently."

"There isn't much time. Gather round, gather round. You too, young princess—" Xith winced from pain. "—Vilmos, the stones."

"Are you dying?" Vilmos asked with the utmost seriousness.

"Your apprenticeship is hardly at an end. He barely grazed my side." Vilmos looked down at the shaman's saturated robe. "Even small wounds bleed and the pain is not in my side, it is in my head. Our friend there has had quite a trial. I shouldn't have attempted to connect to his mind without blocking the flow of feelings. Never have I been so overwhelmed by anything…"

Xith winced again. "But I needed to find out what he knew. Just as I needed to know about you, Princess Adrina."

"Then you heard everything we said before?" Adrina asked.

Vilmos turned to regard the young woman. Before his thoughts had been on other things, he hadn't really noticed her until now. Momentarily he was caught up in her great brown eyes.

"Seated there in the shadows, it was hard not to. Do not worry, your secrets are safe with me. As I said, and as my companion, Vilmos, said, we are friends. We were drawn to this place for a reason. Each of us has a part in changing the many paths, for here the paths converge."

"How do we know we can trust you?" Emel asked.

Adrina asked, "And what of Prince William? Is that him?"

"Emel Brodstson, even the lady of the night knew the way of your heart."

Emel's face flushed red.

"And no," Xith said turning to Adrina, "that is not Prince William… If I probed correctly, our friend's name is Seth. He traveled here across the West Deep from a place called East Reach… They were ambushed and only a few survived. In the end, only two.

"The rest of his memory was rather disjointed, but as the other there is human and he isn't, I can only assume that some sort of struggle took place on this very beach, and here, he lost his only other companion. We will know more when he regains consciousness, but for now we have more important things to concern ourselves with."

"What do you mean not human?" Emel exclaimed.

Adrina put her hand on Emel's shoulder, but he brushed it away. Xith said nothing. He only stared.

"By the Father, it is you!" called out a voice from behind them. Vilmos turned to see an aged man dressed in a dirty black robe. One side of the man's face was swollen and bruised. "How long has it been, ten... no twelve years." The man's expression became sullen. "Returned from under-mountain just as you said. I didn't want to believe it when I heard it yesterday morning."

Xith regarded the elder for a moment, then said, "You, Jacob do not look well, and hear I'd heard you were now King's First Minister... And, it is nearly thirteen."

Jacob said, "I should have known I'd find you at the heart of all this."

Xith smiled now, apparently at the other's expense. "I am merely one of the fools on the board. I hope I know my part and move accordingly."

"Father Jacob, you know him?" asked Adrina.

"Of course I know the..." Xith put a silencing hand to his lips and Jacob spoke no more.

"Do you wish to inquire about my lineage now?" asked Xith of Emel who still had his sword drawn, "Or do you wish to know of the fall of Alderan?"

Princess Adrina's eyes went wide. She turned to Emel and glared at him. "Fall?" she asked.

Father Jacob waved Emel's weapon away. Emel sheathed the sword then said, "All is well in Alderan."

"All *appears* well in Alderan, because that is what was meant. Do we argue now, or do we ride for Alderan?"

"We ride."

"Yes, we ride!"

"To Alderan," whispered Adrina.

***

Father Jacob sat beside Xith, "Yes, we will listen," he said.

Vilmos, Emel and Adrina sat likewise. They formed a loose circle around the shaman.

Xith cleared his throat, turned his eyes around the circle, then said, "The Alliance of Kingdoms is all but broken. King Jarom has been flooding the upper southlands with men loyal to his cause for many months. And where he doesn't have soldiers, he has spies. His spies are everywhere and his reach is long..."

Father Jacob and Adrina nodded fast agreement.

Xith continued. "In all but name, Jarom *is* the absolute ruler of the four kingdoms of the south. Only King Charles was brave enough to oppose him and while this was true up until a few short weeks ago, it is no longer true. The Kingdom of Sever is now without king and its heir, its heir—"

Adrina interrupted, "What of my brother?"

"King Jarom fully expected King Andrew to answer King Charles' call of aid and for the safekeeping of Charles' son, Prince William. He may be quite surprised to find only a prince, but then again, Prince Valam's death—" Adrina's face flushed white. She began to tremble and Xith expected her to say something or to burst into tears, but she didn't. "—will allow him to usurp *all* lands south of River Trollbridge, all the lands of the South. Already troops march on Quashan'. With the cities' commander gone and the garrison sent north, the city will easily fall."

"I was just in Quashan'," Emel said. "The whole of the garrison was in company."

Xith turned frank eyes on the untrusting young guardsman. "If King Jarom can pay off a Chief-Captain of Imtal Garrison right under the king's nose, surely he can likewise persuade Quashan's garrison commander or one of his captain's or even one of his under-captains to relay in incorrect order."

"But what can we do?" asked Father Jacob. "A great force must've laid siege to Alderan. We have no more than forty riders."

"Fifty six," Emel said.

Princess Adrina's downtrodden expression turned upward briefly.

"I suspect Alderan was taken without a fight from the inside," Xith said. "For all we know, they marched straight into the city under Kingdom standards and the citizens greeted them openly."

Xith took a long swig from a water bag. His throat was dry and overworked. The ride to Alderan had gone smoothly, but not quietly. "Once Prince Valam is dealt with. The forces in the city will turn their sights on joining the march on Quashan'. This is what we *must* count on..."

***

"Are your men ready?" Xith asked.

Emel nodded. Xith joined Father Jacob deeper in the midst of the trees and there the two spoke in hushed tones.

Fifty-six ridesmen anxiously waited near the tree line for the dusk shadows to deepen. They had been waiting in the trees for several hours now.

Adrina scratched absently at the mosquito bites on her arms, hands and face. The City of Alderan seemed deceptively quiet. Emel's closeness to her was reassuring, but she was still ill at ease. She glanced to the strange wise man that had told her to stop calling him Watcher. "My name is Xith," he had told her.

The conversations with Xith had left Adrina filled with dread. Especially his seemingly casualness about that fact that Prince Valam would most probably be dead when and if they found him. Adrina hadn't burst into tears then, though it had taken considerable effort not to. Now she could only remember fond thoughts of her only brother—big as a bear and with a heart twice any normal man's. It was in Valam's shadow that she used to walk the streets of Imtal and his dreams of seeing all of the world that filled her young mind with thoughts of fantastic adventures.

"Are you all right?" whispered Emel in Adrina's ear.

Adrina nodded.

"Good. You and Father Jacob will wait here until we return. If we're not back by sun up, leave. Make progress north as fast as you—-"

Adrina cut Emel off with a hiss. "I'll not stay here and worry through the night. Where you go, I go. Remember the words of the lady?"

"Only death awaits in Alderan," returned Emel.

Adrina glared at him. "You expect me to turn away when every hand counts? I am as good with a blade as you are, perhaps better."

"Besting me on the practice field is not the same thing, Adrina," Emel said coldly.

Xith returned. "Keep your voices to a whisper," he said.

Adrina started to speak. Xith raised a silencing hand. He squinted his shiny eyes and stared out into the darkening land. "Everyone back and stay down," he said, "not a sound anyone…"

Soon figures carrying shielded lanterns appeared from the dark shroud. Behind them came horses and riders. Behind the riders, heavily laden wagons. Behind the wagons, more horses, more men. From her vantage point, Adrina began counting them as they passed. She stopped as the numbers swelled over two hundred.

Adrina found it unsettling that she heard only the occasional squeaking of wagon wheels to mark the group's passage. Riders were leading their mounts whose hooves were apparently padded. The weapons and armor of the soldiers she saw were also apparently padded, for as they passed, the normal clink-clink of metal scraping metal was absent. The group was traveling east, east to Quashan' just as Xith had said they would.

The eastward passage continued for more than an hour, and then for an hour afterward nothing. No shielded lights pierced the darkness and no sounds pierced the uncanny silence.

Out of the corner of her eye, Adrina saw Xith raise his hand and suddenly the press of bodies around her was absent. The small band of Kingdom ridesmen were suddenly sweeping toward Alderan City. Split into three tiny groups, they would strike the city from the north, east and west. The intent was to make the enemy remaining in the city think they were under attack by a large force. Adrina didn't know exactly what Xith hoped to accomplish by this, for surely the defenders would discover very quickly only only a few dozen men were carrying out the attack.

Adrina felt a hand on her shoulder. She spun around, surprised to find it was Emel. She stared at him in momentary disbelief. "You didn't go with the others?"

"Xith asked that I remain, and I have." Emel didn't seem happy about the prospect, but Adrina was—Emel wouldn't die with the others.

Adrina's smile died when she saw Xith's glowing eyes upon her.

"Vilmos, Adrina and Emel you'll ride into the city with me," Xith said, in a quiet voice. "Only Father Jacob is to remain behind. He'll watch our new companion and, he knows what to do should we not return. To your mounts! Our route into the city should be wide open soon. Hurry now, there is no time to waste..."

The Kingdom ridesmen attacked the city from three directions. Xith, Adrina, Emel and Vilmos made their way to the city from the south. Adrina was surprised to hear the sounds of a raging battle coming from the northern sectors of the city now. One thing she had neglected to consider, as Emel had pointed out, was that Alderan was a Kingdom city and had been a united city even before there had been a Kingdom. Apparently those in the city thought the King's army had come to liberate them. No true Kingdomer would sit idly if they thought the King's army was storming the city.

Under this shroud of confusion, the four crept into Alderan. After they had safely passed the city gates, Xith signaled for them to stop and gather round.

"We make for the city center." Xith spoke very softly. "Even now all routes to the keep will be guarded. If for some reason anyone is separated, watch your way with care, but head for the keep at once. Remember, all through streets are set up like the spoke of a wheel. They all lead to the center hub, and the keep."

Xith paused, then looked to Adrina. "To get into and around the inner keep unseen, we'll need your help."

Adrina stared blankly at Xith.

Speaking for Adrina, Emel said, "She's never been to Alderan."

"Down to the last detail, Imtal Palace was fashioned after Alderan's keep," Xith explained. "Only the old sections of the palace though. The maze of passageways used by the King's family should all be unguarded. Surely you've walked them a thousand times..." Xith's voice trailed off.

Adrina smiled, she could walk those passageways in her sleep. Then she frowned.

"But—" she began.

Xith cut her off saying, "Once safely inside and set upon the path, you and Vilmos will remain behind. Emel and I will proceed from there. Do not worry, if the prince lives, we *will* find him. Getting out of the city will be the problem..."

***

As anticipated, the southern sectors of the city were nearly deserted. The four, now on foot, blended into the shadows of cobbled streets as best they could. Emel clearly had not wanted to leave Ebony behind, but eventually he had. Twice they had made their way passed patrols without mishap. Fortunately both patrols had been racing north where the battle for the city raged.

Intermittently Adrina's eyes flashed on the small form of the boy, Vilmos, who walked beside her. He seemed a likeable lad, but a bit young and surely inexperienced. She could see open terror mirrored in his eyes and more than once, he had reached out his hand to hers to find comfort. But Adrina too found comfort in his touch and in the rapier still in its sheath that she clutched with her right hand.

Emel had the lead, and at about ten paces ahead, Adrina could only glimpse his form as he passed the infrequent lights of the darkened city. Somewhere behind them Adrina knew Xith lurked. Many times Xith had disappeared down a side street to reappear beside them at the next or the next intersection.

Adrina gulped for air and her heart skipped as Emel suddenly appeared out of the darkness.

"Patrol," he hissed, "they head south, not north."

Emel flashed his eyes at Xith. Xith waved them into a nearby alleyway.

Huddled in the shadows of the alleyway they waited. Soon, Adrina heard heavy footfalls, then she saw torchlight and shadowed faces. The patrol stopped at the intersection of the street and the alley, directly in front of the horrified onlookers. Adrina heard harsh whispers and angry voices. The members of the patrol were obviously displeased about being sent to watch the city's southern gate when a battle raged elsewhere.

From her vantage point in the shadows, Adrina could see much more than the outlines of faces. Light from their torches reflected dully off their armor and the swords withdrawn from their sheaths. The angry man who seemed the leader of the patrol was bearded and though rather gaunt, just from the tone of his voice and the way he stood, Adrina was sure he was capable with a blade and hardhearted. He was arguing with another man who wanted to return to the north. Both men's words were becoming increasingly belligerent.

Then to Adrina's horror, the leader of the patrol set upon the other man. In one swift move, he brought the point of his blade to the other's throat and plunged it inward. Adrina screamed, which would have brought sure discovery, if Emel hadn't clasped a hand to her mouth just prior. As it was, her muffled scream mixed in with the horrible gurgling sounds of the dying man as he sought to speak a few last words.

The leader removed his sword from the other's throat as he fell, and without another word, the members of his patrol continued south.

Emel removed his hand from Adrina's mouth and put his hands on her shoulders. "Are you all right, Adrina?" he whispered.

Adrina couldn't answer. She felt numb and sick.

"It will pass, Adrina," Emel said. "As I said, 'This is not the practice field.' This is real. Are you all right with that?"

Adrina still couldn't answer. Emel shook her.

"Adrina will be all right in a moment," Xith said. "Give her some breathing room."

Xith took Adrina's hand.

"We near the city center," whispered Xith. "Once past the last line of buildings there will be no cover. On my signal move quickly and without stopping across the square to the walls of the keep. Emel, you'll go first. Then, Vilmos. Then, Adrina. Once at the wall, speak not a word. Await my signal to continue…"

***

At a flat out run, Adrina raced across the square. Her heart was pounding in her ears. Vilmos and Emel had already made it safely across the open hundred yards to the shadowed wall and were excitedly watching her run. Adrina glanced from Emel to the archers on the walls. Only one of them needed to spot her and it would all be for nothing.

Halfway across, Adrina no longer held back her smile. The run was strangely exhilarating after the tension of creeping through the besieged city. She glanced back once to look for Xith. She knew he waited somewhere out of sight behind her to make the last mad dash across the square. When Adrina glanced back, her foot caught one of the square's cobblestones. She tumbled and fell. Her face struck cold stones.

Disoriented, she looked up. Emel was edging away from the safety of the wall. She waved him away. Then her eyes rose to the top of the wall, a single figure stood looking down over the square now, seemingly his eyes looked straight at her. Breathless, Adrina waited for him to raise an alarm or notch an arrow to the string of his bow.

Unmoving, Adrina waited, and waited. The archer stood still. He stared down into the darkness of the square. For an instant, it seemed their eyes locked. The archer raised one of his arms—surely he was about to reach into the quiver at his side for an arrow. Adrina's heart stopped and the whole of the world seemingly collapsed in around her. Adrina stifled a moan, held her breath and waited.

As the archer turned away and continued his march along the battlements of the wall, Adrina thanked Great-Father for smiling down upon her and launched herself into a run.

Hastened by her fright, she crossed the remaining distance to the wall in a surprising burst of speed. Emel caught her in his arms and held her for a moment before both turned to look back across the square. Immediate shock registered on their faces, Xith stood in plain sight in the middle of the square.

Adrina heard Vilmos whisper, "Run, run." Then he began waving his arms wildly to the shaman. Heedless, Xith waved them on. "<*Go now,*>" he said in a voice that was strangely compelling and seemed to carry across the square on the wind, *<Do what you must...* >

A cry went up from the walls and suddenly a number of voices were echoing an alarm. Almost immediately afterward Adrina heard the twang of bows and the hiss of arrows. She squeezed her eyes tight. Fool, she thought to herself, sacrificing himself for no gain.

"Quickly now," said the boy, Vilmos, seeming suddenly resolved to action. "Pray my master's diversion buys our way into the inner keep..." His words fell away, and as if in response to his voice, a blue-white streak raced through the air to the wall. Disquieting screams followed.

One of the archers fell from atop the wall and smacked the cobblestones not more than five feet from where Adrina stood. The man's face was twisted oddly toward her. The emptiness in his eyes and the unnatural twist of his body told Adrina the fall had been fatal.

More blue-white streaks raced to the wall. Another soldier fell to his death—Adrina saw no trace of the blue-flighted arrows that had claimed either man. Emel grabbed Adrina's hand and pulled her after him.

The minutes that followed were crazed and everything for a time afterward passed in a blur. Adrina found herself racing alongside Emel and Vilmos. She remembered remarking that the buildings of the inner keep truly did resemble the old wings of Imtal Palace and that true to Xith's word, the King's entryway into the main building was unguarded. She lead them along unlit passageways that were familiar to her feet even in darkness, yet she knew they only seemed that way.

It wasn't until many uncertain minutes later that Adrina abruptly halted. She realized she no longer heard voices and that the footsteps she was running away from were her own and that of her companions. When she stopped, first Vilmos and then Emel slammed into her.

"What's wrong?" asked Emel.

"Nothing," Adrina said in a hiss. She turned to Vilmos. "Did Xith tell either of you where they would hold my brother?"

Even in muted darkness, Adrina could see the boy shrug.

"I thought he told you," Emel said.

After a long silence, Vilmos spoke. "Xith said it would be easy and that getting out of the city would be the hard part. Your instinct is what led you here in the first place. Where were you going?"

Another period of silence followed then Adrina said, "I really have roamed these passageways a thousand times. They are a solitary place. My father never liked them and doesn't use them. It is true that very few even know they exist."

"Where were you going?" repeated Vilmos.

Adrina continued as if she hadn't heard the question. "I wonder if… No, that would be too much to hope for." Vilmos glared at her. "I guess, I was going to my quarters."

Vilmos suggested that she should continue.

Adrina closed her eyes in thought for a moment, then lead them on their way. After ascending a flight of stairs and after a few twists and turns in the passageway, the three found themselves standing before a door. Only Adrina knew for certain what was beyond the door, the others could only guess. She slid the door open, expecting to find her room.

She was about to step into the room, when Emel swept past her, a short blade cupped in his right hand. There was a rather large man standing hunched over with his back to the door only a few feet away. Emel stealthily crept up on him and plied the blade to his throat. Then he spun the man around.

Adrina bit her tongue to stop her scream. Then as she sought to speak no words came forth. Her eyes were wild and Emel stared at her for a moment in apparent confusion.

"Adrina?"

"Valam," Adrina said. "By the Mother, you live." Adrina was crying now and she ran to embrace her brother.

Shocked, Emel lowered the blade from the prince's throat. "Dear Father—Your Highness, forgive me. I had no idea."

Valam embraced Adrina in a great bear hug and swept her from her feet. His joy was short-lived, his expression grew suddenly grim and he let Adrina go. "It is not safe here, you must go."

"But, we are here to rescue you."

The prince put a finger to his sister's lips. "There are things occurring here that you cannot hope to understand. You must leave at once."

"What is wrong with you, Valam? Come quickly." No sooner had Adrina said this than someone off to the side of the room cleared their throat. Adrina turned and from an adjacent doorway, great blue eyes greeted her. Adrina asked, "Prince William?"

The other nodded and grinned evilly.

"Run, Adrina, run," Valam said. He flung Adrina toward the passageway and barreled at the prince.

Complete pandemonium followed. Confused, Emel and Vilmos stood their ground. Adrina recovered her feet and stared in wonder at the struggle between her brother and Prince William. Valam had a firm grip on the other's throat. William was straining to reach a short blade in his belt.

Adrina watched in mute horror as Prince William broke free of her brother's grasp and whirled about to face him. Prince Valam, at six foot four inches and two hundred pounds and fifty pounds, was nearly the largest man in the Kingdom. With bare fists he could take any man, but where Prince Valam had only his fists, the other had a long, curved blade made for close-quarters fighting.

Two guards rushed into the room. Again Adrina tried to scream and no words came out. Seeing the guards, Emel sprang forward, and engaged both.

Undaunted by the menacing blade, Valam circled defensively, waiting to attack. William it seemed was also waiting for the right moment to strike. The end came quick and clean, Prince William sliced in with his blade, Valam countered and then planted a solid blow to the side of the other's unprotected skull. Prince William went down, his knees crumbling, his body collapsing beneath him.

More guards swept upon them from the open doorway. Emel screamed wildly and pointed to the passageway. Vilmos remained deathly still, apparently gripped by fear. Adrina turned. Soldiers were streaming out of the tunnel behind her. Before she could get free, one had her arm and twisted it back forcefully, a burning pain shot up to her elbow.

Prince Valam descended upon the attackers like a hungry demon, his eyes unfocused and angry. He grabbed the man that held Adrina by the throat, lifted him off the floor and flung him to the wall. Without stopping, Valam slapped Emel's blade away and backed Adrina, Vilmos and Emel into the corner. He stood guardedly in front of them.

With the aid of two guards, Prince William regained his feet. He rubbed the side of his head and directed a vengeful stare at Valam.

Valam maintained the face off against the many guards in the room and directed his eyes at William. "Tell them to back off," Valam shouted, "we'll submit!"

"Enough, enough," William said. He clapped his hands together and the soldiers backed away. "Stay your ground. Let's shed no more blood than we need to for now.... We have what we wanted and a prize or two to boot."

Chapter Twenty Three: Prisoners

Through the night Father Jacob watched the strange one, the one called Seth. As the shaman had asked, Jacob placed the healing stones one by one to Seth's forehead. He had seen such stones before in the Temple of the Mother, but never had he witnessed their ability to heal. When first held the strange stones hummed and glowed bright yellow, touched to Seth's forehead, the color slowly drained from them until they were left dull, black and empty.

Then suddenly two hours before dawn Seth had opened his eyes and spoke. "Where is my companion?" he had asked, his words in the old language.

The old language, being the language of priests and priestesses, hadn't surprised Jacob. He had answered without thought in the same tongue. "I do not know, I am sorry."

It was only now that Father Jacob was deep in conversation with Seth that he realized Seth spoke in the old tongue, the language that had once been universal to all peoples and was now preserved only by those of the Mother and Father. Jacob considered Seth's statement for a moment more, then replied. "Then it is true, you are an elf."

There is disbelief in your voice, Fa-a-ther—Seth stumbled over the word—he had told Jacob earlier that he didn't feel comfortable naming a Man father. —*Jacob, yet your thoughts say you want to understand.*

"Myth and lore would have most Kingdomers believe that your kind are akin to fairies, pixies, and sprites."

Seth smiled and regarded Jacob with his blue eyes. He seemed to know Jacob was joking.

Jacob continued. "You must meet a friend of mine. Keeper Martin would write entire tomes filled with your words. There'd be a definite gleam in his eyes as he wrote: Elf of the gold and green forest, most fare and generous..."

Yes Jacob, I am very much mortal, just as you, Seth said, answering the question that had been on Jacob's mind for some time. *Many of my companions journeyed to Great-Father so that I could be here and it fills my heart with sorrow to know it was all for nothing...*

"You will have counsel before King Andrew, friend Seth, this I promise you."

"*You do not understand, without my companion, Brother Galan, I have failed. My fate is here... She was needed to return to my homeland, the land of East Reach.*

"There is something you must know, Brother Seth," Jacob said, borrowing the title as it seemed appropriate. "The one who found you said something that was strange. On the beach where you were found, it appeared there had been a struggle of some sort. One dead man attested to this. Unless there was a man in your party?"

There were no Men— Seth's voice sounded suddenly distant. His eyes flashed, his expression became one of puzzled remembrance. *Yes, yes there it is.* Seth sent surprise and hope into Jacob's mind along with the words.

For the first time Father Jacob realized Seth spoke in thoughts and not aloud. Do you walk in my thoughts? He asked himself.

It is the way of my people. I took open thought as a sign that you wanted me to enter your mind. I am sorry if I have offended you.

"Nothing of the sort, Brother Seth," Jacob said, "you continue to surprise me is all. There really are poor records of the four peoples after the Race Wars."

Tell me of this other, the one who found me and the one you are thinking of now. He is of the four peoples, is he not?

"Xith, last of the Watchers. I first met him thirteen years ago. He came to me in a time of great need. He promised he would return one day when the need was again great, and he has. Great Kingdom is being consumed by the heart of darkness itself."

Would he know where Galan is?

Jacob nodded in understanding. "He might, he just might, but I suspect the disappearance of your friend is tied to the struggle we face. Xith said that we were drawn to you because of a joining of the paths. Our fates are together, my friend."

And more I am afraid. I remember some of it now. At the last, I called out with my mind in desperation. The call, I fear, lead more than just those who wished to aid me. I fear I summoned your enemy as well, and now they've taken Galan.

Seth attempted to stand and did so only with Jacob's help. *I would help you. What must I do?*

"For now, there is little we can do. If Xith has not returned to camp shortly after sunrise, we journey north and return with the King's army marshaled before us."

Jacob looked to the East where dawn was forming on the horizon. "To war," he whispered. "But for now we can only wait and hope against hope… I truly fear the worst."

***

For two days Captain Trendmore drove the column north along the coast of the great sea. On smooth terrain the foot soldiers maintained a steady pace and made good progress. Keeper Martin was hopeful that by afternoon the walls and spires of the Free Cities would be in sight.

Doubt had grown in the Lore Keeper from the moment the column had turned north instead of south, but Martin had no definite proof to act on his feelings. He couldn't act on hunches and doubts. For all he knew Captain Trendmore was indeed following Captain Brodst's orders. But then again, if he didn't take action, who would?

Keeper Martin cast a sidelong glance to the close-mouthed rider to his left, then lowered the hood of his cloak and looked to the sea. A strong breeze out of the north carried with it a salty spray. "On such a hot day," Martin said, "the moisture and the breeze are refreshing. Don't you think so, captain?"

Captain Adylton replied, "The sun near midday is hot here, Lore Keeper, you would do well to keep that hood about your head."

Martin eyed the tall, dark-skinned Southerner who had removed his cloak about an hour into the ride and rode with short leggings that exposed calves and knees.

Captain Adylton quickly added, "Playing in the surf and lying by the sea is about all I did in my youth. My father was a fisher..."

Keeper Martin smiled—a mischievous smile. In a voice that barely carried above the plodding of his mount's hooves, he asked, "Did you sail these waters often with your father then?"

"More often than I cared to."

Martin noted Captain Adylton's annoyance and his apparent wish to end the conversation. "Would an autumn storm have driven your sails north or south?"

"I see," Adylton said, "that troubles you too."

Martin nodded. "I have sailed to High Province close to winter season many times. Always I felt the breezes upon my face when I stood at the bow."

"Aye, the winds change with the ending of summer. Autumn and winter bring cold breezes out the north."

"Captain Trendmore wasn't a fisher's son was he?" Martin asked.

"Hardly, his father was a tanner or was it a smithy—at any rate, no, I'm sure he's never sailed."

"I have known Captain Brodst for many years, yet I cannot recall his father's trade?"

Captain Adylton gave Keeper Martin a stern look. "You know as well as I that..." The captain's voice trailed off. He looked again at Martin, suddenly seeming to realize where Martin was going with his questions. "You are right. The storms would have blown the ship south if it strayed off course at all. Any experienced captain would have had little trouble in those storms. They were early autumn storms, full of malice yes, but not violent like the storms of winter."

Keeper Martin looked Captain Adylton straight in the eye. "Do you have loyal men in your squadron?"

Captain Adylton stared back at Martin. "They are loyal men all, and they follow all lawful orders of their commanding officers. None would turn against the other, if that is your hope."

"What of unlawful orders given by a man who is no longer loyal to his country or his countrymen?"

Captain Adylton reined in his steed, nearly coming to a halt. "Proving such a thing, Keeper—" His changing the pace brought mayhem to those in the column behind him. A wagon driver's team nearly drove over him. Captain Adylton shrugged off the man's curses and spurred his mount. "—How do you propose to do that?"

Keeper Martin judged the captain's receptiveness to the truth by the unease in his eyes. "There is news I have not shared with you, captain. The situation is much graver than you are aware of. It was not just the upcoming departure of a ship from the port city of Wellison that brought me to Imtal Palace to disturb King Andrew's rest in the middle of the night. Prior to this, I had been in the Far South for many months. Secretly.

"At first it was personal matters that brought me to Sever more than anything else. After, much more. It was fortunate that only Keeper Q'yer of Quashan' knew my whereabouts.

Also fortunate that my last visit to Sever had been some years before.

"When I arrived in Gregortonn, all seemed well. The affairs in the capital were running smoothly. Over night, all this changed. King Charles ordered the city sealed. The city garrison turned to the streets. Hundreds were arrested. Dozens killed in clashes. For a full day afterward the city was quiet. Only the flags removed from their poles upon the walls attested to turmoil. Then just before dawn of the second day, the searches began. More arrests, more fighting. Luckily I was able to find reliable accommodations, which did not come without a price.

"Two weeks I was in hiding, plotting my escape. Then one afternoon while moving to a new safe house, I made a most unexpected discovery. Soldiers loyal to King Charles were no longer in control of the city. An agent of King Jarom had somehow usurped power... Everything I'd seen suddenly made sense.

"Soon after I arrived in the new safe house one of my benefactors discovered my true identity. I don't know how, but it was a fortunate turn of events, for it was then that men loyal to Charles approached me. They spoke of a bold plan to retake the city and of a plan to smuggle the heir to the throne from the city to safety. It was with their help that I eventually made my way back to Great Kingdom."

Keeper Martin took a long swig from a wine skin, then cleared his throat. "You know as well as I that King Charles' voice was the only vote of dissension in the Minors when King Jarom last sued for war and the dissolution of the Kingdom Alliance. His aim is war with Great Kingdom, there can be no doubt."

Again Captain Adylton disrupted the pace of the group, he reined in his mount and stared at Keeper Martin. The wagon driver behind the captain screamed angrily this time.

"Is there something wrong?" came an excited voice from behind them. A rider raced toward them. Both Martin and

Adylton recognized the voice and the rider, Captain Trendmore.

"We must act, are we agreed on that, Captain Adylton?" Martin asked as he raised the hood of his cloak.

Captain Adylton signaled agreement and urged his mount onward.

"Is there something wrong here?" Captain Trendmore repeated when he came abreast of the two.

"I was just explaining to the good keeper that if he kept his face to the sun for another hour on a day like today, he would be as bright as a one of Duke Ispeth's apples before nightfall. I think it took him by surprise."

"Yes, yes indeed," Captain Trendmore said, a crooked smile coming to his lips.

***

It was the morning of the second day since their capture and still Vilmos cursed himself. Xith had told him to do what he must and he had done nothing. To him this was unacceptable and as he marched with his hands tied painfully tight behind his back, he hung his head in shame. It seemed of small consequence to know that Prince William and his henchmen had fled Alderan out of fear they might not be able to control the city any longer.

Vilmos knew little of the Prince of the North, Valam, but he was sure there had been tears in his eyes when William of Sever had ordered the city set ablaze and that no building should be left standing. That night, even from miles and miles away, they had seen the unearthly glow of the burning city. Vilmos had seen rage and hatred in Prince Valam's eyes then.

They had been moving since daybreak without respite. The first day they had stayed near the coast, traveling south, but this day they traveled more east than south. Vilmos knew this because the sun shined almost directly in his eyes, making the world around him bleached and hazy. He knew only that

Princess Adrina was to his right and that if he didn't maintain a correct pace, he stepped on the heels of the guardsman, Emel.

Sweat dripping down from his forehead ran irritatingly into his eyes and with his hands tied behind his back, Vilmos couldn't wipe it away. Exhaustion sought to overcome him and he fought to stay alert. He still held hope that Xith would somehow rescue them.

An abrupt kick from behind sent Vilmos sprawling. Screaming, he hit the hard ground face first. He spun around angrily and spat out dirt.

"Rest," said the voice of the figure towering above him.

With his back now to the sun, Vilmos found the haze in front of his eyes slowly clearing. He squinted his eyes up at the shadowed figure, which hovered over him for a moment more before turning away.

"Are you all right?" Adrina asked.

Vilmos said, "I think so." His backside was a little sore but he'd recover. His pride was hurt more than anything. He had done nothing to provoke William's men yet it seemed they had singled him out. More than anyone else, Vilmos bore the brunt of their resentment and anger. He was the one who was forced to watch while the others ate, albeit meagerly. He was the one who was denied water or forced to drink from a bowl like an animal. He was the one who was pushed and kicked.

The brooding prince also regarded him. "You are tougher than you look, my young friend, I am glad." Prince Valam was silent for a moment, then continued. "It seems you have been singled out because you are the smallest and the youngest. Their aim is to break you and thus break us all. Know that I *will* give repayment for every such mistreatment. And know also, that many a man would have already yielded."

Emel seemed to agree. He winked at Vilmos. "Hang in there, we will surely make them pay."

"May Queen Elthia turn over in her grave so that she does not have to see the harvest her son seeks," Vilmos whispered.

Prince Valam turned a puzzled frown to Vilmos. "My father's words," Vilmos explained.

"It seems we were never properly introduced, my young friend. You look of royal blood and you speak like one well educated and Kingdom borne. Yet, I have never seen you in any of the southern courts beside your father."

Vilmos' faced flushed red. "I am hardly of royal blood, my father is a village counselor." Vilmos paused, his tongue growing flustered. "In truth, I am ill at ease in your company..." His voice trailed off momentarily.

"Yours too, Princess," Vilmos said, turning to Adrina briefly before turning back to Prince Valam. "And in truth, I am not as tough as you might think. I was more afraid of crying in your presence, than of my lost pride. Even William of Sever's men respect you."

"Respect and fear are two different things, Vilmos. They fear me only as long as we remain on Kingdom soil. Matters will change when we reach Sever." Prince Valam turned at the sound of approaching footsteps. "Water," he shouted at the guard. "Water for every one!"

***

The passing of another day brought Vilmos only more misery. Prince Valam had told him that perhaps tomorrow they would enter the northernmost forests of the Kingdom of Sever. Vilmos had cringed at the mention of the Vangar, yet it seemed he had always known he would one day return there. Now, even as he closed his eyes and tried to find sleep, he saw the great white fangs and glowing eyes of the beasts called Wolmerrelle.

As the night looked to be a cold one, Vilmos, Adrina, Valam and Emel huddled close for warmth. They bedded down upon the hard ground and could only look with yearning to the fires a short distance away. They had been offered neither blankets nor fire, which was in stark contrast to the previous days.

Behind him, Vilmos could hear whispers passing back and forth between Emel and Adrina. Afraid to close his eyes, Vilmos stared into the darkness and listened in. He wasn't surprised to find they were talking about William of Sever once again.

"I don't understand," Adrina was saying, "the lady told us to find him. As if all would be well once we did. She said he would not arrive in Alderan…"

Emel corrected the princess, "She said the ship would not arrive in Alderan and that only death awaited there. We did not listen and look what has happened. Have you told anyone else of that conversation?

"Only Father Jacob… And, Xith…"

Emel was silent for a time, and Vilmos almost fell asleep against his will. "Should we tell His Highness, perhaps together… No, it is a foolish hope."

"Go on," said another voice. Prince Valam edged closer, pressing Vilmos who was in between the giant and Emel, closer to Emel. "I have long wondered why Prince William would turn against us. Our kingdoms have always been the strongest of allies…"

Vilmos wanted to say something but held back.

"Perhaps we should post a watch. This is something no one else was meant to hear," whispered Adrina.

"Emel," Valam whispered, and the guardsman inched away into the night, leaving only the three.

As Adrina began her tale of the meetings with the lady of the night, Vilmos' thoughts started to wander. He had heard this story once already.

The next thing Vilmos knew Emel was returning. He didn't know how much time had elapsed or what had transpired in the interim, though he suspected somewhere along the line he had fallen asleep.

"They sleep," Emel said. "Now there are only guards around the periphery."

Valam continued to speak without pausing, "Perhaps it wasn't Prince William you dreamed of. What of these others? This Xith you spoke of, perhaps it was him."

"Perhaps," Adrina said. She didn't sound convinced.

"Perhaps not," Vilmos whispered to himself just before sleep found him.

***

With morning came rain, a ceaseless downpouring that made the day all the drearier. To make matters worse, the soft breeze out of the North that had been with them for days was by midday a steady gale. It brought with it a hint of winter's chill. To Vilmos it didn't matter that winter was still months away, he was chilled to the bone all the same. He longed for his hooded cloak, a place next to a warm and cheerful fire, and a bowl of winter stew.

The only good thing about this day was that his hands were free and although Prince Valam said it was yet another sign that William and his men were becoming increasingly bold and less and less afraid, Vilmos didn't care. He only knew how good it felt to have the restraints off his wrists.

Apparently seeing Vilmos' peaked appearance, Prince Valam handed Vilmos his overtunic. Vilmos was hesitant to take it.

Vilmos said, "You'll catch your death of cold, Your Highness."

"Snows in High Province are already knee-deep, and in winter, they are so deep a man cannot walk across them. Take it, Vilmos, to me it will make little difference. The hide is specially treated, rain will not soak it. It will keep you from catching a cold. When the time for action comes, we'll need everyone at their best."

Vilmos accepted the tunic and wrapped it about him. The Prince's overtunic was so big in fact that Vilmos was able to wear it like he would have his hooded cloak. He didn't put his hands into the sleeves. Instead, he pulled the collar up over his head and peered out through a space between the two middle ties.

Vilmos trudged on. Hours passed. Afternoon came. Still rain poured down upon them. Then just when Vilmos thought the day would end much as it had begun, his deepest fears were realized. The green of forest came into sight.

It was then, in a softly whispered voice that Vilmos told the prince, the princess and the guardsman of his previous travels in the Vangar. He also told them of the soldiers in the valley, and of the Wolmerrelle. All the while he spoke, an uncontrollable trembling and dread flooded over him.

"Thank you, Vilmos," Prince Valam said. For a time he was obviously deep in thought, then Valam said, "Be that as it may, we must address other matters. Once we cross the boundaries of the Kingdom into the Minors, our captor will have little use for you and Emel.

"I know not why he has allowed Emel to live, but I am sure now why you live. He is using you to keep me in check. He knew I would brood over the injustices he has given you and think not of other things—escape. That is exactly what I did. His advisors whisper well in his ear.

"But my mind is clouded no more. Tomorrow in the forest," Valam said, "we *will* make our move then. To die fighting is honorable. To die with a blade in your back is quite another thing…"

Emel seemed to agree. "Tomorrow," he whispered.

Vilmos wanted to say that Vangar Forest was no place for travelers, especially a small group of unarmed travelers on the run. Instead, he found himself saying, "William of Sever is at home in the forest more than any man. It wouldn't be a wise—"

Emel cut in. "Would you rather die then?"

Adrina, who had been regarding Vilmos thoughtfully, spoke before he could respond to Emel, "You call the Prince, William of Sever, and there is a ring in your voice as if you know him."

As if suddenly realizing a thing that had passed by him, Prince Valam's eyebrows rose and he nodded his head contemplatively. "You are right." He turned to Vilmos. "Have you met William before?"

"My father is the Counselor of Tabborrath Village."

"You are Minor borne," Adrina said. "And you have met him before?"

"Not directly, though I once saw him at the Three Village Assembly. Everyone from our village circle and many from the forests came to Olex Village that day. It was the first time William of Sever had returned to his birthplace."

"Birthplace?" Valam said, disbelief in his voice. "Queen Elthia was my mother's sister. She was not Minor-borne."

Vilmos started to say something but Emel cut him off with a wave of his hand. Almost immediately afterward, Vilmos went sprawling face first into the muddy ground as he was booted from behind.

"Rest," said the now familiar voice. The guard, who apparently took great pleasure in his misdeed, turned away laughing as Vilmos spat and tried to wipe mud from his eyes.

This time as Valam screamed at the guards, "Bring water," none of them moved.

"Already they find bravery," Prince Valam whispered, "perhaps tonight in the forest would be even better."

"You give the word, Your Highness, and only death will keep me from your side," Emel said.

"I do not think they will kill the two of you just yet. If you truly are Minor borne, Vilmos," Valam said, turning as he spoke, "William may just give you your life. Use that chance, Vilmos, use it for all it's worth. Go back to Tabborrath Village and leave the affairs of men to men."

Vilmos felt suddenly stung. He turned away, hiding the tears in his eyes.

Adrina sat beside Vilmos. She spoke softly to him. "You were about to answer my brother's question. What were you going to say?"

"Nothing," Vilmos said through his tears.

Apparently Prince Valam noted Vilmos' tears too, for as he spoke his voice which had never been truly gentle before was also soft. "Go on, please..."

Vilmos shifted to a more comfortable sitting position. "William of Sever was not born in Gregortonn. Gregortonn is the capital, it is not a place of birth."

Seemingly remembering something from the past, Adrina laughed, "Chancellor Yi's lessons..." Her voice trailed off and for a moment it seemed she wasn't going to explain. "All births are registered according to the ancestral home of the father. For census, tithe and tax."

"Of course," Vilmos said. He found he was smiling. "My father muttered many silent curses in its name. It was the only of his responsibilities that he disliked."

Emel waved a hand under his chin. The conversation stopped. Vilmos turned and saw a guard approaching.

"To your feet!" shouted a gruff voice, signifying an end to the brief rest. Apparently their captors were eager for the feeling of safety being within the borders of Sever would provide.

Vilmos struggled to his feet, and stared glumly at Prince Valam momentarily. Then his thoughts turned quickly to what lay ahead. Whatever their struggle, it would take place in the Vangar. Vilmos was sure of this now as he had been sure of no other thing.

Chapter Twenty Four: Bushwhacked

Like thieves in the night, the enemy army had stolen upon Quashan'. From atop the city's fortified walls, Chancellor Van'te stared out at the enemy host. In the two days since their arrival, they had staged no attacks against the city and though they barred all travel into or out of the city, they harassed its residents in no other way.

Chancellor Van'te turned to the young sergeant-at-arms beside him. "How many do you estimate today?"

Sergeant Danyel' grimaced. "A few hundred more arrived in the night. Still, nearly the same as yesterday, around ten thousand."

"That is my estimate also." Van'te looked glumly to the young recruits on the wall. "How many were you able to rouse to the city defenses?"

"Two hundred more," Danyel' said proudly. "I told them nothing of the garrison's absence. None would've believed me anyway, who would believe the entire garrison, save for the handful which includes me, is gone."

The chancellor scrutinized the sergeant, then said in a soft voice, "You think me the true fool to allow such an order to pass, don't you?"

"The seal was genuine, and what man can refuse a summons by his King. Perhaps Imtal is likewise besieged."

Chancellor Van'te wasn't able to respond. "Runner!" came the cry from the west wall.

Chancellor Van'te grinned, he knew if he was persistent enough one of his messengers would get through. "Give the man some help!" Van'te shouted to the archers on the walls. As archers began firing wildly at the enemy line they couldn't reach, the chancellor moved to leave the wall. "Sergeant Danyel'," he said, "lead me from the wall."

The two hurriedly made their way to the courtyard where they hoped to find good news. It was a short walk. Still Chancellor Van'te, well in his years, found he was wheezing and puffing by the walk's end.

When Van'te and Danyel' reached the courtyard, they found the runner winded and hunched over after his sprint across the field. Still without delay, the runner handed Chancellor Van'te the scroll and in earnest, the chancellor began to read its contents. "By the Father, " Van'te muttered to himself, "it is from Prince Valam…" His voice trailed off and shock registered on his face.

Chancellor Yi turned to say something to the runner and found the man gone, as if he had vanished. "Sergeant Danyel'," Van'te screamed in a high-pitched nasal tone as only he could, "I want that runner found!"

Danyel' signaled to the two soldiers beside him. They hurried off. Danyel' asked, "What does it say? Is the message truly from His Highness?"

Chancellor Van'te showed the scroll to Danyel'. A mute minute passed, then the sergeant said, "Are you sure this is truly Prince Valam's writing? Couldn't this be an elaborate hoax to make us quit the city?"

A pained expression crossed Van'te's face. He blamed himself for what had transpired. He felt suddenly tired and old. "I have schooled His Highness all the years of his life. Surely by now, I should be able to recognize his scrawl… See the loops above the I's, the double slashes on the T's and the way he stops to make an L?"

Danyel' nodded.

"Done that since he was a boy first learning to write, just to annoy me—Yes, I am sure it is his handwriting."

"Do you really believe that if we opened the gates of the city, the army surrounding Quashan' would guarantee safe passage for all who wished to leave?"

"Prince Valam didn't."

Danyel' seemed confused. "What do you mean?"

Chancellor Van'te flattened out the scroll and pointed to the last few lines.

Danyel said, "I still don't understand."

"The handwriting switched here... Can you see the darkening of the strokes?" Danyel' shook his head. "Never mind, never mind. Only a foolish old man or a young boy such as you would think five hundred could defend a city from ten thousand."

"You, Chancellor Van'te, are no fool," Danyel' said. He patted the chancellor on the back. "If any can save Quashan', it is you. Tell us what you would have us do, and we will do it."

"At any rate, there is little we can do now. Soon enough they'll know we do not intend to quit the city, the attack will begin then..."

***

Prince Valam turned to Emel. "How many men are stationed around the periphery of the camp?"

"You mean, is there hope for escape this night?" Emel leaned close to Valam and whispered something that Adrina couldn't hear, but from the expression on her brother's face, it wasn't good news. Adrina returned to her muddled thoughts. Since their capture, her thoughts had been ever jumbled and never clear.

A day of trudging along overgrown paths had left her exhausted and in tears. Mostly she was distraught because she had always considered herself capable of doing anything a man could do, yet every day now she saw how much she depended on Emel and Valam to make it through the day—especially this last day. Here she had found a bitter truth, until now her life had been the pampered and sheltered life of a spoiled little girl.

Adrina was also agitated, because it seemed Valam and Emel left her out of their plans for escape. Disappointed, she remembered a conversation she had with Emel days ago, just before Alderan. She had told him, "I am as good with a blade as you are, perhaps better..."

Emel had replied, "Besting me on the practice field is not the same thing, Adrina." She remembered how coldly Emel had said it, and how bitter the truth of it was now that she understood what he had meant.

Again she heard the words of the mysterious lady in her ears. *The evil brings the change you so wished for. It has found a home in the emptiness of your heart. You care too little for those around you. You see not the servants who toil for you, workers in the fields on their hands and knees with the whip at their backs, drudges scouring the kitchen floors... You must open your eyes!*

Adrina thought back to another time and when she closed her eyes, she saw the quiet fields of Mellack Proper—it was then only two days after she met the mysterious lady and her journey was only beginning. Lying there on the cold ground, her body sore, her stomach rumbling, the fields of Mellack Proper, the orchards of Duke Ispeth, the hills of the Braddabaggon, and even the mires of Lord Fraddylwicke all seemed desperately far away.

Adrina rubbed painfully blistered feet. "My eyes are open, *truly* open," she whispered to the wind. Opening her eyes meant much more than simply seeing the things around her. It meant looking for and finding understanding in the world around her, looking not only with her eyes but also with her heart, mind and soul, and then finding resolve to action. It meant being a participant instead of an onlooker.

"Adrina!" hissed Emel in her ear, breaking Adrina from her thoughts.

Adrina started, Emel clasped a hand over her mouth. Adrina noticed then that the camp seemed suddenly shrouded in darkness. Beneath the forest canopy no stars were visible. Even the central fire seemed muted by the stark darkness. Then she noted that the logs on the fire were all but fiery ashes. Apparently many hours had passed in what to her had seemed minutes. "Yes?" Adrina finally answered.

Emel squeezed her hand. Just then Adrina noticed the ropes that had been tied around her feet and hands were gone. Before she could speak her thoughts Emel nodded his head as if he were reading them. Her eyes went wide. Adrina tried to speak again. Emel put a silencing finger to her lips.

Valam gripped her shoulder and turned Adrina to face him. He showed her four fingers and then pointing to Emel, he lowered three. With two fingers raised, he pointed to her. Three to Vilmos whose eyes were as wide as saucers. Four, Valam pointed to himself.

He then turned her head to look around the camp. In the distance Adrina saw the immense trunks of the great southern trees whose intertwined boughs formed the clearing they were in. At the far edge of the camp a number of watch fires were set, but they also burned low. Only a handful of guards still stood their watch. Valam pointed out two of them. In the dim light Adrina watched them. One kept slapping both hands to his face, apparently trying to erase sleep from his tired eyes. The other was leaning up against a tree and, to some degree, faced their direction.

A long period of complete silence passed as they waited, for what Adrina wasn't entirely sure. Then without preface, Valam raised a single finger and Emel slipped away. For an instant afterward, Adrina saw Emel's silhouette against light cast by the fading fires and then he disappeared into the unshadowed gloom.

Adrina held her breath as Valam gripped her shoulder. Unexpectedly he embraced her, and for a moment Adrina was smothered in his great embrace, then just as suddenly, he ushered her into the gloom after Emel. Her thoughts swam, Adrina didn't move. Valam gave her a push and suddenly she was racing along the ground on her hands and knees.

Many times, she cast nervous sidelong glances to the center of the camp and to the nearest two guards at the perimeter. Any minute she expected someone to shout an alarm and the camp to burst into frenzied activity. As fear and anxiety sought to overwhelm her, Adrina fought to hold them in check.

She knew she had finally reached the edge of the camp when a trunk of one of the great trees appeared in front of her. The next thing Adrina knew, friendly hands were gripping her waist and pulling her to her feet. She didn't pull away from Emel's embrace. Instead she hugged him fiercely. His warmth was the only reassuring thing she had known for days and now it was even more reassuring.

Silently Emel and Adrina waited. The next face Adrina hoped to see was that of the boy, Vilmos. Slowly over the five days of their captivity, Adrina had come to know Vilmos. To her it seemed a strange darkness lurked behind his eyes and also that his thoughts were ever distant and he was distant. She found this oddly alluring, for in him she saw a bit of herself.

Thinking she saw movement amidst the gloom, Adrina leaned forward. She knew at once the burly figure she saw wasn't Vilmos. Panic entered her mind and momentarily, the urge to flee. She pushed back against Emel's warmth, her body growing tense.

Abruptly Emel grabbed Adrina and roughly pulled her back and down. Huddled against the ground they lay together. Adrina saw a figure outlined against the murky pale of the dying lights in the camp. Soon afterward, a second shadowed form joined the first.

"Erravane?" hissed the first. Adrina held deathly still.

The other responded with, "Yes." From the voice alone, Adrina couldn't tell if the second figure was a man or a woman, though the first she thought a man. Among Prince William's soldiers, only a dozen of the several hundred were women. Although they were few, it seemed that they held high positions. Valam had suggested that perhaps they served as William's personal bodyguards, though he had been honestly unsure of this estimation since several of them came and went seemingly of their own leisure.

A long period of silence followed. Adrina couldn't see what transpired, though she knew both figures still stood only a few feet away. Then with a sudden heave, both were on the ground and for a time they rolled around in the leaves. Afterward, again silence. Adrina knew only that Emel's presence beside her was a powerful comfort.

Suddenly Adrina heard muffled laughter and again the whispered voices.

"Quit, you'll alert the camp," hissed the first.

"Not likely."

"What do you mean?" the first sounded at the end of his patience. "Why are you here, Erravane?"

Behind her Adrina heard Emel's barely audible gasp. He had recognized the first voice at nearly the same time as she.

"One question at a time my sweet." Adrina was sure now, the second *was* a woman. Her name was Erravane, and the first *was* Prince William. "I have found what you sought."

"And the traitor?"

"Oh yes, a present for you." Erravane rose to her knees, then dumped something onto the ground. She cackled madly, then said, "His head."

William jumped to his feet. "I trust the other is alive?"

"The southern encampments have proceeded north as planned. The bulk of your army is spread out through the forest. Your commanders will join you here, tomorrow."

"What of King Jarom's army?... Wait a minute, what of the—"

Erravane cut William off, "You are ever impatient. She is well. I believe the deceased—" Erravane kicked the head and it rolled past Adrina. Only Emel's firm and comforting grip around her waist kept Adrina from screaming. "—Was tricked. Though I am not sure how. These creatures have strange powers."

"Then you were right?"

Erravane cooed. "Yes, my sweet."

"Where is she?"

"I was afraid you'd prefer her to me. And what of this princess? I've heard tell she is quite striking."

William said, "She is a child."

"She is the enemy. Have you so soon forgotten the empty stare in your father's eyes?"

"I never will." William began to move back to the camp. "No games this time, Erravane, no games... Dawn is only a few hours away. I trust your pets will harry my men no longer?"

"My dear William, they take only what they need. The disappearance of one or two in the night is of little consequence. Would you rather have them turn on me?"

For the first time as he turned back to Erravane, Adrina saw Prince William's face clearly outlined in the pale light. "Perhaps it would not be such a—"

Erravane put a finger to William's lips. "You still need me, William of Sever. Do not say a thing you will later regret." With that, Prince William strode away, and soon afterward, Erravane. Both went in separate directions.

Emel helped Adrina to her feet. Finally she took a deep releasing breath. Before she had been nearly afraid to breathe and had done so only sporadically. Erravane and William had been so close.

Adrina heard movement in the leaves behind her. She turned, sighed, knowing at once it was Valam.

"I circled around," Valam explained. "The boy?"

Adrina shrugged.

Emel who had been staring intently toward the camp said, "There, on the far side, do you see?"

Adrina and Valam turned and stared. On the opposite side of the camp, reflected in the light of the dying embers of a perimeter fire, was a mostly shadowed face. Undoubtedly, it belonged to Vilmos.

"Were you listening?" Emel asked. Valam nodded and Emel continued. "The time to make our escape is now or never."

"No," Adrina hissed angrily. "Vilmos is one of us."

Valam took Adrina's hand. "Alas, there is little we can do now. We would waste precious time if we tried to circle the camp. We cannot. There is too much at stake. You heard as well as I, the forest is full of William's men... Perhaps it is for the best. He should fare well and, should his instincts continue to lead him south, he will find safety quickly.

"On the other hand, we will not be so fortunate. Our duty takes us north. We will have the whole of an army at our heels until we either reach Quashan' or die trying." Valam paused, took a deep breath, then added, "Quickly now..."

***

Vilmos watched his companions turn away and disappear into the gloom. Disbelief and dread flooded his thoughts. He had no idea how he had ended up on the opposite side of the camp, but *the* one thing he was sure of now was that he was on his own.

Anger quickly replaced disbelief and dread. Valam, Emel and Adrina had deserted him. Vilmos knew dawn was near and that he must act or surely he would be recaptured, but where would he run to? If he made a wide circle around the camp and tried to follow the others, could he find their trail? But, did he want to find their trail? After all, they had forsaken him.

Vilmos caught movement out of the corner of his eye. He didn't wait to find out what it was he saw, he ran away fast as he could. Unsure which direction to flee in, he ran aimlessly. His fear drove him on and only his instinct and the flora of the forest controlled his direction.

Then as dawn lifted darkness from the forest leaving only shadows, Vilmos stopped running. Tired, hungry and feeling desperately alone, he slumped onto a moss-covered stump. He stared up through a break in the canopy where a ray of soft white light radiated down to the forest floor.

Vilmos moved to the spot bathed by the warm ray, and found a sense of security in it. He thought about Prince Valam, Princess Adrina, and Emel then. During his run he had come to terms with what had happened. He was no longer angry or mad at them for leaving him. He understood now that they had done what they had to do. He heard the prince's words in his ears, "... Use that chance, Vilmos, use it for all it's worth. Go back to Tabborrath Village and leave the affairs of men to men."

Suddenly Vilmos was homesick. It seemed forever since he had joined Xith and left Tabborrath Village. He lay back, crossed his arms behind his head and closed tired eyes. For a time he forgot about the dangers. He forgot that he was lost and alone in Vangar Forest. He knew only that images of home played before his closed lids.

***

With Emel leading the way and Valam pulling her, Adrina raced faster and faster. At first she gave her sore and blistered feet little thought. She flitted along, and kept pace just behind Emel.

Soon Valam was pulling her more than she moved under her own power. Soon afterward, Adrina was limping. Seemingly without thought or hesitation, Valam picked Adrina up and with her cast her over his shoulder, continued.

For a time, all was well. Then in between her brother's gasps as he heavily sucked at the air, Adrina heard shouts from far off.

Valam and Emel apparently heard them too and panic urged them to new speeds.

They raced on and on, the voices grew near intermittently and then again distant. Dawn was at hand, and gloom began to lift from the forest.

"Their trackers are worse… than those of… South Province," Emel said between breaths, "but still, what I wouldn't give for Ebony about now… He'd get the three of us… out of this accursed forest… in no time."

Valam started to laugh or so it appeared, then suddenly he doubled over, and dropped Adrina.

"It is a good time to rest," Emel said, as he slumped to the ground.

Adrina forced herself to stand on tender feet. "Are they far behind?"

"We'll know soon enough," Emel said. "Do you think you can continue on your own?"

"If you two can, I must…" Adrina was about to let her words trail off, then she decided to voice her thoughts. "Do you really think Vilmos escaped too?"

Valam stood, then turned and stared in the direction they had just come from. "Let us hope so."

Adrina's face lit with worry and showed her fears to the contrary. Emel took her hand and said, "I think he did, but now is not the time to dwell on things we cannot change."

Shortly afterward the three began running again. Adrina moved as swift as she could. Valam and Emel did their best to help her keep up with them. Shouts came from off to their left now and their feet lead them right. Abruptly they stumbled into a clearing. Adrina tripped over a bound and gagged figure that was lying in the grass on the edge of the clearing.

Run, said a faint voice in their minds. *Forget me. I am lost. It is a trap.*

Emel grabbed one of Adrina's hands, Valam the other. They started to race away. A circle of dark shapes with glowing eyes emerged from hiding. A voice asked, "Where are our guests going?"

Adrina recognized the voice of the speaker. "Erravane?"

Deftly the speaker stepped forward, grabbed Adrina's chin in her hand and turned her face to the pale light. "You *are* a pretty one."

Valam grabbed Erravane's arm and twisted it back as hard as he could, which brought the woman to her knees. Pain was met with sick laughter.

"Do you mock me?" Valam screamed as he twisted the arm back still further, fully expecting to hear the snap of breaking bones.

The arm began to bend and change in Valam's hand, growing thicker and shorter. Valam let go and pulled Adrina back, confusion and perhaps bewilderment showed on his face.

"If you move again," Erravane said, her voice changed as her body changed, "they will kill you."

"Close your eyes, Adrina. This is no thing for you to see," Valam shouted. "Of all the beasts of hell…"

But Adrina couldn't close her eyes, she felt compelled to watch the metamorphosis. Erravane's eyes were glowing now and fangs filled her mouth, a mouth that was twisting and contorting, growing wider and longer as Adrina look on in fascinated horror.

Valam stepped in front of Adrina protectively. "If I had my sword," Valam said, "I would run you through and send you back to the icy pits you ascended from."

Erravane snapped her head and locked powerful, wolflike jaws around Valam's hand. Screaming in agony, Valam dropped to his knees. Adrina closed her eyes and squeezed them together as tight as she could. She waited for the screaming to stop and when it did, she felt compelled to open her eyes. She was just as surprised as Valam obviously was to find he still had a hand.

Erravane, clearly no longer human, spoke with an otherworldly voice. "I said, 'no movement.'" Erravane licked her front paw.

Valam spoke again, but took care not to move. "What do you hope to gain from this? Prince William will kill the lot of you as soon as he has no need for you?"

"Ah, but I ensure that he continues to need me until I have all that I want for. And, now I have you. His precious little bargaining pieces. He will grovel on his knees to get you back."

Chapter Twenty Five: Conquest

The first shafts of golden light from the new day were just breaking the horizon far to the east. A wet spray blew in off the sea, and Keeper Martin shivered. He had awoken early and only he and the mid-watchmen greeted the new day.

A troubled dream had disturbed his few hours of precious sleep. Keeper Q'yer's response to his earlier dream message had been grimmer than he ever imagined it could be. Quashan' was under siege. How five hundred defenders held the city was beyond his imagining. But there had been more distressful tidings in the dream, and this, Martin didn't even want to think about.

The sound of footsteps caused Martin to turn. He eyed Captain Adylton who looked as frazzled as he felt. "You did not sleep well this night?"

"I did not sleep," answered the captain as he stared out across the dark waters.

Martin asked pointedly, "How many days to Quashan' without the Foot?"

Captain Adylton raised an eyebrow. "Two days of hard riding, and only if we can get enough fresh horses in Alderan City. Otherwise, three at best."

"How long would it take for the Foot to catch up?"

"Foot soldiers move like sand caught in those waves," Adylton said, eyeing the frothy surf breaking against the rocks. "Depending on the weather, I'd say seven days."

"At best?"

"Six, maybe five. They'd arrive spent and—" Captain Adylton broke off, apparently he heard the footsteps as Martin did. Both men turned to see who was approaching.

"Mid-watchman," Keeper Martin said. "He's been hawking me since I stepped out here."

Captain Adylton regarded the watchman, then tossed Martin a wink. "My man... My men," he said, waving his hand in a sweeping gesture around the camp.

"And Trendmore's?"

"I gave his watchmen liberty. Told them to enjoy the Free Cities."

Keeper Martin tightened his cloak about him. "Then you've gone ahead. Are you ready?"

"Nearly so. It should all go smoothly. Better than half of his men are on liberty and he isn't the wiser... Have you received word from Alderan or has something happened in Quashan'?"

"You, Captain Adylton, are very perceptive." Martin explained about the dream message and the situation in Quashan'. Adylton grimaced. "So you see," Keeper Martin concluded, "there is precious little time to waste."

"What of Alderan? You didn't say. Did the ship arrive safely?"

Keeper Martin fixed eyes filled with distress on the captain. "Alderan is no more."

"Surely you don't mean—" Adylton began. Martin nodded solemnly. "—And, Prince Valam?"

Martin said nothing.

Martin was sure Captain Adylton was going to collapse. The captain's knees bowed and his face became ashen. Martin grabbed the captain's shoulders to steady him.

Captain Adylton turned to face the salty spray of the breaking waves. He was silent for a long time. Yet, it was clear he was slowly recovering his wits as anger and finally resolve seemed to replace disbelief. "What of the sea?" Captain Adytlon asked. "We could send the foot soldiers by ship down the coast... Better still, up River Trollbridge. In autumn the rivers run high. No deep-hulled ships, but still, with the right winds and heavy oars, they could land within a day's march of Quashan'."

An incomplete smile eased Martin's downtrodden expression. "You, my friend, have never bargained with free traders. It'll take a king's ransom to pay for passage... Still, the plan is not without merit."

***

"Let me untie her. You must untie her," pleaded Adrina, "she is in obvious pain."

Do not worry unnecessarily, whispered the pleasant feminine voice in Adrina's mind. *I will journey to Great-Father, but it will not be at the hand of the likes of this.*

"Enough," snapped Erravane. "My patience is at an end. You *will* now tell me where the boy is."

The first rays of a new day pierced the thick canopy overhead, casting odd shadows about the forest floor. Erravane turned toward the light. Suddenly and swiftly, Valam lunged at Erravane, but just as swiftly, one of the Erravane's beasts leapt upon him and knocked him to the ground. Afterward, it stood defiantly upon Valam's chest, staring down at him, a deep rumbling growl escaping its throat. Adrina shuddered and edged closer to Emel.

"My pets are hungry—" Erravane reverted to human form as she spoke, her voice losing its otherworldly hue. "Do they feast on a boy or one of you? The decision is yours, but do not take too long to decide." There was anger on her face, mirrored in her eyes. She walked in a wide circle around Valam, staring down at him.

"Which will talk?" Erravane said, pointing her finger at each of the three in turn.

No one responded.

"Which will die?"

When no answer was forthcoming, Erravane said, "If you do not choose, then I will choose." With a lightning fast snap of her wrists, Erravane wrapped her hands around Adrina's throat. "I choose the princess."

Adrina recoiled, the hands tensed around her throat until it seemed she could not breathe. Terrified, Adrina stared wildly at Erravane. Beside her Valam and Emel attempted to gain to their feet, but one of the Wolmerrelle had likewise leapt upon Emel.

"Why do you care so about a boy?" Adrina asked, her words coming out through a strained gasp. "Vilmos is long gone."

"His *name*," Erravane said sinisterly. "Thank you. Now, where did he go?"

"Home for all we know."

Erravane tightened her grip on Adrina's throat. Her long, sharp fingernails pierced the skin and drew blood. "That is not the answer I want. I tire of this, and I too hunger for a feast."

Straining ineffectively to raise his chest under the weight of the Wolmerrelle, Emel craned his head upward. "Let Adrina go! I will die willingly in her stead."

Erravane started to laugh, a deep demented cackle. "So noble, so very noble. What about you Prince of the North? Would you die for her too?"

Valam said, "Let them both go and I will do whatever it is you ask."

"Is that a promise?"

"Stop!" shouted a voice vaguely familiar to Adrina. "You do not know what it is you do. Make no promises to her kind." Xith emerged from the shadows and stood with his hands extended before Erravane.

"Watcher," Erravane said, no surprise in her voice. "Age takes your stealth. You clomp around like a Man. I wondered what it would take to make you reveal yourself, and now I know."

"This is <*no game.*> What is occurring is of <*no concern*> to you. " Xith's eyes glowed as he regarded Adrina momentarily. Adrina saw strange emotions on his face and there was a quality in his voice that escaped her ears. "<*Return to Ril Akh Arr and Under-Earth,*> Erravane."

Erravane hissed, then attacked Xith. She knocked him down and stood over him. Xith made no move to defend himself.

"Attempt your guile of Voice on me again," Erravane said, "and I will kill you."

"Then kill me, Erravane, I grow weary."

Erravane hissed again and released Xith's throat. "You sicken me. All of you sicken me. So willing to die. So willing to sacrifice. Is the will to survive in any of you?"

Erravane cocked her head as if listening to the wind. "You are too late Watcher. The hunt is joined. Oh, they are joyous!"

"Vilmos did not kill Rake. It was I who took his head."

Erravane laughed again, the same sickly cackle. "I know, which is why I will enjoy their feast all the more."

"Return to your forests. Nothing that happens here concerns your kind. You tamper with forces you do not understand."

"I will leave in good time, once I have what I came for."

"And what is that?" Xith asked.

Adrina shouted, "Prince William!"

Xith jumped to his feet. "Is that it, Erravane?... Your appetite has changed."

"I already have his child in my womb."

Xith laughed. "If you had so precious a cargo you would have returned to Ril Akh Arr… A half-breed child of royal blood no less…" Xith added the Voice at the last, "<*Let Vilmos go.*> <*You do not need him.*>"

Erravane pounced on Xith and slashed his face with her fingernails. "I warned you, Watcher. I *will* kill the boy now."

As if stung, Xith reeled away from Erravane. "And if he kills your pets, what then? What will you do then?"

"He will not."

"What if? What then? Would you no longer meddle in affairs that do not concern you?"

Erravane was obviously irritated at the course of the conversation. "Yes," she shot back at Xith.

"Is that a promise?"

"And if the boy dies, what then?"

Xith said simply, "I will surrender to your will."

"I would have you surrender regardless."

"You are far from our realm, further still from the forest temple of Arr. Attempt a test of wills here and you will lose." Erravane slashed Xith across the face again. Xith held his ground. "If Vilmos survives, you will return to Under-Earth. If he dies, I will do as you bid. I would even help you birth the child if that is your wish."

Erravane's eyes widened greedily. "You would birth an abomination?"

Xith slowly nodded.

Erravane grinned. "Your faith in a human child will be your undoing."

***

Quite sure what had awoken him, Vilmos stirred. He had been dreaming of Tabborrath Village but thoughts of dreams all spun away. His eyes were wide, his mind in shock. From not far off came another long wailing cry, joined by more, which were still distant. Vilmos had sudden flashbacks to another time in Vangar Forest. He knew with certainty the Wolmerrelle hunted him.

He cast aside the prince's overtunic. The oversized garment had kept him warm during these past dreary days and chilly nights. Now he needed speed and not warmth.

Then as he started to flee, he caught a bit of an old memory. Perhaps he could trick the Wolmerrelle just as he knew he could the hounds of Tabborrath's huntmaster. Without delay, Vilmos retrieved the tunic. He dragged it along the ground, then scrambled up into a nearby tree and left the tunic there.

Then Vilmos ran. He had no idea where he ran to, only that he ran away from the howls. The boughs of trees passed as dark blurs around him and as he ran, Vilmos imagined that Xith was beside him and that the shaman urged him to race faster and faster.

They lead us, whispered an old voice in his mind. Vilmos nodded in understanding. He veered right instead of left where the unnerving calls sought to lead him.

His race became a race of desperation. He ran to escape, only to escape. On and on he raced. He used his hands to ward off branches that seemed to reach out to grab him as he passed. He mounted a rise and started down its backside. There, he found his second wind. The path muddied at the bottom of the rise. He came to a stream, kneeled briefly to drink of its cool waters, then hurried on. The calls were never far off.

Completely winded, Vilmos stopped. Clutching his chest, panting for air, he hunched over. His face, cold despite the perspiration that dripped from his brow, stung where branches had caught his cheeks. He fought to get his breathing under control and bit back the pain of sore muscles.

Gradually the splotches before his eyes cleared and he brought his breathing under control. He straightened up and looked around, noticing then that the forest seemed suddenly too quiet. His face blank and expressionless, Vilmos panned his eyes slowly from left to right.

Out of the corner of his eye, he caught movement and perhaps, a flash of white. Suddenly, the voice of the past was in his mind again, *From this lesson stems the basis of your magical shield, the shield that will protect and keep you in dangerous times…*

Vilmos conjured the magical shield now, just as he had then. Out of the corner of his eye, he watched a great black blur sweep toward him. A yelp followed as the creature struck the invisible barrier. Still its momentum carried Vilmos to the ground with it.

Disoriented, Vilmos shook his head and inhaled. The force of the blow had knocked the wind out of him. For an instant, it was as if Vilmos didn't think at all. All his bewildered thoughts stopped, the magical shield fell away, and then the beast howled and struck again.

Vilmos struck back with his fists. He clubbed the side of one of the Wolmerrelle's two heads. The creature wheeled back. Vilmos crab crawled backwards as fast as he could. Only his back slamming against the trunk of a tree stopped his crazed retreat. Then without Vilmos even realizing what he was doing, a trace of blue-white light danced across his fingertips. The bolt raced outward, toward the Wolmerrelle and caught the beast full in the torso. Howling madly, it staggered backward.

Vilmos pressed his back against the tree trunk, and using his knees, inched up to a standing position. Still he was terrified and his every thought screamed out to him, Escape! Again magic raced from his hands and struck the howling Wolmerrelle. The smell of singed fur and flesh stagnated the air. The creature charged, but managed only a single stride before collapsing.

For the longest time Vilmos didn't move. He sat wide-eyed, his thoughts still racing, still screaming, Run! Escape! Get away! But the Wolmerrelle was no longer moving.

Cautiously, Vilmos crept forward. He reached out with his foot and nudged the beast. He jumped back as it convulsed. Then, it moved no more.

Vilmos was elated, tired from his flight and drained from the brief fight. He collapsed to his haunches, but was given little time to recover. A glimmer of movement out of the corner of his vision caught his eye. Suddenly he knew more of the creatures lurked just beyond his view in the shadows. He raised the magical shield. Again it saved him. Only this time the great beast did not carry Vilmos to the ground with it, and this time, he maintained the shield.

They came at him then, one by one in a great wave. Vilmos struggled to maintain the shield and keep his feet. Magic surged wildly through him as he drew in more and more energy. Consumed by it, Vilmos turned wild eyes on the five Wolmerrelle that circled him, waiting to pounce.

Again Vilmos' thoughts were propelled to the past. In his mind as he poised for the attack and turned in a tight circle, it was the great black bear that he saw. Reared up on its hind legs, it towered over him, a mound of black fur and dark eyes.

Vilmos was no longer gripped by terror as he stared up at it. The voice in his mind no longer screamed, RUN! It was chastising him. *Control! Always stay in control*, it said.

Vilmos fought to gain control of the rampant energies within him. Perhaps sensing a moment of weakness, the Wolmerrelle charged.

Vilmos' shield held them at bay and the charge served to focus his thoughts. Suddenly he realized something. Xith had traveled through Vangar Forest to reach the clearing beyond his village. He had all but admitted it. He had arrived on horseback and no horse could have descended into the valley from anywhere within many miles of that clearing. And that night when Midori had left the camp, she had taken the horse with her, for the animal hadn't been there the next morning.

Vilmos' own voice rang in his ears, *You weren't expecting hunters and trackers were you. Who were you expecting shaman?*

There is no need to trouble over the could have beens, returned Xith's voice, and Vilmos was now sure that the great black bear hadn't mauled and killed the girl from Olex Village. The bear hadn't attacked him during that fateful encounter and it probably wouldn't have. Evident anger in his eyes and on his face, Vilmos turned to face the first of the great two-headed beasts.

Do what you must… rang Xith's voice in his ears.

The urge to let the magic flow unchecked through him was suddenly strong. Vilmos fought to control it and instead channeled that strength carefully to his hands. Bolts of blue-white lightening sprang forth and struck one of the beasts. The creature died.

Vilmos' magical shield fell as the remaining four attacked and overwhelmed him. White-hot fire shot through his right leg as a pair of powerful jaws clamped down on it. Vilmos let out a scream that shook the trees and rang through the forest.

Pain flooded his thoughts, panic took over. Wildly Vilmos lashed out again and again, wielding his magic, punching, even kicking when necessary to fend off the relentless beasts.

Again, he found himself with his back to the trunk of one of the great trees of the forest. The last of the great beasts stared him down. Vilmos could barely stand now, and only the tree at his back kept him on his feet. Too weary to focus, too weary to find his center, he knew only that the magic was gone now, gone with his rage.

Vilmos didn't think it odd that this beast had only one head, though he did take note of it. This Wolmerrelle was smaller than the others, still somehow more powerful. Its eyes, glowing even in the light of the new day, regarded him in an almost human way. Though badly wounded, it dragged its hind legs while howling a tormented wail up at the heavens and came at him.

In an attempt to flee, Vilmos stumbled and fell. The injured leg that had held him while his fervor raged, collapsed under his weight. Vilmos' face slapped the hard earth first, his hands were too slow to brace against the fall. With his face pressed against wet earth, muddied with blood surely his own as well as the fallen beasts, Vilmos lay where he fell, too drained to move.

A shadow blocked out the daylight filtering in through the forest canopy. Vilmos rolled his eyes up to see the Wolmerrelle standing over him. He shielded his face with his arms as it set upon him. The creature latched onto the arm and shook its head wildly.

Vilmos groped frantically with his free hand and kicked at the beast's head with his one good leg. His hand found only leaves and dirt, but there was something on the ground just outside his reach. He could feel the edge of it. *Shape your power, use it to your advantage! Concentrate, control, focus!* screamed the voice in his mind. Vilmos squeezed his eyes tight, fighting the pain, fighting to concentrate.

He focused on the object just out of his reach. It was the clubbed end of broken branch, he could feel it now vibrating on the ground. It wanted to inch forward into his grasp. Then suddenly it was in his hand and Vilmos began bludgeoning the beast.

The weakened Wolmerrelle howled and hissed. Repeatedly, it raked Vilmos' chest with its forepaws. For an instant as he beat with all his might on the creature's head, Vilmos swore he saw a human face—his weary mind and body were surely playing tricks on him. He mustered the strength to deliver a last desperate blow and then dealt it, putting every bit of himself into the blow. The crunching sound of bone and wood followed. The branch broke. The beast collapsed and just as suddenly as the attack had come it was over.

Blood covered Vilmos' face. His hands. His arms. He knew not whether it was his own. He didn't care. He had won.

"I did it," Vilmos whispered to the voice in his mind. *You performed excellently,* the voice whispered back. Vilmos managed a smile. Then weak from blood loss and battle, he collapsed.

***

"If you strike," Xith said, regarding the clawed hand raised to his throat, "know that our arrangement is void. In addition, if you do not kill me with that single blow, know that I *will* kill you. Know also that the boy's powers pale in comparison to my own and that my memory is as long as time itself. One day I *will* return to Under-Earth. It is in your hands whether I make my life's last work the siege of Ril Akh Arr or other matters..."

Deftly Erravane swept back her hand. "This is far from over." She said it evilly. She was hiding something and apparently Xith knew it.

"If you have designs on Prince William, think again. I need him alive."

"So do I," hissed Erravane.

"It is over, Erravane!" Xith grabbed Erravane's throat with a mystical force that Adrina couldn't see but knew was there. Erravane's beasts raced to her aid but crashed against an invisible barrier. Viciously they attacked the unseen wall but couldn't break through.

"Do not dismiss me," hissed Erravane despite the pressure of the phantom's grasp on her throat. A dozen more Wolmerrelle emerged from the shadows and suddenly the woods were full of long wailing cries. "You kill me and you will never leave the forest alive."

Xith pointed his finger at one of Erravane's beasts. A line of fire raced from his hand and engulfed it.

Adrina gasped. She realized the source of Xith's mysterious powers. "Forbidden magic," she whispered.

Erravane screamed a tortured wail that matched the dying Wolmerrelle's. Her face twisted and contorted as she sought to change shapes, but no matter what she did, she couldn't break free of the phantom's grasp.

A figure emerged from the shadows. Deep blue eyes looked in Adrina's direction momentarily, then suddenly the figure was moving with inhuman speed among the pack of Wolmerrelle. "Seth," whispered Adrina. The still figure whose head Adrina held answered, *Yes*, and there was evident relief in the tone.

Xith matched Seth's blows one for one with a stinging magical flame. One by one the Wolmerrelle fell. Eyes bulging, Erravane clawed at the air and before Emel and Prince Valam could gain their feet and join the fray, she cried out, "Enough, enough. Stop!"

Mid-blow Seth stopped, drew up to his full height and cast a sidelong glance at Erravane. The remaining Wolmerrelle made no move to attack him. Dumbfounded, Emel and Valam looked to Xith.

"It is over," Xith said. "If *you* leave here alive, Erravane, it will be up to you… Cease struggling, the grip will be relaxed accordingly." Erravane hissed but ceased to struggle against the unseen phantom. Xith turned to Adrina then, "Ease your fears Princess, those creatures cannot break through."

Xith then turned to Seth. "You are bleeding."

It is only a scratch.

"As superficial as that single scratch may seem, it could kill you if not cleaned properly. Untreated, it will fester like nothing you've ever seen." He paused, then turned back to Adrina, "I must apologize for waiting so long, but I had to be sure—"

"What of our deal?" interrupted Erravane, "You promised I'd go free."

"I made no such promise, though you did promise to return to Ril Akh Arr and meddle no longer in affairs that do not concern you or your kind."

Adrina broke her trancelike gaze on Xith. She looked once more to pitiful Erravane, then beckoned to Seth. "Sit beside me," she said, "let me clean your wound."

Xith smiled fondly at Adrina, as if remembering a thing from the past. Then he turned back to Erravane who had begun to howl.

"Let me go," Erravane hissed, "you have what you wanted."

Xith forced the phantom's grip. "Answer this question with care, your life depends on it. When will William meet King Jarom?"

"I do not know... You must let me go."

"She lies," Emel said. "Adrina and I overheard her speaking to Prince William. His commanders will join him at his camp tomorrow."

Erravane cringed and cowered away from Xith's stare. She began babbling. "His army is ready to march. The encampments are spread out all along the northern edge of the forest. William awaits the arrival of King Jarom's army before he strikes. King Jarom's advanced guard has already struck against Quashan', they lay siege to the city days ago."

"Where is Jarom's army now?" questioned Xith. "Where is King Jarom?"

"Quashan', but the bulk of his army has just entered the southern edge of the Vangar. Even with the paths cut by William's path forgers, days will pass before they arrive."

The unseen hand lifted Erravane off her feet. Xith asked, "William doesn't know this?"

"He knows only what I see fit to tell him."

Momentarily, Adrina saw surprise or perhaps glee cross Xith's face. Xith said, "The games end, Erravane. I would sooner cut out your tongue than listen to you speak. If you lie about King Jarom, I will kill you now and be done with it."

"He is an overzealous man who thinks he cannot lose. My beasts took great pleasure in harrying his soldiers... They are truly afraid of these forests now."

Xith seemed pleased with the answer. "You are free to go Erravane. Know that I make no empty promises. If ever I see you again, I will kill you, and more... Return to Under-Earth for it is there that you belong, and not here."

The expression in Erravane's eyes as the unseen hand released her, matched that which had been in Xith's eyes moments earlier. Adrina and the others watched as Erravane and her beasts slipped away into the shadows. As Adrina had finished cleaning his wound, Seth now saw to Galan's needs. He held a water bag to Galan's lips and she drank heavily.

Emel spoke first, voicing the thoughts also on Adrina's mind. "Do you really believe Erravane will do as you asked? I don't trust her."

Neither do I, sent Seth.

"Though eventually she will keep her promise, Erravane is hardly one to be taken at her word. She is strong willed and wants what it is she came for, this I am counting on." Xith turned to Galan and Seth, "Can she walk unaided?"

Alas no, Brother Galan is weak from thirst and hunger...

Valam who had been quietly regarding Galan's lithe figure, said, "I will carry her." Adrina had never seen such a look in her brother's eyes. Valam was smitten by Galan's angelic beauty or so it appeared.

"Good, good," Xith said. "We have little more than this day and the next to set matters straight... But first, we must find Vilmos."

Adrina turned to Xith. "I must ask," she said. "Where have you been these many past days? Where is Father Jacob?"

"Know that this way matters have turned out better than they otherwise would have. I had very important matters to attend to and, I am truly sorry if you feel that I abandoned you when you needed me the most."

"What of Father Jacob?"

"Jacob is well, but surely irritated," was all Xith said.

Chapter Twenty Six: Full Circle

"Well met, Keeper Q'yer. What brings you to the walls?" asked Sergeant Danyel'.

"A dream," responded the keeper, his voice distant, his eyes searched the horizon.

Sergeant Danyel' turned about on his heel and looked out at the campfires that dotted the landscape like a swarm of lightning bugs. "At dawn they will come again. They attack alternately from the south, east and west, leaving only the north wall alone. They toy with us and keep us occupied though I know not why. Perhaps Great-Father truly smiles upon us, for if they ever once attacked in full force, we would be swept away."

Danyel's voice became soft. "What I would not give for a spy among them."

Keeper Q'yer seemed to only half listen to Danyel' as he stared, then as he turned away he asked, "What of Chancellor Van'te?"

"He sleeps awaiting the attack. I beg you not to disturb him if it is your plan. It is the first he's slept in days. We need his direction tomorrow."

"I bring good news, I think he would approve."

Danyel' regarded the keeper's troubled eyes. "You don't look like a man bearing good news."

"With the good there is always the bad. Will I find the chancellor in his quarters?"

"No, he has taken up residence elsewhere. I will take you to him if I must."

"You must, this is important, a dream message from Keeper Martin."

***

Adrina drove her mount still faster. She tried to shake images of the boy from her mind. They had found Vilmos lying on ground saturated with blood some hours after Erravane had disappeared into the forest shadows. Adrina was certain that death had found him by now and tried to convince herself that perhaps Vilmos had found peace.

She cast the thoughts away and whipped at the reins of her mount. She glanced to Emel and Valam who rode in tight formation on either side of her. She couldn't help noting the defiant pride in Emel's eyes as he stroked his Ebony. How Xith had safeguarded and kept their horses after Alderan was beyond her.

To Adrina, it was clear Emel was both excited and troubled. The reunion between master and mount had been a sweet one and left Adrina a bit envious. Emel had not hid his joy at the sight of his beloved steed.

It was now well into the afternoon. The three had left the southern forests in early morning. Slipping through William's lines had been easier than Adrina imagined it would be. One thing was clear, the soldiers weren't expecting anyone to pass through their ranks. Their camps had no guards posted forward or rear.

An enemy army, worse, an enemy army seemingly without cares, so close to Kingdom soil, had outraged them all. Valam, seemingly the most. More than once Adrina had watched him fight back the urge to charge into one of the sleepy camps and slaughter the unwary louts—"Louts" being Valam's word for them.

As they neared the top of a small rise, Valam signaled a halt. Adrina reined in her mount and dismounted. "Dusk is still a few hours away," she said. "Why do we stop?"

Valam, clearly deep in thought and already preparing to rub down his mount's tired legs, didn't seem to hear Adrina's question.

Emel said, "We can't afford a lame mount now, Adrina, despite our urge to race on. I'll rub down Ebony and if you'll walk him after, I'll do your mount."

"I'll rub down my own horse. Show me what I must do."

"You should rest. His Highness may wish to press on through the night and we will surely end up walking at some point."

"Do you speak for my brother now?"

Emel cast her a glum stare then turned back to Ebony. He removed Ebony's saddle and walked him for a time, then began using a comb from his saddlebags. Imitating his actions, Adrina did her best to rub down her steed. Never had she imagined that rubbing down an animal could be so tiring.

Afterward she found she had to rinse the stink of animal sweat from her hands. Exhausted, Adrina sat cross-legged and unladylike upon the ground. Days of captivity and hardship had nearly numbed her awareness to proper mannerisms, and it was only absently that she felt the moisture in the tall grasses.

As a voice from the past flashed through her mind, Adrina looked to Valam who was stretched out on the ground and staring up at the darkening sky. She knew though he looked relaxed, he was brooding. "I miss you, Lady Isador," Adrina whispered to the fleeting voice in her mind, "perhaps you were right, wintering with Rudden Klaiveson wouldn't have been so bad a thing."

Adrina found Emel's eyes upon her. "I didn't mean to snap at you."

"I know."

"Is there really hope in this race? I mean, Quashan' is east, we ride north and we haven't even crossed the river—"

"His Highness knows what he is doing. There is a ford nearby, we will cross it and then follow the far branch of the river back to the south and east."

"What did he and Xith talk about? They spoke at length. Valam said nothing and we've been riding all day. Neither of you have said anything, what am I supposed to think?"

Suddenly Adrina noticed Valam was on his feet. Valam said, "You yourself saw William's army in the forest. You know the entirety of the second most powerful army in all the lands marches north and that Quashan' is under siege. What is there to say?"

Adrina cast imploring eyes in Valam's direction.

"This is no place for you, Adrina. Why father ever let you leave Imtal when he was aware of the troubles here, I'll never understand. And why Keeper Martin and Father Jacob let you continue the journey when they knew there was danger is a matter I intend to take up—"

Emel put his hand on Valam's shoulder. Valam regarded it but still continued, "These are things that must be said, things I could not find heart to say before. But now that we are clear of danger for a time, I must speak my mind."

"No one is to blame but me, Valam. You know I get what I want—it has always been that way. If you're going to point the finger at anyone, point it at me."

"There will be time for blame and arguments later," Emel said, "with luck we will be upon the road to Quashan' in the morning."

A deep worry was written on Valam's face as he turned away from Adrina and said to Emel, "No, we must be upon our way to Quashan' come morning."

***

"You want me to what?" screamed the galley's captain above the sound of pace keeper's drums.

"I want you to continue up river," said Keeper Martin.

"Captain Adylton, you claim to be a fisher's son, bring some sense to your companion."

Captain Adylton had been watching the rise and fall of the sweeps as they stroked the water and it took him a moment to respond. "If any of your ships is damaged, we'll pay you double its worth in gold from the King's treasury."

"Night is nigh at hand."

"Triple," said Adylton.

The ship captain still seemed hesitant.

Captain Adylton said, "Plus a year's wages for lost revenues during rebuilding."

"Lanterns!" shouted the galley captain, "Bow, starboard, port. Close watch! Drummer, mid beat! Relay the orders to the rest of the fleet!"

Keeper Martin nodded approval. He and Captain Adylton moved away from the helm so their voices wouldn't be within earshot of the galley's captain. With the noise of the drums, the grunts of the rowers and the splash of the sweeps, they didn't have to go far.

Keeper Martin said, "You learn the ways of free traders quickly."

"I didn't say I'd never bargained with free traders before my friend, what I said was 'I disliked free traders.' Yet, I suppose there are worse ills in the world than a hunger for gold."

"Well said, but how much is it going to cost to convince him to continue when one of his precious ships really hits bottom?"

Captain Adylton frowned. "Do you believe the river still so shallow, even with the recent rains?"

"If the Trollbridge was safely traversable at any time during the year, an enterprising captain, perhaps even our ship captain, would've been sailing it long ago, and there would be ports up and down—"

"—I get the point," Captain Adylton said, shifting his stance as the boat swayed. "We will pray then that none of his ships run aground." Captain Adylton tried to change the topic of the conversation. "Did this Keeper Q'yer of yours receive your message yet?"

"The message entered Keeper Q'yer's dreams as I sent it, that is the way of the message. What I don't know is if he understood it, though we will surely find out soon enough."

***

Father Jacob eyed the grizzled commander who stood beside him. Reflecting the light of the new day, his brown eyes shone with an uncanny luster. There was naked rage on his face; he was gritting his teeth and his hand on Jacob's shoulder was trying to crush bone. Then his tone grim, Captain Mikhal said, "A costly attack at dawn it will be, but we must strike now. I cannot bare the sight of this."

Jacob peered out from his hiding place amidst the trees. From his vantage point, he saw most of Quashan' and the amassed army. The emblems on the enemy banners at this distance were hardly identifiable, though the colors were. They were not green and gold, but blue and black. The colors of King Jarom and the Kingdom of Vostok. Jacob bowed his head wearily, but didn't respond.

The two stood there for a time, staring down at the army poised to strike the city as they obviously had in previous days. Quashan's walls were battered. The east wall, which they had the best view of, had large sections missing from its upper bulwarks. Thin trails of black smoke were streaming from the southern part of the city and a section of the nearby wall was charred.

Captain Mikhal turned and started to walk away. Father Jacob stopped him. "I too am nearly at the end of my patience. For days I have done nothing but wait, and while I grow tired of waiting, I made a promise to an old friend that I would wait when it seemed we must attack and he in turn made a promise to me."

"There are exceptions to any promise, and this is surely one, unless this friend of yours is His Royal Majesty or My Lord Prince or—"

"Who he is not important, that I trust him and would give my life for his *is* important. No, we must wait."

Captain Mikhal hissed and cursed in a low voice. He pointed, then spoke, "Look, ridesman, lancers. Hundreds."

"White and red," Jacob said quietly.

Captain Mikhal regarded Jacob. "It cannot be, it doesn't make sense."

Jacob sighed and bowed his head wearily. "Prince William's advance guard, his army comes."

"But, the Alliance?"

"The Alliance died with King Charles."

Captain Mikhal's nostrils flared. "That is as impossible as—"

"—an order sealed with King Andrew's seal rousing the whole of Quashan' garrison to Imtal being false?"

Before Captain Mikhal could respond, Father Jacob explained the last thing he had been holding back from the garrison commander. He spoke quickly and directly, telling Captain Mikhal a thing that he himself had not wanted to believe until he saw it with his own eyes. "The Kingdom of Vostok and the Kingdom of Sever are united in their cause against Great Kingdom."

"If the Alliance is broken, what of Zapad and Yug? King Peter and King Alexas are marionettes, and King Jarom is the puppeteer."

"We must give thanks to Mother-Earth and her divine providence."

"Even the Stygian Palisade has passes, and there are certainly enough ships in the Far..." Seeming to realize what he was saying, Captain Mikhal's voice trailed off.

Suddenly the call of dozens of trumpets broke the air.

Captain Mikhal's face was livid as he said, "They're preparing an assault. The time to strike is now while they muster. Nothing you say will make me change my mind. Nothing."

"Who will you serve by charging to your deaths? You must trust in—"

"—I've little faith, Father Jacob, I must confess this, for if you are going to tell me that I must trust in Great-Father, you'll find me lacking."

Father Jacob put his hand on Captain Mikhal's shoulder. "I've faith for the both of us. I was about to say that you must trust in me."

Jacob paused and took a deep breath. He was about to speak when more trumpet calls broke the silence.

"The attack begins," said Captain Mikhal, his hand returned to Jacob's shoulder was again trying to crush bone. "My hand yearns for the hilt of my blade, can you know what it does to me to see this?"

Jacob winced. "Yes, I do know."

"We strike," Captain Mikhal said, "we strike."

***

In the midst of a circle of trees they sat. Seth beside Galan. Vilmos opposite Xith and the mysterious lady.

Vilmos listened carefully to the tall light-haired woman who he was sure had saved his life when no other could have. Mid-sentence she had turned to him and Vilmos knew she was now speaking to him. He wondered if she had read his thoughts.

"—like a tree with many limbs that branches out forever. With each new branch comes a choice and for right or wrong you follow one or the other." The lady paused, then stood. "Sometimes, two great boughs touch and for a time, their branches intertwine. Sometimes, the great trees form a circle such as this."

She gestured to the circle of trees. "And for good or evil, they form an ever continuing chain. The evil that plays upon the hearts and minds of the disenchanted has its part in the chain. You cannot cleanse yourself of it forever though you can hold it in check. You, Vilmos, have found yourself. Do not lose or waste what you have gained."

The lady turned to Xith. "Go with my blessing. Remember, you will find help in a most unlikely source. And, to Quashan' you hasten—" She looked at the others each in turn. "—Galan, Seth, Vilmos, remember what I have told you. Sometimes, it is best to remember our roots, for a tree without roots cannot grow."

She stood and Xith bowed his head. Seth and Galan did likewise and then Vilmos. Vilmos had only just looked down—for an instant, no more—but when he glanced up, the lady was gone. He flashed excited eyes to Xith, suddenly realizing something else. *The trees were gone?*

Vilmos felt emotions flood over him—first surprise, then alarm—a chill ran up his back. He looked to Galan and Seth—to him, their abilities were both strange and wonderful. He turned then to see what they saw. He was on a hillside, there was a walled city in the distance. However, the sun virgining in the East shrouded all detail in a golden haze. Faintly, he heard what could've been trumpet calls.

"There is much to be done before this day is finished," Xith said, waving for Vilmos, Seth and Galan to follow him. "I pray that we are not too late and that Father Jacob still waits."

***

Sergeant Danyel' burst into Chancellor Van'te's chamber. "The attack comes, we must hasten to the walls!"

Chancellor Van'te looked to Keeper Q'yer and when neither spoke, Danyel' repeated, "We must hasten to the walls."

Chancellor Van'te stood then and as he did, he again looked to Keeper Q'yer. Keeper Q'yer raised a hand to his lips. Instead of responding, Chancellor Van'te indicated Danyel' should lead the way.

As Danyel' turned to enter the hall, a runner, panting and out of breath, appeared in the doorway. "Hurry, the enemy..."

The runner paused to inhale and to wipe sweat from his forehead.

"We know," Danyel' said, wiping sweat and grime from his own brow.

Danyel' stumbled as he took a step toward the runner. Van'te grabbed his arm to steady him.

The runner continued, "No, you don't understand..."

Danyel' said, "Go on."

Chancellor Van'te looked to Keeper Q'yer again. He already knew what the runner would say, still, he listened.

"They come from the south... the east, and the... west in a great swarm."

Sergeant Danyel's face turned ashen. Chancellor Van'te steadied him as he nearly fell, then handed him off to Keeper Q'yer. "He is the one who has not slept since the siege began. Take care of him. I'll go do what I can.

"And keeper—" Chancellor Van'te stared directly into Keeper Q'yer's eyes. "—I pray that no more of what you've told me comes true."

Chapter Twenty Seven: Battle

Vilmos saw Captain Mikhal glance toward the city then heavenward. From the direction of the city came the sounds of a raging battle. It was midmorning, only two hours after they had found Father Jacob, and things looked surely grim for the defenders. Smoke was rising from the eastern part of the city as well as the southern part now.

"They'll come. <*Patience,*> Captain Mikhal," Xith said.

Captain Mikhal fixed eyes filled with rage on Xith. "No more, your promises are empty. For the life of me, I don't understand why I listened to—"

"Please," Father Jacob said, "don't you see the folly in such a pointless attack? Only united with the soldiers of Imtal do we have a chance."

"I see only that the defenders will soon be overwhelmed. The Quashan' garrison isn't the largest in the Kingdom, isn't the strongest, isn't the best equipped, but we'll be damned if we stand by and watch our homes destroyed. Never underestimate the determination of men defending their homes. We'll fight. We'll fight like demons possessed."

"You should <relax,>" Xith said.

Father Jacob said, "I pray that you will listen to reason."

"Save your prayers for the enemy when we drive them from our lands. The burning in my heart is matched two-thousand fold by the burning in the hearts of my soldiers. We fight."

Before Jacob or Xith could respond, Captain Mikhal turned about on his heel in military fashion, and strode away.

Xith stopped Jacob from going after him. "You cannot change the minds of those who are already convinced to the contrary."

Captain Mikhal didn't waste any time, already he was barking orders to his men. Vilmos didn't know military tactics, still, it was clear Captain Mikhal did. Vilmos was about to speak when a masculine voice sounded in his mind.

He deems himself a failure. He will charge to his death if you let him.

"I know," Xith said. "Can you ride?"

Seth sent an odd sensation of warmth that Vilmos had slowly come to realize meant a curt yes.

Xith motioned to an attendant and indicated the man should bring three horses. Xith said, "Brother Galan, watch well young Vilmos. He is an apt apprentice, and I shouldn't like to see him do anything that will sever our relationship prematurely."

At the hearing, Vilmos smiled. Xith had expressed genuine feelings for him. Then when he realized Xith aimed to race off without him, Vilmos frowned.

Before Vilmos could voice an objection, Xith said, "A very important task falls to you, Vilmos and Galan. You must go up into the highlands, then circle west until you can see Quashan's west gatehouse. There you must await the arrival of His Highness, Prince of Great Kingdom. Explain the situation to him as you know it." Xith looked directly at Vilmos. "Remember what I said about Erravane."

Xith paused and cast a sidelong glance to Captain Mikhal. A runner had just returned. "Captain," the runner said, "the sub-commander of the Foot, awaits your orders."

Captain Mikhal nodded to the sub-commander of the horse soldiers who was beside him. The sub-commander came to attention then departed. Captain Mikhal went off in the opposite direction.

Just then, attendants returned with the horses. Xith, Seth and Father Jacob mounted. It seemed Xith was going to say something more, but then Captain Mikhal ordered his foot soldiers to begin their advance. The three squadrons of foot soldiers, some fifteen hundred men, began their charge. They burst from the tree line and raced down the slopes that they knew so well into the Quashan' valley basin, using the contours of the land to hide their movement as best as they could.

Meanwhile, the horse soldiers waited. Captain Mikhal had divided the Horse into two files. One would later sweep in along the northern flank of the Foot, the other the southern, but only when the time was right, for Captain Mikhal hoped the Foot would cover considerably more than half the distance to the city before the enemy would spot them and turn about to set up a rear defense. Only then would the Horse begin their charge.

Captain Mikhal's stallion pranced anxiously as the captain held the animal's reins taunt. Xith, Seth and Father Jacob, on horseback, were beside him now. Captain Mikhal reached into his saddlebags and handed each a strip of green and gold cloth. "Field insignia," Vilmos heard the captain say, "tie it around your right arm. Do not lose it, it is the only thing that will identify you with the Kingdom forces in the mayhem to come. Father Jacob, stay close, I will do my best to protect you, for we will surely have need of your healing abilities."

"Would that I were a priestess," muttered Jacob.

From high overhead, Vilmos heard the call of an eagle. He looked up, and saw it circling above the city. He looked to Xith. The shaman's eyes were glossed over.

The Foot was nearly halfway to the valley floor. Vilmos expected at any time to see the enemy host turn to form a defense. But they didn't. And the Foot continued their silent race.

Vilmos glanced to Xith again, then back down the hillside. He looked beyond the Kingdom foot soldiers to the great walled city of Quashan'. He couldn't see the men upon the walls, though he knew they were there. They were the ones pushing back the breaching ladders and responding to the enemy's relentless charges with catapult volleys.

Suddenly the eagle dove from the heavens and just when it seemed it would crash into the walls of the city, it disappeared. Xith came out of his trance and said something to Captain Mikhal that Vilmos couldn't hear. Captain Mikhal raised his sword arm high overhead, momentarily his broad-bladed sword glistened in the late morning sun, then he thrust the blade forward. The charge began. More than five hundred riders spurred their mounts into a race.

Vilmos stood enthralled, unable to break away. The thunder of hooves blocked out the sounds of the distant battle. Galan at his side was silent. She too watched and listened. Eventually though, the plodding of hooves grew distant. The first excited shouts erupted from the enemy host and men scrambled to set up a frenzied rear defense.

Midway down the valley's slopes now, the Kingdom horse soldiers spurred their mounts, driving the animals as fast as they dared. Arrows of the Kingdom bowmen began to penetrate the enemy lines and soon afterward the first wave of foot soldiers struck the enemy's rear ranks. Privately, Vilmos cheered for the Kingdomers, but he was also torn between loyalties. Some of those on the field were from his homeland.

As Vilmos watched, Sever's Knights of the Lance, their red and white banners waving in the wind, rallied for a clash with the Kingdom riders. Instead of turning to engage them, Captain Mikhal's horse soldiers continued directly into the enemy ranks. Even from this distance, Vilmos heard the screams of despair, agony and panic that followed.

It is time, imparted Galan into Vilmos' mind. *We have a long walk ahead.*

***

Captain Mikhal's mount reared up onto its hind legs. All around the captain was the press of enemy soldiers. He removed his foot from the stirrup, kicked out an approaching soldier. The heel of his boot struck the side of the man's skull. Abruptly the soldier stopped, his knees crumbled under his weight. Captain Mikhal didn't pause. He turned his mount, struck down with his long blade, and like a cleaver, it hew a defender before him. Captain Mikhal continued his charge.

Xith tried to stay close to Captain Mikhal. He defended himself as best as he could, relying largely on his magic shield while he concentrated on other matters. There was a breach midway along Quashan's east wall and in just a few seconds as he watched, dozens of attackers had pushed their way up onto the wall. There they were carving out an ever-growing section. At the base of the wall, many more were preparing to raise breaching ladders and behind them, hundreds waited to climb to the top of the wall.

Xith regarded Seth, the elf's prowess in battle was awe-inspiring. In the midst of the enemy ranks, Seth had leapt from his horse, seemingly undaunted by the fact that he had been surrounded. Now, all around him lay the dead and the dying.

"I wish I had a hundred like him," shouted Captain Mikhal to Xith above the din of the battle.

"I wish there were a hundred more like him." Xith pointed to the breached section of the wall. "Do you think we can reach it?"

Captain Mikhal's eyes went wide, apparently he hadn't seen the breach until now. He raised his sword high and behind him, a trumpeter's call rang out. He pointed his sword in the direction of the wall.

"To the wall," he shouted and charged his mount.

The trumpeter's call rang out again, and while the bulk of the Kingdom forces were caught in attacks from both sides, hundreds rallied and raced after their commander.

Xith turned his mount about and charged it in Seth's direction. Two bolts of lightning, cast first from his left hand then his right, cleared the way through the enemy ranks. He wheeled his mount in front of Seth. "Now is not your time to journey to Great-Father, Brother Seth, they have need of your skills upon the walls. Climb on!"

Xith helped Seth onto his mount.

"Hold on tight," Xith said. He kicked his mount sharply.

They raced off.

***

Galan had followed Seth in his thoughts, looking out through his eyes to the battlefield. She had watched the green and gold of the Kingdom banners clash with the blue and black. For a time, it seemed those of the green and gold held a strategic advantage on the field, where the others held an advantage solely in numbers.

Then she had lost contact with Seth's mind. She knew only that he was caught up in the frenzy of battle and she had been content to look down from her vantage point to the city below. The boy, Vilmos, walked silently at her side. She could sense conflicting emotions in him and a great urge to race to the field to join his master.

When they were directly north of the city, Galan and Vilmos began the long westward circle. Here they followed the rim of the valley. The sounds of the battle were reduced to a faint din in the distance and both the attackers and defenders were reduced to tiny figures moving about on the fields around the city's walls.

Galan lashed out with her thoughts, *Where are you, Seth?*

Galan felt Vilmos' subconscious shiver at the sound of the voice in his mind. *I am sorry, I should have directed the thoughts. I am ill accustomed to your ways, please forgive me.*

Vilmos asked, "Can you really talk across such a distance?"

Only if Brother Seth maintains the link and as long as we do not journey too much farther away from the—

Galan broke off as Seth's vision filled her mind's eye with second sight. Seth was atop the east wall. The wind was blowing in his hair, and he was looking across the basin to the battlefield. Still, the green and gold were holding their own. With the Kingdom defenders back in control of the east and south walls, they could now lend considerable aid to the Kingdom soldiers in the field. Catapults hurled rocks. Arrows from Kingdom archers rained down upon the enemy. But the enemy still held a tremendous advantage in sheer numbers. They outnumbered the Kingdom soldiers at least five to one.

Several large columns of the enemy army had fallen back to regroup. Three lines of shield bearers hundreds long amassed. Behind them, bowmen, prepared to fire on the move, would provide cover. While swordsmen and pikemen waited to strike. The enemy commanders rallied them, then ordered the attack. The shield bearers, pikemen and swordsmen surged forward, a great moving wall that clashed with the first line of the Kingdom defense.

Enemy bowmen focused on the heart of the Kingdom's defenses. Pikemen used the shield bearers for cover, their long pole arms felling nearly all who came against them. Swordsmen filled in the gaps of those who fell and again and again, the enemy wall surged forward. In short order, they cut off several groups of Kingdom soldiers from the main forces and gained control of the field.

Vilmos grabbed Galan's hand. "Look. They march, from the east!"

Seth, to the west, the forces west of the city are on the march. You must find a way to bolster—

***

—the forces upon the southern wall. I will pray for you and for reinforcements, sent Galan.

Seth severed the link and turned his attention to the defenders on the wall. One of them must be in command. He watched for a moment to see who was giving the orders, but there was so much chaos it was difficult to tell. He stopped a man rushing past.

Who leads?

A puzzled frown crossed the man's face. He turned and pointed, then hurried off. Seth raced off in the opposite direction.

Do you lead? Seth asked.

"I am Sergeant Danyel'."

This man was also puzzled but was too exhausted to understand why. Seth switched to spoken words. "From the west, the enemy comes. You must send reinforcements to the southern wall."

"There are no reinforcements. This is it. The Father must truly hate us."

"The enemy does not attack from the north. How many men do you have positioned there?"

Sergeant Danyel' wiped blood and grime from his brow. "Twenty. No, fifteen."

"And, you will have to bring more from the west and the east."

"I cannot bring any from the east and in the west, I have more wounded than able." Sergeant Danyel' stopped abruptly, cocked his head, then reached for his sword. "Who are you? You wear Kingdom insignia, yet—"

There is not time to explain who I am, you must trust me, you simply must. I rode in from the east with Captain Mikhal, it was he who gave me this. Seth indicated the green and gold cloth tied around his right arm.

Sergeant Danyel' furrowed his brows momentarily, then grabbed one of the soldiers rushing by. "Send runners. Strip the north wall, any able-bodied men from the west wall and twenty from the east to the south wall."

"Sir, I go to the north wall. You know the enemy hasn't attacked at all from the north, Chancellor Van'te expects a strike there next."

"That was an order! I will deal with Chancellor Van'te if needs be." Sergeant Danyel' stumbled, and Seth had to support him or else he would have collapsed.

The soldier held his ground, eyeing his sergeant and Seth.

Lead me to this Chancellor Van'te and I will talk to him, Seth told the soldier, then turning back to Danyel', he said, *You must rest, you are of little use in this condition.*

"No, I will go with you. Soldier, lead the way!"

***

Arrows poured down upon them like a ceaseless rain. Xith extended the radius of his magic shield to protect those around him, but could only extend its protective envelope so far. He was tired and his mind was on other things, mainly, trying to pinpoint a weakness in the enemy lines through which they could escape back to the Kingdom lines.

While they had managed to push the attackers back from the walls, the enemy had only to regroup and come again. In the end, it had cost the Kingdom forces dearly. Only one in ten of the hundred horse soldiers and countless foot soldiers had reached the base of the wall. Now fewer than fifty men remained. Yet while they were cut off from their lines and trapped amidst of sea of the enemy, the soldiers did not relent. They were determined to keep the enemy at bay.

Xith sat his mount beside Father Jacob and Captain Mikhal. The Kingdom commander was nearly exhausted, but remained tall in his saddle. There was defiant pride in his eyes. His soldiers guarded him with a fierceness rarely seen, and with their lives.

Xith wheeled his mount in a tight circle, continuing his search for a weakness in the enemy lines. He knew Captain Mikhal must survive, for in him lay the power to deliver the day from the hands of the enemy. The Kingdom forces were rapidly losing momentum. Without the leadership of their commander, and more importantly the strength he lent to his men, all would soon be forever lost. The time to act was now.

Xith's mount whinnied and reared up. Xith fought to control it, and as he struggled with the animal, a flash of color waving not far off caught his eye. He steadied the horse, soothing it with gentle treatment. He stared, squinted, his eyes went wide as he realized what he saw was a royal banner. For an instant as the press of bodies around the King parted, Xith looked straight at King Jarom.

Yet Xith wasn't the only one to see the banner. When Xith looked back to Captain Mikhal, he found that the captain had already raised his sword. Xith knew at once the captain was preparing for a direct charge against the monarch's defenses, a charge Xith had to stop before it was too late.

But when their commander raised his blade high, the ten remaining horse soldiers around him did likewise. Before Xith could act, Captain Mikhal dropped his sword and spurred his mount. His men followed. The foot soldiers parted to let the riders through, then took up position along the riders' flanks.

Xith held his ground for a moment, considering what to do. Again, he saw Vostok's royal banner fluttering in the wind, so close, but yet so far. It was a hopeless charge, Xith knew it, but he also knew he could not dissuade it. He followed.

Abruptly the call of countless trumpets broke the air. Fighting on both sides broke off. Captain Mikhal and his men cut short their charge. All eyes turned southward. Poised along a ridge of the foothills was a line of horse soldiers a thousand across. The Kingdom forces began to whoop and cheer. Prince Valam and reinforcements had surely arrived.

A second time, trumpet calls broke the air. The riders began their charge, a great black wave racing downward. The Kingdomers continued to whoop and cheer, then gradually their cries turned to murmurs of dismay, for behind this massive wave came a line of flag bearers. The banners they bore were bold red and stark white, and not Kingdom green and gold. Behind the flag bearers came long lines of foot soldiers. It was not Prince Valam at all, but the army of the Kingdom of Sever.

***

Vilmos' mouth fell open. He gawked at the red and white banners, and the force of thousands on the move to the battle around Quashan'. The Kingdom soldiers would soon be hopelessly outnumbered, and if there had been even the smallest of hopes for winning the battle before, it died with the arrival of Sever's army.

Before he knew what he was doing, Vilmos found he was racing down the hillside.

Vilmos, stop, called out Galan, *you will only get yourself killed. We are to wait here and give instructions when reinforcements arrive.*

Vilmos paused only to turn back and regard Galan. Magic flowed through him like a tidal wave. His eyes focused with rage told her what he couldn't say. Then he cast off the voice in his mind that told him what he didn't want to hear and raced off.

Worriedly, he studied the distant battlefield. King Jarom's forces had fallen back to re-form and wait for the fresh troops. The Kingdom soldiers also regrouped, but they did not wait to attack afterward.

Vilmos, panting and straining for breath, forced himself to maintain a breakneck pace. Behind him, Galan with her longer strides was catching up to him. Vilmos fought to stay ahead of her but couldn't, and soon they were running side by side.

Vilmos, what good will dying do? This is pointless.

"I am a magic-user, just as Xith. I do what I must."

You are an apprentice.

Vilmos didn't answer, he pushed himself to race still faster. Sever's horsemen had already clashed with what remained of Quashan's garrison. The Kingdom soldiers fell back, tried frantically to re-form, but each time they formed a hasty shield wall it crumbled, forcing another retreat. Soon it became painfully clear that the Kingdom army was on the run.

Only a hundred yards to go now and Vilmos would be on the flat fields surrounding Quashan'. There he could stretch out his legs and, there he was sure he would leave Galan behind. He ran to the pace of the thump-thump in his ears, which drowned out the cries of despair and anguish that the wind carried. Once on the flat fields, Vilmos stretched out his legs, lengthening his strides. As he did this, his foot caught Galan's. Both stumbled and fell.

Vilmos was quick to regain his feet. He screamed at Galan, "You did that on purpose!"

Galan turned Vilmos about, so he was staring up at the valley's rim from the direction they had just come from. He had just started to protest when he saw them, a line of horse soldiers. The banners at the fore were green and gold. Prince Valam had come. He had found Keeper Martin and those of Imtal garrison.

Behind the horse soldiers came the foot soldiers, thousands of them, and far more than Vilmos or Galan had anticipated. Amidst the green and gold banners were banners bearing a blue circle on a field of white. Galan asked Vilmos without words and strangely with only emotions who the others were. Vilmos could only shrug. He didn't know.

Prince Valam, there! shouted Galan.

"Where?"

There! repeated Galan. She grabbed Vilmos' hand and pulled him to a start, and he chased after her.

Chapter Twenty Eight: Last Play

It was now late afternoon. During the day the battle had taken many turns. The arrival of nearly ten thousand troops, Imtal soldiers and free men, had changed the tide of the battle for a time. Still, this had only made the field more even and not equal.

Adrina was in the midst of relating the story of their journey and of how Keeper Martin and Captain Adylton had managed to persuade the free men of Mir and Veter to join the Kingdom's cause. "Most are oarsmen from the free city fleet, not soldiers, though still good with a blade," Adrina said. "Gold surely persuaded their loyalty, also a fear of losing their freedom, for after he had captured the whole of the South, King Jarom surely wouldn't have let the Free Cities remain outside his rule."

"Surely we cannot just sit here," Vilmos said. "We must do something."

"I aim to do something, all right." Adrina grinned. "Tell me exactly what the lady told each of you. She did speak to each of you right?"

Galan and Vilmos quickly told Adrina what they remembered of the conversation, though much of it seemed a blur.

"She spoke of choices being like the branches of trees and for right or wrong you follow one of the other, and of good and evil," concluded Vilmos.

Adrina asked, "Did she tell you to remember something?"

Vilmos was pacing. Adrina knew he was growing restless. She turned to Galan, and found an unexpected expression in the elf's eyes. "What is it Galan, what do you see?"

Galan was staring off into the distance, her eyes were unfocussed. *Seth upon the walls.*

"Really, you can see him from here?" asked Adrina.

Galan didn't answer. She was apparently lost in what she was seeing and Vilmos explained what little he knew of her gift, which he deemed akin to corpeal stasis.

It is not, Galan said, *it is a projecting of thoughts. I can project feelings and images too.*

"Like an image in a dream," Adrina said.

Galan didn't reply she was again distracted by what she saw.

"Is there a way we can see as well?" Adrina asked.

Perhaps.

Suddenly, Adrina saw Seth standing atop the upper battlements along Quashan's southern wall. She could feel the wind blowing through his hair and the despair ravaging his heart. Seth's emotions flowed to Adrina, mixing with her own, and soon despair ravaged her heart as well. The enemy had breached the southern gates of the city and a wave of humanity was pouring in. Torches were being distributed and many buildings were already burning. Cries of panic rose to a clamor; she heard women and children crying as they ran from homes they reluctantly evacuated.

When Galan broke the link, Adrina found she was trembling beyond her control and her cheeks were wet with tears. From their vantage point, they saw the billows of smoke, and eventually the flames as well.

Adrina asked, "Is there no hope?"

Neither Vilmos nor Galan spoke.

Adrina turned to the group of guardsmen who Valam had insisted remain to see to her protection in case the worst happened. Their faces were racked with anguish and lament. She knew they wanted to join the fight, though it would surely cost them their lives.

She stood and wiped the tears from her eyes.

"I order you into battle!" Adrina shouted.

The ranking soldier said, "His Highness ordered us to remain."

Adrina glared. "And I am ordering you into battle! Now, mount your horses and go."

"We cannot."

"If Quashan' falls, I will have no need for fifty guards. I will have no need for guards at all." Adrina turned away from the speaker. "I will count to five, when I turn around you *will* be gone, and I will speak never a word about this. One, two—"

Adrina waited until the sound of hooves mixed in with the din of the battle before she turned back around. She was surprised to find that six guardsmen remained.

She glared at them, but they held their ground.

"We must stay," one of the men said. "If it comes to it, we will ensure you reach Imtal."

Adrina didn't offer a response.

Vilmos seemed suddenly inspired by the sight of the retreating guardsmen and there was the same twinkle in his eye that Adrina had seen in her brother's eyes earlier. "Take my hand," Vilmos told Galan.

Vilmos' eyes glossed over, and it seemed he was in a trance. Adrina and Galan waited. Adrina was unsure what to expect.

After a time, Vilmos released Galan's hand. "In the foothills, the Wolmerrelle. Erravane." His voice betrayed dismay. "William of Sever, she certainly is seeking him out."

Galan's voice whispered in Adrina's mind, *You will find help in a most unlikely source.*

"To think, I once called him cousin," Adrina said, "If only we understood why he turned against Great Kingdom."

"Perhaps we do," said a voice from behind them.

The Kingdom soldiers rushed to protect Adrina. Adrina, Vilmos and Galan turned around and stared into the afternoon shadows. A man with gray hair and a distinctive salt-and-pepper colored beard slowly made his way from the shadows. Adrina said, "Keeper Martin."

Recognizing the lore keeper, the soldiers backed down.

"You must excuse me," Keeper Martin said, "I have been listening to your conversation for some time. I circled back about an hour ago."

Keeper Martin walked toward them. Adrina saw that his face was drawn and pale, and then she saw the deep stain of blood on the right side of his cloak.

"An arrow." Keeper Martin said simply as he eased to a sitting position.

Adrina's eyes went wide.

"Yes, I will live." Martin motioned for them to sit. Adrina, Galan and Vilmos sat.

"I was in Gregortonn when King Charles was poisoned and, finally I understand why King William has joined with King Jarom."

"King? What—" Adrina began.

Jacob raised a silencing hand. "King Charles has passed on. The grippe took Phillip. William is heir. As you can see by the display in the field, there was no contest to his ascension. Yet, I am sure that it is with little pride and no love that the army of Sever sides with Vostok.

"The truth is that I myself did not understand what I had seen in Gregortonn until some hours ago, but by then I thought it too late to act on what I knew. Yet, I can see the error of that now and you are responsible for opening my eyes."

Adrina furrowed her eyebrows.

"Babbling, aren't I? Perhaps—" Keeper Martin coughed and gripped his side. "—it is the wound. Yet, I tend to do that normally. It is the green and the gold."

"Green and gold?" Adrina asked.

"All along I was sure agents of King Jarom had somehow seized power in Sever's capital, for you see, I saw through the disguises and when I saw banners of green and gold—Kingdom colors—to me such colors were not out of place, but those of Sever knew at once the colors were foreign."

Keeper Martin's face became extremely pale. He bit back pain, then took a long drink from a wine bag. "Do you understand?"

"I am beginning to," Adrina said.

"Brother Galan, as Lore Keeper of Great Kingdom, I know much more about your kind than the average Kingdomer, still your gifts are truly amazing. Can you truly project images into the minds of others?"

May I? asked Galan, suggesting she wanted to take a closer look at Martin's side. Keeper Martin nodded approval and then seemed not to notice Galan's hands probing the outside of the wound. *You did not remove the shaft of the arrow.*

"The shaft snapped."

Shock crossed Adrina's face as Galan's hand melted into Martin's side. Keeper Martin gave no indication of sudden pain, in fact, he seemed at ease. Adrina, torn between repulsion and attraction, watched. The skin around Galan's wrist rippled as if fluid, and as if nothing was happening, Keeper Martin turned to Vilmos and said, "What little I know of the Watcher, through Father Jacob, leads me to believe that you are gifted with the forbidden as is he and while I do not condone its use, I believe as does Father Jacob, exceptions must be allowed if they are for a greater good. Yet, you are also from Sever. Yes?"

"My home is Tabborrath Village," Vilmos said.

Martin said, "Your Highness, come here, let me look at you."

Adrina didn't move. Galan was withdrawing her hand and in it, she held the broken arrow.

"Your Highness," Martin repeated.

Adrina looked up. Martin looked into her eyes. "You are the image of your mother, and Queen Elthia as well. Can you braid your hair in a triple braid and let it flow over your right shoulder?"

Adrina caught a glimpse of a pink-yellow glow out of the corner of her eye. She looked back to Martin's wound to find it was gone, as if it had vanished. Adrina turned back to Martin and said, "I think you should rest, you are not thinking clearly."

"On the contrary, I have never thought more clearly." Keeper Martin waved one of the guardsmen over. He was a short, thin fellow. "Soldier, change clothes with the lad here, he will have need of your uniform."

***

Xith kneeled beside Captain Mikhal and cradled the man's head in his hands. Most of the southern quarter of Quashan' was ablaze, and a full evacuation had begun. The Kingdom army was divided and they were now defending against two fronts. King Jarom's foot soldiers came from the west. The army of Sever pressed from the east. The horse soldiers of both kingdoms controlled the middle of the field.

It all seemed so utterly hopeless.

"Can you save him?" Xith asked Father Jacob who also kneeled beside the fallen commander.

"The wound is grievous, I can only ease his suffering."

"Do so, he has earned a peaceful passing from this life."

Xith had been sore pressed to convince Captain Mikhal that his men needed his continued strength and guidance and that a single last rallying of his horse soldiers for a final charge would have been sheer folly. Xith found it a bittersweet irony that the commander had met the lethal blow while trying to return to the ranks of his soldiers a second time.

"He is gone," whispered Jacob.

"He was a brave man."

Father Jacob bent his head for a moment of prayer and Xith did likewise.

Shouts erupted from not far off. "Fall back, fall back," the voices screamed.

The former sub-commander beside them stood and urged them to retreat. Xith and Jacob stood and followed the new commander as his forces fell back to regroup.

***

Beside Adrina, Galan and Vilmos marched silently. Adrina could only vaguely see the silhouettes of the five soldiers who preceded them amidst the glare of the setting sun. Slowly though, more and more shadows shrouded the foothills and nightfall steadily approached.

Vilmos, dressed in the guardsman's uniform, held tightly the prize Keeper Martin had given him. He was their eyes. He kept watch from overhead and Galan at his side directed him. She read his thoughts, and thus they were able to steer clear of any patrols set up in anticipation of an ambush as the field became blurred.

Keeper Martin's plan had seemed bold as he had revealed it to them, but now as they moved ever closer to the ranks of Sever's army, it also seemed suddenly desperate and simple. They were to sneak into William's camp, find his tent and convince him that Great Kingdom had no part in his father's death.

The guardsmen disguised as Sever soldiers and the banner Vilmos held but did not display would help them on their way. Still, the most difficult part—moving through the camp, finding William and convincing him—would fall to Adrina, Vilmos and Galan alone, and mostly to Adrina. Yet, she wasn't entirely sure she could convince William of anything, though she knew she must try.

***

Darkness fell, and still the battle for Quashan' raged.

Prince Valam conferred with his field commanders, the captains of the Imtal and Quashan' garrisons. Only a short time ago his forces had finally managed to break through the enemy lines to join with the soldiers of Quashan', and he had just now learned of the death of Quashan's commander.

Kingdom forces held the base of the southern and eastern walls of the city, yet the fire within the city still burned out of control. The enemy came at them along two fronts but fortunately could no longer attack from the rear or squeeze them into a killing zone. At last, they had driven back the enemy horse soldiers and erected an inner and outer defensive line. In an ironic twist, they had taken control of the trenches dug by those that had besieged the city initially and, it was this that was helping them fend off the superior force.

"The attack slows, Your Highness," Captain Adylton said. He wiped fresh blood from his face and sheathed his blade. "I answered the call as soon as I could."

A soldier offered the captain water and he drank heavily. Captain Adylton continued, "It looks as if they'll soon fall back to their lines. The night comes."

Prince Valam said, "That is indeed news worth waiting for." Valam surveyed his commanders. "Has anyone seen Captain Berre?"

A sergeant with a soot-covered face answered. "He commands on the left flank, Your Highness. He sent me in his stead. He has the devil's own fury in his eyes. His home, a wife and three children, was along Cooper's Walk."

"Stand at ease sergeant." Valam looked to the burning city, then to Captain Adylton. "What of the other Imtal commanders?"

"Captain Ghenson's position was overrun. He was dragged from his mount, I believe he is dead."

Valam turned to the sergeant. "What news from the left flank?"

"Your Highness—"

"Save the pleasantries for another place and time. Be frank and quick."

"The line holds, the men are tired, hungry and thirsty. The wounded and the dying lie about the field. Their sappers are digging another trench line, and Captain Berre fears it is a sign they await reinforcements."

Valam gripped the sergeant's shoulder, then turned to Father Jacob. "Father Jacob?" he said.

Father Jacob stood a little taller and nodded.

"At last, we have a stable position. Care of the wounded is in your hands. I want all wounded who can still walk, but cannot wield a sword, on relief brigade. Without food and water, soldiers cannot fight."

The soot-faced sergeant's downtrodden expression brightened.

Xith stepped forward. "May I speak?"

"Speak freely."

"Light skirmishes and raids will continue through the night, the enemy hopes to keep us expecting an attack that will not come and to wear us out. An all out attack will not come until just before dawn, but if we switch to a defensive and do not continue to press the attack, all will surely be lost come morning."

Valam was puzzled. "How can you possibly know this?"

Father Jacob said, "There are those who have divine gifts of sight, and Master Xith is one of them. You trusted him before, you must trust him again. Without him Quashan' would have already fallen, and none of us would be standing here now."

Valam extended his hand to Xith's shoulder. "I am sorry, it has been a trying day. You must know that you have my eternal gratitude and when this is all over, one way or another, I will repay you."

"If you want to repay me, do what I say." Xith paused, and for a moment, it seemed as if he heard something far off. Valam heard it too, perhaps it was the call of an eagle from high over head, but he couldn't be sure. "Before moonrise, every available man must be mustered and assembled for an all out assault against Sever's army. At precisely moonrise, the attack must begin."

"We cannot desert the left flank," interrupted the sergeant. "There are two enemy armies—"

Valam raised a silencing hand and Xith continued. "Yes, it is very important that the enemy not know we have stripped our left flank. Moonrise is not for some hours and the night sky looks to be dark and clouded. We can use this to our advantage…"

***

Vilmos unfurled Sever's banner. Adrina tried to imagine that she heard it flapping in the wind instead of pitiful moans and screams of agony. She forced herself to maintain a steady pace. Her heart pounded in her ears and she bit her cheek to remind herself to stay calm. Frantic thoughts flashed through her mind and more than once she almost cried out at the ghastly sight of the dead and the dying that littered William's camp from end to end.

For a moment, Adrina thought of Emel and wondered where he was amidst the fighting, then the thought was gone. Ahead lay a tent with many guards posted around it. Adrina was sure it was William's. Expectantly, she inhaled a breath and held it, but when Galan continued past the tent without even turning an eye toward it, Adrina let the breath slip out.

"You passed his tent, is something wrong?" Adrina whispered.

There is nothing wrong, said Galan, carefully directing the thoughts.

After passing the last tent on the end, Galan paused. *This is William's tent. The other was meant to catch the eye of anyone bold enough to sneak into the camp.*

Galan did not hesitate long, instead she continued until she found a place with few campfires and no torches. *There were two guards just inside the entrance, but cleanly out of view. William sits at a table with his back to the guards. There was another in the tent, but he was preparing to leave.*

Vilmos tossed aside the banner. "You read their thoughts?"

In a way, yes.

Adrina asked, "Is there a chance we can replace the guards with our own?"

One of the guardsmen stepped forward. "We will try. They are surely hungry or tired, or both. I can tell you there have been many times I wished for relief and would never have questioned it if it came."

Galan smiled, seemingly approving the show of bravery. She closed her eyes for a moment. *They are both hungry and tired. You are quite wise.*

"I am but a simple soldier who knows what it is to stand watch." The soldier broke off, his face showing concern.

"Go quickly," Adrina said, "may Great-Father watch over you."

Two soldiers slipped away.

While they waited, Adrina took in the activity around them. Everywhere soldiers hurried about the camp, singly, in pairs, and in large groups. The camp was in a state of confused frenzy, but this was changing, order was being restored from chaos. The sound of the battle was fading. More and more fires were raised both along the camp's perimeter and its interior, and lines of torches were being put in place to mark hastily cleared paths.

Princess Adrina?

"What is it, Galan?" Adrina whispered.

They are inside.

Adrina saw two figures leave the tent. "Is it safe to proceed?"

Galan said, *It would seem so.*

Quietly the small group moved toward the tent.

"What would you have us do, Your Highness?" asked one of the three remaining guardsmen.

"When we reach the tent, we will go in, you three will continue past. Do not stray far though, we may have need of your sword arms. Keep a close eye on the tent, and do not start a fight unless it is absolutely necessary. If an alarm is sounded, we will surely never leave this camp."

At the front of the tent, they stopped. Adrina signaled to the guardsmen to continue on their way. They did so reluctantly.

Adrina started toward the tent's entrance. Suddenly everything Keeper Martin had told Adrina flooded through her mind. She knew that in order to convince William of the truth, she must first find confidence in herself. Still, she didn't see how her resemblance to Queen Elthia would help anything. Or why it was important that Vilmos was a native Severian. Nor did she really understand how Galan was supposed to project Keeper Martin's memories of Gregortonn into William's mind when Keeper Martin wasn't even with them.

Galan grabbed Adrina's arm and pulled her back. *Wait, there is something wrong. I am not sure—No, I am sure, Erravane.*

"The Wolmerrelle," Vilmos said. He gasped. "We must act now or all this will be for nothing."

Galan stopped Vilmos from hastily running into the tent and indicated that they should move back in the direction they had just come from. *As unlikely as it seems Erravane's presence may actually help us. We should wait to see what occurs.*

"I agree," Adrina said, "we should—" From far off the sound of angry voices exploded into the air, followed by panic-filled screams. More shouting followed. Soon an alarm was sweeping through the camp.

Frenzy followed. The camp was in an uproar. Men were running about the camp screaming, "To battle! To battle! The enemy comes!" Then, Adrina heard shouting and screams from

William's tent. She turned bewildered eyes to Vilmos and Galan. Together they rushed into William's tent.

The two guards lay face down in the dirt. Adrina did not doubt that they were dead. Apparently Erravane had cut her way in through the back of the tent and aimed to go out the same way. In a half human half animal state, Erravane was dragging William out of the tent. Abruptly she changed directions and pushed her way back into the tent. Behind her came the three Kingdom guardsmen, their swords drawn.

Erravane spun around. Her eyes were wild. "Princess Adrina, you of all people should not stand in my way. William's disappearance will most certainly serve you."

William shouted, "She aims to kill me."

"Hush, or I'll rip out your tongue, I will only kill you at the end and though you deserve much anguish for abandoning me, I will do it swiftly."

"Even William doesn't deserve to die," Adrina said, her voice strong and with no hint of the alarm that raged through her mind. "Release him, or you will never escape from this camp."

"If I do not escape, neither will you."

Vilmos pushed past Adrina. Blue-white fire danced around his hands. "Xith warned you not to meddle in affairs that do not concern you."

"It is you, the boy who killed—" Erravane was shocked. "No, it cannot be. You and the Watcher should be—"

"Not in the Vangar, we are here—" As Vilmos spoke, he walked slowly toward Erravane, his hands poised menacingly "—And, should he find you, he will most assuredly keep his promise."

Erravane howled and with inhuman strength hurled William at Vilmos. She turned to make an escape, the guards barred her way. Adrina knew for certain they'd be killed if they tried to stop her.

"No!" Adrina screamed. "Let her pass."

The guards stepped aside and Erravane fled into the night.

Vilmos and William were in a jumble on the ground. Galan and Adrina helped them to their feet. William's eyes were agape and shock was evident on his face. He started to say something, but before he could say anything, a soldier rushed into tent. Adrina turned about. The Kingdom guardsmen began shouting and rushed forward to intercept the soldier who had drawn his sword and also had begun shouting.

The Kingdom guardsmen engaged the lone soldier of Sever.

Adrina began shouting, "No, no, Stop," but the combatants didn't.

The soldier lay dead on the dirt floor before other soldiers answering his call rushed into the tent. Soon the three Kingdom guardsmen were being pushed back by the sheer number of newcomers arrived to save their king.

Adrina turned to William. "Do something, make them stop!"

William seemed disoriented.

"Do something," Adrina repeated. She grabbed William about the shoulders and shook him.

"I am in no danger, I think, I mean—I need to sort this out." William paused, flustered. "Sergeant, soldiers, I order you to halt!"

The soldiers grudgingly broke off the attack. William pointed to two of them. "Find Commander Stenocco, tell him to come at once. Five more stand guard, the rest of you outside."

The soldiers didn't move.

"Throw down your weapons," Adrina told the Kingdom guardsmen. They hesitated. "Do it!"

Their swords clanked as they hit the ground.

A puzzled frown returned to William's face as he turned to Adrina. "Why did you save me? I mean, Erravane was right, you should have rejoiced. Why are you in my camp in the first place, if it is not to kill me?"

"We came to talk." Adrina wanted to say more but she was trembling and there were tears in her eyes. Suddenly it seemed lead weights were around her shoulders and her legs wanted to collapse under the weight. "May I sit?"

"A chair," William said.

A soldier quickly brought a chair.

Adrina cleared her throat, then looked to Vilmos and Galan in turn. She started speaking, determined to convince William using Keeper Martin's plan. Yet somehow, things didn't come out the way she planned, and instead she told him everything the plan entailed. She explained how they had come to the camp and sneaked through it intent on finding him, how they had planned to trick him and finally how they had planned to convince him of the truth. During the telling Sever's commander hurried into the tent but William ordered silence.

Adrina concluded by saying, "I tell you the truth when I say I harbor no hate in my heart for all you have done. I know what it is to grieve for one so dear it seems they are all you had in the world. I know what it is like to feel you are all alone. I know how such loss can cloud your mind and make you want to lash out at all the world, but if you loved your father, and I know you truly did, you will listen to reason. Great Kingdom had no part in your father's death. This you must believe."

Indignation crossed William's face. "How can you possibly know what I feel? How can you possibly know what it is like to lose a mother, father, and brother all in the space of a few years?" William's eyes turn wild. His tone became icy cold. "Kill them, kill them all!"

The Kingdom guardsmen raced for their swords. Adrina leapt from her chair and started screaming at William. Galan grabbed Adrina and pushed her back. Vilmos stepped in front of them both.

There was joy in Commander Stenocco's eyes as he withdrew his great sword from its sheath. He ordered his men to stand at ease. "Leave them to me," he said arrogantly, "I want them all."

The Kingdom guardsmen held their ground as the enemy commander advanced on them. When he was within striking distance, Commander Stenocco stopped and laughed, mocking the tension on the guardsmen's faces. He spat, then with surprising speed, heaved his massive blade toward them. Adrina squeezed her eyes together and winced in anticipation of the sound of clashing blades. When she heard a dull thud instead, she opened her eyes, expecting the worst. The worst hadn't happened, however. Nothing had happened.

Commander Stenocco's eyes were wide and filled with rage. He lashed out with his sword. Yet the sword couldn't reach its mark. Again and again Adrina heard a dull thud. For a moment, the commander stood unmoving, a muscle in his cheek twitched nervously, then he cast aside his sword and began ramming the unseen barrier.

Adrina was as confused as the enemy commander was, she turned to Galan. Galan pointed to Vilmos.

"Princess," Vilmos said, "I cannot hold him back long. Do what you must!"

Adrina's thoughts spun inward. She turned back to William and felt suddenly sick to her stomach. She knew what she had to do—something she wished someone had done to her long ago. She struck William across the face with the back of her hand. "How dare you speak to me like that!" she screamed at him, then with her eyes she backed him into his chair.

"King Charles is gone, your self-pity will not bring him back! Great Kingdom and Sever have always been the strongest of allies. My father, King Andrew, has no desire to sit upon Sever's throne. That seat belongs to the line of Charles, to you… Think. Who stands to gain the most from such treachery? Think, and no longer let blind rage control your actions."

For a long time, William said nothing, then he turned to the soldiers inside the tent and dismissed them all save for his commander. "It is no easy thing to stop what has already begun," William finally told Adrina, "I know you are sincere and though I want to believe you, I cannot. You spoke of proof. If you have proof that King Jarom was behind the poisoning of my father, I would hear it."

Commander Stenocco screamed, "This is a trick, their forces attack as we speak!"

William raised his hand, commanding silence. "You spoke of proof, I would hear it," he repeated.

Adrina turned to Galan. "Are you ready?"

***

False dawn was on the horizon and still the battle raged. Seth looked down from atop the wall to the fields south of the city. The Kingdom forces were falling back to reform for another charge, to the west Sever's army was also regrouping, and to the east King Jarom's army was mustering for their first attack of the new day. Vostok's soldiers were fresh, few soldiers stood between them and the middle of Prince Valam's camp as the bulk of the Kingdom army was engaged in the fighting to the west. Seth knew that once the attack came, the camp would be overrun.

Seth watched the men upon the walls prepare for the attack. Bowmen notched arrows. Soldiers loaded catapults. Others hunkered down behind the battlements and waited to counter the press of enemy siege ladders.

Trumpets chanted to the east. Vostok's army began to form in long lines. Shield bearers at the fore followed by pikemen, swordsmen and lastly archers. Horse soldiers in column formation waited with swords raised high.

The trumpets sounded again. Thousands of foot soldiers screamed and charged. Seth turned his eyes westward, expecting Sever's army to begin their charge. They had reformed, but held their ground. Poised to strike to the west, the Kingdom army also waited. Their rear ranks began to turn about and prepare a defensive, but did not move fearing a deception.

Perplexed, Seth watched the two unmoving armies. He squinted his eyes, trying to see why neither attacked. *Was there something on the field between them?*

Galan? Seth called out.

Seth, came Galan's voice into his mind

What is happening?

Sever's army is quitting the field, Galan replied, and it was then that Seth saw the white flag and six figures moving toward the Kingdom lines.

Seth was puzzled. *But to the east, the attack comes.*

By the Mother, I did not realize—you must find Prince Valam. William has decided to quit the field. Seth, he knows the truth. But he also says he cannot fight against King Jarom.

Vostok's army came. The clash began. The Kingdom army seemed unsure of which direction to defend against. Seth started running along the top of the wall. He was sure disaster waited in this indecision. He tried reaching the prince's mind, but he had no idea where Prince Valam was among the mass of men in the frenzied camp below.

Sergeant Danyel'? Chancellor Van'te? Seth screamed.

Fatigue clouded Seth's mind, allowing panic and dread to flood over him. He raced faster and faster. Then Sever's army began to quit the field, and when it was clear they were not just falling back and were actually retiring, a wave of cheers erupted from the mouths of the Kingdom soldiers. The men atop the walls also began to cheer.

Seth stopped running. The whole of the Kingdom army turned about, and weary or not, they began a driving charge. King Jarom's army hadn't anticipated such a massive counterstrike. Their shield wall was weak and it fell quickly.

In retaliation, Vostok's horse soldiers began their assault, but this came too late. The two armies were too intertwined and the enemy riders trampled their own soldiers as well as

Kingdom soldiers. And when the riders met the first solid Kingdom line, horses and men collided, lances met readied swords and pikes, and large numbers of riders were pulled from their mounts or had mounts cut out from beneath them.

The Kingdom army had its own horse soldiers and they were driving into the heart of the enemy army. Vostok's army stunned and surprised, could only fall back again and again, but without support from the other flank, they no longer had superior numbers in the field. It was now they who were outnumbered.

One last time the army of Vostok tried to raise a defense so they could reform, but this was shattered quickly and the Kingdom army made good their rout. The men upon the walls began cheering louder and louder. For days their city had been besieged and now the enemy was on the run. They were elated and suddenly no longer weary.

Seth watched the Kingdom horse soldiers pursue the enemy army to the valley's rim and beyond. It was there that Seth lost sight of them. He too was joyous, and he joined in their cheers.

***

A full celebration was underway.

The fires in the city were at last extinguished and rebuilding would begin as soon as possible. Already priests and priestesses had arrived, answering Prince Valam's call for aid. The Priestesses of the Mother were caring for the hundreds wounded. The Priests of the Father were interring the dead upon the fields south of Quashan', and the former battlefields would forever more stand as grim reminders of the devastation wrought by even the briefest of wars. Great Kingdom's losses had been heavy and numbered nearly one thousand.

Adrina's joy was tainted with sorrow. She felt so alone, even though Galan was beside her. Vilmos had gone off in search of Xith, and while Adrina was sure Galan would have rather sought out Seth, Galan had stayed with Adrina to comfort her. Emel had not been among the fit or the wounded and she had searched through every one of the dozens of relief houses set up to care for the wounded. The only thing she could do now was to search among the dead for his body, a task that seemed too grim for her to bare alone, yet she was determined to find Emel and to say her goodbyes.

"Father Jacob," Adrina called out.

A very weary Father Jacob turned to greet her. He took her hand. "Your Highness, I heard of your deed, you have done well, very well indeed. " Jacob grinned, and a bit of fatigue lifted from his eyes. "I knew you would."

"Emel," Adrina said, "you haven't…"

"No, I have not seen Emel, yet I do not think you will find him here."

"I have looked everywhere but here, Father Jacob." Adrina was in tears. "He is nowhere to be found."

"I have lain to rest too many familiar faces, I remember each, and none was Emel's. Perhaps you searched in the wrong place."

Adrina was convinced otherwise. "No, if Emel were alive, I would have found him."

Galan took Adrina's hand. *Riders are still in the field.*

Father Jacob sighed. "A few, yes. They help clear the fields. Most have returned to the city to join in the celebrations. Emel is not among them."

A few, Galan said, sending disbelief along with the words, *I see hundreds.*

Father Jacob and Adrina followed Galan's gaze, a confused call going forth from the walls matched their surprise. That the large band of riders was Kingdom horse soldiers there was no doubt, but the rout of the enemy army had been completed before the day had even begun, and now the day was nearly over.

The jubilant soldiers' swords and lances glistened in the late afternoon sun. They did not race their mounts, instead they held them to a steady trot. The animals must have indeed been weary.

"Could it be?" Adrina asked.

Neither Galan nor Father Jacob had to respond to the question. At the fore of the group was a great black stallion. In Adrina's mind, there was no mistaking *Ebony Lightning,* Emel's beloved mount.

As the riders approached, their faces slowly became clear. Adrina knew that it was Emel who rode *Ebony.* What's more, Emel wasn't just at the fore of the pack, he was leading it and behind him were over three hundred Kingdom riders. Their shouts and cheers rose to the walls of Quashan' and trumpets returned their jubilant cries with increasing vigor. Those celebrating in the streets of Quashan', curious as to the commotion, came to the field and soon thousands covered the near end of the field by the city's southern gate.

Father Jacob said, "His father would have indeed been proud of him this day."

"Indeed," said a voice from behind them. At once Adrina recognized the voice of her brother. Prince Valam put his hand on Adrina's shoulder. "Captain Brodst will surely hear of it, for I will tell him myself on the day I see his son is promoted to Second Captain, Imtal Garrison."

"Second Captain?" Adrina asked surprised.

"Imtal Garrison is without two of her captains, and who better to fill the place than one who has proven himself worthy."

Adrina pointed a finger at Valam. "You knew where he'd been all along didn't you." Adrina wiped tears from her cheeks. "And you let me worry and fret—"

"I had a hunch, but I wasn't certain."

Before Adrina could reply, Emel reined in *Ebony* beside them. He was grinning ear to ear. He leapt from the saddle.

Adrina ran to him and hugged him fiercely. "I thought you dead. Where have you been?"

Emel laughed then said. "Making sure Jarom's army never returns to South Province without giving precious thought to the consequences. We chased them so far, and they ran so fast, I'd be surprised if they weren't still running."

"You will make a good captain, Emel," Valam said.

Adrina was still hugging Emel fiercely, and now Emel's face was a bit red. "Captain?" Emel asked.

"Captain," Adrina said, and she kissed him on the cheek.

Valam cleared his throat. Adrina stepped back, and Valam gripped Emel's shoulder. "Second Captain, Imtal Garrison. Captain Ghenson was a good man, and I know you will lead well in his stead."

A surge of celebrants and music came toward them. Dancers and musicians had made their way to the field from Quashan's many squares, stirring ever more excitement into the already boisterous crowd. Valam, Emel, Adrina, Galan and Father Jacob found they could do nothing other than join in.

Chapter Twenty Nine: Parting Ways

The celebrations continued for three days and nights. Every day since, Quashan's artisans had been hard at work rebuilding the city. The Master Stonecutter had seen to the walls and his laborers and masons had them nearly as strong as they once had been. Already the city's smiths had the ironwork of the southern gate and portcullis restored. The city's woodworkers had started construction on dozens of new homes. And the fact that there was already a shortage of nails, timber and bricks, proved how hard everyone was working toward the city's restoration.

Vilmos was growing restless. It wasn't so much that he was tired of life in Quashan's keep, but he was unaccustomed to people paying so much attention to him. Serving girls made him uneasy by catering to his needs and treating him as he imagined visiting royalty must be treated. The room he and Xith shared held riches beyond anything he had ever dreamed of. The mattresses on the beds were made of hundreds, maybe thousands, of goose down feathers, as were the magnificently plush pillows. He had never imagined a bed could be made out of anything other than straw covered over or that a night's sleep could be so abiding.

The sheets also were soft and silky smooth. Servants would draw him a bath each evening and he used scented soaps to wash with. He had been given fine clothes, a jeweled dagger to put in the scabbard at his belt, and handsomely crafted leather boots. No more ill-fitting boots.

Oddly, it was the absence of his old and worn boots that made him yearn for home. He wondered how Lillath and Vil fared, and hoped that no harm had come to them. He had told Xith of his vow that one day he would return home, and Xith had said that perhaps one day he could go home, but that day would be a long way off.

Vilmos looked at himself in the mirror again, made a face, and started to undress. Xith came into the room.

The shaman smiled, then said, "You look like a fine young man, come quickly. We cannot keep His Highness waiting."

Vilmos frowned, looked back into the mirror, then wordlessly followed Xith. He knew something special was planned for this evening, but what Xith hadn't told him.

They were descending the central stairs to the keep's great hall, when Vilmos asked, "Why all the secrecy? What is afoot?"

Xith stopped and faced Vilmos. "Enjoy yourself this evening. We will be leaving Quashan' in the morning. It is time to begin your education."

"Education?" Vilmos asked.

Xith didn't answer, instead he continued down the stairs. Vilmos heard playful laughter in his mind and before he followed Xith, he glanced to the top of the stairs. Galan and Seth stood at the top of the landing. Galan wore a deep blue dress befitting a princess and Seth wore princely clothes matched to Galan's dress.

We will leave in the morning also, Galan said. Galan took Seth's hand as he offered it to her, and he led her down the stairs toward Vilmos. *Perhaps you will come with us to Imtal to speak to King Andrew.*

"I would like that," Vilmos said, "but I think Master Xith has other plans."

"Perhaps, perhaps not," Seth said. He spoke aloud. "But I fear we are nearly late and should hurry."

Vilmos smiled at Seth's spoken speech. Seth was working hard on his Kingdom accent.

Galan laughed again, and Vilmos heard its echo in his mind as she prodded him to chase after Xith.

Vilmos raced off to the keep's great hall. Seth and Galan followed.

***

Hundreds of guests were seated at the many tables encircling the hall's main table. At the head of the table sat Prince Valam. Seated to his left were Chancellor Van'te, Keeper Martin, Father Jacob, Sergeant Danyel', Captain Adylton of Imtal and Captain Berre of Quashan'. Princess Adrina, the soon-to-be captain— Emel, Vilmos, Xith, Seth and Galan were seated to his right. Vilmos was glad to be surrounded by a few friendly faces, for most of the others in the enormous hall were strangers to him.

Wonderful aromas rose from the kitchen at the northern end of the hall and, nearly out of sight, attendants waited to bring food to the tables. Vilmos glanced to the four empty seats around the table and wondered who they were reserved for, then bowed his head as Father Jacob began the before meal prayer.

Father Jacob concluded the prayer as he had the past six evenings, by giving thanks to Great-Father for divine providence. Afterward, for a brief time, a discord of voices returned.

Vilmos looked about the hall.

Emel to his left said, "Still not used to it, are you?"

"To tell the truth, I would much rather eat somewhere more private."

"And miss all this?" asked Adrina. "Just wait till you see Imtal's hall."

Vilmos shrugged.

Emel whispered, "Me too."

Adrina asked Vilmos, "You will be coming with us to Imtal, won't you?" When Vilmos didn't answer immediately, Adrina glared, then added, "You must."

Vilmos turned expectant eyes to Xith.

"Alas," Xith said, "it is time we were on our way. Vilmos and I have much to do. He has an education to begin."

Adrina made a face.

Xith said, "Do not fret Princess. Seth and Galan will accompany you to Imtal, yet, I suspect that you have not seen Vilmos and I for the last time."

Vilmos was about to say something when Lord Valam cleared his throat, then stood. A sudden hush spread throughout as Valam's gaze swept around the hall.

"On the eve of the seventh day of the cleansing of our home, we celebrate." Valam raised a golden goblet. "We commemorate those who have fallen in the defense of their kingdom and honor those who helped achieve victory.

"It is unfortunate that this hall cannot hold each and every soldier presently residing in Quashan', for down to the last man—" Adrina cleared her throat. "—or woman, they contributed to victory, and none more so than those of you seated here today. I, the citizens of Great Kingdom, and your king, thank you."

Valam raised the goblet above his head in salute, then drank from it until it was empty. A cheer went up, then everyone likewise honored the toast, Vilmos included, though he did not drink wine. Xith had warned him that he shouldn't and for good reason, because it was customary for each of the honored guests to likewise make a toast. Cheers followed every toast, empty wine bottles were hurled against the walls and attendants hurried about the room with new bottles.

When it came time for Vilmos to make a toast, he was so nervous that all he could manage to say was, "To Great Kingdom," and still the crowd cheered.

The last toast made, the cheers faded. Prince Valam stood. He raised his hand, commanding silence. "Several matters have come to my attention that demand addressing," he began. "First of all, the heroic deeds of those seated here—" Valam swept his hand around the central table. "—are largely unknown to all save a few. I wish to make public the knowledge of these deeds so that all may know and none will forget."

Keeper Q'yer was admitted to the hall. He carried a large tome and placed it before his prince.

"Inscribed on these pages are the deeds of the twelve seated here before you as best as can be ascribed," read Valam aloud.

Valam looked to those around the table. "Please stand and be recognized, as I read your name. Chancellor Van'te, once King Andrew's advisor who now serves Lord Valam. Keeper Martin, Head of Lore Keepers. Father Jacob, First Priest of Great-Father. Sergeant Danyel', Quashan' garrison. Captain Adylton, First Captain of Imtal garrison. Captain Berre, First Captain of Quashan' garrison. Princess Adrina, daughter of King Andrew. Sergeant Emel Brodstson, son of King's Captain Brodst. Brother Seth of the Red Order who are the Queen's Protectors. Brother Galan of the Red Order who are the Queen's Protectors. Master Xith, of Oread and wise shaman. And lastly, Vilmos, son of Vil, Counselor of Tabborrath Village."

Briefly Keeper Q'yer began recounting the deeds inscribed in the tome. Lastly he spoke of Princess Adrina, Galan and Vilmos' venture into Sever's camp and an audible murmur passed through the crowd. It was clear few knew of this event.

Valam said, "From this day hence, this tome shall be put in a glass case which will stand at the entrance of this keep so that all may look upon it and read the inscribed names, and those who stand before you shall be known as Quashan's protectors, heroes of the realm. Let the word go forth from this hall so that all may know."

Unrestrained cheers followed and it took Valam a few minutes to calm the enthusiasm.

"The next matter concerns my sister, Princess Adrina, who has decided to return to Imtal instead of staying the winter in our fair South." Keeper Q'yer handed Valam a scroll. "This scroll contains a message to my father, King Andrew, that Adrina will conduct to Imtal. With my regrets that I must stay in the South, I send a request that the King grant Brother Seth and Brother Galan an audience that they are surely due."

Valam put his seal upon the scroll. Keeper Q'yer raised it for all to see. Then Valam said, "Now, I think it is about time we eat!"

A cheer went up and attendants hurried heavily laden plates to the tables. Keeper Q'yer sat at an empty place, and they were about to start eating when a page entered the hall. Valam took the roll of parchment the boy held. After reading the message, Valam whispered something to the page then the boy hurried off.

With his eyes, Vilmos followed the departing page until the boy disappeared into an adjacent corridor. A few seconds later, the page returned. Behind him were three men. One was a burly man dressed in a captain's uniform. The other two by their attire and poise seemed to be nobility, but their hair was fair and not dark as Adrina's or Valam's.

Vilmos turned back to regard Valam. Valam was grinning.

"One last thing," Valam said. "Please welcome, King's Captain Brodst and the guests he brings from Klaive. The Baron of Klaive, and his son, Rudden, conveyed a supply caravan of lumber from their hardwood forests and metal for nails from their mines to Quashan'."

Adrina, who was apparently shocked, seemed about to try to slip under the table.

"Greetings My Lord Valam," said the Baron of Klaive and his son.

"Please join us," Valam said. He clapped his hands and attendants rushed forward to seat the newcomers.

Rudden was seated directly across from Adrina, and Vilmos was now positive that she would at any moment slip under the table. Then she seemed to notice Emel, as Vilmos did just then. Emel was clearly jealous of the tall, good-looking southerner. Emel also seemed about ready to pull the arms off the high-backed chair he sat in.

Adrina's pout relaxed, faded, then she burst into laughter. Valam was quick to join in, as did most everyone else around the table, even Rudden who seemed a good sport.

"Let us eat!" Valam said.

And, the meal began.

***

Vilmos and Xith left the great hall and slowly made their way to their chambers. To Vilmos, it seemed Xith was disappointed or concerned, and certainly, the shaman's thoughts were elsewhere at the moment.

Vilmos stood in front of the chamber mirror and regarded his stomach. He smiled a boyish smile and whispered to himself, "Imagine me, a hero of the realm."

His mind still spun with the wonder of the hall. So much had happened. He had never seen so much splendor, never eaten so much food and never drank so much. His belly felt as if it was about to burst. This evening's events had certainly lived up to his expectations and would be something Vilmos wouldn't soon forget.

Still, he felt uncomfortable in the finery he wore. In the reflection of the mirror, Vilmos saw Xith changing into his customary robe. His eyes darted to a neatly folded pile of clothes. He picked them up and laid them out on the bed. He found the chambermaid had darned his socks, patched the knees on his pants, and mended his shirt just as she had promised.

Without a second thought, Vilmos changed into his old clothes, and while they weren't silk, they felt just as good. He turned back to face the mirror and found Xith standing in front of it. Xith was grinning.

"You look a fine young man," Xith said. "Those are clothes befitting one who is about to begin an education."

"I'm not sure I'm ready," Vilmos said.

Xith looked Vilmos up and down. "You are right, you aren't ready."

Vilmos frowned and a flood of disappointment swept over him.

Xith maintained his grin. "First I must—" Someone knocked on the door. Xith went over and opened it. Vilmos heard him say, "Your Highness, please come in."

Prince Valam stepped into the room. "I trust I am not disturbing you?"

Xith glanced to Vilmos then said, "Certainly not. Please come in."

"Adrina told me you planned to leave early tomorrow, so I slipped out of the hall for a moment to give you this." Valam handed Xith a rolled parchment. "It is something Father Jacob, Keeper Martin and I discussed at length—a writ, signed and closed with my seal. It is not as good as changing the King's law regarding magic, but I think it a close substitute. It guarantees safe passage for you and Vilmos through Great Kingdom and proclaims you lawful magicians."

The prince looked directly at Vilmos for a moment then back to Xith. "I truly wish you would reconsider undertaking the journey to Imtal. I would rest easier knowing you were with Princess Adrina and the others as they return north. You would then be able to talk to my father, for only the King can change a law. But you would have my backing and that of Father Jacob and Keeper Martin."

Xith took the writ. "You are most gracious. This is much more than I'd expected and, it is a first step. Yet centuries of superstition and fear cannot be erased with the wave of a hand. Let us not forget the reason magic is forbidden in the first place.

Perhaps the day will come when the mage may again walk free and without fear. That day is not today nor tomorrow, but tomorrow's tomorrow."

Prince Valam's face lit up with mirth. "Father Jacob said you would say something like that, but I had to try… I will let you two get back to whatever it was you were doing before I arrived."

"Thank you, Your Highness," Xith said and he closed the door behind the prince.

When Xith turned back to Vilmos, some of the concern that had been in his eyes earlier had lifted. Vilmos started to say something, Xith hushed him and just then, Xith revealed what he had been hiding behind the mirror. It was the staff Xith had been whittling, what seemed to Vilmos forever ago.

Xith asked, "Do you remember when I first showed you this?"

Vilmos knew all right, it had been the night before he and Xith entered Vangar Forest for the first time.

"Well, I have finally finished it and you have proven yourself worthy. What I was going to say earlier was that, first I must give you this before you are ready to begin. The staff is an extension of you."

Vilmos reached out for the staff, Xith pulled it back.

"Take it," Xith said, "and you will set your feet irreversibly upon the path to becoming the first Human Magus in five hundred years. What you have learned so far are simple cantrips to a true Mage. But be warned, you, Vilmos, are different. Just as I did not know if your dreams were truly gone, I do not know where the end of this path will take us."

Vilmos' heart was racing. His eyes were wide. He reached out and took the staff from Xith. Never had he been so sure of anything as he was right then when he touched the strange soft wood. His place was with Xith and wherever the path took him, he would follow.

Xith crossed to his bed and laid down on it. "Tomorrow will be a long day, there is so much we have to do."

Vilmos faced the mirror, grinned, then turned back to Xith. He asked, "Is Imtal truly as grand as Princess Adrina claims?"

Xith smiled, but didn't reply.

The story continues with:

Ruin Mist:
Keeper Martin's Tale Part II

About the Author

Robert Stanek is the author of many previously published books, including several bestsellers. Currently he lives in the Pacific Northwest with his wife and children. Robert is proud to have served in the Persian Gulf War as a combat crewmember on an electronic warfare aircraft. His distinguished accomplishments during the Persian Gulf War earned him nine medals, including the United States of America's highest flying honor, the Air Force Distinguished Flying Cross.

We Need You

Reagent Press is a small publisher. Without the help of you the reader, we will not be able to produce future works. If you liked the book, please tell your friends and associates or submit positive comments to your favorite online bookstore. If you didn't like the book, please tell us.

Thank you for your continued support!

Printed in the United States
3966